Simon Williams

Embers Drift

For J and K

I - Desperate Beginnings

I

They no longer recalled when they began to name one another numerically. They could not even remember whose idea it had been. Perhaps the decision had been made eight hundred years ago, or eight hundred and fifty. More, less, it didn't matter. Such gulfs of time, so important to their mortal subjects, had become a needless detail to the Mothers.

One, Two and Three had all but forgotten their names from that so-distant time, when they too were mortal. Yet they occasionally recalled with bitterness the distant events that had conspired to place them here, as absolute rulers of a dynasty that could not end.

One winter's evening, as swirling blizzards ground the Citadel to a halt and citizens huddled for warmth wherever they could, Three knelt by the fire that raged in the hearth of the Southern Tower's meeting hall. She preferred the austere, cold architecture of this section of the palace to any other. Some innate bitterness attracted her to the many marble columns, the chequered floors, the stark contrast of light and dark. The hard surfaces and simple coloration brought a degree of clarity to her conflicted emotions.

Her alabaster countenance showed none of this inner turmoil. Her pale blue eyes appeared washed free of all emotion, nothing more than gems set into stone.

Two watched dispassionately as Three extended her hand to the fire. The crackling flames leapt eagerly to consume the flesh from her offering. Three grimaced

5

in pain but remained resolutely silent before she finally removed that flaming ruin. Acrid smoke curled up from the cooked and charred meat. Two and Three watched in silence as the flesh slowly mended itself and skin grew back, black char replaced by new pink flesh and skin. In the space of four or five minutes the repair was complete, and the hand looked no different to how it had before its temporary combustion.

"Do you remember the time when you threw yourself into this same hearth?" Two remarked.

Three scowled. "I remember well enough. Mostly I recall the days after that. The pain. The *punishment,* I thought."

"I watched as the flames appeared to consume you whole. But they died down eventually, starved of fuel, and you lay there for half a day, blackened and still."

"You watched me the whole time?"

"I had nothing better to do. The afternoon wore on and as the sky grew dark, I saw you move from out of the ashes, nothing more than char tinged with raw slashes of exposed flesh."

"The pain was excruciating," Three said with a shudder. "I lay still, but I didn't lose consciousness. Perhaps *that* was my punishment- to feel every cell and nerve made again."

"I've noticed something." Two knelt next to her and took Three's hand in her own much darker one. "With every attempt we make to end our existence, our physical forms are replenished more quickly. One might say it *is* a punishment. The Great Power pushes back harder with each attempt at unmaking."

"I wasn't trying to *unmake,*" Three pointed out. "I only wanted to feel the brightness of the pain." She flexed and moved each finger in turn and traced the

6

finger of her other hand along the contours of flesh. "It's gone now. It always goes."

"More quickly each time?"

"More quickly each time."

Two let go of her hand and pondered. Finally she asked, "Are the finger prints exactly the same as before?"

Three blinked in surprise. "How would I know? It isn't something I've thought about. I never studied the old prints. Does it matter?"

"Such things may hold clues as to how we might eventually die. A pattern hidden in the detail, perhaps. Or a pattern that can't be faithfully replicated."

Three smiled sadly at that hope. "Eternity will be unbearable if you fail to accept it. The Spider blessed and cursed us at the same time, and you presume to fight your way through her web a thousand years later? We belong to her, now and forever."

"Unless," Two said, "we displease the Spider sufficiently."

Three laughed, but then felt a prickle of unease stir inside her. "How could we possibly do that?"

"If we began the cycle again..." Two left many things unsaid, and Three's unease only grew as she considered the ramifications of unleashing such forces-technology whose remnants they had inherited, but which they had long given up trying to understand. "We would stir an ancient hell into life," she said.

Two only smiled at that.

A day later, the Mothers sat around a granite table in the adjoining hall. Today, they preferred the temperature to be savagely cold, and their even, measured breaths rose visibly to be lost in the vastness of their meeting place.

"What if the Spider has learned from the previous cycle?" One asked, fretfully twisting ringlets of her dark hair. "Is she not omnipresent? All-seeing, all-knowing? What if she has already sensed this treacherous little get-together?"

"Her power is vast, but she has never observed little details," Three pointed out. "If we begin and accelerate the cycle, the response will be swift. The old ways will rise again- this time, to destroy us. *She* is the core of that power, and the one thing that *can* destroy us."

"You forget that we're not like our predecessors." Two shook her head dismissively. "I thought of this idea, but I say now that we should abandon it."

"What frightens you?" One demanded.

"That this time the cycle will be different. We are a *part* of the old ways, vessels that carry the echoes of that time when they were wielded freely in the world. The Great Power runs through us, in our blood, even if we seldom use it."

"No. Those who came before us were the same, in all the ways that matter." One's voice echoed harshly in the emptiness. "She gave *them* the powers to rule, to change, to transform... and to live forever. But eventually, they died. They were destroyed. Oh, they struggled against it, but their time came. And ours will come too, a punishment for unlearning the universal lesson. We know what needs to be done to stir the Spider into action- the terrible mistakes of the past must be made again. We won't fight the inevitable. We'll let it overcome us. The darkness in our veins will expand to fill us entirely. We'll be annihilated."

"We all wish for the one thing we cannot have," Two warned.

"But we *can* have it. Oblivion will fall on us like a black wave. Do you think the Spider will allow such horrors to be recreated?" One grew restless and paced up and down across the tiles. "Let's look again at the technology and rebuild it if we can. Over time we'll understand the science well enough to make progress. We have an almost limitless supply of subjects, more than they would have had in the old days. Humanity's endless capacity for multiplication will serve us well."

"If nothing else, it would constitute a change," Three remarked. "The days would be different."

"Setting foot outside the Citadel walls would be a *change,*" Two added, and the others stared incredulously at her.

One night a thousand and eighty-three years ago, the three women had gone to one of the ancient gateways of the Citadel. These exits had remained closed and sealed for the last one hundred years, ever since the Mothers had decided the city-state would shun the outside world. But at last they had agreed to taste the bitterness of it for themselves.

An icy wind blew through the entryway, and nothing but darkness could be seen through the bars and patterns of the thick metal gates. The three women had forced open the barrier, suppressing the immense sound of metal as it scraped against stone, so that the entire deed was done in silence and with no one to see it.

Then they had stepped through the tunnels carved in the great stone walls, and on into the gloom beyond.

They had taken no more than five or six steps beyond the Citadel's outer perimeter when the agony and the nightmares began. Visions from their distant past sprang up before them- mortals they had once known and even loved, when they had possessed the capacity for love- all long gone from the world. Events from that time unfurled and played out, many of them terrible reminders of the things they had seen and done. All these things, along with the terrible guilt they aroused, ate away at the Mothers of the Citadel.

They stood held in place and in unimaginable pain, like butterflies on pins, until finally they learned that they could at least retreat, back towards the lights of the Citadel, back behind their defensive walls.

They staggered like dolls or puppets played and taunted by a cruel universal force, until at last they had fallen back within the shadow of the Citadel walls again and the searing agony ebbed away. Then they wept silently, for now there could be no doubt: not only were they condemned to live forever, but they could never leave this place.

Until now, none of them had dared to speak of that night. The paradox of their immortality and invulnerability, juxtaposed to their imprisonment in this vast metropolis they had nurtured and built, was almost unthinkable. They could not fathom it. They could not bear this unsolvable existential riddle. Nor could they adequately express their despair and rage and bewilderment and so they internalised their torment.

In so doing, they slowly crushed the remaining humanity from their selves, and over time the three women felt nothing but contempt for their subjects and hatred of their mortality.

"We were trapped here because *she* engineered it, in her spite," Two continued at last. "Who knows what may happen if we stir the Great Power by doing this? I should never have suggested it."

"On the contrary. It's the best idea you have had," Three argued.

"It offers us a chance." One had ceased her pacing. "The horror of eternity is certain, but *this* is not. Why haven't we considered this before?"

None of them could say. But within each of the Mothers stirred the faintest of hopes, that they might yet cheat the curse woven around them by the Spider- the name they had given the consciousness of the world, the intelligence behind the Great Power.

The next day they went down to the unused, labyrinthine dungeons in the western section of the palace- a vast maze of cellars and antechambers that had not seen footfall for hundreds of years. The warmth of the air and the closeness of the dark and rotting ceilings pressed around them, and dust lay inches thick in places.

Had they memorised the layout of this labyrinthine place when they last walked here, the three women would have known that its structure had changed over time, in ways that should not have been possible. Inexplicably, new rooms, passageways, staircases and other details had all appeared over the long centuries and continued to do so, a vast exercise in meticulous stealth.

But the Spider worked in ways too subtle for their cold, impatient hearts.

In the catacombs the three women rediscovered dreadful remnants of the past- parts of the virulent technology initially worked on by those who ruled in the days before the Citadel. In the months and years that followed, they attempted to understand and build upon this incomprehensible science. They struggled for a length of time that would have forced mortals to give up in despair, but these women were not mortals, and they had an inexhaustible amount of time in which to unravel the puzzle.

However, they needed people to become receptacles for the strange power that had now stirred, for it had been designed for a singular purpose- to meld with human flesh, to enhance the human condition and perhaps in time overcome it entirely.

The Mothers had at their disposal a vast supply of citizens who could be put to this grim purpose. Over time, hundreds of felons, vagrants and others who would not be missed disappeared from the Citadel's cold and filthy streets. They were used, assimilated, stripped of their humanity in many different ways- and the three women who called themselves the Mothers of the Citadel tried to recreate the perfect fusion of human flesh and science powered by a force that, even as they grew to understand how it worked, they could never fully comprehend.

Their experiments failed quickly at first. No synergy resulted between the two vastly different systems. The parasitic technology simply ravaged and overcame the biology to which it was introduced.

But as time wore on and they learned from their dreadful mistakes, the women observed that progress was being made, of a sort. Their unspeakable creations remained alive for longer, albeit in a state of intense suffering. Yet they perished eventually. The hybrid creatures became erratic and violent and eventually self-destructed in spectacular fashion, tearing themselves apart.

They would have given up eventually, but their only alternative was the implacable horror of eternity. And out in the vast city-state they ruled, stories filtered through to the Mothers which could only be signs of the

Spider reacting to their abominable work. Inexplicable events, anomalies and observations filtered through to them- not enough to become universally believed by their mortal subjects but enough to make the Mothers certain that the Great Power had stirred and begun to touch the Citadel.

The Mothers also bore witness to the slow reconstruction of one of their predecessors- the only one of his kind who had survived the great war that had brought the Mothers to power. But his was no survival that anyone could understand.

This unfortunate man, discovered by the Mothers shortly after the end of hostilities, had been all but obliterated by someone or something. The Mothers guessed that some violent force wielded by one of his comrades caused his demise. Yet they eventually discovered, as they returned again to the place of his apparent death- for nothing fascinated them as much as death- and observed his ruined flesh, that not only did he not decay but his body had begun to repair itself. The head had been crushed and its contents ejected far and wide, but they bore the shapeless remains to a place where they could better observe this phenomenon as dead flesh shrivelled away, and new flesh gradually appeared in its place. Over many decades they found that not only did the body repair itself, but the *head* began to reform.

"He lives," they declared, "or, there will come a time when he lives and is whole again."

With that in mind, for he had been an enemy of theirs, the three women locked the process and the subject away in an indestructible prison- a glass cage in one of the palace halls to which only they had access. Making use of the Great Power, the Mothers rendered the glass unbreakable, but made the prison permeable so that air could enter and leave.

Over the countless years, his physical form continued to slowly repair as the mysterious force that nurtured the rebuilding worked at its own deliberate pace, following an unknown blueprint.

At least once a month, the Mothers would gather around this transparent prison, whose fragile contents would have confounded any mortal who observed the situation. Their captive was held upright and in place by forces that they had brought to bear on the area within the cage.

As they stood around their prisoner in his transparent box, the Mothers would sometimes ask questions that none of them could answer:

"Does he think, yet?"

"Is he aware of us standing here?"

"Is he conscious in the way that *we* are conscious?"

"Does he feel pain?"

"What do you think it feels like, to *re-grow* by tiny increments?"

"When the process is complete, will he be the same man as before? Are memories retained?"

Over the long centuries they continued to ask themselves and one another these fundamental questions, in the hope that by meditating on them they might learn answers.

They didn't, but as they gathered around the prisoner the Mothers wondered if, perversely, this other immortal might hold the key to their eventual death.

The Mothers persisted with their dark work in the catacombs beneath the palace. Day after day, month after month, year after year, they laboured. Out in the

Citadel, entire generations came, went and were forgotten, specimens taken from each. By tiny and frustrating increments, the Mothers learned the workings of the grim technology. Over time, despite the vast number of people who were destroyed through their experiments, they made further progress. The hybrids lived for longer. Some were even capable of basic speech, cognition and in some cases, tasks that they would not have been able to carry out prior to their transformation. They died after only a short while- some managed to kill themselves- but their brief, chaotic lives sometimes proved useful.

Eighty years spent working on this exhausting project had passed when Three declared to her companions one day, "We're almost done. There's harmony now, between the flesh of the human and its infection by the *illuminance*." They had coined that word to describe the technology with which they had worked and struggled over the years.

"The time for messy trials is over," she continued. "We're on the verge of being able to *produce*. But I think we must ask questions of our prisoner. We must know what *he* knows about the process. Have you seen that his healing has accelerated? A threshold of some kind has been reached, and now his flesh repairs and grows back more swiftly. He may have a unique insight that could help us."

"He won't tell us anything," Two sourly responded. "He doesn't even have the physical capacity. His mouth is not yet whole."

"But he *will*. One way or another, we'll extract the information from his brain. He is functioning..."

"Do you remember the question we asked one another, years ago? Are memories retained?"

15

"We will find out," One said curtly. "We'll discover and taste those memories and sooner or later we'll locate the knowledge we need. The answers are in his head. They can be extracted."

The next day they visited their prisoner.

"We haven't spoken to you in such a long time," One remarked.

The man said nothing, of course‑ as Two had pointed out, his jaw had only partly formed after so many centuries, although the rest of his head was now almost whole. But the Mothers detected a faint shimmer within the glass cage‑ a barely perceptible disturbance. And without any doubt, only one living creature within the confines of the cell could have caused that tremor.

"We've been busy," Three said, as if their prisoner required an explanation for their absence. "But now we need an answer to a very important question. A question for the Ages."

One began to pace around the square perimeter of the cell, taking five measured steps to traverse each side. "Obviously you cannot talk‑ *yet*‑ but we've concluded that you *are* able to communicate with us. You are conscious. You think. We sense you. And *you* sense *us.*"

Two, who sat in silence some distance away, to concentrate fully on their subject and his microscopic responses to their presence and their words, sensed a sudden *spike* from the prisoner‑ fear, defensiveness, secrecy, determination. "He doesn't wish to help," she concluded, "but he fears what will happen if he doesn't."

"As well he ought." One ceased her movement and pressed her face against the glass as she stood directly behind him, where she observed in exquisite detail his spine and part of his brain, which although not yet fully enclosed, was- as far as they could tell- intact and functional.

"The miracle of your remaking can be reversed," she murmured. "All this painfully slow progress- *is* it painful, I wonder?- can be obliterated in a moment. But perhaps you long for that black sleep, which we can only imagine. You're almost whole again- soon you'll be complete. Ready at last to taste eternity. Then again, you and your kind despised eternity every bit as much as we do. So I offer you release from it, if you answer the questions we pose."

She paused and considered for a moment. "You may wonder how it is that we can grant such release, given that we share the same curse. But the answer is simple. We know what will bring about the ultimate retribution from the great power of this world. *Her.* Even you, a technocrat from another time and place, know what I mean by that."

"The Spider," Three murmured.

"He doesn't know that name." One turned her attention back to their captive. "But he knows what we mean. She is alive. You know she's alive. The world, the Great Power, the web that holds it all together, the weaver of the web. It's all the same thing. You saw it when you lost the great war so many long centuries ago. Your comrades were destroyed either by her, or by one another's hand. But she played a part in each death, didn't she?"

Three faced the prisoner directly. "How do we set the process free? The process of creating and recreating the hybrids. We are missing something- what is it? We need the process to work better and faster- and with consequences."

One looked questioningly to Two, who gave a barely perceptible shake of the head.

17

"Perhaps I'm not being entirely clear," Three admitted. "By *consequences* I mean the rage of the Great Power, which destroyed your empire so long ago- the same force that we ourselves employ from time to time, to remind the masses of our power. It has remained largely silent for so many centuries as the Citadel makes quiet, calm technological progress- neither too slowly nor too quickly. It's not a tool, however much we might treat it as one. We are its unwilling, cursed servants, and if we commit the most dreadful act of all- as your kind once did- then we will be annihilated."

Two had closed her eyes during this explanation, but now they flickered open and she hissed, "You shouldn't have spoken of our aims!"

"Then we destroy him," Three said, perhaps a little petulantly.

One shook her head. "An easy death? No. He shan't have that luxury until the day we have it ourselves."

Two continued, "The question we posed is too complex, and requires articulation. And even if he was able to describe how this was done before- if he remembers- would we comprehend it properly?"

One frowned, frustrated. "So what do you suggest?"

"We're on our own, for now. Only we can unlock it."

"One day soon," Three said hopefully. But she, and the others, knew that their triumph might not come one day soon- or ever.

II – The Engineer

"What do you see, other than the darkness?"

I see nothing, she thought, but that was both correct and the wrong answer.

She offered words which were both a compromise and a lie. "I don't know." At the core of her being she *did* know- but had no way to describe how she felt and what she could *almost* see, with her mind's eye.

As Lena peered down the steep flight of stairs, a nameless existential fear took hold of her, as if she stood on the threshold of a void into which she might easily spiral as the ground crumbled away. She almost lost her footing and would have done had her father's hand not steadied her.

The cellar lamps lit the way down as far as the eleventh step, beyond which the darkness appeared so absolute that the steps might have extended into space, and anyone who stepped beyond the eleventh and possibly final stair would fall forever through the nameless void that so frightened her. Lena tried to comfort herself by considering all the special properties of the number eleven, but the juxtaposition of absolutes transfixed her and made any mathematical recall impossible.

"It calls to you," he said, and she heard a wonder and inexplicable sadness in her father's voice. "It calls to you, but I'm not sure you can answer."

"What is it?" she whispered plaintively. "I don't understand. What is it?"

He placed his arm around her shoulders but didn't answer. Did his hand tremble a little?

"I often imagined what lay behind the door." At last Lena dared to look away from the void and up to her father. "You would never open it for me. I think you *wanted* to, but something always stopped you."

"Had I shown you when you were a child, you might have rushed thoughtlessly into the gloom to be lost forever. Do you remember those headstrong days, when you embraced the unknown without thinking?"

"I remember," Lena admitted reluctantly.

"And now you think all the time but embrace nothing. This is the right time to show you, or it *should* be- but maybe it's already too late."

"I don't know what you mean."

"Perhaps too much of the Citadel exists inside you now that you're a part of its... *system*. I trust you, Lena- but what if I have nothing left to trust you with? What if you walk away?"

Lena stared at him and wondered if her father had asked her to solve a complex riddle or equation. "Are you ready?" he asked, and his voice sounded as if it came from far away. Momentarily cast adrift from reality, Lena felt with her other hand for reassurance that her father still held onto her, even though she knew he did. He continued, still in that oddly distant voice, "There are places where another version of the world touches this one. Threads of that touch persist in some hidden places, and this is one such place. Men and women of science would refer to it as an *anomaly*. Certainly it was a cosmic embrace that can't be readily explained. I didn't expect to find it when we came to live here, but perhaps I should have done."

"I don't believe in mysteries and miracles," Lena said with sudden, reactionary ill will. Nevertheless, she looked down again and kept her eyes fixed on the bottom stair as if it might suddenly be stolen by the blackness and wink out of existence.

"I don't ask for belief Lena. I'm not sure *what* to ask for."

Lena shook her head. "I don't understand. Why show this to me now?"

"Because you had to be shown. What you do with it is up to you, but we *must* do it together. We can't let it *react*. Not without taking measures to hide ourselves from discovery." Suddenly he seemed frightened.

"*Do* with it?" Lena was nonplussed. "What have *you* done?"

"Nothing," he admitted. "If we're less than certain, we should go back and close the door on it."

"Do you know what's down there?"

"No. I've kept all knowledge of its existence to myself, which is the one thing that you *must* do. I don't even know if I'm doing the right thing, Lena. I only know that there's reason to this. It isn't coincidence."

Lena said nothing but tried to imagine how it *couldn't* be anything other than simple mathematical coincidence.

"It has changed slowly over time," he added quietly, "and I think it's responsible for other things that have changed." A distant smile creased his lips for a moment. "Perhaps you ought to do nothing other than be its guardian. Then you can pass on the fact of its existence, as I did..."

"No," she said forcefully. "I won't have anyone to pass it down to. Anyway, it's just a dark cellar. It's part of the house. Bricks and mortar and measurable dimensions. There's a wall somewhere down there." As she spoke of comfortable certainties, Lena found her confidence return and the odd sense of an indefinable

21

other place recede swiftly. "You shouldn't have shown it to me. Shut it away forever, like you said."

He knew better than to argue. His fourteen-year-old daughter had vociferously denied that she might ever find someone to spend her life with. *I don't need anyone else,* she had defiantly declared, more times than either of them could count.

They left the cellar without speaking. Lena felt uncomfortable and frustrated by her father's silence, as if she had disappointed him without quite knowing why-but she couldn't think of any questions to ask. Nor could she find any words to lessen his disappointment.

Her father locked the door to the cellar, and they never spoke of the matter again.

From time to time as the years went on, she would observe in his expression a strange yearning, as if he had wanted to fall into that blackness or walk with her hand in hand to open a world beyond their understanding. But fear and protocol kept him tethered to the ordinary, and Lena knew that nothing stood in the shadow of the stairs but a brick wall.

Even then she understood the boundaries and constraints of form, shape and structure at an intimate level- to Lena this was the mathematics of the real- and it was from that world that she would draw temporary comfort over the ensuing years.

And so she could never explain why she averted her eyes on the rare occasions when she passed by the door to the cellar.

II

Lena had gone out for a walk later that morning. The day was bright and sunny, with a light breeze and a faint

22

promise of spring. More tiny white clouds than she had ever seen before dotted the azure sky.

She headed down towards Barrows Verge, a raised area of scrub that overlooked tightly packed terraces and, further towards the Eastern Quarter, the tall dark chimneys of industry. Thick black smoke belched from some, wisps of steam or lighter smoke from others. Their combined haze lay over the Citadel's shimmering expanse, fading gradually into the sky.

Lena observed the shapes and contours of these familiar sights, took deep breaths to calm herself, and concluded- for no reason that she knew- that she must now force her life to take a direction. She would study as hard as she could in the mathematical and engineering disciplines- areas she already excelled in at school- and one way or another she would make a living from her toil. Her success would be tangible but modest. It would quietly please her but draw no more attention than she could cope with.

She applied for work at one of the Citadel's sprawling power plants a month or so later. Perhaps she felt more determined than ever to distance herself from an unnerving experience that could not be described, measured or quantified- even after many days had passed and the episode no longer even felt real. Over a period of six years, with grim determination she hauled her way up from the lowly rank of sweeper, carrier and general drudge to become a qualified power engineer. She proved her intelligence, insight and attention to detail at every given opportunity. Eventually she became senior engineer and supervisor in charge of one of the sets of steam-powered generators and associated appliances that provided light and heat for the Citadel's millions.

She attained this position at a younger age than anyone before her, although the fact was not widely known and Lena herself was not inclined to boast about it. Attention was only ever drawn to the results of teams that worked together and strove for ever greater efficiency, so Lena's relative obscurity suited her well. She had no desire for recognition. Some of her colleagues might have claimed her motto- if she had one- would be *Hard work is its own reward.*

But all Lena wanted was to immerse herself in the real, the familiar. She strove for a life of defined boundaries.

Lena appeared to have no desire for reward of any kind. Some of the men and women with whom she worked wondered what motivated her, but even Lena couldn't have answered that question. The solutions her work required came easily, and so she drifted from day to day, consistent in her dutiful approach and the exemplary quality of her work, and seldom thinking beyond the horizon of her immediate existence.

Progress was an inevitable part of her environment. Her schooling had focused a great deal on the last hundred years of scientific and industrial advancements- the growth of so many hundreds of factories, deep mines and most importantly, the harnessing of steam power and now electrical power. Her occupation lay at the heart of its slow but relentless march.

The population grew at a greater rate year on year despite attempts by the authorities to control it, and despite the dreadful diseases for which no cure had yet been found. The pool of intellect within the Citadel- of which she was a small droplet- required more innovative ways to reasonably accommodate the burgeoning number of people. The vast walls of the

Citadel had always marked civilisation's perimeter and so it remained now- instead of building outside the Citadel walls- where no one ever ventured- those responsible for housing devised and built structures that clawed ever higher into the sky. Many were built in a great hurry only to be later deemed unsafe and destroyed. A few had even fallen of their own accord and killed hundreds in dust and rubble. Little was learned from these tragedies. Buildings with hasty, often cosmetic modifications quickly replaced those that had fallen. *How fast can it be built?* was an oft-spoken question, along with *How do we build it more economically?*

The wheels of industry spun ever faster over time. Lena supposed that this surrounding acceleration was intended to make people happier or more content with their lot- what better or other reason could there be, she reasoned. But did it? New solutions created new problems. Were the folk of the Citadel happier now than, say, a hundred or two hundred years ago? To her knowledge no one had considered measuring such an abstraction. Besides, electricity everywhere in the Citadel remained sporadic and unpredictable, even dangerous. The harsh winters routinely killed a hundred thousand or more of the very old, very young and those with underlying health problems. The smoke from the factories created a thick smog whenever weather conditions colluded with particulate matter. Over half the sewers in the city were open, prone to flooding and the cause of many diseases suffered by the people.

No-one is happier, Lena often told herself. *They simply expect more.*

Hers was a highly analytical nature- she could not have done her job as well otherwise- and she had long observed that her fellow workers were not unlike the machines they looked after. They worked, they ate, they drank, they slept and the cycle continued until ill luck or age cut through it. In short, they fed and replenished themselves without thought. The only difference between Lena's taciturn colleagues and herself was that she was acutely aware of her condition and increasingly found it intolerable, no matter the quiet and methodical life she had carved for herself, whereas they appeared to live in bleak acceptance of their fates.

Sometimes she wondered if they existed on a lower level of awareness.

Lena survived her black moods‑ of which there were many‑ by telling herself whenever she could that resignation, acceptance, limitation were not for her, no matter that she saw and felt no alternative existence, nothing outside of the fanciful dreams that sometimes floated through her head in the small quiet hours before the morning light.

Except for that day when, as she stood on the cellar stairs, she had felt the caress of something that might have been revelation, or oblivion, or both.

Lena's father had once told her that humankind yearned to find other life even as it collectively conspired to destroy itself, but the Mothers had decreed that the use of farscopes to scan the skies for other places was forbidden. Shortly after that, the sale of farscopes had been made illegal except to the various professional Guilds around the Citadel‑ and the work they conducted and any findings they made were endlessly scrutinised by the authorities.

Much of the Citadel, he hastily pointed out, now lay under such magnitude of light that the practice had become of little use. "It's for the best," he had said as he set his glass of wine down with a sigh. "We live in the light- why peer into the darkness?"

"You don't believe yourself," Lena had pointed out. His smile- sad, knowing, perhaps even a little proud of her for pointing that out- had simply confirmed as much.

Her father was indeed proud of her in his understated way, although Lena thought of her engineering skills as a product of simple luck, a position somewhere on a sliding scale. Yet she felt that her path had contributed to his sadness and wondered how that could be. How could he be simultaneously proud of her *and* saddened by the path she had taken?

Lena had no answer and so she tried to push the question aside and never challenged or delved into his quiet frustration.

Her job brought useful money into their household, which became of even greater importance as she reached the age of twenty. Her father, a Guild assistant, became unable to work after contracting a blood infection that had ravaged his body and then started to affect his mind. But did she love her work? No, and in the quiet hours of the night Lena would wonder if she had the capacity to love anything or anyone other than her father- and if she even wanted to. She had no need of other people. She was entirely competent in every practical area of existence that mattered and had begun to prepare herself for a life of lonely independence, knowing that her father would not live through another winter. *Only fools fail to plan,* she would sometimes remind herself.

I've become an adult and he has become a child, Lena thought more than once as he shouted his frustration at being unable to string sentences together properly at times or remember anything from the last few days.

He died four months later in the depths of winter. Two days before he slipped from the world, he spoke calmly to her about regrets and secrets, more lucid than he had been for many days. He regretted his life spent anchored to the grimly mundane. He said that he had secrets to tell her, but he could find no way to speak of them. "I'm frightened, Lena," he confessed. "There are things I swore I would reveal, but the years wore on, and you chose a different life."

"You let me," she quietly pointed out.

"Yes. And now I don't have the words. It's like a faded dream. It doesn't even make sense to me now."

Lena shifted uncomfortably. "I'm sorry."

"No. You're not, and you shouldn't be. Just... do your best and try to be happy."

He sighed and looked away. Presently he began to talk of other things- recollections from days gone by, mundane trivia from a time she couldn't remember. Lena sat and listened patiently as the snow drifted silently down outside.

Her father stopped talking a while later. Perhaps he knew that Lena, try as she might, couldn't muster enough interest to make him continue. He watched the snow in morose silence as the day grew dark. His mood darkened too, and he made less sense as the evening wore on.

"Hell is inside us, and we made it that way," he mumbled. "I'd give anything... to hold her in my arms. Anything to see them. Anything for us all to..."

Lena listened in confusion and waited for him to continue and perhaps even explain, but he added nothing to those words.

"So many terrible things," he said as she finally got up to light the gas lamps. "So many terrible people. We become the things we do. We're not made to be slaves on the wheel. No, we're not painted that way."

"How, then? How are we painted?" Suddenly, Lena was desperate to know.

But he turned away and drifted to sleep.

In his last moments two days later, he screamed nonsense at his daughter as snow still drifted gently down outside, his eyes wild with fear directed at the woman he no longer knew, the stranger in his house. He threw aside the water she had set on the bedside table, and when Lena looked up from collecting the jagged pieces of glass he lay still and silent. Later, she would try to recall the last lucid thing he had said to her, but she couldn't.

She stared at him for an age, carefully holding the shards of glass. *What now?* she thought finally. *What happens now?*

But, being Lena, she went back to collecting the pieces of the water jug.

Lena was his only living relative, and so four days later a total of three people clustered around the grave- herself, the Officiator and his assistant, a pale and nervous young man who the Officiator had brought along as part of his training. "This is a very straightforward example," Lena overheard him explain to his assistant. His voice carried across the wind. "Most ceremonies will be more complex for one reason or another. This is a lucky first case for you. Usually the relatives will have things to say, stories to tell."

He had spoken with Lena that morning and asked her if she wanted to say anything. "No," she said. "I should have said more when he was alive."

"I meant, a summary of his life, perhaps," he began, but she shook her head. "Why? We had no friends. No one is coming to the funeral except me. Who will hear my words?"

Lena watched as the two men carefully laid the coffin in the ground. *Straightforward. Simple. Unknown. There's very little that tethers me to this world. When I leave, only two will attend me - because two must attend, by law.*

They will comment to each other on how very straightforward a procedure this is and how easy I made it for them.

On this unusually mild day the snow had turned to rain borne by dense heavy clouds that raced overhead carried by the stiff breeze. Lena listened absently to the solemn monologue of the Officiator, which simply listed the main events of her father's life. She had written the list for him at his request, so that he had something to say, but they sounded like points of summary in one of her technical documents. Why did he need to recite it at all? She already knew each event, and no one else knew or cared.

She longed for tears that wouldn't come, for something greater and deeper than the calm resignation that had cloaked her since the wintry afternoon of his death. Guilt at the relative ease with which she had dealt with the emotional and practical matters of his passing wore away at her. *I'm much as I was before,* she thought. *Just a little greyer, a little emptier. Some part of me has fled into the sky, or into the ground to be with him. What's left is cold dust. Hell, maybe it's all dust.*

Lena tried to tell herself that guilt made no sense. His illness hadn't been her fault. It was simply bad luck, brought to its ultimate and inevitable conclusion. *Don't try to feel anything,* she admonished

30

herself as she wiped wet strands of her mousy brown hair away from her face. *You're a logician, not an artist or a composer. You don't need emotions. If you become like one of your machines, then so be it. It may help you understand them better.*

But the simple truth, though Lena would stubbornly deny it, was that she was nothing of the sort. Hard technicalities and logic defined her day to day existence but her inner life retained a quite different shape. Now the veneer of sense and practicality began to slowly peel away, for she had lost all that mattered to her.

When she returned from the funeral, shivering after being caught in a brief but heavy rain shower, a restlessness came over her, and Lena wandered through every part of the house that afternoon. If anyone else had been there to observe her, they might have thought she was looking for something. But Lena was simply exploring rooms and passages, nooks and crannies, all the forgotten places where dust had gathered. She had done much the same, though more quickly, as a child. Now she moved slowly and deliberately, touching with reverence, remembering. Every so often she imagined the sound of her laughter from long ago, peals of mirth that echoed down the hallway or across one of the landings.

At last, Lena sat in the hallway and stared at the wall. *What now?* she asked herself.

That night, she dreamed not of her father, nor the funeral, or memories of past times, but another house, a little like her own home in design. This distant building had been created far beyond the Citadel. Thousands upon thousands of trees surrounded it. Lena walked through the open door, and although the place lay dark and abandoned, when she stopped to listen, she

31

could hear the murmurs of a hundred or more voices. She tried to concentrate on individual voices, desperate to understand them, but when she did, although the others obediently faded away, she still couldn't understand the words that single voice uttered.

Each window gave her a different view‑ not simply by virtue of its position but in terms of time and location. From one upper window in a dusty bedchamber she saw a night‑time scene with distant mountains under the moons. From the back window of the lower level she saw a vast, sunlit garden that appeared to stretch away forever.

When Lena woke the following morning, the dream filled her thoughts for a full minute. Then a cold, heavy feeling clawed at her insides as she remembered everything that had happened in the last few days. She uttered a low, miserable sigh and wished that she could go back to sleep‑ and sleep forever.

Two days after her father was placed in the earth, Lena stood upon the threshold of the staircase in the cellar once again.

III

Lena pushed the door closed behind her and set one of the two oil lamps she had brought into the wall bracket. She stared down the flight of stairs for a long while. The lamps flickered and spat and cast thick greasy shadows across the walls of the stairwell.

Lena listened intently to her breaths and the steady, fast thump of her heart. She imagined her father at her side, telling her quietly about this phenomenon and others like it, supposedly hidden from sight and discovery. What had he expected of her that day? Had he hoped for some revelation, a leap of logic from his daughter that might explain that which had never been understood? Had he thought she might unleash her formidable but rigid intellect upon the puzzle, and use the power of reason to point the way to its solution?

If so, her response had disappointed him.

Now I have only myself to disappoint, Lena thought as her gaze fell upon the final visible stair and the total darkness that lay beyond. She wondered if it had simply been a joke of his, conjured when he observed the odd trickery of light that made the darkness appear greater than it ought to be. *The joke's on you, Lena,* she imagined him saying. *The steps merely continue through the shadow and end at the bottom of the cellar wall. Just as you said. What else did you think might happen?*

Where else did you think they might go?

But no, he wouldn't have concocted such casual cruelty. He had never been cruel.

Lena attempted to weigh up the risk of taking that extra step and however many others lay beyond. She couldn't. All she could do was fretfully wonder if it led to something both miraculous and terrible- or, worse, simply ended at a wall.

On the one hand, the dull predictability of months and years spent in familiar routine stretched ahead, dependable and ultimately pointless. On the other, a sharp and literal step into something truly unknown waited- unless this was indeed a bizarre and implausible joke, Lena reminded herself. She wondered what she might do then, if all the hopes and fears she had left in the world were to be dashed.

Do it, she urged herself.

Without knowing why, Lena took out her pocket watch and made a mental note of the time- half an hour past five in the evening- then returned it to her pocket.

33

That calm generated by a firmly made decision had settled over her. Lena made her way slowly down the staircase. The air temperature grew a little colder with each step.

She sat down a few steps away from the final visible stair, lowered herself further and watched as her leg disappeared into the gloom. One moment she could see her leg, the next it couldn't be seen at all.

When she moved her leg further down and felt nothing more ethereal or otherworldly under her boot than another step, Lena felt an odd sense of shock. She took a deep breath and began to make her way down again, shifting her weight step by step. The lantern she held in one hand glowed faintly but did nothing to illuminate the surrounding gloom, which shouldn't have been possible. She ought to have been able to see several steps in front of her but instead, there was only light and blackness and nothing between.

Lena stopped and carefully turned to look behind her. The door and visible steps together with the lantern she had set in place on the wall, all looked as if they floated in a wider darkness. She found the effect deeply unsettling. Based on observation alone, elements of reality had started to come apart and drift away from one another.

The light of the lantern faded, and as total darkness surrounded her for the first time Lena felt genuine fear. She turned around again, set the lantern down and reached a hand across the step, first to the left and then the right. The steps ended abruptly and she could feel the stonework only in a downward direction. *No wall to either side now,* Lena thought, and wondered how far the descent would be if she stepped over the edge. *This is no longer a staircase, but a bridge. Over what?*

Finally, she continued down the steps. She no longer worried that the steps would end in empty space- if she continued forward and didn't stray to either side- but barely any time passed before her further progress was stopped abruptly by a solid surface.

Lena reached out and determined that it was made from wood. After a moment her hand found something colder and harder- a handle made from a thick circle of metal. She found no keyhole anywhere on the surface.

She turned the handle and pushed on the door. It opened into further darkness, in silence.

Lena felt cautiously with her foot and found solid stone beneath. She went down on her hands and knees again and moved slowly forwards until, to her bewilderment, she encountered steps that led upwards.

But these stairs must lead up into the waste ground near the house, Lena thought as she worked out the approximate position of their emergence above ground. *This isn't possible. I would know if there was an exit. I used to play there.*

She crawled slowly up the steps, counting twenty of them before she finally reached another door, whose surface and handle felt identical to the previous one.

Lena stood up, opened the door and stared out into the cold grey drizzle of a late winter day. She stepped through the doorway and stared around. Finally, as she saw a nearby street that sloped down towards the south, she realised where she was.

"No," she whispered as she took another uncertain step forward. "No. This can't be right."

This area, a high point overlooking the far south of the city, was a place she had been to only a few times before. It was over two days' walk from her home- or the best part of a morning on the Earthline, the subterranean railroad that ran through some parts of the city.

Lena pulled out her pocket watch with a trembling hand. "Ten minutes," she whispered, and wiped moisture from the curved glass lid of the timepiece. Looking at the numbers distorted by droplets of water she wondered if time itself had also been distorted. She could not have reached this place in only ten minutes. "Not possible," she mumbled again. "*Think*, Lena. Work it out."

Suddenly she remembered the door and turned quickly around.

But the exit had vanished. Only rows of grey bricks could be seen. They joined with their neighbours as if no door or any kind of aperture had ever stood there.

Some people were giving her curious looks. Lena managed to adopt a neutral expression as she turned away from the wall. She walked away half a dozen paces then looked around as if she was simply about to decide which way to head. The onlookers soon lost interest and moved on.

Go home, she told herself. *Maybe you're dreaming. Maybe you've gone mad. Whatever happened - and whether it happened in the outer world or in your own head - just get home and then try to make what sense you can of it.*

Lena inwardly marvelled at her composure as she headed down the road. *It's because I don't believe it,* she told herself. *It didn't happen. I'm dreaming.*

She passed by a hundred or more people - all of them wrapped up in their thick coats and their unknown thoughts and worries, their breath steaming into the thin, cold mist. Finally, she arrived at the squat, grey structure of an Earthline station building. The sign above the arched entrance read *South Hill Central*

Station. She would be able to get the Earthline train from here to the station nearest to her house.

Or would she? Lena's hand dived into her pocket and she searched anxiously for some money to pay for the journey. She found enough to get her two thirds of the way back. Her pass-card for free travel along the entire Earthline- one of the benefits of her occupation and position- had been left at home. *I didn't think I'd need it,* she remarked to herself and managed to stifle the harsh giggle that rose suddenly.

Lena made her way into the station hall, paid for a ticket as far as Blackstone and then walked down the grimy spiral staircase to the subterranean platform. Her boots echoed harshly in the stairwell as one hand clutched the cold curve of the bannister and the other trembled at her side until she forced it into her trouser pocket. *This is not real,* Lena told herself several times, but it certainly *felt* real.

She noted the sight and sounds and acrid stench of her environment, which worsened as she walked out onto the platform area. Oil, steam and grime mingled with a faint stench of sweat and urine. Nearby, a tall man in a long coat coughed up mucus and then spat it onto the platform. Lena glanced at the greenish fluid as it glistened in the faint light.

A beggar called plaintively, his voice muffled or coarsened by some affliction or other, and on a whim, Lena went to him and stooped down. She asked abruptly, "Is this real?"

His mouth closed to a line and his eyes narrowed, perhaps wary of the strange, confrontational woman. Then he looked away and down at himself and his piss-stained clothing, perhaps hoping she would leave him alone.

"You see me," she decided.

"Got any..." His request was curtailed abruptly by a fit of coughing and shaking.

Lena wandered slowly away to the other end of the platform. The intermittent buzz and crackle of the lights fixed to the wall would normally have annoyed her, but she barely noticed. Her only interest was in absorbing the entire scene. She tried to work out whether her environment was real or imagined but couldn't decide.

It occurred to her later, as the train carriage rattled its way through the dark, that she had suffered memory loss. A part of her cautioned against trying to rationalise the experience. But what else could she do? Perhaps she had suffered brain damage and forgotten the time between her opening of the cellar and her sudden appearance in a distant part of the Citadel.

But what about the time?

Lena constructed another theory. Maybe a whole *day* and ten minutes had passed.

She looked out at the soot-encrusted walls of the tunnel as the train screeched painfully along and wondered if she might not have opened the cellar door at all. *I was at home and reminiscing,* she recalled. *Did I take some wine or spirit from the pantry? Maybe I had too much to drink and fell down the cellar stairs. Maybe I hurt myself.*

Another possibility took root in her mind.

What if I consumed so much that I spent the entire night walking the streets until I blacked out, and only realised where I was the following afternoon? Maybe in my stupor I thought I'd got there through the cellar, through the magic door, because I miss Father and I want the things he implied to be true.

I can't bear this grey and dismal life.

Lena blinked back tears and forced her rambling thoughts away. She looked straight ahead at nothing and tried to ignore the old woman in the wet raincoat who stared at her from further down the carriage. The woman had no shoes and her feet were dark with dirt.

Everyone was too interested in her, Lena silently fumed, her fear replaced by resentment as she alighted at Blackstone later. What was it about distress that attracted and discomforted people at the same time? Why couldn't she make them all go away?

When she arrived back at her house Lena suddenly wondered if she was supposed to be at work. She figured eventually that today was a ninthday, and exhaled slowly, relieved. She had no need to be at work today, or tomorrow.

Perhaps that explained why she had lost control of herself last night. It seemed likely and it made as much sense as anything did right now. It wouldn't have been the first time she'd drunk too much for her own good on an eighth-day evening. That sort of episode had happened all too frequently in recent days. But this time, perhaps she'd tipped herself over the edge of sanity. She had become so intoxicated that not only had her memory of the night been destroyed but she had somehow replaced it with a wildly insane dream or recollection.

Maybe I dreamed as I lay in the gutter in the small hours, Lena reasoned as she turned the key in the door and made her weary way inside. She looked down at her clothes and wondered why they didn't smell worse than they did.

She couldn't find much evidence of late-evening drunkenness in the house. Some glasses sat in the kitchen sink, but they had been there for several days. *I took the bottles with me,* Lena decided. She looked in the store cupboards and pantry, in the hope that she could work out what she had taken and how much, but she couldn't remember what had been there to begin with. She then considered pouring away what remained but couldn't bring herself to.

Lena returned to the living room and stoked up the fire in the hearth. The ashes were still hot and glowed sullenly as she disturbed them. She put some wood and paper on and managed to coax the fire into life. Then she sat in her armchair as flames leapt from the new fuel.

She stared across at the chair on the other side of the hearth where her father had always sat. He alone had made its unique dents and creases. Had she ever sat there? Lena didn't think so, and she had no desire to sit there now, although she couldn't help but illogically wonder if observing the room from that unused location would lend her some unimaginable insight.

A solution. Her life required a solution.

What if it happens again? Lena worried suddenly. *What if I'm caught in a never-ending loop? How do I break out of it? Am I lost inside my own head, asleep and condemned to never wake up?*

Her mood changed abruptly several times that evening. She panicked and paced around the room, unable to decide what to do but certain that she must do something, anything. Then she sat and wept in desperation and fear, half-believing that she had gone insane and had been incarcerated in one of the terrifying hospitals for the mentally incapacitated. She screamed her anger at the injustice of her situation, despite having no idea what that situation was. Later, as the warmth from the fire temporarily lulled her into a quieter mood, she fell asleep only to wake up shouting at some imagined foe and unable- for a short while- to determine if she was truly awake or simply transferred to another dream.

"Please," Lena whispered. But she didn't know what she begged for, or who she pleaded with.

She considered making her way up the creaky wooden stairs to her bedroom as the small hours came but decided against it. It was warmer here, and for some reason it also felt safer.

"What should I do, Father?" she asked the empty chair across the room.

IV

Lena left the house the following morning and went for a long walk towards the centre of the Citadel.

She stopped at the midsection of a long, high bridge that spanned the Great River. Minutes passed as she stared down at the fast-flowing river far below, a murky churning torrent which entered the Citadel from the unknown, unexplored land north of the metropolis. It poured through a great wide tunnel that had been built into the walls many centuries ago. The river followed a winding path through the Citadel and then disappeared through another tunnel, in the south-facing wall. From there it cut through an abandoned harbour, parts of which could be seen from the highest points in the centre of the Citadel, before it emptied into the ocean.

Lena's thoughts drifted as she surveyed the swirling patterns. She imagined the almost infinite complexity of the process as movements and counter-movements played out endlessly in the water below.

Her exhaustion was complete. Alone, empty of hope and at the end of her ultimately pointless road, Lena felt an oddly detached sense of peace, as if she had begun to move gradually into death and fade from a world she only partly occupied.

Maybe her experience was a symptom of that approaching death.

Lena turned away from the waters below and walked on. She wondered if her displacement was the effect of a different reality, one that she would eventually occupy all the time. For now, she was still fading from one and into the other- being *poured,* Lena thought. She would see it again, and the frequency of such experiences would increase, until eventually she would have drained permanently from *this* dreary world to one of eternal peace.

As she drew near to the other side of the river, Lena asked herself how she could validate that theory, but surprised herself with her answer.

She didn't need to explain it. She had limits. All minds had a finite perimeter. So maybe all she had to do was believe in it.

Lena wondered if her theory would provide comfort or solace as she got used to the idea. It felt strangely hopeful.

But by the time she reached the end of the bridge and stood with hands deep in the pockets of her coat, Lena had decided that it wouldn't.

It was too easy an answer. It was the answer she wanted, so it was either wrong, or incomplete at best.

Cold rain began to fall. She turned and hurried home.

Two days later, Lena returned to her workplace. Around mid-morning she was summoned to an interview with Faral Whitewood, the chief counsellor at the Department of Industry. A bald, middle-aged man with an oily smile, he attempted to give an impression of

42

understanding and sympathy as she was admitted into his cramped little office high up in the Administration block of the power station.

"Lena. Thank you for giving me some of your time this afternoon."

"I wasn't aware I had a choice."

Faral did not appear to have heard her. "Before we start," he continued, "I should express my sadness at the passing of your father."

"Did you know him?" Lena asked. She knew perfectly well that he hadn't.

Faral merely paused and blinked at her as if the question was worthy of casual recognition but not an answer. "How are you feeling?" he asked presently.

Lena wondered how often he had uttered those words in the last year, the last five years, or the whole time he had worked as a counsellor. "I don't know," she said eventually. "How should I be feeling?"

Faral peered at her over the top of his glasses. "What a curious question," he murmured at last, in the manner of a man who had found a new specimen to inspect.

And you're a curious man, Lena silently retorted. *I don't care to be one of your subjects, to be held up and scrutinised. You have even less empathy than I do. Mine is a technical, inquiring mind like yours, only I prefer the workings of machines to those of people. I don't care to know what makes people do the things they do. I don't care for people very much at all. I never did.*

If they passed a law to allow it, would you pin your subjects to the walls of your laboratory to peruse forever? Would you open their heads and attempt to work out why their brains didn't work in the way you thought they should?

43

Under the desk and out of his view, her fists clenched so hard that they shook. Lena didn't notice, and neither, as far as she could tell, did the counsellor. She only managed to stop when she imagined that a door had appeared in the back wall, behind Faral's desk.

Oh, to step through and never return.

"The standard of your work remains excellent," Faral remarked, and scratched at his hairless, pockmarked head as if he couldn't fathom why it would.

"I've lost none of my mental faculties." Lena shifted uneasily in her chair as she listened to her own lie, unable to precisely fathom where the conversation was headed.

"No, of course not, and why would you?" Faral gaped at her as if she had uttered something that astonished him.

"I wouldn't," Lena retorted.

The counsellor made a show of reading through his papers again. Lena watched as he shuffled them pointlessly. She wondered what his next question would be.

"Lena, do you feel angry?" he asked finally. He didn't bother to look up. Had she disturbed his equilibrium? Lena hoped so. "It's quite normal to," he added, as if that might encourage her into confession.

"No," she lied. Anger could be viewed as something that might compromise the quality of her work and the accuracy of her judgement. "It's just one of those things that happen sometimes. Bad luck."

Faral's puzzlement appeared to deepen, yet he continued, "But you *do* feel depressed, don't you?"

Lena struggled to maintain her composure. *I need to answer him,* she told herself, and finally came up with, "A little, of course, but I'm sure I'll feel better eventually." She then added, "As you know, I have a great deal to offer the Department's many engineering and infrastructure projects. I'm looking forward to putting everything that's happened behind me."

Faral smiled faintly. "Thank you, Lena, especially for your honesty at this difficult time. You may go."

As she hurried down the corridor towards her sector, Lena reckoned she felt worse than before their conversation. Her fury, not properly expressed, had made her weak and tremulous.

A couple of hours later, she sat in the low-ceilinged and poorly lit canteen, her meal cold and abandoned. One of the senior engineers, a man called Shen, sat further along the table, making loud snorts and grunts as he consumed his lunch, pausing only to wipe errant food from his beard. Lena felt a twinge of nausea at the thought of eating anything. She wanted to tell him to shut up or go elsewhere but couldn't bring herself to speak. In any case, she wasn't his superior or even in the same maintenance team.

"Sorry about your father," Lena heard him say as he glanced in her direction. The words were muffled by the food he hadn't yet swallowed. *Couldn't you at least finish your mouthful first?* she thought angrily. "Thank you," she said aloud without looking at him.

"If there's anything I can do..." he added, leaving the pointless offer unfinished.

"No. There isn't." But Lena's forbidding tone had little effect on Shen, or perhaps he simply didn't notice. He swallowed the rest of his food and leaned across towards her. "If you ever want some company, I'm around whenever you need me. I expect you're lonely."

Ah, how swiftly you show your true colours, Lena thought contemptuously. *Although I already knew what sort of man you are.*

She turned slowly to face him. "You're not my type of man, Shen." A couple of other men seated at a table nearby sniggered, and Shen's mood immediately soured in the face of that further humiliation. "So, what *is* your type of man?" he spat back, wiping his hands on his oil-smeared vest. "Or maybe you prefer women?"

"Maybe I just prefer to be left alone."

He pushed his lunch tray away and stood up. "Just trying to be friendly," he said. Lena looked back at him and saw a cold hardness in his eyes that belied his words. *That's the look all men get the moment they're denied,* she reminded herself. *They're nothing more than dangerous children.*

"You'd better watch yourself," he added darkly, followed by, "I'll bet my salary you're a virgin." Then he turned and strode away, kicking a chair out of his path as he went.

Why do they behave that way? Lena pondered a little later, alone now in the canteen. But the question reminded her of the only man she knew who hadn't worn misogyny like a badge of honour.

Father, why did you have to leave me?

V

Lena made her way home later that afternoon under a sullen sky. Sleet lashed sporadically from fast-moving clouds as she hurried along Downspiral Street. *Such an apt name,* she thought as she glanced up at the sign on the brick wall at the corner of the road.

Despite the damp and chilly weather, Lena dreaded the simple act of walking into the house long before she took her key from her pocket and turned it in the door. Her home felt simultaneously empty and filled with memories, some of which she had only recently begun to remember properly again.

Useless, she thought angrily as she finally made her way in, slammed the door behind her and walked through the hallway. *Why should I recall such times now, when I need to shut them away? If Father was still here it might have been different. But no, if he was still here it wouldn't occur to me to talk about old times. We would both be distracted by our mundane day to day existence, just as we were until it was too late. We'd play out the days as pointlessly as we did before.*

She stopped at the entrance to the sitting-room and pulled the cord for the lights, which flickered on with an accompanying groan as the generator grudgingly responded. Lena reasoned that she could fit a new one. She could change everything inside and out. She could even sell this place and buy a house on the other side of the city. The borrowers' bank would let her. She had been working continuously for years and had no debts.

There were a great many things she *could* do, but the idea of doing anything at all made her exhaustion more acute than ever.

Later that evening Lena opened the drawers of her father's desk, searching for important papers such as the certificate of ownership for the house- one of the documents she would need if she decided to sell it. She finally located the yellow-cornered certificate and placed it on the table in front of her. Warm shadows danced in the corners of the room, produced by the fire and the lanternlight.

Where would she go? It didn't matter. Somewhere small and manageable, whose exact dimensions and shape could be easily known. After all she told herself, she didn't like nooks and crannies and pointless corners and alcoves.

But Lena remembered that she had taken great pleasure in the illogical design of this house during her childhood. She had even imagined that their home had changed in subtle ways over the years. Hadn't her father implied as much, once? She couldn't be sure but thought he might have done.

It changes, Lena. But you mustn't tell anyone.

Who built it? she wondered suddenly as the light buzzed and flickered.

Then she came to the absurd, but absurdly plausible idea that, to some extent at least, the house had built itself.

Lena's imagination had burned brightly in those days. She had spent long hours immersed in worlds of her own making. She had chased imaginary villains or monsters through the house, especially during the dreary winter days when dismal weather meant few chances to venture out.

But as the years went on, the logical and structured side of her personality gained the upper hand and refused to let go. Her drawings and musical compositions- written using a code she had devised herself- were put aside and forgotten. Artistic endeavour was seldom appreciated in the Citadel, and the authorities generally discouraged it unless it also served a practical purpose or fulfilled a pressing need. Drawings and music did not tend to be useful, in their collective opinion. They represented a distraction from progress.

That morning in the cellar, Father's words finally broke me, Lena recalled. *No doubt he intended the opposite effect. And here I am, possibly at the end of the wrong path.*

She listened absently to the solemn thud of the wooden clock on the shelf across from her and wondered suddenly if any of her works from long ago had been kept somewhere in the house. She almost went in search of them, but then sharply reminded herself that such childish randomness had no place in her world now. What use could it have?

The Citadel is everything, she tiredly reminded herself, and repeated the mantra instilled in children throughout their years of education. *The Citadel is everything, the last bastion of civilisation, the envy of the monstrosities that lurk in the wilderness. The Citadel is the pinnacle of human endeavour and the light to hold against the darkness of the abandoned outer world. The Citadel provides every one of its people with a purpose in life. A goal, a talent, a niche fulfilled.*

Perhaps those words held some truth. Lena's father had once said that the best lies of all were those that contained elements of truth, which gave them a veneer of plausibility, lessening the leap of faith required to believe them.

"Think about what we know to be true, and what we are *told* is true," he had said during one of the many philosophical conversations they had held during her teenage years. These were conversations that could be entertained nowhere but behind closed and locked doors, for the authorities would have considered them treacherous. "The people have no real idea what lies beyond the Citadel. The world stretches away into the distance, an unpainted canvas. It hasn't been documented, or if it has then they have no access to the documents."

"You said *they*-not *we*," Lena noted. "The people. Not *us*."

He didn't respond to her observation. "What people do you suppose live out in that unending wilderness?"

"There aren't any. There haven't been for over a thousand years."

"Well, let's suppose you're right. What *creatures* then?"

Lena thought. "I don't know. We're taught that terrifying monsters roam out there. There must be a good reason why the Citadel hasn't been expanded out into that land."

"Exactly. You don't know. None of us do. The High Walls have guardsmen who patrol constantly. They look out over the vastness. Sometimes monsters *are* sighted, apparently. Never any people, though. Evidence enough that whatever world exists outside our civilisation is indeed a dark and savage place. It may be, it may not. Why struggle to survive, when we can all exist adequately here in the Citadel?"

But something about his smile made Lena pause. She thought for a moment. "You said exist *adequately*," she pointed out.

"Did I?" He looked at her for a while and then leaned forward. "Maybe that's because very few of us can do anything more than exist adequately. Why, with all our mastery of engineering and technology, can we not colonise whatever vast areas await outside the Citadel?"

"Because of the dangers..."

"...that very few of us have ever seen."

Lena felt deeply troubled. "We shouldn't even be discussing this."

"You're right, of course. In fact, such discussion is ultimately pointless. The Citadel is everything and we have everything we need. Why go against that? How would that be logical?"

But his sardonic, strangely sad words had planted in Lena a sense of disquiet that had never truly left her. There was something more that he'd wanted to say, she had no doubt. But he was as frightened of taking that metaphorical step as he had been of taking the literal steps into the dark a few years before.

For days after that conversation, Lena spent a lot of time with her head in history textbooks, her intention to piece together a better understanding of the Citadel, of society, of how their isolation had come to be.

But her intensely enquiring mind remained dissatisfied with the half-answers and platitudes she discovered.

The further back in history she delved, the vaguer and more piecemeal that history became. Lena could not find anything much beyond the assertion that the Citadel had been founded by the Mothers perhaps over a thousand years ago, from an existing smaller settlement- which had in turn been built by people who migrated from other settlements, of which no detail could now be found. The Citadel was, to all intents and purposes, everything. It represented both the core and the limit of civilisation. Beyond its vast triple walls that stood a thousand hands tall and a hundred thick, nothing but wilderness and savagery held sway. Thus it had been for all of recorded history. The smaller settlement from which it had formed had been built by a group of people dedicated to the creation of a better place, with more hope than the miserable, far-flung pockets of humanity that existed around that time. It grew steadily as more and more people flocked there, drawn by the promise of a safer place where their children stood a reasonable chance of reaching adulthood, where future families might be raised in relative peace, and where justice might prevail and those who sought nothing but chaos and lawlessness would be suitably punished.

"And what existed before *them*?" Lena wondered aloud several times. "Where did everyone live before the time of the Citadel?"

No doubt those same questions had been asked many times before over the centuries. But why had they never been answered?

Over centuries the Citadel had become home to many millions of people. The most learned and gifted of them contributed discoveries and inventions that eventually changed it beyond recognition. Even so it stood then as now, a single city-state, empire as much as settlement- and apparently the only one of its kind.

If other lands, other societies had once existed, then their names had somehow passed out of history altogether. They were not individually recorded in the books that Lena found. Everything about those failed places- except the simple fact of their existence- had been forgotten. They now warranted only a cursory mention in the few books that covered the subject.

No maps existed of the lands beyond the Citadel, nor of the great ocean to the south. *What lies beyond that sea?* Lena had also wanted to know. But she could find no book to inform her.

Neither could anything be found from that distant time that concerned the Mothers - their origins, their powers, their mysterious immortality.

Frustrated and growing ever more fearful of discovery, Lena eventually put the matter aside and lived with her unease and the lingering feeling of discontent that tainted her life. She continued to immerse herself in study. She devoted her life to the learning and execution of things that could be designed, created and relied upon, that *worked* manifestations of truth and reliability.

She became a cog in the Citadel's vast mechanism.

Her dreams, meanwhile, were often frightening visions of places she had never seen.

Lena stared at the certificate for a while longer. *I must leave,* she told herself, but at the same she could think only of the staircase in the cellar and the mad but exhilarating notion of exploring beyond the limit of the light again. Where might she end up next time? Somewhere beyond the Citadel?

It was a dream, Lena cautioned herself.

Her stomach churned uneasily at the thought. She swallowed, her throat suddenly dry as her palms prickled with sweat.

She felt helpless, frightened and yet excited, as if a hitherto unknown freedom might lurk just beyond the periphery of her life.

The thought of never going back to work took root in her mind. *I could try the door again,* Lena thought. *I must go through it once more and figure out how it works. That could be my work now, and from this point on until everything ends.*

The sleet intensified and pattered in a harsh rhythm against the windows. Lena placed the certificate back in its drawer and then paused. She had always loved the sound of the rain. She could open a bottle of wine and sit in the living room, immerse herself in sad, drunken warmth and perhaps read a book and be lulled by the rhythm of the downpour outside.

No, she decided forcefully.

Lena went through to the door that led onto the staircase, taking a lantern with her. The key was already in her hand.

She opened the door. Soon she moved into shadow, felt her way along in the dark and reached the door at the bottom of the staircase.

Then sudden panic set in. Abruptly she removed her hand from the handle as if it was red-hot, no matter that it felt like ice.

No, she told herself angrily. *What are you doing?*

Then an answering voice spoke up- *Walk away now and you'll hate yourself forever. You'll remain a prisoner of your dismal existence, measured and defined by your profession, your supposed calling.*

"It's not that bad," Lena said aloud, but her heart spoke differently.

She waited by the door for a long while, as if in fanciful hope that the decision to go forward or back would be taken out of her hands by some unseen force or entity.

But when Lena eventually grasped the door handle again, pulled it and scrambled through into the darkness beyond, she moved with an almost savage speed.

VI

Lena slowly breathed in the surrounding darkness. The door closed quietly and unnoticed behind her. She marvelled at the sudden *difference* she felt, as if she now weighed half as much or possessed twice her usual energy. It manifested as an inaudible hum of power, or at least potential. *As if I'm a machine,* she thought. The irony of being a woman whose life had been consumed by the maintenance and fine-tuning of machines did not escape her.

The area behind the door was different to how she remembered. She stood at the base of another staircase but in a low-ceilinged passageway lined with ancient bricks. A faint yellow glow lit her environment, but she found it impossible to pinpoint its origin. The air felt dank and cold against her skin.

Lena turned to look back at the cellar door, but- as a part of her had expected- it was no longer there. She marvelled at the seamlessness of the transformation. *Perfect,* she thought as her hands caressed the places where she estimated the edges of the door had been.

She felt no fear. This in turn led her to wonder again if she had become insane and trapped in a place of her own design.

But if that was true, then the rules of this place- if any existed- were fashioned by her subconscious. Lena wondered if that meant she wasn't here at all but sitting in her lonely living room by the fire with her eyes fixed on empty space. Perhaps a forgotten book and a few empty wine bottles would be somewhere nearby.

Or had she already been incarcerated, judged to be a danger to herself or others? Had her interview with the counsellor proceeded differently to how she believed?

Lena began to walk along the passageway. Later, she wouldn't recall whether she had turned left or right, but she felt oddly certain that direction didn't matter here in any traditional sense.

As she walked carefully along, holding the lantern in front of her, Lena concluded ruefully that she had never been the woman she had tried to sculpt herself into. Maybe that was why this had happened. She had pushed herself too far, forced herself into an occupation she never fitted into, and tried to convince herself that it was her calling.

Then when her father died something snapped inside her.

I should be frightened, Lena thought. *Instead I'm ever the analyst, peering at an unfixable problem.*

A faint green glow could be seen through a crack in the wall. Lena stopped and pulled hesitantly at the surrounding material, which crumbled away in her hands. Then she peered through the gap. She immediately recognised the first object she saw- the main tower of the materials factory that stood a short distance away from the power plant where she worked. It stood about five hundred hands away, she reckoned, and it looked a little taller and thinner than it ought, but Lena recognised the structure nonetheless. No smoke emerged from the chimneys clustered at the top of the tower. The windows dotted at various levels along its length all glowed with a faint green light.

Lena stared transfixed and for a short while that light became her world.

She longed to be a part of that outer place, to step into that light. The thirst for discovery almost engulfed her. Her hands pulled and strained against the brickwork as the urge to escape the confines of the passageway became too strong to resist. Eventually enough pieces of the material cracked and fell away for Lena to force herself through the gap.

She emerged into a dimly lit street, beyond which the factory stood. *This place is not the Citadel,* she reminded herself. *This is a dream of the Citadel, or a picture of what it might have been.*

Great towers and spires rose high into the gloom, pockmarked with windows of all shapes and sizes. Light poured from some of them. Lena thirsted for secrets that she knew *must* lie beyond every doorway and through every aperture. What if entire, different worlds existed behind each window?

She breathed in the oddly flat air and listened. Utter silence filled this ghostly version of the Citadel and no movement disturbed the pristine stillness. When she began to cautiously walk along the deserted road her footsteps sounded muffled, almost distant.

Disquiet stirred within her. What if she became trapped here forever?

That notion led quickly to other unpleasant thoughts. If there were no people here- an idle assumption at this point- did that mean that nothing to eat or drink could be found? Was it night-time and would it lighten to become day at some point- or might this vague gloom be eternal?

Lena stopped for a moment. *Don't be silly,* she chided herself. *You're inside your own head. You've lost your mind, at least temporarily. How else do you explain the disappearance of the cellar door? How else do you explain some of these structures all around you, which cannot physically remain standing and yet defy every natural law regardless?*

But she couldn't deny how *real* this place felt. She looked to the starlit sky and tried to identify the constellations but couldn't. Would they move over time, or remain as if they were painted onto a backdrop?

The street opened out into a vast cobbled square. It looked a little like Traders' Arena just east of the Citadel's centre, but the surrounding architecture had taken on a violently different form. Wherever Lena turned, buildings of every shape rose up to scrape the glittering heavens- thin towers with sharply pointed turrets, blocky high-rise structures with hundreds of square windows, misshapen ugly factories infested with chimneys that sprouted like brick mutations from their blackened, grimy roofs.

The scene looked like a nightmare of the Citadel.

Lena felt a frightening emptiness open inside her. If every part of every building here was abandoned, if the entire vastness of this place might hold nothing but silence- what of any worth could exist here?

But then, she had no need of people and never had. She came from a place that had far too many of them. She had watched them struggle through the dullness and drudgery of their existence with the spark of imagination snuffed out forever. And so, a part of her had always wanted to be free from the expectations of others.

But then, even if this place could be hers alone, what would the point be of dominion over an empty world?

Utter helplessness overcame her. She had discovered this miraculous, impossible place, yet it held no discernible purpose and fulfilled no need. It was a riddle without words.

Thin tendrils of smoke began to drift from one of the tall industrial chimneys of the building that looked like the power station, as if this gloomy world had finally seen fit to respond to her thoughts. Lena watched as it swirled to become lost in the sky. Had some combustive process caused it?

Then the music began.

It sounded a little like some of the songs she had heard on the factory floors and occasionally in the engineering common rooms- shambolic, bawdy and yet somehow urgent. Lena tried to identify its source and eventually decided that it came from the factory where smoke had started to rise into the night.

She approached the nearest door in the building, one of the side entrances which- in the world she knew- was used for the delivery of goods and supplies. She walked down the corridor beyond the entrance, then turned left down another passageway. The lighting flickered and the faint, doleful hum of distant machinery sounded. What use could an empty world have of industrial processes?

Lena stopped suddenly at a set of double swing doors. They looked identical to those that led into the canteen at the engineering plant where she worked.

It doesn't matter here. The rules of reality are more fluid in this place.

Cautiously she pushed open the doors and walked on, to find that this was indeed the canteen she was used to, or at least an approximation of it. *I'm making all this up,* she reminded herself. *But even I can't seem to get all the details right.*

As she surveyed the emptiness and breathed in the silence, Lena caught sight of something that moved near the rear of the room, flitting amongst the tables and against the wall. She couldn't understand what she saw at first, then realised that it was a *shadow*- darkness whose shape and position changed continuously. But that couldn't be possible. A shadow needed not only an object but a source of light, and none of the lights in here had been positioned in the right place to make it.

She backed away and out of the canteen and hurried on along the corridor, which now seemed narrower than before, its ceiling higher. The sounds of machinery became a little louder, accompanied by a low, almost musical humming noise that sounded as if machines and humans made it together.

Lena finally found her way out of the building and into a yard that led to a back alley. Here she became suddenly aware of a presence that she couldn't define- a pure malevolence, evil without true form.

Then she saw it- a sliver of absolute darkness. It flickered against the dimly lit wall, a vileness that silently screamed its hatred into this still world. She wondered fearfully what it might be. Maybe not anything alive, but the essence of something that once lived, now trapped here for all time.

How could something that wasn't truly alive feel such hatred, or anything at all?

Lena hurried away from the factory, towards another vast, tall building across the silent road. Here she saw movements in the light that poured from the windows, and the song had started again now. After a moment Lena realised that this was not truly music, but an aural representation of something entirely different. A process, she decided. A joining together of two different complex processes- one of them human and natural, the other cold and mechanical, rigidly structured. It was the combination of two fluids, such that the two could never be separated.

It was a symphony of evil, and- Lena decided- a prophecy.

She stepped slowly towards the dreadful pulse and flow, and as she drew near to one of the windows, Lena saw something that looked both like a shadow and a human-shaped area of darkness. It writhed in the strange illumination, and Lena realised that she could sense other things inside its form- distinct areas of light and dark, objects that she could not hope to define or describe, movements that at first appeared chaotic but which she soon realised were all part of an overarching plan.

She concluded that this was a visual interpretation of the song she had heard. *Someone or something is trying to describe this to me,* Lena decided. *They use the song to describe it aurally. They use this patchwork of impossible things to describe it visually.*

There's a message here, and I must learn to understand it somehow.

But the more desperately she tried to comprehend, the more Lena sensed revelation move beyond her reach. She could not solve this mystery by forcing her intellect upon it, nor could she apply the wisdom of experience, because she observed something that existed far beyond her horizon.

"No!" she pleaded, as the scene faded, and the accompanying sounds drifted away into silence.

The ground slowly crumbled beneath her feet, and Lena tumbled away into darkness.

III – The Voice

One task above all others filled the man known as the Voice with irritation and unease. This meaningless and baffling chore- carried out away from the sight of any others, like most of his work- elicited no reaction from the prisoner he questioned. Only the Mothers of the Citadel, absolute rulers of human civilisation, knew anything about it.

Never speak of this, they had said to him, *until or unless you receive a response.*

He had obeyed without question. To disobey the Mothers was unthinkable.

The prisoner, parts of whose face and body were missing, stood held in place by force fields that operated from every direction- great powers that even Seneth, with his knowledge of mathematical and physical laws, couldn't understand. The Voice had no idea how long this unresponsive creature had been incarcerated here, nor did he know the purpose of the questions that he asked every day, if indeed they had one. The prisoner could not have pre-dated the Citadel of course, but Seneth sometimes entertained the far-fetched notion that the metropolis had been built around this curiosity. *A civilisation built around an unspeaking ruin of a man,* he had silently scoffed more than once- and then tried not to dwell on how strangely plausible the concept seemed.

"What is your name?"

"What do you know of other worlds?"

"What does the mirror mean to you?"

Silence had always met every question he asked. The third question had always interested him more than the others. He wondered which mirror was being referred to. He also wondered how the prisoner was expected to respond, given the obliqueness of the question.

Perhaps, rather than provoke a meaningful verbal response, they were intended to provoke another observable reaction- rage, perhaps, or fear.

Other worlds. The mirror. Seneth did not know of other worlds- the study of such things was forbidden, and even *this* world had, except for the Citadel, long been abandoned by humanity. It had been left for monsters and demons that few books dared shine a light upon.

The three questions were then always followed by others which, to the Voice, seemed more directly useful. The Mothers referred to these as the *lesser* questions. They related to dry, routine matters such as the efficiency of machines, or the automation of a process, or an obscure mathematical sequence. Many of them *he* already knew the answers to.

Useful or not, none of his questions had ever caused a reaction. Only the steady rise and fall of the prisoner's broken chest and the faint pupillary dilation and constriction in the single (unseeing?) eye in his three-quarter head showed that he lived at all. His jaw and throat appeared intact, which, Seneth surmised, might be why the Mothers had assigned the interrogation to him. They clearly believed that their captive could visibly respond to it, no matter that a vast chunk was missing from his brain.

One of his arms appeared healthy and whole whilst the other was nothing more than a bloodied set of bones held together by thin threads of musculature.

Seneth had no idea how that could have happened. It didn't look like the result of any wound or affliction that he could imagine. How had this prisoner been *rearranged* in this way, and how had he survived the ordeal? Had the Mothers brought about his disintegration in the distant past- and if they had, then why slowly reconstruct him and demand answers to questions that- aside from the first one- had no obvious short answers?

Seneth had many questions of his own, but no one who could answer them- except the three women who he dared not ask.

During his daily visits to the prisoner in the glass box he sometimes imagined that he felt a faint presence, which belied the unresponsive nature of the prisoner. Seneth could not measure or understand it. Often during his tenure as Voice he had wondered what secrets lay locked within the prisoner's brain- if his brain still functioned at any higher level. *If he's aware,* Seneth had surmised on many occasions, *he should be able to respond. Does he choose not to?*

He likely wouldn't find out in the next five years, before his role as Voice came to its natural end and his private execution was carried out.

Seneth sharply reminded himself that no greater honour existed than to serve as Voice. How many others could in honesty say that they had beheld the faces of the Mothers of the Citadel- their *true* faces? How many others held such power, answerable only to the Mothers? There were none. Many men would kill many other men to become Voice. Indeed, many men *had* killed others in such desperate attempts to prove themselves.

Seneth had no idea how many he had killed.

Still, every morning he felt the taint of dissatisfaction lurk in the back of his mind. He would have liked to be the one to whom the silent prisoner finally spoke, even though the Mothers would inevitably claim such progress as their own. He even considered asking questions other than those he had been assigned, but he dared not.

Know your limits, he would tell himself.

Seneth was reminded daily of the Mothers' great power and ruthlessness. When he went to his meetings, he traversed a vast chamber known amongst the servants and administrators of the Palace as the Great Hall of Flesh. This forbiddingly chilly area had a thick glass floor which held the bodily remains of at least a thousand men, women and children- a small fraction of those who had committed crimes against the Citadel in the past. Each body had been perfectly preserved. Some faces bore looks of unending astonishment or horror, others no expression at all. Perhaps this was how each had looked at the point of death, a snapshot frozen for eternity.

Only the Mothers decided whether to incarcerate a wrongdoer within the glass. Seneth had never seen the process but reckoned it involved cutting or melting the glass, placing the body inside and sealing it quickly, all of which those women could do without mechanical tools. Their powers were, as far as he knew, boundless.

Today, as he lingered in the hall and knelt to peer at some of the bodies- naked, shaved and perhaps even embalmed, not that he could tell through the thickness of glass- sunlight poured from the great windows that stood in the east-facing wall and brightened the glass and its pale preserved contents even further.

Seneth exhaled slowly and watched his breath drift into the icy air. He never tired of peering into the eyes of the condemned, wondering idly if some of them might, against all logic, still somehow be alive‐ staring back at the surface dweller in unblinking despair.

"Beautiful," he murmured.

Finally, he left, not because he wanted to but because‐ as ever‐ duty called.

One of Seneth's duties involved the interrogation of certain suspects before deciding whether they should be passed back to the Ministry of Law or simply executed. Only particularly unusual cases were brought before him, and one such person was due to be handed over today by Dalan Moran, the Chief Balancer and head of the Citadel authorities.

The Chief Balancer, his prisoner and a retinue of guards were already waiting in one of the outer halls when Seneth arrived.

He observed the prisoner dispassionately, and the trembling creature averted her eyes. She stood unclothed like all the felons who were brought before him. Seneth idly counted the ribs that pushed against her skin and imagined that skin softly bursting to reveal her glistening interior.

He made a mental note to offer her food in exchange for information as he scanned through her identification papers that the Chief Balancer had already placed on the table. *I'll have the servants bring me my lunch in the interrogation chamber,* he decided. *It does them good to see that place from time to time. I'll enjoy my meal in front of this wretch, and then we'll see how long her resolve lasts.*

According to the arrest papers, her name was Rhion Freeward. She appeared to be a vagrant and petty thief with a chequered but otherwise unremarkable criminal record. As Seneth finished his perusal and glanced at her again, he wearily suspected that this would turn out to be a complete waste of his time.

"We believe she's carried out forbidden practices," Moran told him unnecessarily. His gimlet eyes surveyed the prisoner and a small, pink tongue darted quickly back and forth across his lips for a moment. Seneth wondered if the Chief Balancer was hungry, or had carnal thoughts concerning his charge, or was simply nervous. "The report suggests the use of an accelerant of some sort, but no such substance was found. That said, we have six independent witnesses who, under oath, gave consistent testimonies."

"I can see what the report says." Nevertheless, Seneth glanced at it again. "I assume you've ruled out membership of a chemical terror group? It isn't clear on your report."

"She has no prior incidents of this type on her record. There's nothing to suggest she's the member of any group at all. The suggestion of an accelerant is as standard, my Lord Voice. Reports must always make reasonable suggestions."

"Must they, indeed?"

"Will you take her? Or shall we lock her up?"

Seneth frowned at the Chief Balancer's fractious tone. "You've brought creatures such as this to me before, Moran. None of them ever admitted their crimes."

"Oh? That must have disappointed you, my lord Voice."

"Their deaths went some way towards making up for it."

Moran flashed a quick smile. "Of course. But wouldn't it be a worthy challenge? Perhaps for the first time, one of these... oddities may succumb to your persuasion. Do take her off my hands. Rhion has been *so* looking forward to meeting you at last."

"I'm sure she has." Seneth laughed as good-naturedly as he could. He had never yet lost his temper in front of the Chief Balancer, although he had thought many times about arranging his assassination. The problem with that was twofold- no assassin anywhere in the Citadel would be able to take on such a task even if they were mad enough to show an interest in it, and more importantly the Mothers would easily trace the act back to him. Was there anything in existence that they could not see, or discover?

If he wanted Moran dead that badly then he would have to beg them himself, in person. And he had no desire to seek an audience with his mistresses, for something that they might consider petty and punish him for.

Can I break this one? he wondered. Already the prisoner looked sunken in defeat, but that didn't necessarily mean anything. Moran was right about one thing. To break one down would be a worthy achievement. One of Seneth's great frustrations- aside from the curious matter of the silent prisoner to whom the Mothers attached such strange importance- was that all of the previous five whose criminal reports included observations that couldn't be explained, had somehow resisted his interrogation, which would have swiftly had words tumbling from the mouths of other men and women.

They had been meek, apparently submissive, and yet none had revealed one ounce of their trickery. What made them different? He had no idea.

Seneth shrugged. "I'll take her off your hands and see what can be done. If I fail, well..." Again he forced a bright and almost amused smile. "Each of us will fail sooner or later, Chief Balancer. Our lives all end in failure."

"As you say, my lord Voice." Moran bowed slowly and perhaps a little too deeply for Seneth's liking.

The Chief Balancer turned and left. Seneth led the woman slowly away in her chains. As per protocol, two guardsmen from nearby archways fell in on either side of him, hands resting on their pistols in case the prisoner attempted the most unlikely of escapes. Seneth found their presence an irritation more than a reassurance, but he would dismiss them once they reached the interrogation chamber.

A man who saw what went on in there might never be the same again.

II

Seneth had always reckoned that the interrogation room was unnecessarily large for its purpose, but then almost every part of the great Palace was oversized in one way or another. Year on year the structure grew larger still, as orders filtered down from the Mothers through himself for new parts to be built around its perimeter, not that most of them served any function that existing areas couldn't. Seneth had no idea why the Palace needed to grow at all, but he knew of many construction merchants who had grown rich and fat and retired early simply because of the pointless yet lucrative work their companies had been commissioned to carry out here. Aside from the prestige associated with it, Palace work paid far better than its equivalent elsewhere in the Citadel.

Seneth motioned for Rhion to sit opposite him. He looked around the dismal, mildew-spotted walls of the chamber, barely reached by the light from the single bulb that hung from the ceiling. For some reason he had never understood, the brickwork in this room retained a persistent dampness, as if the structure sweated. None of the surveyors and geo-engineers he had brought down here to look at the problem had offered a satisfactory explanation or a solution. *Bad rock,* one of them had had the audacity to claim.

Rhion placed her hands on the cold metal table. She no longer trembled, although this room was chillier than almost anywhere else in the Palace- another feature that had never been adequately explained. She looked him directly in the eyes, which was something very few people managed to do for longer than a moment. Seneth decided that the woman had steeled herself against whatever torture she might suffer. He wondered if her earlier distress had been a facade- but what would that achieve? Was her behaviour nothing more than the freedom of a condemned woman to behave as she wished?

Maybe he could convince her that she still had a chance of walking free. But then, she might already know that very few survived an audience with him.

"Well, Rhion- you've achieved something today," he commented as he put her papers to one side. "Your previous crimes resulted in nothing more than fines or short-term imprisonments. In fact, it looks as if most of your imprisonments came about from your inability to pay the fines levied for your previous crimes. A downward spiral."

"I'm a lady of limited means." Her voice sounded soft. *Almost liquid,* he thought.

"Nevertheless, you've displayed an impressive level of persistence in disregarding the law, which has helped you to achieve your audience with me."

Rhion blinked. "Is that an achievement?"

Seneth gave her a chilling smile. "Oh, you *know* it is. But I won't begrudge you your little victory."

"I'm hardly the victor in this situation." She rustled the chains around her wrists and ankles.

"Your predecessors all sat in the same chair you occupy right now. Over time they died there. Do you feel their unquiet presence?"

"I don't believe in ghosts and spirits." She peered at him, seemingly puzzled. "Why ask me such a thing? Perhaps you sense something that I can't?"

Seneth ignored the questions. "None of them succumbed to my interrogation. They were, in fact, the only five who resisted me successfully."

Rhion shook her head. "I wouldn't know these people."

Seneth leaned forward. "They were like you. They carried out acts- *crimes*- that could not be explained and were brought here. They died in the most excruciating pain and, much to my frustration, took their secrets with them. I can't let that happen again, so I'm quite willing to play a very patient game with you, over many days if that's what it takes. You'll recover just enough to keep playing, and we'll begin again, differently."

Rhion stared expressionlessly back at him. "Why tell me of your failures? You spoke of *predecessors*, but I'm quite alone. I've no family, no ties to anyone. I don't know who else you've questioned, and I don't know about these acts which can't be explained."

Seneth smiled. "Of course you don't. But let's see if your opinion changes today."

"Let's."

"I will ask you a number of questions. If I'm unhappy with any of your answers, I'll hurt you and ask

71

the question again. The process continues⁻ no, it *intensifies⁻* until I'm satisfied."

"That's how I thought it would work," Rhion commented.

Seneth thumbed through her papers again until he found the page he wanted. "A fruit trader in West Castle Square reported that you caused every single one of his products to spoil in under a minute as you passed by two mornings ago. His claim is supported by six independent witnesses."

Rhion smiled. "Are you going to ask me if I did it, or *how* I did it?"

"The latter. I already know you're responsible. My interest is in the mechanism, not the fact of the matter."

"But a magician can't possibly divulge the tricks of her trade. Also, doesn't it seem like a rather trivial matter for the Voice of the Citadel to be involved with? I mean, *fruit?* What do you suppose the total value of his produce was?"

"The value, the produce and the trader are all scenery. You know very well what I'm after." Seneth got up and went to sit on the table next to where she sat. The woman gazed coolly back at him. "How did you do it?" he asked her quietly.

"Perhaps I had a chemical agent on my gloved hands, which I used to greatly accelerate the natural process of decomposition..."

"No such agent was found. There is *always* a residue."

Rhion simply gave him a blank look. Seneth felt her appraisal sweep over him and just for a moment, an irrational fear. Of what, he couldn't say. Was there something familiar about her? Had they met before, perhaps long ago? It was unlikely. She was about half his age and he had an excellent memory for faces.

"Do you like my chains? You keep staring at them."

Chains. The word crept through his mind, a laughing whisper. He walked away, making sure that his back was turned. An image bloomed, of a boy strapped and chained to a filthy mattress in a small room that stank of mildew. He would be released later, but only after...

The Voice willed the nightmare away and walked back to Rhion, his expression carefully neutral. Rhion looked at him with overdone concern. "Are you all right?"

"Perhaps I work too hard sometimes." Seneth perched on the table again. "I expect to be working *very* hard today, and every day until you break. And you *will* break. I won't let you slip away with your secrets."

As Rhion leaned forward, Seneth heard several faint cracking sounds, as if every bone in her body was being moved, rearranged in some subtle way. Seneth pictured her insides, the sounds they made amplified in the wet darkness. When he closed his eyes for a moment, he imagined himself crouching near his prisoner's opened body, licking her ribs dry and breathing in her salty odour. He could almost believe that Rhion's internal workings were different to those of other people- a world that bore little resemblance to that which he explored when he cut open the bodies of his interviewees, whether alive or dead. She was *different,* and when he rummaged around in her darkness- to capture the last of her heat, despoil her innards, perhaps even eat a little if she was healthy- he would touch and taste that difference.

He stared at her now with renewed, helpless interest. He could see past the thin frame, the insignificant breasts, sunken cheekbones and green, watchful eyes.

Oh, I'll enjoy you.

In his growing lust, Seneth assumed that that thought was his own.

Rhion observed the man dispassionately as he stood up. She allowed herself a faint smile as she saw the bulge of his full erection through his trousers. She had worked him out the moment she had set eyes upon him, and nothing she had seen or heard since had surprised her. The Voice of the Citadel- such a pretentious title!- had a deserved reputation after all. He was a sadist whose greed and lust were normally tempered by a need to maintain rigid control over every facet of his life. In his position, he could never allow the mask to slip.

And yet now it had, without his knowing.

She understood his urges. To an extent she even shared some of them. Rhion was a creature of primal forces and raw emotions, and where an act did not put her in danger of discovery, she took whatever she wanted whenever she wanted. Freedom sang through her veins.

You, however, need to work within your own regulations and those of the Mothers, she thought as she watched and breathed in the hunger behind his eyes. *You're a powerful man, but you're still only an insect caught in a web.*

The chains that had bound her fell unnoticed to the floor. If they made a noise, the Voice did not hear it. Rhion shifted herself up onto the slate table in one lithe movement and lay down, shivering for a moment as her clammy skin pressed against the cold unyielding surface. Seneth's eyes followed her helplessly as she slowly moved her legs apart.

He swallowed, cleared his throat and said, "I'll kill you quickly afterwards. I'll grant you that mercy."

She watched as he removed his clothing. He was taut, muscular- physically excellent, she silently admitted. "What will you do with my body?" she asked idly. "I'd like to know. Please tell me."

"I'll take you apart," he whispered. "I need to see how it all works." He clambered onto the table and loomed over her.

"Oh, you can't possibly *begin* to imagine how it all works," Rhion told him as he thrust himself into her. She directed her body to respond to the foreign flesh, to caress that part of him inside her, and Seneth's expression became nothing less than crazed. For a moment he looked confused, perhaps wondering how he had reached this point without the usual ritual of interrogation and torture. The mask had melted away entirely now, and a confused monster leered at her through the gloom. Rhion imagined for a moment that it bore many different faces simultaneously- and yet she also imagined him as an empty, hopeless man, an unsatisfied and insatiable killer.

Beneath her coy smile, Rhion was terrified. But she was determined to hide her emotions. He might be an expert on fear, but he wouldn't see hers. *Just a moment longer,* she pleaded with herself. *Keep calm.*

"I... need to know what you are," he mumbled.

"Ask me a more precise question," she whispered.

"Are you human? Are you a machine?"

"A *machine*?" Rhion laughed as her thin fingers reached up to caress his cheek. "Even *I* couldn't tell you what I am. I'm many things, my Lord Voice. What would you *like* me to be?"

His flesh had become numb in each of the places where she had touched him with her fingers, but Seneth remained oblivious to the fact. Perhaps the novelty of their intercourse had sent him into a mad little world of his own.

A glazed look entered his eyes, and his mouth opened slightly. Rhion felt the faint warmth of his seed coat her womb, and immediately she directed her energies towards its neutralisation. The Voice's ability to feel anything at all or realise what was happening to him vanished in the aftermath of his climax. He had become little more than a passenger.

Rhion stroked his cheek and wondered idly what it might be like to live a life such as his- devoid of the raging chaos that defined her own existence.

They were both monsters, but so different.

She could destroy him. But would that set in motion the destruction of the Citadel's delicate balance? Would it even cause the slightest ripple in this vast infrastructure? No, of course it wouldn't. The Mothers would appoint a successor, and everything would continue as it always had. Other men like him could be found in the Citadel- creatures with similar shapes and similar cravings.

Besides, he was far more useful to her alive. He had become her window into this fortress.

Rhion managed to push Seneth from her and sit up on the table. Her vision swayed as she leaned over to one side and vomited.

The Voice collapsed to the floor. Rhion wiped her mouth and glanced at him as she got off the table. His eyes still held that faraway expression, but she had no idea how long the trance would last.

As they joined, she had caught a glimmer of his knowledge of the hidden ways in and out of the vast Palace. Rhion had hoped this would happen. She had received flashes of insight about other men when she allowed them to have their way, and perhaps that had been the catalyst for this daring (some would say reckless) plan. She had been shocked at the sheer power of the insight that accompanied this union.

She could now visualise entry points and exit points from the Palace, the routes taken by little-used passageways and tunnels, and even a rough idea of their dimensions. Many of these obscure routes even the Mothers had likely forgotten about. How many more halls, passageways, catacombs and a myriad of other structures had been built in the last fifty years alone?

She looked again at Seneth's prone form. An inner voice urged her to forget her desperation for knowledge and to do the Citadel a favour.

No, she sternly reminded herself. *We're linked now, and I need him. And I can only imagine the effect if the Mothers were to discover his body.*

Know your limits, Rhion.

Odd, she thought a moment later. *Know my limits? When have I ever told myself to do that?*

She left him lying on the cold stone floor with a look of pure, almost childish wonder in his eyes.

III

Rhion used her new-found intimate knowledge of the Palace's warrens and catacombs to leave through a subterranean passageway that wound down and away from the Palace grounds and opened out at a disused sewer sluice gate. Soon afterwards she found herself above ground, under the cover of night. Slipping silently through narrow, pitch-black alleyways and taking shortcuts across poisoned waste ground, she reached one of her hiding places, a storehouse where low-value foodstuffs were kept but rarely utilised. She had concealed some spare clothes here a few days ago, and they were still where she'd left them, behind a wooden box in a corner.

She dressed, found the three nickel pieces that she'd also hidden nearby and headed to a late-evening market that took place in Butcher's Square which was only ten minutes' walk away. She bought some fruit ale and a pie and headed back to her lonely storehouse.

After eating and drinking, Rhion sat and leaned against the dank brick wall at the back of the storehouse, exhilarated and exhausted. *I did it,* she thought, but her euphoria was tempered with anxiety. What would happen now? He wouldn't remember what happened, surely- but might the connection have some unexpected effects?

Blood thumped a liquid drum beat inside her head. *My special blood,* she thought, and closed her eyes for a moment as she imagined that dark river coursing through her body. "And he thought I was a *machine,*" Rhion whispered aloud. "Guess again, my Lord Voice."

Outside, cracks of thunder rolled and echoed in the dense and heavy sky. Inevitably, rain began to fall through the unseasonably, oppressively warm air. Rhion sweated and listened to the first fat drops and then the comforting hiss of the deluge that followed.

She loved the sound of the rain. It never failed to make her smile, but she didn't know why.

Her body eventually calmed, but her thoughts grew more complex.

Where does it all end? whispered an enquiring voice.

"It doesn't matter," Rhion muttered. "Go to sleep."

She slept for twelve hours without stirring once. Eventually she woke and sat up, listening to nothing more than the beating of her heart and sound of her breaths for a while. Finally she got up and opened one of the nearby doors a little way. She peered down at her reflection in nearby puddle. Already her appearance had changed. She looked less tired and haggard. Watchful eyes stared back at her from a well-proportioned if ordinary countenance. Her hair had a shine to it that had been missing for days. "You don't look like a monster," she whispered, and the puddle blurred and rippled suddenly as a gust of wind blew down the alleyway.

Rhion was used to the subtle changes in her appearance that came and went as the days passed. They depended more than anything on what she had eaten the previous day- if she'd eaten anything at all. To be in such continuous flux had served her well on more occasions than she cared to count.

The force that was intrinsically a part of her, present in and coursing through her blood, lay quiet now, more seething fluid than raging torrent. Years ago, Rhion had named this continual companion *liquid darkness,* although Rhion's mother had given it a different name when she first explained these mysteries to her confused and frightened daughter. Elia had simply called it *the Great Power* or sometimes the *Old Great Power,* but Rhion had a quick and enquiring mind that worked in odd ways. "How long has it been old for? It must have been new, once. There's always *something* older. And we must find a better, more precise word than power."

"As you say, Rhion." Elia had smiled at her daughter's earnest enthusiasm. "Why don't you think about it and find a suitable name?"

I still miss you, Rhion thought as she moved a finger through the water to further disrupt her reflection. *I should have been with you at the end. I shouldn't have said the things I did.*

Should, shouldn't. What does it matter now?

She neither loved nor hated that undefinable, often monstrous side of her being, nor could she truly understand it. This permanent, internal shadow possessed a voice, after a fashion, perhaps even a kind of consciousness, but no personality beyond that. It reacted to things that happened. It protected her when required. It had gifted her with astonishing skills in abundance which her mother, with her similar powers, had helped her to nurture and control- the ability to regenerate and swiftly recover from wounds, a talent in placing even cautious and intelligent people in a captive trance, and others that she used less often. Some talents she knew that she possessed but had never dared to use, certain that she would be unable to control them.

But many of Rhion's days were dark and miserable, and she would imagine what might happen if she gave free rein to those mad, locked-away powers, sank into the unspeakable depths of her own self and let loose every black little sliver of chaos from within.

Sometimes she would think about the acts and events that pockmarked her life, the decisions either made or left unmade. She could never decide which was the monster- the liquid darkness, or her. On her better days, she wanted to be able to give rather than take, but did she want it enough?

Who is in control? she would ask herself. *Which is master and which is slave?*

Rhion breathed in the fresh morning air. She felt elated at having finally gained entrance to the Palace and a meeting with the Voice of the Citadel, but this was mixed with disbelief. He could have had no idea how long she had worked on the setup of that apparently chance interrogation. Hopefully he would never learn what she had done during their brief connection, never sense the source of that link to him that would help her to discover more about the Palace's secrets.

Of course, many secrets existed that he knew nothing about- eternal matters that were the domain only of the Mothers. Perhaps one day she would see a glimmer of their obscure truth, perhaps not. But she had achieved one of the goals she'd sought desperately for years- inside knowledge of the Palace. That information was patchy, little more than a glimmer in some areas, but it nevertheless made a beginning. With luck, it would grow.

Rhion had yearned to know these things simply because she already knew everything useful there was to know about the Citadel *outside* the Palace. Her knowledge of the vast city's geography could match anyone's. She had made it her task to learn the ways between all places, to memorise routes to wherever she wanted to go. But her urge to learn the secrets of the Mothers' inner realm simply for learning's sake had grown stronger over time until it became a struggle to control. She had used her abnormal abilities in subtle ways, to attract the right people amongst the defenders of the law, until finally she came to the attention of the Chief Balancer, second only to the Voice himself in the strange hierarchy of the Citadel's lawkeepers and enforcers.

I should be pleased, she thought- and she was, but as she stood and tasted the morning, something happened to remind Rhion that forces played in and around the Citadel that neither she nor anyone else- perhaps not even the Mothers themselves- fully understood. A prickle of uneasy excitement shuddered through her, and an intangible sensation rippled along her skin. The Great Power was about to stir, but Rhion had no idea *how*. The phenomena she had seen recently took on many forms.

The puddle near to where she stood rippled again, but this time no wind moved it. Some other force disturbed the water. Rhion stepped hastily away but kept her eyes fixed on the water as it became increasingly agitated. She watched, utterly transfixed, as the liquid moved slowly across the breadth of the alleyway and part of the way up the wall until it stopped and remained still.

Then the puddle- if it still deserved such an ordinary name- gradually shrank as if powerful heat had been applied to it to boil the water away. But Rhion saw no steam rise from the water on the wall. The water simply *disappeared,* as if it had been sucked into some other realm altogether.

A while later, Rhion stirred from her thoughts. She sighed almost regretfully, turned away and walked along the alleyway towards the sights and sounds of normality.

In the aftermath of each impossible event that she witnessed, Rhion felt empty, deflated, oddly frustrated that she could see such things and yet, elsewhere in the Citadel, normality persisted. Rhion longed for the chaos to become greater, more tangible, so that she might observe the reactions of other people to these impossible things. She wished that she knew why they existed.

But she believed, deep within herself, that these phenomena were related to her own nature, that she could see them because she was different to other people.

They happened more often now, she reminded herself as she reached the end of the alleyway and made her way along the main thoroughfare without looking back. A time might come when more and more people saw them. The scales would fall the other way.

How odd, Rhion surmised, that chaos had chosen a direction.

As she moved amongst bovine humanity, the faint warmth of the sun on her back, Rhion felt sudden, acute isolation. This was not unfamiliar but tended to occur when she least expected it. After all, she had eaten well, she had witnessed a beautiful secret, and she answered to nothing and no one.

"Cheer up, Rhion," she murmured, and walked on. She chose streets and walkways at random through the bright morning, until the sounds and the movements and the smells melded to a sensory blur.

IV

Seneth opened his eyes. For several minutes he had no idea where he was and couldn't move to find out. He felt impossibly, unutterably cold.

Finally, he managed to move his head left and then right, sufficiently to realise that he lay upon the stone floor of his interrogation chamber like the corpse of one of his interviewees, naked and as cold as stone.

Why was he here, alone?

His strength returned slowly, as if he had to coax the life back into his body.

He couldn't recall how he had ended up here, nor how his recent memory had become confused. He remembered that Moran had passed a prisoner to him for interrogation, but nothing after that, and certainly nothing about the prisoner.

Seneth breathed in deeply and caught the sour tang of vomit in the air. When he found his clothes abandoned a short distance away, he also saw a spatter of disgorged matter nearby. He inspected both but found nothing to shine light on his memory loss.

He sat for a moment to contemplate and try to make sense of his situation. Was he ill? Had something affected his mind? He couldn't afford to be ill, or weak. He had to maintain control.

He had to find out what had happened, and how.

Seneth dressed in grim silence and then searched the chamber thoroughly for clues as to what might have happened to him. He found none.

He wondered what he had done with the prisoner's body. He burned many of them· after having committed whatever violation took his fancy that day· cut others to pieces and finally sent them for further rendering. Most of the remains ended up as dog food, as far as he knew.

But he always kept a note of what he had done and how he had done it. It would be in the notebook. He always entered the details into the notebook. There might even be a few sketches.

But he found his notebook in his office later, and he saw no entry whatsoever for the prisoner. The last notes had been entered fifteen days ago, which correlated with his interrogation of the previous captive sent his way.

Why hadn't he followed proper protocol?

Seneth furiously threw the notebook to one side, enraged by the missing data. Might this be the manner in which all Voices of the Citadel died or expired· in a protracted fit of confusion spread over days, a panic that set it in as they realised that they could no longer carry out their jobs effectively? Perhaps the Mothers, with their absolute yet subtle power, had means by which they could instigate such fog in the minds of whomsoever they chose. That, Seneth concluded, might be how the role of Voice was filled only for a fixed term of ten years. Perhaps there were no executions at all, and the process was much subtler. Were all those who held the position of Voice destroyed from the inside out when the Mothers decreed that their time was up? Did their minds disintegrate as they lost the capacity to tell reality from delusion?

What purpose could that serve? Why would the Mothers want their highest servants to die so pointlessly?

Stop it, he told himself. *That's a ridiculous, baseless theory. Control yourself.*

He put an abrupt end to his self-questioning. The application of reason and common sense to the habits of the Mothers was pointless, because logic did not dictate their moves. They did what they did for reasons that only they knew.

Besides, he reasoned, he had held the position of Voice for only five years. Could they be so dissatisfied with his work that they had decided to end his tenure early by breaking him down from within? He thought it very unlikely. His work had been faultless. He carried out their accords and rulings- through his network of direct and indirect servants including the Citadel Police- with clarity and precision. His efficiency was matched only by his ruthlessness, and anyone who failed to meet his high standards failed only once. The Mothers knew about his preferences of course, but they had no interest in how he did his job, only the effectiveness of his methods. They were interested in the clear and powerful communication of their laws.

The Voice was the link between the Mothers and the various practical powers of the Citadel- the Chief Balancer, the head of the Citadel Police, the ministers of the governing Council, the leaders of the more important industries. All those who kept humanity in check- dutiful, compliant.

Yes- he had fulfilled his functions as well as, if not better than, anyone before him. But that only deepened the mystery of his sudden mental malaise.

Seneth remembered vividly the night before his Summons, the secret process by which a new Voice was appointed. A letter had arrived at the police office where he worked, directly from the Chief Balancer of that time. Seneth had worked his way tirelessly up through the ranks of the Citadel Police for many years and had often wondered if his diligent work had caught the eye of his superiors. The letter, delivered by the personal servant of the Chief Balancer, confirmed that it had- but also swore him to absolute secrecy in the matter.

That night, he had not slept at all. He had been utterly certain that he would be the greatest Voice in all history, the one to whom the Mothers would still refer a hundred or five hundred years hence. His name would echo down the ages.

He could not fail.

Seneth spoke to no one about his mysterious disappeared prisoner. A man in his exalted position existed in splendid loneliness and had no colleagues, no friends. He reported only to the Mothers, and they could not be told about this inexplicable problem. He would find a way to fix it.

The Mothers summoned him the next day. He discovered a note sealed with their specific marking, left on the table in his office that he used for writing reports.

As ever, the summons was simply that and nothing more. The Mothers never gave away any detail in their written communications. Nor had he ever seen any such note arrive. He assumed that they came in person- no servant could be trusted with their communications- but they always arrived when he was elsewhere.

With trepidation Seneth trod the long corridor to their designated meeting hall. His boots made no detectable sound, one of many odd features of this part of the palace for which the Mothers were responsible.

At the end of the passageway stood a vast door with ornate panelling. No guards were ever posted at this door or anywhere else where the Mothers chose to convene. They had no need for guards.

No one other than Seneth was ever summoned to appear before the absolute rulers of the Citadel. The Voice was named as such for a good reason. No one so much as glimpsed the Mothers unless they decided on a public display of their powers, which happened only once in a generation- just often enough for their great power and their immortality to be verified continuously by anyone and everyone.

Seneth recalled that the last such occasion had been fifteen years ago. He had been a young man then, a member of the Silent Guard in the police, the division concerned with interrogations and- where necessary- assassinations. The Mothers had walked from the Palace to Apex Square in the middle of the Citadel. The surrounding streets and the edges of the square teemed with a great crush of people desperate for a glimpse of their immortal rulers- not that the faces they showed were their own. They had given their witnesses a show of absolute power which was talked about in hushed tones of reverence even today, which had of course been their intention.

The Mothers had created a tornado whose vortex cut through the ground and created a deep borehole. They had summoned an ice storm from out of the clear sky, and balls of hail the size of fists hammered down. At least twenty people had died from injuries sustained during that onslaught. Dissatisfied even with that show of terrifying and lethal force, the Mothers had then made a column of light appear between the three of them and their citizens, and that light became a window of brilliance that hovered above. Everyone present had felt the intense heat generated by that light. Many people had suffered burns, and some of those unfortunate enough to be nearest to the spectacle had died from their injuries, baked and blackened as they screamed their agony.

Seneth made a point of reminding himself of the things he had seen the Mothers do, whenever they summoned him. *Know your place,* he always told himself. *Know your limits.*

Seneth immediately bowed his head as he prepared to step through into the stark hallway beyond. He walked forwards with his head down, shoulders stooped and eyes fixed determinedly upon the floor. The doors closed behind him and he shivered in the chilly air. The temperature in many of the halls was either oppressively hot or icy cold and never anything in between.

Following protocol, he walked as far as the single black tile in the room and dropped obediently to his knees. He stared intently at the tile and strove to imagine the shape as a void. The exercise helped him to maintain his concentration throughout these ordeals.

"Seneth." The voice, a perfect match to this harsh and soulless chamber, sent a further shiver through him. "How long has it been?"

With a calmness borne of long practice Seneth replied, "Fifteen days, Majesty. Perhaps a little longer."

"No, I think forty or fifty. Things have happened during that time. They always do."

"As you say, Majesty." Seneth had no idea what words other than a banal, non-committal response would suffice.

"Especially after the rain, it would seem. The air is damp and oppressive, filled with an electric surge that swirls around. We catch only a glimpse, like a colour never seen before... just beyond reach. Sometimes she mocks us. These little displays, they're made to remind us..." The words drifted regretfully away into a low and unintelligible mutter, and Seneth felt a nameless fear take hold of him. What was she talking about?

He had no idea what to say, so he kept silent even as he felt every inch of his skin crawl. Despite the painfully low temperature, beads of sweat began to form on his forehead and under his arms as he waited for minutes, perhaps even an hour. He reminded himself that their perception of time was different to his own and to everyone else's. Sometimes slower, other times faster.

Should he have understood? Were they testing him?

Whenever he felt his attention wander, he refocussed on the void, the black tile.

"What are you *doing* here?" The question cut through him suddenly like a harsh reprimand.

Seneth flinched. "I..." He struggled to understand. If they had decided to test him, how could he possibly pass that test?

"Are you retarded, mortal? Have you forgotten how to speak?"

"Forgive me, Majesty. I... you summoned me, or perhaps one of..." With an effort he managed to stop the babble of words that threatened to spill from his mouth. *Think before you speak,* he told himself. *Maintain your wits or lose your head. Look at the tile.*

"Yes. I did. Or rather, *we* did." Now she sounded thoughtful, pensive. Seneth ached to steal a look at her- no matter that the idea also filled him with fear- but he hadn't been permitted. Likely he would be killed on the spot if he so much as raised his head unbidden. He could tell apart the distinctive voices of all three, but could never remember which voice belonged to which face. Might they even be interchangeable in some way?

Time passed. Pain spread through Seneth's knees and worsened until he almost gasped in pain. Finally, the Mother spoke once more, and her icy tones startled him. "Do you fear for your life, Seneth? Sometimes?"

"Sometimes, Majesty. Yes." Now his whole body trembled.

"Stand up. Look at me."

Filled with fear, Seneth stood and forced his gaze upwards until it fell upon the figure that reclined in the tall, glass chair at the far end of the hall.

The woman was young- no, not young at all, he reminded himself. She was eternal, ageless. In her eyes he saw something inhuman, merciless, but also a cold rage. Despite this her face remained impassive, an ocean with a storm that swirled somewhere deep in its fathomless depths.

She regarded him for a long while, and having been given no other instruction, Seneth had no choice but to fearfully meet that implacable gaze. He dared not look away, and more than likely couldn't have even if she had offered the choice.

This entity could crush him to dust in an instant, or slowly. In this miserable moment, he ached for nothing more or less than simple death- to be put swiftly out into the dark. Hatred and lust had both powered and empowered him for so many years, from the time of his training and determined climb through the ranks of the Citadel's law keepers, and on through his tenure as Voice of the Citadel. But all trace of the cold fire that burned constantly inside him fled to some other place in the presence of this ancient woman. He became a stone sinking through her sea, and he feared that if she wished it, he might fall forever.

"Something wonderful is about to happen to you, Seneth," the Mother informed him at last, and the words filled him with a nameless terror.

"Majesty, I... may I..."

"Ask what it is? You may, although I can't describe it using words that you might understand. After all, you're a man of the Citadel, tethered to the laws in which that place is grounded. What can I tell you? You've been chosen because you're the Voice, and we need a different Voice. No, that's inaccurate. Specifically, we need *you* to be different. Have I ever told you that you're a prime example of your kind?"

"I... no, Majesty. I don't think you have."

"Well, consider yourself told. Your chances of survival are accordingly high."

His chest tightened as he heard a faint murmuring sound, as if some other, hidden presence agreed with the Mother's lack of explanation. Were the others somewhere in the hall, standing in the shadows? "Majesty, is my time at an end? It has been an honour to..."

"On the contrary, Seneth. Your time has only just begun."

Inexplicably, a quiet but insistent voice whispered in his head. Seneth was used to voices but had never heard this one before. *Run,* it beseeched him. And he almost turned to flee, pointless though that flight would have been. He would run to the door, but the exit would be somewhere else, or he would start to sink through a floor that grew increasingly liquid as he struggled. Perhaps he might attain a sort of glazed immortality like the trapped specimens in the Great Hall of Flesh.

An invisible force now held him in place. He felt an unseen weight bear down upon him on all sides. Seneth cried out in fear and tried to plead with his tormentor as she observed and remained unmoved by his distress. But he could not speak. His eyes bulged, his lips may as well have been sealed together, and a moment later he suddenly lost control of his bowels. *Please spare me,* he silently implored as he collapsed to the floor. He no longer wished to die. Had she read that idle thought and decided on a whim to act and grant it?

But she said that my time had only just begun!

Shadows and an explosion of colours flickered at the edges of Seneth's vision like ephemeral creatures come to witness his final moments, as his consciousness faded to nothing.

V

"We need to see if it's possible, after all this time," a voice whispered. "You *do* understand, don't you? We must keep trying, and as I said, you are a *fine* example of your kind. The odds are good. Better, anyway."

Seneth's eyes flickered open. He had no idea where he was. Old-fashioned oil lamps lit the grimy, low-ceilinged room, one in each corner. Machinery and cables ran throughout the place. He could smell dust and grease and the harshness of metal. Small glass screens were set in some of the machines. Most were dark, but one looked as if a bright green light shone from inside through the screen. The light flickered.

What is that machine? he wondered. *Why is there a light inside it?*

His eyes followed the box's attendant cables to the dingy wall where they entered the cracked surface and disappeared into some other place. Electricity powered the equipment here, but Seneth felt certain that it was different to the sort he was used to. The light looked wrong, and he felt a crackle in the air that made his skin crawl.

He turned but couldn't find whoever had spoken. He thought one of the Mothers had whispered to him but could no longer be certain. Had she left, or was she still watching him from somewhere? How much time had passed? Only a moment, he had thought, but it might have been longer.

The Voice realised suddenly that both his wrists and his ankles had been shackled, and the chains to which they were attached disappeared into the smooth stone surface of the floor. *How did I not notice this before?* he wondered as he looked down at his naked form.

The Mothers had placed him here, but why? To punish him for wanting to die? For some other perceived slight that he might not even know about? What form would his punishment take?

Something moved under the skin of his left arm, and he almost cried out.

"We need to know where the intrusion came from," the voice continued softly, this time from behind him. He jumped and the chains rustled harshly. "It's very unusual, and the particular energy that made it happen is even more unusual. It hasn't been seen... lately."

"I..." He tried to speak but his voice came out as a dry rasp from his parched throat. "I don't know," he whispered.

"No, I don't believe you do. She did her best to make certain of that. But the memory is buried somewhere within your mind, and we'll draw it from you one way or another." Amidst his rising panic the voice added quickly, "There's no need to be afraid. Fear is only helpful if you have a means of escape. I can assure you that you don't. You'll emerge from this ordeal as a far superior being, Seneth, and you'll give up the secrets buried in your head. You can be sure of that."

He looked down at his body. *A far superior being?*

"This is a good time for you to undergo the process," she added. "You would have been subjected to it regardless, but the recent... *intrusion* adds some urgency to the situation."

"Intrusion." He had no idea what she meant.

"Soon you'll come to realise that almost everything is temporary, including the life that you lived. You were human and mortal, and you made an error. Others before you made grave mistakes of their own. We've always accepted that this is what you *do,* sooner or later. But we can't allow it to continue. The Voice must be perfect. That's the foundation. The blueprint for the future."

"Majesty..." he whispered hoarsely. "I can only..."

"*No.* Don't speak. It may interfere with the process, and everything needs to run as smoothly as possible. If it doesn't, then bad things may happen. We don't want bad things to happen, and neither do you. Must I sew your mouth shut?"

Seneth blacked out abruptly. When his consciousness returned he saw that wires, cables, lights and boxes surrounded him. Some of the cables had been attached to his hands and feet. No, not attached. They had been inserted directly into his limbs while he stood strapped and dead to the world.

Every part of his body had become numb. A cold wave pulsed from his toes through his legs, torso and down into his arms and hands. It crawled through his neck and face and up into his skull. He could no longer move any part of himself, even the muscles in his face. He couldn't even blink.

Without any warning Seneth's vision inverted. The darker parts of his environment became unbearably bright while the brighter objects and areas darkened. A fierce agony surged through his body, from his extremities and towards his core, then deep into his head, a savage burst of light and sound. He couldn't scream his pain.

Seneth begged silently for death. But the torture continued. At times it would ebb back before surging forth again like a dark, malevolent tidal force. In only a short while his ability to frame any cohesive thoughts was obliterated. Colour and illumination flooded his mind, along with horrific images that he couldn't hope to describe. They swarmed through his tattered consciousness- scenes of worlds he had never known and never would, of ages long gone and times yet to come.

He witnessed far more than a human brain ought to have the capacity to withstand. On one level he understood none of this horror, and on another he comprehended everything. It made a terrible, logical sense.

Years, centuries came and went. Civilisations were born and died. People and cultures that had long since passed into oblivion and would never be known again flared up in his mind like transient sparks, miracles that flowered in brief defiance of a universal darkness.

Finally- perhaps hours or even days later- a hard and insistent voice pulled Seneth gradually back towards the cold light and contours of the world he knew. *Wake,* it commanded him. This was the voice of one of the Mothers, calling across a great distance.

But he also sensed a great blackness- an entity that existed outside all the worlds whose lives and deaths he had witnessed- reach out to him, hungry and curious. *WHAT ARE YOU,* he thought it whispered.

The words echoed through his head even after he opened his eyes to the room of cables and screens and dim lighting and saw one of the Mothers standing before him.

He could not speak coherently. The sounds that came from his mouth were animalistic and uncontrolled. Saliva escaped one corner of his mouth. Shame at his reduction to a simple creature filled him, but he could not express his frustration and the only movements he made were fitful and useless.

The austere beauty before him observed his continued disarray with a perfect lack of expression. Then she motioned towards the wires that burrowed into his body and Seneth uttered a hoarse scream as they slid abruptly from his flesh. Patches of crimson bloomed and burst at the perimeters of his vision. He looked down at his wrists and saw that the wires' exit points shrivelled and closed, and no blood spilled from them.

They've taken my blood, he thought dazedly. *Why would they take my blood?*

As he shivered, the Mother approached until she stood close enough for him to feel her faint breath against his face. He stared helplessly into her eyes as she studied him, and for a fleeting moment he saw pictures not unlike those from the endless nightmare to which he had been subjected. He could not keep that fearful vision at bay. It danced clearly in her eyes, like memories that had a life of their own. Had she tasted the visual aspects of his torture, collected them somehow from his traumatised mind?

Within a moment her expression changed utterly. He saw bewilderment, alarm- and before he could read anything further an invisible wall stood between them. No longer could he sense anything about whatever emotions and memories lurked within her. "You've seen and heard... the *beneath*," she whispered eventually. "That which makes everything disappear over time. It's singular, isn't it? The dark? The abyss?"

The words meant nothing to him, but he suddenly found his voice, and the fact that his tongue had been loosened startled him, as if his speech had jumped ahead of his scrambled thoughts. "What... happened to me?"

The Mother looked into his eyes in the same way as he had hers, except that *his* history, everything about him, was laid bare before her and he had no defence against the interrogation. Her eyes rummaged through the debris of his being, and as she conducted the search her expression remained static, a stone that knew everything.

Finally she spoke. "Today is a great day for us, Seneth, and for *you*. At long last, the process has worked as it ought. Perhaps it finally encountered the correct vessel. It makes sense, I suppose. You were a man with no need for humanity. Perhaps you were ready to accept the change, ready to be filled with purpose, whereas your predecessors all tried to fight it. This is all for the greater good."

She smiled then, as if she had noticed a subtle shift in his expression. "Oh, I don't for a *moment* think you have any consideration for that, but you've always displayed thoroughness, diligence and discipline which enabled you to do your job well, in our name."

Seneth dimly sensed that a response of some kind might be required, but he could offer only a slow, bovine nod of the head.

"After so many centuries, we have found a starting point. We now know the *recipe,* and over time there will be others. You are the rock that starts the avalanche."

Seneth did not know what an *avalanche* was. "Please... Majesty." His voice had been reduced to a cracked whisper. "What..."

"...happened to you? You've simply become something *more,* something greater, so that you may better fulfil the requirements of your station. I've looked inside you and seen for myself that we'll never again need to recruit another Voice. Who knows- you may be Voice for all eternity, Seneth, although it remains to be seen who your new masters will be. Perhaps *you* will be master. What do you say to that? I admit I'm curious to know the shape the world will take after we're gone."

She smiled. "But not *that* curious."

He gaped helplessly at her, and at the same time an image opened like a chasm before him- a recollection of falling forever through a cold void and being ripped slowly apart only to be remade again.

I WILL KNOW YOUR NATURE, came a whisper through his mind, as if from out of that abyss.

Seneth began to sob in the face of that coldly mechanical voice, until a sudden icy touch from the Mother- a gentle scrape of her porcelain finger against his cheek- pulled him back.

"Don't cry, Seneth," she said softly.

"Together we sail uncharted territory," she continued. The phrase was unfamiliar to him. "After all these failures, finally we have a healthy, working receptacle. You know, I envy you in some ways."

"Envy me, Majesty?"

"In the days to come you'll find that the world is quite different to how you thought. You'll see things that you thought impossible, and yet your insight will be quite different to ours. And then- if the world corrects itself over time, you'll become familiar with one thing above all else."

"Eternity," she murmured when he failed to respond.

VI

He didn't see her leave.

Seneth's sharp, shallow breaths echoed harshly against the walls. One of the lanterns sputtered and went out. *I mustn't be alone in the dark,* he thought, and the frightening idea forced him to take several faltering steps forward. For a short while he was in two places- this room and another, from his childhood- a room that would always stay with him.

The bedroom is dark, warm and full of odours and shadows. The chains hurt. But he won't call out. He won't cry.

"No," Seneth whispered. "Go away."

99

His joints and muscles protested at first, but he soon found the strength to walk without staggering. *Are my movements faster?* he asked himself in puzzlement. He thought they were.

Then his legs collapsed from under him.

He remained on the cold stone floor until sometime later the door opened and he was lifted and taken somewhere.

His vision came and went. His hearing became painfully sensitive and then muffled. He sensed the Mothers walking nearby, but they didn't carry him. Something invisible bore him along.

He was placed on a bed- perhaps his own- and strange energies swirled around and inside him. His vision remained blurred and gloomy, but at one point he glimpsed the Mothers standing together and observing him from across the room. Strangely, the three of them looked identical.

Finally, he slept.

He dreamed that the Mothers, dressed in the dark robes of mourning- although what could they possibly have to mourn?- carried him on a bed of air along the icy corridors before laying him down on a vast granite slab. So cold was the surface that it turned the flesh of his back to ice. One of the Mothers sang to him, and another kissed him upon the lips. When she did, her memories of a forgotten age dissolved into his passive mind and he cried out regrets for terrible things he had never done. Then, as they departed in silence he cried again in the darkness, but his voice had grown small and weak as the humanity leaked from him to be crushed by the waiting abyss.

No one is coming for you, it whispered.

Seneth woke, many hours later, on his bed.

He briefly chased the dying remnants of his dream. *Yes, I belong to it now and I do its work,* he thought, still half-asleep as he sat up. A moment later, that notion- meaningless on its own- was all he could remember of his dream.

The Voice immediately observed his reflection in the full-length mirror, transfixed by his appearance in a way he had never been before. *Something is different,* he decided. *What is it?*

At first glance he saw nothing that gave him pause, other than that he bore no outwards signs of the trauma from whatever the Mothers had done. *I look better than ever,* he told himself as he stepped nearer to the mirror. *Yes. Better than ever.*

But something different lurked behind his eyes. He only noticed it when he looked slightly away and saw a subtle change from the edge of his vision. When he quickly looked directly back at his reflection, he saw nothing out of the ordinary, nor could he determine what the difference might have been.

Seneth had no duties to perform that day, other than his routine visit to the Mothers' silent prisoner. He walked along the maze of corridors with barely a thought as to what he was doing or where he might be headed. He was aware of his task but felt half-asleep throughout the well-trodden journey, almost as if another entity carried out his duties for him. An alien calm cloaked him like a shroud. Whatever fears he had- and they were receding to nothing now- no longer felt consequential.

He unlocked and opened the door to the hall where the remains of the prisoner awaited him in his glass cell.

Seneth prepared to ask the first of his questions, but he immediately sensed that something about the prisoner had changed. *Or perhaps I simply see him differently now,* he reasoned.

The Voice drew nearer until he stood close enough to touch the glass. Then something astonishing happened.

His vision leaped through the transparent barrier and as far as the half-face of the container's occupant. Onwards it went, into the substance of the prisoner, and it was here that Seneth lost all understanding of the things he saw, and instead silently marvelled even as a part of him railed fearfully against this revelation.

He saw an internal world he could never hope to comprehend, and within it a slow, miraculous healing process which gradually made and put together the remainder of the prisoner's head, his torso and limbs, complete with all the inner workings that would make him properly alive, functional and aware.

This process, Seneth finally understood, had been ongoing for a long time. It had been set in motion from the smaller remains of tissue from this man, and some innate memory or detailed set of instructions carried within that flesh had been preserved. Those instructions had been interpreted and put to work, their purpose to recreate the man who, presumably, had once been all but destroyed.

How? Seneth wondered. *Why? A great force must have disrupted the natural order of things. Something changed his nature and is intent on rebuilding him.*

Abruptly he was forced out of the prisoner's consciousness and thrown fully back in his body. He stumbled and his vision swayed. He knelt near the ground until the spiralling sense of vertigo and sickness dissipated.

Seneth realised that he had not yet asked his daily questions. They seemed ridiculous, banal now after all he had seen. But it remained his duty to ask them.

He raised his head and addressed the man in the cell. "What is your name?"

The prisoner didn't answer.

"What do you know of other worlds?"

"What does the mirror mean to you?"

But the prisoner said nothing.

He dwelt on the minute detail of his visual journey within the workings of the prisoner in the glass cage. A man, Seneth reminded himself. But one whose constituent parts built upon one another to recreate him. Surely the Mothers knew this as well- why else would they have imprisoned him here? What did they hope to discover? Did they also expect him to discover something about the prisoner in time?

What secrets did they hope to unlock?

Having asked his three initial questions, Seneth forced himself through the remainder. "Still, the task is a little less tedious now," he said finally. "Now that I can see inside you."

But as he left, his thoughts were suddenly filled once again not with the enigmatic captive but instead with the memory of his torture and the abyss to which it had sent him. Details seeped slowly back as he hurried away.

He remembered the harsh, mechanically whispered question from the void, a question that he could no longer answer.

WHAT ARE YOU?

VII

"I smell the odour of their copulation," One said.

The Mothers stood around the table in Seneth's interrogation chamber. They bore angry, disbelieving looks. It ought to have been inconceivable that someone- a descendant of the Forgotten, no less!- could criminalise themselves into the Palace, into the hands of the Voice, only to subvert and turn the situation on its head.

"There can be no doubt." Three had already touched the semi-dried remains of Rhion's vomit, and the stains on the table. "It's only a residue, but so powerful," she whispered. "There's no other explanation. I know her name too- it's Rhion. Isn't the name always linked with a particular pattern of the Great Power?"

"How can *any* of that line still live?!" Two exclaimed. "We made efforts to root them out *centuries* ago. Does this mean there are others?"

"Undoubtedly." One gave her a scornful look. "Those dozens responsible for numerous unexplained events. Their hold on the Great Power is weak- I doubt any of them even knew what they were doing- but they must have some dilution of the Forgotten's blood. Didn't we fear at the time that a few may have slipped through the net? But we gave no pause for that possibility at the time. The blood has weakened over the centuries, and the powers of those who survived have grown dim."

"But not Rhion. She is *so...*" Three began, only to stop when the other two fixed their irate stares upon her.

"If she is, then she will be a favourite of the Spider," One reasoned. "If we were to disturb and pursue her..."

"...then the Spider sees us." Two nodded. "Of course. Bringing us into chaos and conflict..."

...which is what we want. I think we need to talk with our loyal servant, the Voice of the Citadel."

The room to which Seneth had been called lay in complete darkness, but he immediately detected three indistinct shapes in front of him. He saw them as faint red glows and knew immediately that what he saw was the heat emitted by the bodies of the Mothers.

"The last few days must have been quite confusing," one of them spoke up.

"Do we look different to you?" another asked, and faint, cold laughter ensued for a moment.

Seneth suddenly realised he had forgotten to bow and hastily began to do so, only to be told to stand up and look straight ahead towards their incandescent forms.

"We're envious of your transformation," the first voice said. "And yet *not* so envious."

"It's a remarkable journey for you to undertake," the second remarked. She sounded eager to observe this journey for herself.

Seneth shivered. "Majesties, I can only thank you..." he began, but a third voice cut him short. "Be quiet and listen. You will not speak unless we expressly permit it."

"With the passage of time we realised that we required the use of old techniques to solve new problems," the first voice intoned. "The process is far from perfect and requires a vast amount of energy."

"We think it causes power cuts, out in the Citadel- although it shouldn't be linked in any way," the second voice added. She seemed amused.

"It failed us more times than we remember, and the results of such failures had to be disposed of. Such disappointment, such waste, over so many years! But we

105

persevered, and you, Seneth, are the product of that perseverance. You're the first of your kind to be created in a *very* long time. So long, indeed that you may consider yourself a pioneer. No doubt problems will come to light, but we don't expect them to be insurmountable. We require you for some... novel uses, so you can rest assured that if obstacles appear, we'll do whatever it takes to ensure you overcome them. In time, perhaps others like you will be made. But you... well, you can be their king, if you like."

Again, a ripple of icy amusement echoed softly in the dark. Seneth listened fearfully. He longed to ask them what they meant, but at the same time he imagined his tongue being torn away at the root and his mouth filling with blood- the grim price of such insolence.

"You were a man. Now you are more. You may have already seen that your transformation has granted you insights beyond anything you could possibly have imagined."

"Now, to a separate matter," one of the others spoke up. "A trick has been played upon you, by someone who was brought under your jurisdiction and subsequently escaped."

Fear stabbed through him.

"You were a diligent and thorough Voice, a careful and rigorous man who fulfilled his duties to the best of his considerable capabilities- but nevertheless a *man* and prone to eventual failure. In this case you allowed your lust to blindside you, which in turn meant that your prisoner escaped justice."

He jumped, startled and frightened as a buried memory slowly unearthed itself. "Don't speak," one of Mothers warned him as he opened his mouth, about to babble some incoherent excuse for which he would have been punished severely.

"We visited your interrogation cellar," she continued, "and there we discovered the residue of your union, the nature of which greatly concerned us. By the time we arrived, the prisoner had long gone. She played with your mind and your body, and she may well have gained a certain insight into the nature and topography of the Palace and certain things within it. That woman must be found, Seneth. Everything- the entire preservation of order and sanity throughout the Citadel- depends upon this."

"Pay particular attention now, Seneth," another of the Mothers instructed him. Her faintly glowing form rippled as she leaned forward, and Seneth felt the air grow thick and heavy around him. "When she is found, she must be destroyed instantly. She is to be summarily executed. Nod your head if you understand."

Seneth nodded. His mind whirled with conflicting emotions. He had been found out. But the Mothers had, if not forgiven him, at least allowed him the mistake. Unbelievably, they didn't appear unduly concerned about the fact, and they had given him a chance to redeem himself.

Relief swept through him, yet he remained terrified.

His memory of what had happened trickled relentlessly back through his mind. *Rhion,* he thought hatefully. *That was your name.*

"Allow us to give you a little more background, Seneth. Wider issues are at stake here. Throughout the Citadel, certain anomalies have appeared at a greater frequency than ever before. By anomalies we mean events that should not be possible, but which are nonetheless observed- although only by a very small number of people so far. Most of these phenomena go unseen, but as their frequency increases so does the likelihood of their being seen by enough citizens to cause unrest. For the sake of order and peace, impossibilities cannot be allowed to become known facts. It now falls to you to ensure that such anomalies are contained."

"We believe that your former captive may be linked to them," another one of the three spoke up. "*She* is an anomaly of sorts. This may explain what happened when she became your prisoner for a short while. Your reality and her reality are not quite the same thing."

Seneth silently struggled to understand. Desperate to speak, he held his tongue and wondered what they would ask of him.

"You now see things that you couldn't before," one of the Mothers remarked. "Scale and detail have become different to you. You're the first to be granted this gift for a very long time. We believe that this is the key to learning the reasons for the anomalies."

"Order must not be allowed to break down," another spoke up. "Peace must be preserved at any cost."

The Mothers were correct, he realised- and why wouldn't they be? They knew everything and he had been foolish to hope otherwise. The memory of the failed interrogation continued to slowly blossom in his head, and Seneth marvelled as each facet of it came back into sharp focus in his head.

But with that sense of wonder came deep shame, followed by rage. He had been outwitted and made a fool of. Images flashed through his mind, violent depictions of how he would slowly ruin that woman when he captured her again. Immediately he willed them away. He could not fail a second time, and he could certainly not be seen to be a slave to his baser instincts again. The

Mothers would not forgive that. They would find a way to torture him for all eternity.

But for the first time in many years, Seneth found himself ill at ease because of someone other than the Mothers. He had been tricked by a creature that he couldn't understand. Might there be a chance, however small, that the same could happen again?

"She is the enemy of all things ordered and sane," came a sharp voice. "She is the darkness that finds a way in when the forces of logic and progress are lax, and the guardians of civilisation look the other way."

"With much effort and energy, we have given you more than anyone has ever received," another pointed out. "As things stand at the moment, you would live..." In a quieter voice, she consulted with her companions. "What did we estimate? Another two hundred and fifty years?"

"A figure in that region," another of them concurred. "But inevitably, further improvements would be made during that time. Great steps forward arising from important discoveries. That's why we believe you might live forever."

Filled with a maelstrom of joy and horror, Seneth let out a wordless sob. They permitted him the sound, and then one of them suddenly pulled his attention back to them with a sharp reprimand. "You won't make us regret this investment, will you, Lord Voice?"

"No, Majesty," he murmured.

She had neglected to mention his fate if he *did* cause them such regret, but Seneth's imagination filled the silence with a more than adequate image of that eventuality. He thought for a moment that he heard a short, sharp laugh as the awful picture took root in his mind.

"You have twenty-three days to find and destroy Rhion Freeward," one of them told him. "Bring us Rhion's body as soon as you can."

"Yes," another echoed. "The body is important. The body is the key to it all, perhaps."

"What was it like?" a third voice asked suddenly.

"I..." He blinked. "Forgive me, Majesty, but..."

"Laying with Rhion. What was it like?"

"Why does that matter?" another of the Mothers demanded.

"I want to know. Tell me what it was like, Seneth. You *do* remember?"

He did. He remembered everything. Her face. Her knowing smile. Her warmth wrapped around him and her feet touching his back as he pushed himself into her. But there was more. Something about her, something inside her, in her blood, her nerves, every cell of her body... why did it feel so familiar?

"I enjoyed her, Majesty," he confessed.

"I'll bet you did. Was she... different?"

"I can't describe how, Majesty. It's beyond my intellect, I think. But now- all I feel is shame for allowing this to happen. I will make amends."

"You'd better." He felt the cold crack of her smile settle on him.

As he sat in confounded silence in his quarters later that day, Seneth felt as if he had drowned slowly in darkness and then opened his eyes to see nothing but a faint circle of light above. That imaginary light grew dimmer with each passing moment. His life no longer made sense.

He had no choice but to accept reality. Certainly he had no hope of escaping his fate. He couldn't beg to be released from this impossible task. Only two options remained- success or failure.

How quickly could he find her?

Seneth made a rough calculation of how he might locate, apprehend and kill Rhion Freeward. In a city of almost ten million people that would be an impossible task for most, but whatever else he had become he remained the Voice of the Citadel. He could find anyone, whoever and wherever they might be. He had useful servants to call upon.

He decided he would give her exact description to each of the four Lawmasters of the Citadel, so that they could make the best use of their most talented spies to unearth the woman. If she had any sense Rhion would have gone to ground and would remain extremely cautious for a long while. But it wouldn't take them long to find her. He would need to give strict orders that she was not to be approached, much less harmed. He would do all the harming himself.

A quick kill, he reminded himself. Probably the quickest he would ever carry out.

But why couldn't the Mothers find her themselves? Why rely on him to locate and destroy this woman? What was it that he could do, that they couldn't?

Questions to which he would never find answers.

After some time, Seneth noticed that darkness had fallen. He went to his window and looked out over the lights of civilisation.

He stood by the window as the night wore on. He found that he didn't need to sleep despite having remained awake last night. Was sleep also to be denied him? Had he no longer any need for it?

Everything he looked at felt oddly *sharper,* more detailed- even the light of distant illumination. The entire Citadel had been drawn into greater focus. He could not only see far better than before, but further. If he concentrated, he could also hear things he would never have been able to before, and from those sounds extract information that shouldn't have been accessible. About two thousand hands to the south-east, a group of stray dogs fought in an alleyway. From that faint and muddled sound he knew how many there were and the approximate size of each one. When he closed his eyes he could even picture the largest of them, a hideous one-eyed beast whose fetid breath steamed into the chilly night air as she dominated the fight and then- her foes cowed at last- began to pull apart and eat the dead body that had attracted the pack's interest to begin with.

Seneth could have stared out at civilisation's contours until dawn- but after a while he went to sit on the edge of his bed and found that every part of his body had begun to slow down. His pulse slowed to a powerful, low staccato. *A beat every two point four seconds,* he thought, and wondered how he had calculated that. *That's too slow, or it ought to be.*

The flow of his blood changed, directed to different areas one after another. When he closed his eyes, Seneth marvelled at what happened- for he could see inside his own body just as he had witnessed the internal miracles within the Mothers' ancient prisoner.

He navigated that reddish gloom with his mind's eye and soared through himself as if he traversed the heavens. Threads of silvery light and impossibly thin, metallic substance cut through every facet of his inner workings. The Mothers had made this impossibly strange technology as much a part of him as his flesh and bones.

He sat quietly with his head bowed, perfectly still. Had anyone else been with him and happened to look closely, they would have seen none of the little inconsistencies that normally mar the human countenance. Seneth's face and body, much like his new view of the world, had been subtly corrected. He had, as the Mothers implied, been reborn. His human aspirations, the dark desires that had long marked his life, remained- but they now occupied a very different space.

As the small hours of the night wore on, he looked only inward, lost in a new universe he could never understand.

VIII

Three gave a long sigh of satisfaction. "He will disturb the fabric. His vengeful pursuit of Rhion will antagonise the Spider. Consequently, more anomalies will be stirred into being."

One nodded, pleased. "I believe she was *chosen* by the Spider. There can be no doubt that she's a descendant of the Forgotten. Over time, Rhion's abilities will change and grow."

Two shrugged. "Perhaps. Do you remember when we were not unlike her? In the previous age, there were many..."

"We don't need to be reminded," Three said quietly.

"We must seize the chance when the time is right," One declared. "When everything is collapsing into chaos- when we approach the last moments of this existence- then we'll destroy Rhion ourselves. Let that be our last act, before we're crushed to atoms."

"The Spider will consider Rhion's demise an atrocity."

"So much the better- our end will come swiftly. Her spite is boundless."

"Is there a chance that Seneth might reach Rhion before any of this can happen?"

"He won't," One said firmly. "Remember that we will not only know where he is at any given time, but we maintain a subtle hold over him, enough to slow or confuse him very slightly as and when we need to. This will be enough for her to elude him each time. And the more we disturb Rhion's life, the more we disturb the fabric of the world."

"At last," Two declared, "our end is near."

The three women looked to one another and smiled as hope flickered in their cold hearts.

IV – The Dark River

I

Rhion dreamed.

In her sleep she travelled with shadowy figures that might not have been human, or even living creatures. The journey felt as blurred and imprecise as it ought- Rhion was vaguely aware that she dreamed- but finally she arrived at a place which, although she had never been there before, nevertheless felt intensely familiar.

Here, as her strange guardians drifted away to some other place, the contours and details of her environment suddenly sharpened.

A young girl stared intently through the wide window of an otherwise featureless room, into a sky festooned with stars. Rhion had never seen the heavens blaze with such fury. *I'm somewhere distant,* an inner voice told her. *This is the place we come to when we step out of the maze, when our worldly affairs are done with.*

"Where are we?" she asked, but the girl didn't hear, or perhaps chose not to answer. Instead she said, "They move slowly apart, until we're alone in the dark. Once, a very long time ago, many different worlds held life. We can't imagine what forms it might have taken, what paths it followed. But the technology of just *one* world proved to be a tipping point that forever changed the course of time. The cycle continues, but it's a different cycle now. The wheel is warped."

I know you, Rhion thought as she half-listened to her companion's cryptic mumblings. *I'm certain of it. How do I know you?*

"It was so different," the girl continued wistfully. "When I was ordinary. Before the world changed me."

Then, without any warning, she turned to Rhion. Her pale blue eyes were bright with suffering. They led into an inner hell, Rhion realised- a maze that could never be escaped. "It will change *you* too..."

Rhion's eyes flickered open, and she sat up.

She had slept in an abandoned outhouse near to the river, one of her many hiding places around the Citadel. The only sound she heard was of the water passing by. A harsh, chemical smell hung in the air, possibly from something that had been dumped further upriver.

That dream was important, Rhion thought. A shiver passed through her spine. *It pointed out a universal truth to me. But, as usual, it was something beyond my understanding.*

Rhion rarely kept a close eye on the time, but it was clear that evening approached. She wandered along the riverside for a while, and her memory of the dream faded. Houseboats were moored in an almost continuous line here, and from within some of them she heard sounds of merriment or violence or fornication. *Little lives,* she thought, not contemptuously but a little sadly.

Yet she wasn't sure if she felt sad for the people she passed by, or for herself.

Sometime later she stopped and looked out across the river as the lit city lay under a fully dark sky. Her thoughts drifted like the water for a while and she wondered what to do tonight, and where to go.

Danger, Rhion thought suddenly.

116

She turned and peered down the river towpath along the way she had already walked, sensing that someone or something approached. Mist had started to drift up from the river and languished near the edge of the path as the temperature dipped. Nearer to the walls of old warehouses, impenetrable shadows gathered. A dilapidated boat creaked quietly as the currents of the water moved it gently back and forth.

Rhion drew breath, willed herself to be calm and exhaled gently. Her inner warmth drifted visibly into the chill night air. She wondered worriedly if it was the Voice who approached.

No. It couldn't be. She was linked to him, no matter how tenuously, and would know if he was anywhere nearby.

Who else, then?

She visualised her foe just before he appeared at the corner of the towpath. The faint connection that she had created made a sudden warning bloom in her head, but too late to be of use. Rhion recoiled in shock. It *was* him. How could she not have known?

Filled with fear, she frantically considered her stark options- fight or flight- but before she could decide, he ran straight at her, faster than she could have imagined.

The human-shaped blur of darkness almost killed her there and then. Rhion's instincts alone saved her- but her enemy caught her a glancing blow that sent her reeling and into the wall. Rhion's world went black for a moment and she fell to the ground as blood seeped from her ear and cheek.

She sensed her assailant turn and head back towards her, slower now but intent on finishing her off. The Great Power responded and coursed through Rhion's body as she crouched low and prepared to strike.

She held a knife in one hand- a weapon that she had once dubbed the sharpest in the Citadel- and her other hand stretched out, utterly still. If she could, she would drive a finger or two through his eye with one hand, or the knife with the other. Either way she would wound him. Then, she would make her escape. Where to, she would work out as she fled.

He sprang at her, so quickly that Rhion barely had time to escape the whirl of blades that whistled past her face. She had been an inch away from her throat being cut through.

The next moment she seized her opportunity to strike. It would likely be her only one.

But he sensed her intent and her knife only cut through his cloak and slashed the skin near his ribs. Rhion saw something she could not understand- a silvery glow that shone from his wound for a moment and then winked out of existence. *What in hell was that?* she wondered fearfully. *What does he have inside him?*

Perhaps that glimpse of something so far beyond her experience and understanding, forced Rhion's hand. *Get away,* she silently screamed at herself. *Get away now or you'll die.*

She made a split-second decision, powered by instinct, fear of her foe and a raging desperation to survive.

Rhion dropped the knife, ran as fast as she could to the edge of the river path and dived down into the water.

The cold blackness of the canal enveloped her, so icy that for a moment Rhion was almost convinced she'd thrown herself into a void, that the river was a gateway to a much deeper place. The shock of immersion almost made her forget to hold her breath.

Rhion fought against panic as she dived about twenty hands down and then levelled out, but the same shrill words repeated over and again through her head as she swam through the impenetrable blackness.

He'll come for you, no matter where you go.

He knows what you did. Your tricks won't work against him again.

Rhion struggled on through the icy depths, until finally the pain in her lungs and her head forced her to surface. Exhausted, she trod water for a moment and looked around to find her bearings and work out how close her enemy was.

Mad little notions drifted through her mind as she forced the fresh night air into her lungs, her entire body shuddering. *Chased by the Voice of the Citadel! How the humble have risen. From a petty thief to most wanted in the space of days. I brought this on myself. I bring everything on myself!*

Rhion heard nothing but the flow and lap of the water and her own forced, tremulous breaths. But then, she had heard nothing untoward before the Voice's arrival. Premonition and instinct had bought her only a little time.

Finally, she came to the startling conclusion that her foe remained underwater· not headed in her direction but somewhere deep within the canal, possibly even near the bottom. She faintly sensed his presence like a concentration of energy diffused through the water. How could she still detect him? It couldn't be down to hardened instincts, nor the connection she had foolishly sowed between them. It felt different. *He* was different.

As she continued to tread water, vaguely aware that he had slowly headed in the opposite direction,

Rhion wondered how he could have remained so long underwater. He had no special breathing pipes.

Rhion suddenly felt something pull at her from beneath. For a moment she felt certain that her instincts had been wrong, that the Voice had located her. But it was something else.

She looked desperately to either side of the river but saw no one to whom she might shout for help. Likely it would be too late for anyone to help regardless, and if she did call out then her enemy would surely hear her- no matter that he remained deep under the water.

Her adversary drew nearer again now. She turned and saw a figure reach the surface of the river some distance away, perhaps a hundred paces. At the same time, the curious downward pull became stronger and she struggled to remain on the surface. *What is it?!* she wondered fearfully.

The Voice drew closer. He knew exactly where she was now. He remained little more than a silhouette except for his eyes, whose intense gleam she could clearly see.

Rhion turned and began to swim towards the other side of the river. Perhaps if she reached the water's edge before him, she might gain a head start and find somewhere to hide. That vain, desperate hope was all she had.

But she felt her chances dissolve into the icy darkness of the water within a few strokes. She no longer had the energy to get to either side of the river, nor did she stand a chance of staying ahead of him if she simply swam on with the flow. She was almost numb with exhaustion. Her arms and legs felt heavy and slow.

"No," she mumbled, and coughed as she swallowed some water.

Then the water began to swirl, as if a whirlpool had formed with herself at its centre. Desperately paddling water to stay afloat, Rhion stared around in each direction, bemused as the river flowed around her in an ever-tightening circle.

But it was also dragging her down.

The Voice struggled to break through the accelerating circular current of water. The same force that pulled at her, somehow pushed him away even though that ought to be impossible. If it claimed her, he would fail. Rhion would have laughed at the irony of her situation had she not been consumed by terror and so exhausted that she could do nothing more than try to keep herself afloat and breathe in ragged gasps of the cold night air.

She was done for, she realised as the downward force dragged at her ever more urgently. Here came death at last, to drag her through the darkness and the water and bury her in the unknown mud far below.

Even in this tired misery Rhion knew her fate would be a far better one than that of the Voice, if he failed to capture her.

Either way, I'll die, she thought. *I'd rather let the river take me.*

Rhion stopped paddling and trying to stay afloat. She gave herself up.

The whirlpool cast her swiftly downwards. The volume of the rushing water increased to a crescendo, the roar her requiem.

A faint scream of frustration and despair cut through the noise. It did not sound human.

Her journey through the whirling chaos lasted only moments. As she hurtled downwards, the way below her widened and a void opened below the circular wall of water.

There are stars down there, Rhion thought in astonishment. They glittered more brightly than she had thought possible, as if to light the way to her demise.

I knew my dream had to mean something.

Rhion felt a curious sense of detachment as the noise and the water became her entire world. She tumbled and turned, and the stars and the water became smears and lines of white light and fluid chaos as she fell to her oblivion.

II

Seneth hadn't realised how much he had ached to destroy the concentrated mass of wonder and chaos that was Rhion Freeward, and snuff out the strange light of her existence, until he encountered her again by the river.

And then she was taken from him, pulled down by a vortex that formed as if to deliberately thwart him.

She could not have survived for that length of time underwater, and after the whirlpool ceased Seneth had swam back and forth through the river, into the deepest depths and even as far as the distant Southern Gate where the water raged through a giant, never-opened portcullis to cascade down a cliff and into the abandoned harbour.

Rhion had undoubtedly perished, and yet he could not find her body. He wondered desperately if her corpse had become lost forever in the mud, to decay over time.

The river took her, he raged. *It should have been me.*

Seneth had watched in mounting horror as the mystical light of his prey dimmed gradually to nothing like a star in the morning. He had fought grimly to reach her, but no matter his superhuman strength, the strange currents of the river had been stronger and pulled her away from him forever, through the gloom and down.

He had sensed her soon after stepping outside the confines of the Palace. He hadn't needed any information from the Lawmasters' spies. In a moment his vastly enhanced senses had lain her open to him, a beacon to which he couldn't help but be drawn, and then it had been a matter of going where the beacon blazed more strongly. He thirsted for that force, reached for it desperately even as he knew that he had to extinguish that miracle.

At one point, as he drew close to her before the whirlpool stirred, Seneth almost cried out in the submarine darkness, exalted but confused. *Could* he destroy her? He yearned to experience the internal beauty of this creature before he executed her, just for a moment. Would the Mothers begrudge him that? The energy that radiated from Rhion felt familiar, no matter that he had no understanding of it. He had been desperate to be close to it, to *feel* it, if only for a brief while.

What could a moment mean to immortal beings, anyway? Would they know if he delayed the execution?

But now it was too late.

As he sat by the river's edge and screamed his fury to the night, Seneth pictured his enemy as she plummeted to the riverbed. He imagined the muffled sound of her rupture and implosion, and the sight of her blood and innards as they darkened the water. But not even that implausible vision could dent his frustration.

Later he went to the Southern Gate again in the hope that Rhion's remains had now carried in the current and were caught there in the ironwork. But he found no evidence of them.

Then he went under the water again, hoping beyond hope for the faintest glimmer of her light, suffused through the sludge.

He found nothing, he sensed nothing- and at first light he crept away.

She's dead, he told himself later as he sat and half-heartedly looked through some unrelated paperwork.

And what now? How long until the Mothers summoned him again?

Consumed by a sudden, unstoppable rage, he strode through to his bedchamber and struck the mirror as hard as he could with his fist. Shards of polished glass flew in every direction. Seneth stood shaking as the fury gradually dissipated. *Have you forgotten how to control yourself?* he asked. *Control is everything.*

"It still hurts," Seneth murmured. "But it hurts less."

He looked at his bleeding hand. The blood shone with a peculiar light. Then he looked up, into the jagged remains of the mirror.

He felt no pain- not only that, but he had, almost without thinking about it, directed his own body to subdue much of the pain that he should have felt. *Something else new,* he observed. The Mothers had remade him- so could they unravel this patchwork of wonders they had created?

They don't know everything about what they've done, he decided suddenly. *Why would they deliberately give me such a power, permitting me to subdue or even remove physical pain? No, they're only partly in control of whatever process they followed. They admitted that they'd worked on it for centuries. Was that admission*

124

itself accidental, brought about by the untold glee they felt at their long-awaited success?

Seneth returned to his work room. The hour grew late and the sounds of the Citadel became faint. His paperwork, routine information and requests that attempted to tether him to a world he no longer fully occupied, lay strewn haphazardly and forgotten.

He grew restless. As before, he had no need for sleep- maybe he would never need to sleep again, although the idea was far from pleasant. At last he decided to wander through the little-used north-western area of the palace. He descended to a vast maze of low-level passageways, many of which hadn't been used for years. Seneth estimated that much of this area hadn't been in active use since his ascension to Voice, and likely far longer than that.

As he walked along the dusty abandoned corridors, an unsettling sensation accompanied every one of his steps, perhaps augmented by the questions that would not leave his mind- questions he had pondered before and never found answers to.

Why was the Palace so much larger than it needed to be? Much of it lay empty and served no purpose- purely design without function. Even some of the design made no sense.

How many servants and administrators lived here? They could easily be housed in a structure less than one tenth the size.

Might there once have been a far greater population here?

He trod the silent corridors for hours. He theorised and contemplated, but found no answers waiting in the gloom. He even considered the idea that the palace had slowly expanded and grown of its own accord over many centuries without anyone knowing-except, perhaps, the Mothers.

Above all else, he tried not to think of Rhion.

The lighting had failed entirely in some of the passageways. Seneth stopped at one of them, and as he stood on the threshold of absolute darkness, he thought that he heard faint whispers from somewhere down that corridor. Mechanical and repetitive in nature, they rippled and echoed against the walls and finally faded away. Seneth stood and listened intently but the sounds did not return.

Something beyond his experience and understanding, the Voice decided.

But wasn't everything beyond his understanding now?

III

Despite his fear that he might never sleep again, Seneth drifted into a slumber much later when he returned to his quarters, and a short while after that, he dreamed.

The chasm opened wide, before him and behind, above him and below. Seneth remained caught, held in place like a specimen in the centre of the eternal, abyssal darkness. From out of the void, something unimaginably vast and impossibly ancient shifted, and although it had no eyes the Voice felt its gaze upon him, a single stare like a billion baleful orbs. YOU, it said.

He could neither speak nor move. He had no way to express the absolute terror of hanging lost in the great void with this entity. It could tear him apart and make him whole again. It could cause him to fall forever through a never-ending nightmare. But for now, the low, boundless rumble of its voice rattled through his frozen body. Seneth felt its immense power rupture his insides, and yet he remained in place, impossibly broken and whole at the same time.

THE LIGHT WILL BE EXTINGUISHED AND THE CYCLE WILL END IN DARKNESS, AS ALL THINGS MUST.

ALL MATTER WILL SLOW TO STILLNESS AND GROW COLD. I WILL HAVE DOMINION OVER ALL THINGS, AND THE ABYSS WILL TAKE THIS PITIFUL EXISTENCE.

He felt something solidify beneath him. Now he stood on a narrow, jagged pathway of grey stone. On either side, the ground fell steeply away into a chasm of absolute darkness. As he stared over one edge of the precipice and then the other, a voice spoke up at his side.

"If everything is destroyed, then what can it possibly have dominion over?"

When Seneth turned he saw that the Mothers' enigmatic prisoner stood next to him. But now he had become whole, his healing process complete.

"You," Seneth said.

"Me," agreed the apparition, unsmiling as it appraised him. "You are its servant, nonetheless. You have *made* yourself its servant- infested with an emptiness that eats away at you constantly."

"I serve only the Mothers."

"Of course you do." A mocking smile appeared on the man's lips for a moment. "But they seek to knowingly repeat the past when the void- with the horrors of the technology made by its human servants- almost extinguished all life. Does it matter whom you claim to serve?"

Seneth had no answer to that.

"You're the first meaningful product of their long and desperate project- but you're also the start of a new

127

chapter. In their efforts to stir chaos, the Mothers may attempt to make others like you, now that they believe they know the secret to the process."

"And do they?"

"It doesn't matter. The power of that technology finds a way, sooner or later. But the Mothers will accelerate the process. They still- remarkably- have the will to work together for their common goal. And so, the universal cycle turns again. Progress, loss of control, destruction. Over time, all lessons are unlearned."

"And you also know the void. You know it intimately, don't you? It's everywhere- universal, but also personal to you. The gleeful, primal urge that ends your interrogations. The pain in your victim's eyes, the misery, the search for death's door and the release that lies beyond."

"Are you expecting remorse?" Seneth asked coldly.

"In past ages people thought it ended in white light- pure white light, perhaps at the end of a tunnel. Others suggested that this was an artefact created by the dying of the eyes. Regardless, there grew a consensus that beyond the light- that euphoria as the body collapses- lies the void. Eternal, cold darkness. Humans have killed thousands of their own in the name of discovery, desperate to know the answer to what lies beyond, desperate to be certain. And then, of course, they grew desperate to believe that something existed beyond or after the void. Hope is as part of their nature as much as self-destruction."

Seneth said nothing, but the words troubled him.

"You know the darkness and the darkness knows you. But you touch only a small part of something far greater. Yes- something about you changed momentarily. When you were subjected to that violent change by the Mothers, you were taken somewhere, or you broke away from that bubble of physicality. It doesn't matter. What matters is that on a deep level you're aware of it. You've seen over the horizon a little way."

Seneth looked down at himself. His veins bulged alarmingly from his arms and legs. No, not all of them were veins. Some were...

"Look again, over the edge and into the abyss."

"I don't see anything." Nevertheless, the infinite chasm stared back at *him*. What did it feel? A dull, contemptuous curiosity, perhaps. Fear gripped him again. That universal emptiness had no need to reach out or spend effort of any kind on his destruction. It could flatten him over a wide area and somehow keep him alive to feel the agony of being pulled slowly apart. It could put him back together- mind and body- in an ill-fitting way that would cause unspeakable agony. It could force him to eat himself piece by piece until he was done and, impossibly, whole again and ready for the dreadful cannibalism to start anew.

"Through you, the Mothers have unlocked the ills of the past. Those from that distant time that were like you either evolved or were changed by their human creators, their Gods if you will. At some point the balance tipped. They no longer required that their creators mastermind changes to their infrastructure. They re-engineered themselves at will. Over time the flesh became redundant. And so, it went on, until a time came when these entities developed forms that you would neither recognise nor comprehend. They had evolved far beyond the understanding of primitive humanity.

"But there must be a reaction to what the Mothers have done. That's their intention. The process

129

that started with you will run out of control. The Great Power will be stirred into a response."

"Who were you, once? How do you know all these things?" Seneth murmured. He looked down again and saw that he had started to sink into the ground a little way, as if their stage was about to disintegrate or melt into the surrounding darkness, its work done.

The Mothers' prisoner said nothing and gazed steadily at him without expression.

Seneth sank further into the grey mire, and when he looked up again, he was alone on the edge between two infinite canyons.

IV

I'm swimming in an ocean of my own blood.

That impossibly strange thought was Rhion's first conscious notion. Behind closed eyes she pictured a red, liquid expanse, thick and eternally wide, fathomless under a crimson sky through which black clouds drifted even without a wind to bear them.

Her eyes flickered open.

Numbly she surveyed the hellish landscape before her, which was not entirely unlike the one she had imagined. She sat in the shallows of a vast lake whose waters looked like blood and lapped slowly against jet-black sand. A cluster of jagged, dark rocks formed the hostile topography of a shore, and behind it, buildings of many shapes and sizes rose into a dusty red-tinged sky.

Rhion turned and lifted her head slowly, wincing in pain. *This is the Citadel,* she thought, as she observed distant buildings that she thought she knew. *No, this is a make-believe of the Citadel.*

"He came for me," she whispered. "But I fell." She looked down at herself. Her clothes and skin were dry. She felt no pain and appeared not to be wounded.

She had drowned, but instead of lying in eternal darkness she was here, wherever this was.

A hot breeze blew across the desolate shore, and Rhion felt beads of sweat prickle her skin. "It can't be hot," she said. "Not in the winter."

More distinct memories flooded back, so suddenly that she cried out in anguish and clutched her head in her hands. "I must be dead," Rhion told no one as she observed the hell of her surroundings, and a grim thought came to her. She had wished for eternal peace and been given eternal damnation.

She stood up and the water dripped languidly from her and created ripples in the lake. Why was everything so *slow*?

Finally, she picked her way along the rocky shore and walked alongside the edge of the alien city. After a few hundred steps, she arrived at a vast, crumbling archway that stood by itself, perhaps the remains of a wall.

The uncomfortably warm breeze blew persistently. It carried a faint but unpleasant odour, one she didn't recognise. But she saw no sign of life whatsoever. *So this hell is a private place,* Rhion thought as she reached out to touch the stone of the archway. The surface felt dry and warm, as if heated by an unseen sun.

Who or what had created all of this?

Rhion stepped through the archway. It opened out into the desolation of an empty Citadel. She stood and observed, looking in each direction and then up into the red-hued sky. She thought that she recognised the junction of streets where she stood, but felt certain that they didn't belong here, not together.

Rhion looked down at the surface of the street. Had it felt oddly soft as she walked on it? She thought so. Hesitantly she knelt and touched it, then quickly withdrew her fingers at the unpleasant sensation.

She needed to eat. She needed water too.

Rhion felt and heard her stomach rumble a moment later. She swallowed down the saliva that had flooded her mouth, got to her feet and wiped sweat from her brow.

If she was dead, how could she need anything? Might this be another facet of her damnation‑ being wretchedly hungry for all time?

"Please," she whispered brokenly. "Let this be a dream. Even if it's the last dream of my dying brain."

The thought echoed around in her mind and would not let her be.

Rhion gritted her teeth and chose one of the streets to walk down. One of the supposed hells that some people believed in took the form of a maze where lonely souls walked forever, unable to find one another. Sometimes they would hear the calls and cries of loved ones, but they could never reach them, never hold them again. They could only draw desperately, cruelly close.

Rhion wondered if this empty likeness of the Citadel might be such a place.

"Mother," she heard herself say, and shuddered. The thought of Elia helplessly wandering this place, crying out in abject confusion, was unbearable.

Wherever she looked, no building had any doors in doorways or glass in windows. The foul breeze blew in and out of the open structures and changed direction as if on a whim. When she peered into any of the houses or shops or storage buildings Rhion saw no evidence that anyone had ever lived or worked in them. All were stripped bare.

I should stop looking for people, she reminded herself. *Why should there be any evidence of other people here?*

Rhion turned down one of the many side streets. Here the buildings were closer together on either side and leaned lopsidedly towards one another across the narrow road. Great cracks ran along their surfaces in many places, revealing a vivid darkness. Rhion squatted down and stared into these thin chasms but saw nothing and heard nothing from within. Nevertheless, she felt certain that they *went* somewhere.

The breeze died down to absolute calm as she wandered slowly along. Rhion took deep breaths of the flat, warm air, but no matter how deeply she inhaled she still felt perpetually out of breath.

As she leaned against the wall of a nearby building to rest, Rhion thought that she heard faint sounds of laughter, like childish giggles. They came from further down the narrow street, and when she turned to look that way the sounds changed so that they came from the opposite direction. Finally, they came from both up and down the street and even from somewhere above her, although she couldn't see anyone up on the roofs of the buildings.

Rhion listened to that cold merriment and fear stirred as she realised that it didn't sound as much like laughter as she had first thought- at least, not of any living being. The noise more closely resembled something that had *learned* the laughter of a living being, had figured out the essence of it and decided to broadcast it pointlessly, over and again.

What else could laugh, other than something that lives? she silently retorted.

The noise of amusement - if such it was - faded away quickly after that.

When she reached the end of the street, Rhion felt certain that the area no longer looked as it had a short while ago. The buildings leaned closer together on each side of the other roads that led away, and almost half of them had crumbled in places, as if this dry and empty version of the Citadel had both shifted and aged incomprehensibly in only a short time.

For a moment she glimpsed marks on some of the nearer walls, which faded when she tried to peer at them more closely.

Hell is changing, Rhion thought.

V

For an immeasurable time, Rhion headed along dusty thoroughfares, winding side-streets and perilously narrow alleyways. She descended winding staircases to uninhabited slums and found paths that led across rooftops and wound around spires. She searched inside buildings, desperate for clues but not at all certain that she would recognise any if she found them.

It occurred to her, as she rested and looked out over the jungle of silence and stone, that looking for clues was pointless. After all, if she was condemned, then she was condemned.

Wearily she rested in the shadow of a structure that looked like one of the great Guilds, although this, like every other building she had seen, was desolate. In her exhaustion Rhion drifted off into a light sleep as she sat on the steps leading up to the grand entrance doors, and when she woke, she felt a pit of despair open within her.

"No," she croaked, wiping sweat and dust from her face. "This is impossible. I don't want to be here forever."

And yet it's real, a calm and worryingly amused voice reminded her.

But as she struggled to her feet and stared in each direction in turn, not knowing where she ought to go or if she ought to head anywhere at all, Rhion concluded that she must be dreaming. *I'd rather believe I'm dreaming,* she reasoned as she made her way up one of the streets away from the Guild building. Had she walked this street before? Maybe. Why would it matter, if she was asleep somewhere?

Sometime later, she came to a large square surrounded by ornate but empty buildings. A tree grew in the centre and Rhion stared at it, perplexed. She had encountered nothing else living, not even plants until now, but this tree gleamed with rich colour. Pink blossom fell languidly to gather on the dusty paving stones, and the leaves were the sort of healthy, burgeoning green that Rhion associated with the humid days of late spring. She could smell the heady scent of the blossom even from fifty paces away, along with a different, unknown fragrance. An image came to Rhion of many kinds of tree, a vast city of them that went on for a distance far greater than the breadth of the Citadel.

A forest, she thought. *That's what it's called. I remember Mother telling me.*

Rhion approached the tree and stared down at the place where it rose from the ground. How could it be here, when apparently nothing else lived in this world?

None of the slabs and cobbles had been disrupted by the growth. The trunk of the tree grew from the stony surrounds without cracking or dislodging them, almost as if the stonework had been cut into shape to

135

accommodate it. Rhion wondered, as she knelt and touched the bark, if the tree had been here first. Then the Citadel- or this shadow version- came after. Maybe the builders of the Citadel had decided to build around it.

Abruptly she silenced her wandering thoughts. This was not the Citadel, but some patchwork of fragments and features from that place, and besides, she was dreaming.

Wasn't she?

Rhion felt certain that the tree was trying to tell her something.

She picked up one of the pieces of blossom that had fallen. It felt smooth and velvety to the touch. Suddenly she remembered sitting under a tree not unlike this one, holding out her hands to catch blossom as it fell, coaxed gently by a warm spring breeze.

A deep and troubling sense of isolation came over her. "Am I really the only living thing in this world?" she asked the tree. "Aside from you, of course."

Then Rhion asked, "Am I alive at all? I'd like to know. I need to know. Will I wake?"

The tree could not answer, yet she felt something nearby stir- a presence without form.

Then she recalled where and when she had sat under a tree like this before.

She had been seven years old. Rhion and her mother would often visit a park near to where they lived, where trees, bushes and flowers grew. One time, during the spring, they had gone there to find blossom falling from one of the trees- pink and white fragments that descended slowly to the ground.

Rhion breathed in the scent of the blossom, which was exactly as she remembered.

She closed her eyes and memories of that day flooded back, sharp and poignant.

"Why aren't there more trees in the Citadel? Why aren't there more parks?" Rhion wanted to know.

Elia responded quietly, *"Perhaps you ought to ask yourself why there are any parks at all."*

"I don't understand." Rhion scowled in frustration. She had wanted a quick and satisfactory answer. It was a warm, sunny day and she didn't want to spend it thinking.

Her mother turned to her. *"They were here before the Mothers, and they couldn't remove them."* She now spoke even more quietly, so Rhion had to strain to hear. The air felt different now, somehow thicker. The sounds of other people in the distance faded to nothing. Elia had weaved her trickery without her daughter even knowing at first.

"Of course they could," Rhion said immediately, recalling all the stories she had heard of the Mothers' terrible (but seldom seen) powers.

"No. There are places steeped in the Great Power, Rhion. Even here in the Citadel. True, the Mothers can weave and shape it, but there are places that even they cannot destroy. The Great Power gave them the capabilities we all know about, and it gave them immortality. The universe is like a coin. The Great Power is one side - a presence which is everywhere at the same time. The other side..." Elia looked troubled as she paused.

"What? What's on the other side?"

"Emptiness. An absence of hope. A void where evil grows." Her mother stirred and forced a smile. *"It's best not to think about that. But the world is the Great*

Power, and the Great Power is the world. The heart of the universe."

Rhion shook her head in bewilderment. "I don't understand."

"I know you don't. Neither did I, when I was your age. In time, you will." Elia's smile faded. "But even I can't say how the Great Power might shape you as you grow." She pointed to the nearest of the trees. "They are shaped by it. Everything is. Remember that."

Rhion's eyes flickered open. "And how *did* it shape me, Mother?" she murmured. "I see it. I feel it. I know that great presence, but I also know the void. I've grown close to both. What does that make me?"

She looked up and across the square, and for a moment a clear picture came to her of the same area under darkness. A gloomy green light spread across the sky, and a frightened child ran across the stones. She stopped and looked fearfully back at one point, then ran quickly on, as if something terrible followed.

A sound, Rhion thought, the picture still bright and sharp in her mind. *She was followed by the sound of the void, a pestilence eating away at the world and all its people.*

The girl disappeared into a narrow entrance to a street between two large, block-shaped storehouses on the far side of the square.

Rhion reminded herself that this event had played out in a distant age. And yet, somehow, she knew that lost child.

The picture in her mind and her view of the square were the same. She could see the street down which the girl had disappeared, long ago.

She found her way back, Rhion thought. *I'm sure of it. If I follow where she went...*

Rhion stood up and walked across the square. The glassless windows of the surrounding architecture gaped silently at her. She reached the start of the narrow street, then stopped and peered along its crooked length. Cobbles gleamed faintly in the diffuse light and harsh shadows painted the edges of the way ahead. Narrow, lopsided buildings formed a continuous, ramshackle terrace.

The brickwork on either side of the street appeared darker than it ought. The shadows hung black and severe, like sections where nothing existed or parts of the world had been cut away with nothing to replace them.

Rhion made her way slowly along the street, pausing to look at the buildings as she went. Where would the girl have gone?

Then she stopped outside a building which was unlike all the others she'd seen- it had a door.

The door hung slightly open. A faint yellow glow came from inside but had no obvious light source. Rhion peered into the space beyond and saw only an empty room.

A picture came to her of the little girl as she stood in this same place, so long ago. *She went in,* Rhion decided. *I'm sure of it.*

Rhion took a deep breath, pushed the door wide open and stepped inside.

To her right, an open doorway led through to a passage, and beyond that, another room. She made her way into the room, where an entirely different light shone through a window in the far wall.

A light that was instantly familiar.

Rhion blinked in astonishment. *It's lanternlight,* she thought, dumbfounded. *The light of streetlamps.*

She walked over to the window, transfixed by the illumination. Through it, a night-time scene of the Citadel was revealed. She saw people passing nearby, and heard sounds of rowdy but recognisable nightlife.

I must break the window, she decided. *It's the only way through.*

Rhion struck the window with her fist, as hard as she could. A web of cracks spread from the point of impact until the weakened pane fell apart. Cold night air swept in, heavy with rain. Rhion pulled herself onto the ledge and half-climbed, half-fell through the broken window.

She staggered and slipped on wet cobbles and lay on the ground. Her hands had been cut in several places, but she barely noticed. Nor did she see that the window through which she had escaped was no longer there.

Rhion took breath after ragged breath and raised her head to the night, tasting the rain. She didn't even notice any of the curious looks from occasional passers-by.

I'm here, she thought over and over.

She wept with relief. *I'm here and I'm alive.*

VI

Too exhausted and confused to find her way to one of her usual hiding places, Rhion slept in a hole cut into the underside of a stone archway. It stank of piss and something had died nearby recently, but in her overwhelming relief she didn't care. Late trains squealed and rumbled overhead into the small hours, a harsh punctuation against the persistent hiss and spatter of rain.

She couldn't sleep despite her exhaustion. Another conversation that she had had with her mother would not leave her thoughts, and as the night wore on it became bright and urgent.

They walked into the conservatory area which overlooked the little back garden. When Elia closed the door behind them, Rhion felt certain that they had somehow also closed themselves off from the entire world, that if she opened it she would see nothing at all.

Her mother had noticed Rhion looking at the door. "No one can hear us, for a short while at least. I can't keep the block in place for long."

"Why not? You've done this before when we need to talk without anyone else hearing. Even outside in the park."

"Never for long, Rhion. There's every chance that they would detect it. The more the Great Power is used, the more the lattice is disrupted. A small fly might dance across the web without being noticed- a large one makes ripples. The Mothers call the Great Power the Spider for a reason."

When Rhion's eyes widened in alarm, Elia quickly raised a hand to placate her. "They can't hear us. I wouldn't tell you what I'm about to, if I wasn't certain. But I don't have long. I need you to listen, Rhion- and listen well. This is important."

Her daughter tried to swallow down her agitation. "All right," she said eventually.

They sat at the wooden table in the conservatory, amongst the plants. "I've told you a little about the world outside the Citadel," Elia began. "The Great Power is an overarching consciousness, aware of us even as the many millions in the Citadel remain unaware of it." She paused. "I think of it as she. *I don't know why."*

"What does this have to do with the Mothers?" Rhion asked quietly.

"They were once the chosen ones, the saviours of the old world. They defended her against the rampant technology that threatened the entire universe. Perhaps she trusted them." Elia's *expression grew sad.* "That great gift of immortality carried the greatest responsibility of all. Over time they grew resentful, they shunned relations with the people of the outside world..."*

"There are people out there?!" Rhion *exclaimed.*

"Not just people, my love. Many wonders exist in the wider world- not to mention the mythical inner world known as the Halflight- and perhaps one day, if you fulfil the promise handed down through our family for so many generations- you may see them for yourself."

The very idea stunned Rhion into silence.

"The Mothers, as they became known, remade this place in their own image. New laws were made. Old stories and histories were abandoned, even banned. Over many centuries, the true history of how the Citadel came to be was erased. The people were made to look inward, and the door was closed on the outside world as the Citadel grew large enough to be self-sufficient. The Mothers largely forgot that they were creatures of the Great Power, except of course when they considered their own immortality, or when on rare occasions they chose to display their terrifying powers to the people of the Citadel. And so it continued, as the age that came before was entirely forgotten."

"Except by our family," Rhion *said softly.* "How is it that we remembered, when so many millions didn't?"*

"Because, Rhion, we are like them. Oh, the world has chosen not to grant us immortality, but that's something to be thankful for. We have similar powers, if not quite on the same scale- although ours are passed down the generations. And sometimes, remnants of our

142

ancestors' lives, some of their memories, are passed down. There are other families who hold something of the Great Power. Not many, but some. Usually, different families avoid contact with one another. It's too dangerous to do otherwise."

Rhion saw a desperately sorrowful look in her mother's eyes. "What is it?" she asked pensively. But Elia brushed the question aside and continued- although her voice now sounded a little different- "Our ancestors were known to the Mothers. They were allies once, during the great war that came before the time of the Citadel."

"The great war?"

"Against the power which came from the stars to snuff out all life. It failed. It may have failed many times, with each universal cycle." Elia smiled and tousled her daughter's hair. "That's for another time, Rhion. It's time for bed now."

But Rhion couldn't remember Elia ever talking of that long-ago war after that day.

"What should I do, mother?" Rhion's quiet, plaintive words were lost in what had become a thunderous deluge.

How often had she asked Elia that question while she was still alive? A few times perhaps, but not enough. Rhion, headstrong and fierce even then, had tended to reject the patient guidance that Elia gave, and by the time she was twelve she had decided that she no longer needed advice of any sort, even from her mother. *Especially* from her mother.

Something Elia had said when they talked about the Mothers came back to her then. *Sometimes, remnants of our ancestors' lives, some of their memories, are passed down.*

That's what had happened when she was trapped in that other place, that shadow of the Citadel, Rhion realised. The little girl was an ancestor of theirs. She had also been trapped there, long ago, although it looked different then.

She would never have escaped if it hadn't been for her.

Rhion tried to think of the last conversation that she and her mother had. At first she couldn't, but as sleep had already proved impossible, she concentrated until finally she recalled pieces of that bitter half hour or so. Rhion was shocked by the things that she now began to remember.

"Rhion..."

The sound of her name, uttered in that dry, breathless rasp, sent a shudder down her spine.

"I have things to do, Mother." She didn't, of course- she was fourteen and had neither a place at academy nor a job- but Rhion didn't want to push open the door to Elia's stale, gloomy bedroom. She didn't want to see her mother's almost skeletal form, her sunken eyes. She didn't want to talk about anything, and least of all about something meaningful. Just let me go, *she silently begged.*

"A moment," Elia murmured as Rhion paused on the other side of the door. "A moment's all I ask. Then you can be on your way."

Uneasy, embarrassed and with her eyes averted, Rhion trudged reluctantly into the room a little way.

"There's... something I've kept from you." Her mother reached for a glass of water. Rhion observed her violently shaking hand and with a put-upon sigh she

went around to the bedside and helped the glass into her hands and to her lips.

"*Kept from me.*" Rhion frowned. "*You told me the dark secrets of the universe. What could you possibly have kept back?*" She heard the flippant tone of her words but couldn't help it.

"*Quiet. They may sense words like those.*" Elia regarded her in silence for a while longer, as Rhion fidgeted and occasionally looked to the window, where the light of a dull, cold spring day provided the only illumination in the room.

"*You have immense potential, Rhion. There's vast power in you. Far more than me, or your grandmother, or even her mother. Perhaps the most to be seen in many generations. But that's why...*" Elia blinked and looked away. Rhion was dismayed to see that she was crying. When had she last cried? "*I did a terrible thing, Rhion. We did. But we had no choice.*"

"*Why what?*" she asked, already fearful of the answer. "*What did you do?*"

"*That... concentration, that potential in one place... at first we tried our best to keep it hidden, but it took all our strength- it was eating us alive. They would have come for us all, and that would have been the end... the end of all hope...*" Elia wiped clumsily at her eyes.

Rhion shook her head. "*I don't know what you mean. What are you talking about?*"

Elia managed to sit up and take a deep breath. "*I have to tell you now, Rhion. I don't know if you can find her, or if you even want to find her. But I know that sooner or later, you must.*"

She gave her daughter a sorrowful look, full of regret and shame.

"*You have a sister, Rhion. A twin sister.*"

Rhion couldn't move. She couldn't even think properly. She felt as if her entire brain had lit up.

She moved out of the dark gap in which she had huddled and sat on a boulder under the arch of the great bridge. Rain thundered on the ironwork above and rivulets from the downpour snaked this way and that down the bricks. Rhion lost herself in the torrent of sound and the depth of shadow. All she could think of was her mythical lost sibling.

How could I have forgotten? she wondered dazedly sometime later. *Did Mother make me forget? Or did I make myself forget? Why? How?*

The rain had eased off and far to the east the sky began to lighten. Rhion stared at the emerging architecture and thought back again to the day of that shocking revelation.

It was, of course, also the day that Elia had passed away.

Rhion had not been at home at the time. She remembered the conversation- at least, she remembered it *now* but recalled nothing of the moments afterwards- nothing, in fact, until much later that day when she had been groped by a man in a tavern and had responded by stabbing him in the stomach with her knife. The episode had roused her sufficiently from her drunkenness to allow her to flee the scene, and get the train back home, where she had arrived sometime in the small hours.

By now she had sobered up enough to start thinking about how she could ensure the authorities didn't catch her, and what she would tell her mother.

But when she had peered into Elia's room to see if she was still awake, Rhion could immediately tell that she wouldn't ever need to tell her anything again.

Elia had passed sometime in the afternoon, maybe only a short while after Rhion left the house.

I stood there for a long time, Rhion recalled as she shivered in the gathering dawn. *I didn't walk nearer to the bedside, but I knew she'd gone. Even by the lamp light she already looked grey.*

The regret, the rage and the self-loathing would come much later. In that moment, and throughout the following day, she felt nothing at all, even when she went to the Department of Deaths to report her mother's passing. The fear of being apprehended by the Citadel Police faded to the back of her mind. She wondered absently, as the mortician arrived the next day to take her mother's body and advise her of the next things that would happen, how long her freedom would last.

But as she sat alone in the empty house and waited, no authority came to arrest her. Nor did they appear the following day, although a woman from the Department of Deaths called to discuss legal matters and see if there was anything that Rhion needed. Rhion found the idea preposterous.

"The house will pass to you, of course, but there *is* the matter of your age," the woman had told her with what she presumably hoped was a comforting smile. "A custodian must be appointed. It seems that you have no other family..."

"That's right," Rhion had said. "I don't."

"And so we must appoint someone from the Department of Society to help look after you, just until you reach the age of sixteen. You do understand?"

"I do understand."

"That's good, Rhion. I will come by again tomorrow once an appointee has been organised."

Presumably the woman from the Department of Deaths did call again the next day, but Rhion never found out whether she had or not. Early that morning, she gathered what little food, clothing and money she could carry and left her home forever.

That day was bright and sunny, with a light breeze and a faint promise of spring. The azure sky was dotted with more tiny white clouds than Rhion had ever seen before.

She walked away from the life that had crumbled in a day, unaware of a shifting balance, and only vaguely aware of the dark river's currents within her, swirling with a grief and rage that she had yet to properly feel.

"Why did she make me forget?" Rhion quietly asked herself as she stepped out from under the bridge. "I would have remembered *that*. Despite everything."

She had no answer.

V - The Descent

I

Lena woke in her bed, short of breath. Her eyes flickered open and she looked up into the gloom for a long while, not thinking, only observing. She hadn't drawn the curtains the previous evening, and dawn light seeped through the window. She turned her head for a moment and saw birds wheeling on the breeze.

They go where they want, Lena thought. *They have no walls. The world is theirs. Where do they go and what do they see?*

What does the rest of the world look like?

She had pondered those questions before, as a child. She had even drawn maps of how the rest of the world *might* look. "Why can't we go there?" she had demanded one time when she showed one of her maps to her father.

"We just can't," he had said.

"But there must be *so many* places to explore..."

"And don't forget about them," he had told her, "but for now, *do* put them aside."

Lena sat up. Why could she not remember where she had been yesterday?

"I had a dream," she murmured, as the memory of something incredible and impossible gradually seeped back into her mind. "The *door.* I went through the door."

She laughed and then shuddered. She couldn't recall what day it was, or when she had last been to work. Was she coming apart? Would she lose control and drift away as she'd already theorised?

Lena got out of bed and noted that she was still wearing her shirt and trousers. A cautious sniff suggested that she'd been wearing them for at least three days. What had she been doing? She couldn't have been asleep all this time.

After walking downstairs Lena stopped at the wall clock in the hallway, which told her it was past four o'clock in the afternoon. *Which afternoon?* she wondered.

She was still struggling to decide whether to go to the power station and try to explain her absence from work or wait until the morning, when someone knocked on the front door. Lena jumped and stared down the hallway, frozen with indecision.

She walked to the door and stood still for a while with her hand poised above the handle. When she did eventually open the door, she found Faral Whitewood standing on the threshold. Rain had started to fall, and dark droplets marked his ill-fitting suit.

"Lena." He gave a brief, taut little smile. "I'm so glad to see you. I called here yesterday, and the day before, but you didn't answer."

"I've been... asleep." Lena hastily ran a hand through her hair, suddenly reminded that she had only moments ago got out of bed and walked downstairs.

"Of course," he said, as if being asleep for days could be a perfectly normal and reasonable excuse. "May I come in?"

Before she could answer, Faral pushed past her into the hallway and inhaled slowly as if he wanted to taste the air itself, no matter how stale it might be. Lena felt the heat of humiliation rise in her cheeks. A long time had passed since she had opened the windows or cleaned the house properly. She seldom had either the time or the inclination.

"I don't normally do home visits..." Faral began.

"You're not a physician," Lena pointed out.

He turned and gave her a quick smile, then looked her up and down. "Quite right! But physically, I can see there's little wrong with you. My expertise is in matters connected to the mind."

"Really?"

Her sarcasm appeared lost on the counsellor, whose good cheer remained undimmed. "Shall we sit down?"

He strolled through into the sitting-room, and much to Lena's agitation he seated himself in her father's chair. Reluctantly she occupied one of the other chairs and stared unhappily at the foreign object inhabiting the space where her father had spent so many hours reading or talking with her.

The counsellor steepled his hands and made a concerted attempt to look more serious. "Lena, I'll come directly to the point. Management are a little concerned about you. Now, it's nothing to be overly worried about," he added quickly as he noted the sudden look of alarm on her face. "But it *is* an issue that we need to look at, together. I feel that you're... how can I put it? Not giving yourself the opportunity to grieve your loss properly."

"Oh. Is there a handbook on how to grieve *properly*?"

"I'm afraid not," he said with a sad smile. "Sometimes it falls to professionals such as me to provide the necessary guidance."

"My work..."

"...has been of an excellent standard as always, although you do have a little catching up to do after three days' absence."

"Three days." Lena felt the walls press in more closely and nausea stir inside her.

"I'm sure you're more than capable of doing everything required. So, I can assure you that there isn't any need to be afraid."

"Afraid? I'm *not* afraid," she lied. "I just don't see why anyone needs to be concerned. You said yourself that my work hasn't suffered, and I'll make sure I'm back at work tomorrow, so that ought to be the end of the matter."

"Hmm. If only it were." Faral frowned and uttered a deep sigh as if a complex puzzle perplexed him. "You see, management have raised the issue of... erratic behaviour, and your absence has only made them more concerned."

"Erratic behaviour?" Lena shook her head. "That's a lie! I haven't been erratic..." She paused and tried to calm herself. "Do you have examples?"

He ignored the question. "I quite understand, Lena. But they've decided- subject to my own analysis of the situation- that it might be best to refer you for a short stay in one of the special hospitals for..."

"No!" Lena's sharp exclamation would have betrayed her panic even if she hadn't leapt to her feet like a startled rat. *No one ever comes out of those places,* she told herself. *I can't let them imprison me there!*

"It would only be a short stay. Just until you get well, you understand." Faral opened his hands expansively to illustrate how reasonable his suggestion was.

"There's no such thing as a *short stay*," Lena retorted. "You know what happens in those places.

152

They... they *change* people. They carry out procedures to see what will happen when people are pushed beyond their mental limits..."

"Oh, that's nonsense." Faral looked thoughtfully at her. "Pure nonsense, my dear."

Why did he call me that? Lena wondered fretfully as she sat down.

"But supposing there might be a grain of truth to such stories- you don't need to worry. You see, I don't agree with management's appraisal of the situation.."

"You don't?" Lena relaxed a little.

"I have a plan that can keep you out of such places and away from the arms of medical progress."

"Medication?" Lena nodded before he had a chance to reply. "I'll take whatever you prescribe as long as it doesn't impact on my job."

"Yes- I could make a prescription to get you through. But I think management would be much more satisfied if I made a supervision order." He took a paper from his pocket and handed it to her. As Lena unfolded it and began to read, he continued, "That's a copy. The original is filed safely away. Now, if I come here and spend some time with you, let's see... eight times a month- would that work?" Faral pulled a battered paper notebook from his jacket pocket, opened it and thumbed through the pages for a moment. "Yes, I think eight would be about right. Maybe a little more often in time, depending on how we get on."

"Spend *time* with me? Doing what?"

"I'd like to know you a little better, for one thing. That would help me to help *you.* My work is all about finding out how people's minds work. Of course, I would expect certain favours in return for mine. That would be only fair, don't you think?"

153

Lena's skin crawled as she saw the smile on his lips and the hard look in his eyes. "No. No, I don't think so at all."

"Oh." Faral looked quite taken aback. "That doesn't sound like a master logician speaking. Consider the alternative, Lena. And then remind yourself-*objectively*- what little you must do to maintain your freedom. I'm quite good company, believe it or not. I might even make a conversationalist out of you. And I'm not a violent man. I wouldn't want anything from you that most men wouldn't want from their wives. Nothing... *unusual*." He got up and walked over to her, and Lena jumped to her feet, trembling. "Are you a virgin?" he asked.

"What?! How is that relevant?"

"Lena, *I* decide what's relevant and what isn't. Unless you want to be locked away in the madhouse, you are, or will be, the subject of a supervision order. Are you a virgin?"

"Yes." Lena's cheeks burned. She looked away from him.

"That's good," Faral said quietly. "That's *very* good. I'm gentle with girls like you." He reached out and pulled at the top buttons of her shirt, and she reacted instinctively by slapping him. In response he seized her wrist with surprising strength and pulled her nearer. He forced his free hand down her shirt and squeezed her breast until it hurt. "You will cooperate," he told her. "I can send you to hell, Lena."

Lena's other hand brushed against something cold. She didn't glance down but knew it was a heavy brass figurine that had always stood on the little table next to her chair. She had never really thought about it much before.

A voice whispered in her head: *This is where everything changes.*

All men and women have breaking points- those critical events when they can yield no longer, and they must either lie down and die cowering, or give in to ferocity and the state of mind that Lena's father had once called the *inner scream.*

Lena had never, until this moment, believed that she possessed such a thing.

She moved back, brought the ornament in a sideways motion and smashed it against the side of Faral's skull.

Lena knew that she had only a moment to act decisively. The blow had been nowhere near strong enough even to render the counsellor unconscious. But he relinquished his grip, and while he was still too dazed to defend himself properly, Lena swung the makeshift weapon and hit him again, harder, shocked at the ease and speed with which she moved.

Faral fell to his knees, attempting to protect his cracked skull with shaking, bloodied hands. He sobbed and shouted something at her, but Lena had no idea what it might have been. She swung the figurine again, now with both hands and harder than ever, and this time she shattered his jaw. Spots of blood spattered the nearest wall and several teeth flew across the room.

The furious onslaught continued. As Faral lay on the ground Lena knelt at his side and rained blow after blow upon him until no one would have recognised the man. Streaks of gore spattered the furniture. "I'm sorry, Father," Lena sobbed at one point- long after her foe had ceased to move- and then, to her horror, she laughed hysterically.

Finally she flung the figurine down into the chaos that had been Faral's head. She stared, transfixed by the carved grandeur of the ornament as it gleamed with the fruits of her labour. The brass idol of an unknown figure shone as if the violence had awoken something inside it, the arms raised towards the heavens even as the body lay in a nest of gore and bone shards.

"No, no, no, what have I done, *what have I done*," Lena mumbled. She looked at her hands and then down at her shirt, soaked with the counsellor's blood. "I'm dreaming," she told herself then. "Thought I'd woken up, but *no*. Maybe I *can't* wake up yet. No, there's more to do."

She slowly pulled Faral's body out of the room, leaving a thin dark trail on the well-worn carpet, and down the passageway as far as the door that led down to the cellar. She would tip him down into the darkness to the side of the staircase. How far would he fall? Far enough to never be found, with luck.

But when she attempted to open the door Lena was aghast to find that her key no longer worked. Her hand trembled violently as she tried again and again.

I could smash it down with an axe, she thought wildly. *No! I can't let the cellar and the doorway be discovered.*

It occurred to her that she ought to chop him up into small pieces, put the pieces in a sack and take them to be incinerated.

Then she would clean the house from top to bottom. Wasn't it about time she cleaned anyway?

She dragged Faral through to the kitchen and chopped and cut through his body as best she could. Exhausted and traumatised, she could barely summon the energy to dismember her counsellor. She rested more times than she could count, taking shallow, shuddering breaths of the pungent air. His blood dried on her hands and other parts of her body and she

156

scratched it off. She stared in fascination at the innards revealed by her painstaking progress. Sharp fragments of bone lay scattered on the floor. They reminded Lena of a porcelain cup that she had broken when she was twelve. She had cut herself as she picked up the shards, hoping that she could mend the cup. But she hadn't been able to put the pieces back together.

She had been much more upset about that.

Finally, Lena placed all the body parts into a thick sack from one of the cupboards. She wearily stared at the bundle for a long while.

Lena came to the desolate realisation that she would not get away with this. This was not her area of expertise. She had never killed anyone before. She hadn't even contemplated the act- not seriously, anyway. How could she get rid of the evidence? Even the most thorough cleaning this house had ever seen would never scrub it all away. Management must have known that Faral had come here- mustn't they?

She took a deep breath and uttered a swift rebuke to herself: *You're an intelligent and resourceful woman. You're not doomed to fail. You can't afford to fail. You know what will happen if you're caught. You'll either be executed or incarcerated.*

Lena considered bleakly that intelligence and reason hadn't prevented her from making the most unwise choice of her life- deciding to bludgeon her counsellor to death with a heavy brass ornament in her own sitting room. She could barely remember the event now, beyond a blur of temporary, uncontrollable rage.

I wasn't myself, she thought. But that was not exactly true. She had become something more than herself- as if the free spirit that she might once have been had slipped back into her skin.

Joy, Lena thought. *I felt something like joy, amidst the wreckage and the fury. I shouldn't have. What sort of creature am I, under my cold exterior?*

It might be better for everyone except herself, if she was caught and incarcerated.

But she couldn't let that happen.

Lena breathed slowly and deeply, inviting the tang of blood into her body. She had tasted freedom and imagined that it might be like the sensation and sight of the open world to someone who had lived their life surrounded by walls and artifice.

But didn't that describe all life in the Citadel?

"Find a way, Lena," she whispered. "Find a way."

She again considered taking Faral's remains to the incinerator, which was perhaps an hour's walk from the house. It stayed open throughout the night, providing not only a service for anyone who needed items destroyed but also some power for nearby businesses and properties. But supposing she was seen and questioned? The authorities sometimes carried out spot checks on people who brought materials to be incinerated. Besides, she would need to carry a heavy sack of meat that would no doubt attract any number of stray dogs and cats.

Maybe it was worth the risk though.

Or maybe she could just feed him to those feral beasts.

No, that wasn't an option. There was always the possibility that his body would not be entirely consumed, and gnawed remains might later be found strewn around the gutters and alleyways. Of course, the chances of such mangled pieces being identified as Faral were small, but she wanted them much closer to zero.

"Too messy." Lena jumped at the sound of her voice.

Could she even carry Faral's remains? It had taken a lot of effort simply to drag him through from the living-room.

Then she considered dumping the body parts into the bath in the back room and adding concentrated acid to dissolve it to a sludge. She could then wash most of it away, and if there was some bone left maybe she could grind it up or crush it somehow.

But although a small amount of acid had been kept in one of the store cupboards for months- she had no idea what her father had kept it for- the quantity was nowhere near enough. Maybe she could obtain some from one of the storage chambers she had access to at the power plant, but that was the last place she wanted to go now, and what excuse could she possibly have if one of the guards questioned her?

I need a plan, Lena thought. *And I need it quickly.*

She looked down at herself and realised she would need to change her clothes. They were caked and stained with drying blood. Lena undressed, washed the worst of the blood from her hands and face and fetched clothes from her bedroom- a plain grey shirt and dark trousers. These were not much cleaner, but at least they weren't steeped in her counsellor's blood.

On a whim she took a bottle of rye spirit from one of the kitchen cupboards and poured herself a generous glass of it. Her hand didn't shake at all. *Will I feel remorse at some point?* she wondered as the first gulp of the harsh liquid warmed her stomach.

Lena finished the glass and poured herself another straight away. She drank this one a little more slowly and sat at the kitchen table to contemplate. *Plan,* she reminded herself as she reached the bottom of the second glass. *Don't forget about that. You need a plan.*

What about the river?

The main trunk river was half an hour's walk from here. But the problem of attracting the attention of animals- or the authorities- remained. Aside from that, somebody- or some process- might recover the body parts.

Finally, she settled on an idea that filled her with dread and shame, but which appeared to be the only one that might work. She would need to disappear afterwards, but Lena decided that she would break down the problem into manageable chunks- something an old supervisor of hers had fervently believed in.

She would burn Faral's remains here in the kitchen, and then she would burn the house down.

Lena found a third glass of spirit in her hand. As she took a sip, the languid warmth made her smile even as conflicting thoughts swirled in her head.

This is Father's house!

Not anymore. He's dead in the dirt and gone forever. It's yours now and you can do whatever you want with it.

Lena knew that she would be attempting to cover for one crime by committing another. Burning down her own house was far lesser a crime than murder, though. Not only would a fierce fire consume Faral's remains so utterly that no one could hope to recognise them, but it might lead the authorities to suspect that she too had been consumed by the flames. After all, they wouldn't think that she'd murder her counsellor and then burn down her own house, would they?

Or did they suspect her of such instability that they *would* think so? Might Faral's visit have been the precursor to something far worse, no matter his clumsy and ill-fated attempt at bribery?

Maybe, maybe not. For all she knew, the supposed concerns of management were all lies.

Lena drained her glass and pondered the matter of what came after the flames. She had no family now, which meant the authorities had no relatives to call upon. No one knew her well. No one understood her. No one had any meaningful insight into her life. Very few clues could be gathered by talking to those few people who knew of her existence.

Lena's quiet. Lena's clever. Lena doesn't like to talk.

And that would be the end of the matter.

II

Lena put some clothes, a few books, a little food and a large flask of water into a large bag which she placed in the hallway, and took a large knife which she put in her belt, vaguely aware that she might need something to defend herself with. She poured some alcohol-based cleaning fluid over the sack containing Faral's body and then over almost every part of the kitchen floor and worktops, careful to keep her hands and body free of the substance. Finally, she lit some paper and stepped quickly back as she threw it into the kitchen.

Within moments the entire room was ablaze. Lena watched in helpless fascination, astonished and horrified at what she had done as a wall of intense heat and light formed in front of her. As the fire spread, she quickly retreated down the hallway and picked up the bag. She opened the front door, stepped outside and closed the door behind her. Already the light from the flames danced like a dozen gleeful creatures in the window.

Now I have nothing, Lena thought numbly as she hurried away.

Not even that other place, came an answering whisper. *How will you escape into the darkest recesses of your mind now? No house, no cellar. No cellar, no staircase.*

Lena ran along street after street, measuring her progress by the sputtering gas-lamps she passed. Each sharp inhalation of the cold evening air hurt her throat and lungs. She stopped only when she heard, from the direction of her now-distant house, a low rumble followed by a roar of primitive, subterranean rage. She turned, fearful of what she might see but unable to stop herself.

The sky above the contours of buildings held a faint glow, not an orange hue created by the flames from a burning house but an illumination that flickered and writhed madly and changed colour over and again. Lena wondered fearfully what had caused it. It couldn't be anything to do with the house. Could it?

She turned and ran again, full of dread. An inner voice wailed at her, demanding to know what she had done. It occurred to Lena that her actions might somehow have condemned the entire Citadel to the wrath of an unstoppable power. Had she set free something terrible that would spread and devour civilisation?

Sometime later Lena stopped and collapsed at the side of the street, exhausted. She wept, and then finally drifted into a light, unsettled slumber. But after only a short while she woke suddenly, flailing at a shadow she thought obscured her vision. Not many people were about, and those few who were within earshot gave her only a cursory glance before hurrying about their business, eager to be away from the madwoman squatting in the gutter.

Lena sat and shivered, now too cold and fearful to sleep.

With the dawn came the beginnings of acceptance. The matter was done with, she reminded herself. There could be no going back, no difficult decisions. She had cut out the complications from her life.

But those thoughts offered no comfort. Realisation that her situation had become more rather than less complex started to sink in. She had no idea how to survive as a vagrant on the streets of the Citadel. How would she find enough food and water? No one liked beggars. They were a nuisance at best and to many people they were nothing more than vermin in human form. As a rule, anyone luckier in life than street people regarded them as cautionary tales, warnings of what might happen if they weren't careful in their own lives.

For a while however, Lena's fear of being found by the authorities surpassed any concern she had about day to day survival. She had money in her bag which would keep her going for a short while. She could stretch it out if she ate and drank a minimal amount.

Then what? she asked herself. *I can't ask anyone for work. They'll want to know where I worked before, and they'll need an address. No one offers lawful work to someone who doesn't have those two things. Maybe I'll have to do the sort of work where no questions are asked.*

She moved on, uneasy that she had sat in one place for so long, and so it continued for the day. As the sun sank over the rooftops and the chill of twilight came, Lena pulled her coat tightly around herself and

163

wandered along perhaps her hundredth street of the day. She had found herself in the Old Barrows, a polluted and foul-smelling area whose waste ground pits and ponds were used as dumping grounds by those who preferred not to pay the levy on legal disposal. The streets here were little more than muddy tracks, the houses mostly abandoned.

There must be a solution, she silently insisted, as if her life was nothing more than a puzzle that required lateral thinking and the application of logic.

Lena wondered if any other people in her situation might speak to her or offer advice. None had yet. *Could I ask someone?* she wondered. *What would I say?* She had seen other vagrants from a distance, but none had approached her, perhaps because she didn't look like them. Not yet anyway.

A bedraggled, knot-haired man clad in a thick greasy coat and fur hat sat a short distance from her as she rested at one point. Lena thought about striking up a conversation- not that she had any idea what to say- but he spoke first. "Anything to spare, lady? Coin? Food?" he asked, his voice rough with phlegm.

"Sorry," Lena said. "I'm like you. I don't have any..."

"Something to drink then. It'll be cold tonight. Might snow."

"No, I..."

"I can sell you a keepsake," he interrupted, and pulled what looked like a child's toy from one of his bags. After a moment Lena saw that it was a rudimentary and badly painted wooden model of an Earthline locomotive.

"What would I want with that?" she asked. "What use is it?"

"Belonged to my son." His eyes fixed on hers, intent and suddenly filled with a bright, sharp

164

intelligence that Lena found frightening although she had no idea why. "It has power."

"It has no power. It's made of wood," she said unnecessarily and without thinking. Immediately malevolence filled his eyes. "You'll die without a heart," he told her, and Lena had no idea if he meant he intended to cut it swiftly out of her before she drew her last breath, or if her perceived cruelty would be her downfall.

Taken aback by the turn their short conversation had already taken, Lena opened her mouth to apologise, but couldn't. At the same time her hand grasped the hilt of the knife in her pocket and pulled it free. She didn't brandish the weapon but drew enough of the blade out into the dusk to show that she was armed. Finally, words struggled from her mouth, meaningless fragments. "I... I mean, I didn't..." She found it impossible to make any sense and wondered desperately why she sounded like an imbecile.

But the street-dweller had seen enough. He cast the toy back into one of his bags, scrambled to his feet and hurried away. He looked back once to make sure she hadn't followed him.

"I'm sorry," Lena whispered at last into the gathering night.

Sometime later, under the cover of full darkness, Lena found herself near a large guesthouse opposite an Earthline station. She had never visited this area before. Every building here looked in poor repair, with cracked walls, peeling paint and chipped stonework, and the guest house at least looked sturdy compared with its neighbours. The streets in this area had not yet been electrified properly, and oil lanterns flickered madly, creaking on their pole hooks. Bags of rubbish lay piled high in places and other refuse blew around in the chilly breeze. Lena caught sight of a long-tailed rat hurrying busily from one shadow to another. Rats would always have enough to eat.

The large sign in the front window of the guesthouse advertised rooms at two copper pennies per night. Lena reckoned that was astonishingly cheap, although the outer decor gave a clue as to why that might be, and when she tentatively opened the outer door and stepped inside a faint smell of damp and decay hung in the air.

She almost turned and left, but then reminded herself that as this was surely one of the cheapest places she would find, she could afford a roof over her head for a long time- if the authorities failed to find her.

Maybe enough time to think of a plan.

She walked along the narrow hallway. At its end, dismal staircases led up into gloom on either side of a cramped little office from which an old woman peered warily at her. Near-skeletal fingers clutched a roll of paper stuffed with smoking herbs, still unlit. The woman surmised Lena slowly, looking her in the eyes before she allowed her yellow-tinged gaze to fall upon the rest of her body. Lena wondered for a moment what toxins had made their way through this creature's body over her decades of existence. "You need a room," the landlady said finally, as if only by such a lengthy inspection could she determine that fact.

Before Lena could respond the woman continued, "Minimum stay is three days." She had the worn, cracked voice of someone who had spent a lifetime uttering the same rules and regulations. "Unless you break the house rules, then you forfeit your deposit and you leave immediately. You pay six pennies now to cover those three days."

"What about the *maximum* stay?" Lena asked.

The landlady gave her an odd look. "There isn't one. You stay as long as you have enough money, unless you want to leave." She coughed and wheezed and eventually continued, "No refunds may be given under any circumstances. You may not bring anyone back here. It's not a whorehouse."

"And I'm not a whore," Lena replied immediately, taken aback at the assumption.

"More rules can be found printed on the sign on the back of your door. Make yourself familiar with these. You *can* read, can't you?"

"Of course I can!"

The landlady shrugged. "Have to ask." She held out a scrawny hand in expectation of payment. Lena rummaged in her pocket and handed over the money almost without thinking. "Ought I sign anything?" she asked suddenly. A formal arrangement of some sort made sense to her. Wasn't this a form of contract?

But the old woman gave her a blank look and took a large iron key from a hook on the wall behind her. "Number thirty-seven," she said unnecessarily as Lena noted the number written on the paper attached to the key.

Lena looked left and then right, then behind her, where a half-open door led into what appeared to be a common room of some kind. "Which way should I go?" she asked. To her bemusement the old woman just shrugged and lit her smoke.

Lena sighed and made her way up the staircase to her right. She held the banister firmly as each step took her further into the odorous gloom.

When she reached the landing, she was surprised to see that three long corridors led away, straight ahead and to her left and right. *This place is bigger than I*

167

thought, Lena mused, and looked first at the numbers on each side of the left-hand corridor. "One hundred and seven... one hundred and eight," she observed quietly. Then she looked at the numbers on the right-hand side- "Eighty, eighty-one"- and straight ahead- "Fifty-six, fifty-seven."

"Straight on," Lena said, and made her way down that corridor. Electric bulbs fitted in the ceiling flickered on and off and made a strange fluttering noise as if giant moths were trapped inside the light casings. She wondered how the landlady could afford to fit electric lights here.

The deep, dark red of the décor unsettled her. Looking at it, Lena imagined that blood filled the cavities of the walls, floor and ceiling and had seeped through to their surfaces. It was, she decided, the colour of despair and depravity. If hells truly existed, as some people thought, then this grim, putrid red would be the colour of their rooms- if rooms or buildings occupied such mythical places.

And what about the world *she* had imagined? Had that been some sort of hell that she glimpsed? All the stories said that people never came back from such places.

But her experience was simply the result of a mental breakdown, neither more nor less. There was nowhere to come back from. And even if there had been, now there was nowhere to go back to.

Lena reached the doors to rooms forty and forty-one and then stopped. The following room numbers were one hundred and twenty-six and one hundred and twenty-seven. She stared at the numbers for a moment, perturbed, then walked a little further on and saw that the numbers began to decrease. "Who *designed* this place?" she muttered.

Finally she arrived at a crossroads of corridors. The last numbers in the corridor she had walked down were one hundred and eight and one hundred and nine, but to her left she saw - at last - the door to room thirty-seven.

I'm back where I was, Lena thought at first. But no, she couldn't be. Besides which, there were no stairs here.

As she stood helplessly, it occurred to her that someone or something had decided to play a trick with random numbers as a way of mocking her, telling her that mathematical skills were of no use here.

"Don't be stupid. You're doing it to yourself," Lena said aloud. "Get some sleep."

But she feared that sleep wouldn't help at all.

Lena reached out and turned the door handle. It swung gently open to reveal a tidy if stale room. The large window in the far wall let in murky, greyish daylight that fell upon an immaculately made bed and set of drawers. As Lena's gaze continued to take in the other furnishings, she realised that everything in here was a shade of grey. Inside the wardrobe that had been placed against the left-hand wall she found only dust and a couple of old coat hangers.

Lena put her bag down by the bedside, idly drew lines and curves in the dust that had gathered on the bedside table, then walked soundlessly across the grey carpet to the window. From here she had a view of the street she had walked down to get here, and the Earthline station on the opposite side. Lena yawned. She desperately needed to sleep.

But she waited and watched by the window for a while, and a deep unease stirred within her as time dragged on. No citizens or vehicles passed by. She didn't hear the subterranean rumble of Earthline locomotives. A dead calm hung over the area.

After a while Lena opened the window and listened intently but heard nothing. She breathed in the still air and exhaled slowly, willing herself to maintain control.

She closed the window. *You're sinking back into the blackness in your head,* a spiteful little voice told her. *You're melting into the morass of insanity that's always been a part of you. Oh, you tried to build a wall to shut out the creature that you really are, but the wall's coming down now.*

Had she started to imagine things again? What a fate that would be- to go mad in this grim place, hidden away from everything. And yet it made a sort of grim sense- that she might imagine everyone else in the Citadel had simply disappeared and she was the only living person left.

"Go to sleep," Lena said.

She locked the door and lay down on the bed, exhausted.

Lena woke with a start.

It was night-time, or perhaps evening. She got up and crossed to the window again and saw that there were now some people around. Two men were laughing about something as they passed by. A large coal-cart squeaked along, pulled by a heavy-footed horse. Lena counted its plodding steps until they faded into silence after the horse and cart negotiated the street corner.

Her stomach growled. Maybe she ought to ask if any food was provided here, although she also worried that it might be less than palatable and possibly even dangerous to eat.

She opened the door and made her way down the corridor outside, but no longer noted the room numbers or even the direction she had chosen. Much to her relief she reached a flight of stairs and made her way down them to find herself back in the reception area.

To Lena, the landlady looked older still, and- she thought for a moment- a little darker and smaller, although surely that wasn't possible. Veins protruded alarmingly from her neck like the roots of an ancient tree.

"You took your time," the landlady accused her.

Lena blinked. "I did?"

The woman fumbled with some paperwork on her desk. "Kitchen needs to know if you're dining here. You can go out but there aren't many places to eat in the area. Best if you sign here and then..." She glanced up, and Lena felt a cold feeling wash over her as the woman's eyes widened in terror. "What... what is it?" she managed to ask.

When the landlady didn't respond, Lena turned fearfully round but saw nothing. "I don't see anything," she said, and eventually turned back. "What's..."

But her words faded away as she saw that the old woman had gone. Only the acrid smell of her smokeweed indicated that she'd been here at all.

"You *were* here," Lena whispered.

A door that led into another room at the back of the reception area stood slightly open. Lena became convinced that the landlady had hidden herself in there, and yet, bizarrely, still looked out at her through the doorway.

"You were going to ask me to sign something?" Lena said hesitantly. But she sensed that the old woman had retreated further into her back office or storeroom or whatever lay in the gloom behind the door. After a short while Lena heard a faint sobbing which only baffled her further.

"I should never have let you in!" cried the landlady, and then the door to the darkness slammed shut.

Lena didn't want to go to her room. Something about the washed-out greyness of its furnishings made her feel that if she spent too long in there, she too would lose her colour and become nothing more than a drab artefact, an ornament, a painting on the wall that no one ever looked at.

She turned and wandered through the common room door whose glass façade was criss-crossed with rusted wire. The door handle almost came off in her hand. Lena tutted to herself and tried to tighten the loose screw she'd spotted but gave up as it protested against the rust.

A faint odour of sweat, grimy carpet and another sour smell she couldn't identify greeted her as she walked in. Yellow, dim lanterns and two electric lights which were only slightly brighter provided the illumination. Two middle-aged men sat at a low gaming table at the far end of the room. One of them glanced briefly at her and wiped a flank of greasy hair away from his eyes. His bald companion was too intent on the cards and dice on the table to look her way.

Lena noticed a bottle of turnip spirit and two glasses on the table. The greasy-haired man lifted his glass and looked towards her again as if enacting a wordless toast. When she failed to respond- Lena often had no idea how to respond to people, and so she tended not to react- the man took a sip from his glass, set it down and leaned back in his chair, watching his companion's continued analysis of whatever game they played. After a moment he slipped his right hand into his trousers and began to stimulate himself.

Is everyone disturbed in this place? Lena wondered. She contemplated leaving the room, but oddly this place felt safer than her bedroom, although she had no idea why. She averted her eyes and wandered over to the nearest wall where a thinly populated bookcase had been placed, along with two soft chairs. One of the chairs had been covered with the mouldy remains of some food-bread, Lena thought, along with some sticky substance-so she sat carefully on the edge of the other one and took a book from one of the shelves.

"Uh," said the greasy man from across the room. "Uh. Uh."

Lena stole a quick glance in their direction. The man who had decided to pleasure himself had stopped. The other man, whose bald head was covered in a faint sheen of sweat, still looked intently at the cards and dice on the table. For a moment Lena thought his head, like a polished ball, looked like Faral's. She imagined the sound of it shattering and the sight of bone shards flying in all directions.

She quickly returned her attention to the book. The title on the front cover read *The Gentle Decay of the Past,* but Lena could see no indication of the author's name on either the front or back covers or the spine. When she opened the book and thumbed through a few of the pages she found that the words were mostly nonsense to her. *Like oblique poetry,* she thought. *Where nothing is what it appears to be and meaning is supposedly a choice of the reader, not the author.*

Father and I talked about this, years ago. I don't remember when.

"D'you want some cleanfire? I'll go out and get some," she heard the masturbator ask his companion.

Cleanfire was one of many names for cheap, poor quality spirit, usually bought from vendors who camped near stations and on the fringes of markets. A few years ago, she had tried some out of curiosity. It tasted neither clean, nor particularly like fire but had a harsh, sour taste and usually a yellow colour with a pungent froth. Lena had thought it looked like urine. She had no idea why it was called cleanfire.

"If you want." The bald man didn't look up from the game, Lena noticed as she cautiously glanced in their direction again.

"Don't cheat while I'm gone. I'll cut you."

His companion didn't respond to the threat.

"How many shall I get?" The greasy man scratched rapidly at his head as if the question had made him start to itch. Lena thought his voice sounded dirty and thick, clogged up with earth or mud.

"Don't know. Two. Three. Get the yellow. Don't get the green."

The greasy man stumbled away from the table and passed within several paces of Lena, then stopped. Lena looked down at the book, feigning sudden interest in its contents, but almost gagged as she caught his odour.

"You could have a drink with us," he said abruptly, slurring his words a little. "Shouldn't be alone."

"No thank you." Lena concentrated so hard on the text that her vision blurred a little.

"You're not looking at me."

"I'm reading."

"You're pretty," he said then.

"No. I'm not."

Perhaps that confused him, because he didn't say anything else. He stood there for a moment longer, then turned and walked to the door, weaving slightly from side to side. Lena glanced up quickly as he left and breathed a sigh of relief, although she wondered darkly if the stinking drunk might be the less dangerous of the two men.

Lena took another book from the shelf and began reading. When she looked up sometime later, she was alone. She hadn't noticed either the drunk returning with his bounty of cleanfire, or the two men leaving. She got up and looked around. Daylight poured through the window. How could it be morning already? Or even afternoon?

Lena felt her heart begin to beat more quickly. For a moment she thought she might be panicking, but the feeling was more like euphoria.

Something was about to happen, she decided.

The handle of the door turned, and someone stepped slowly into the room.

A young woman who looked almost exactly like her.

The moment that followed felt impossibly extended, stretched to cover a lifetime. Lena felt as if she stared through a rip in the universe into a different reality where she had been made slightly differently- for this woman- this *stranger* was immediately, intensely familiar.

I really have gone mad, Lena thought helplessly.

She watched in mesmerised silence as the woman crept nearer and stopped several paces in front of Lena, who stared into the stranger's eyes. "But you're not a stranger," Lena heard herself say aloud. The book fell unnoticed through her trembling hands to the floor.

"So it's true," the woman said. "I had to find you, and somehow I knew how- I knew *where*. You're real. It's all true. You're *real!*"

The hairs on Lena's arms stood up and a shiver went down her spine. Inexplicably, she wanted to curl up, foetus-like on the floor and cry. "I don't... I don't feel real," she said brokenly. "I'm mad and I'm alone and I don't even know what's happening..." Her voice had started to shake alarmingly.

The apparition continued, "I thought- how could I find you if I didn't know where you were? And yet I *knew* I'd find you once I remembered. Like touching across a great distance and a small distance at the same time. But I suppose you would know that. You *did* know about me? Maybe you didn't?"

Lena strove to collect her thoughts and cling on to the last few threads of sanity that she could. "Not real," she mumbled.

"Of course it's real. Why wouldn't it be? Oh. Do *you* see the same things I do?"

"Never mind," Lena whispered. "I see all sorts of things." All the strength had left her body. She didn't know whether to laugh or cry, or scream- but she hadn't the energy for any venting of emotion. She looked helplessly into the other woman's vivid green eyes.

"We were together before," the woman said. Her cracked, hoarse voice trembled. "But we were separated."

Lena nodded. It made sense. She wasn't imagining her miraculous twin. Tears rolled down her cheeks. "Why?" she managed to say at last. "Why did he never tell me about you? He could have told me so much and he *never did!*"

A hand reached out to touch hers, and Lena's world changed forever.

III

They walked down towards the river and stopped at the west-facing end of one of the smaller bridges, where unused waste ground sloped towards a muddy embankment. The earlier rain had eased off. Lena observed the fast-flowing river and thought it looked more swollen than usual. As the two women stopped and looked out over the water, Lena feared briefly that a cruel trick was being played- the ultimate trick, one that she played on herself.

"Am I imagining you after all?" she whispered under her breath. But today her environment appeared resolutely real and solid, uncomfortably so. The air held a biting chill. The mud had a sour, pungent odour. A few spots of sleet angled spitefully across them, threatening but not delivering more.

Her twin sister's name was Rhion. She had lived with her mother- *their* mother- until the age of fourteen. Then after their mother's death- "She told me that *you* existed, but then she made me forget, I think, before she died," Rhion said- she had left and found herself struggling for survival on the streets.

"I didn't struggle for long," Rhion added, as if to make a point of pride. "I learned what I needed to do very quickly. And I already knew how to... do things to help myself." She smiled faintly. "She taught me more than I deserved to know."

"I wish I could have met her," Lena said, and Rhion's expression grew dark and regretful.

Lena wanted to know why the two of them had been kept apart, but Rhion had no answer. "Did you know you had a twin?" Lena asked.

"No. I didn't know until I was told. And then I forgot until a few days ago. That will take some explaining." Rhion looked across at her. "I never felt complete. I felt that something was missing. But many people feel like that, for many different reasons. I never imagined that she might be keeping something like this from me."

"Father never said anything. He kept it from me. Even when he knew he was going to..." Lena couldn't complete the sentence.

"Yes. So you said. What was he like?"

"What was he *like*?" The question had more answers than Lena could hope to give. "Sad," she said eventually, and shivered as the cold breeze blew across the waterfront.

Lena was desperate to learn about her mother, but her sister's description was of a woman who over the years had become insular and paranoid, even before her illness. "I remember how confident and sure of herself she had been when I was younger," Rhion said. "But as time went on, she worried more and more about the Citadel authorities. Her fears grew worse. Maybe they even made her ill. She grew fearful of speaking to anyone about anything. Her fears made *me* afraid. So, I began to distract myself in bad ways. I try to remember happier times, when I was little. But I remember the bad times more easily."

Lena nodded ruefully.

"Towards the end she suffered nightmares most nights. They got worse. Sometimes, I think they remained with her for a short while after she'd woken up. She would struggle to tell dreams and reality apart."

Something cold stirred inside Lena. She didn't dare to look at her twin, but she said quietly, "I have had

178

that problem recently. I never used to, but after Father died... no, I don't think that has anything to do with it. Maybe we're all destined to die that way, Rhion. Father lost his mind as well, towards the end."

"Maybe that's what happens if we lose what control we have of the Great Power."

Lena stared at her. "The what?"

"Oh." Rhion blinked in surprise. "He didn't tell you *anything*, did he?"

A hesitant trust began to grow between the two women. "I have to warn you- I'm being hunted by the authorities," Lena said. "If I'm caught, and you're with me..."

Rhion laughed. "They're looking for me as well. At least, they were. Or, *he* was."

"He?"

"I'll tell you all about it when we're somewhere a little safer. I think sooner or later he might find out that I've returned. I shouldn't be surprised if he did, although what he makes of that... anyway, it was all my fault. I have a habit of bringing things on myself."

"You're not making any sense, Rhion."

Her sister looked away and across the expanse of river. Steam from power-carriages that were crossing over the bridge drifted into the air, and occasionally horns blared their indignation at perceived slights by other drivers. "Something happened to me. Well, it's been happening for a while, and maybe now it's happening... *faster.* Let's go somewhere where we can talk. But we shouldn't stay there for long. We shouldn't stay *anywhere* for long."

IV

Rhion took her sister to an abandoned factory set back a half hour's walk or so from the river. The buildings here were red brick monsters dotted with broken windows, dark and ruined doorways and roofs which had gaps where tiles were missing. As the two women walked they had to navigate between jagged pieces of old machinery and tendrils of bramble or creepers that had already worked their way through the foundations of the site.

"Do you hide out here?" Lena asked doubtfully.

"I've come here a few times." Rhion couldn't recall if she had ever hidden or slept in this place. She had stayed⁻ sometimes for days⁻ in many different parts of the city, but this was not the sort of place where one could sleep soundly and safely. Vagrants⁻ *other vagrants,* she corrected herself⁻ who had fallen through the widening cracks of society would sometimes come here at night with substances to change their internal chemistry and sit in mutual stupefaction. That was a mystery she had noted but never solved⁻ that they would often appear in the small, dark hours, but were never to be seen during the day. They were like ghosts.

Rhion had no idea what to make of Lena and suspected that her sister felt likewise. As they stepped amidst the rubble, she stole a glance at her, confused. She didn't know how she was supposed to feel now that they had met. She felt oddly frustrated. Surely she had remembered Lena now for a reason⁻ so why hadn't anything happened? When they met, Rhion had been certain that something momentous would occur⁻ a coming together of all the strange events she had seen. A collision of chaos.

The idea had frightened and excited her.

But no. They had talked and talked- not that Lena appeared to be a natural talker- and now they were heading into the quiet ruins to talk some more. Lena hadn't even heard of the Great Power- or more correctly, had forgotten what it felt like. She had neglected her own nature.

Not that it was her fault, Rhion reminded herself, but the fact remained.

She led Lena into a large room with small, high windows. The floor had been swept mostly clean of industry's detritus some years ago, but weeds pushed through the cracks. Rhion pushed the door shut and marvelled at the silence for a moment. Yes, the daytime was always quiet here. She could almost imagine that this derelict place was a part of the other Citadel she had walked through, or at least a gateway to it- a location that was somehow *thinner*, more tenuously real. That might be why it felt a little safer- safe from the Voice, at least.

"I'll tell you what happened to me," she said. "It was several days ago, I think. I don't know for certain. I've lost track of time a little."

"I know what that feels like."

"Lena, I'm being hunted by the Voice. I believed that I could find a way into his mind and in so doing, a way into the palace. Into the lair of the Mothers themselves. It didn't quite work out as I'd hoped."

Lena, to her credit, did not panic. Perhaps she didn't even believe her. Rhion watched as her sister worked out a response. *How orderly,* Rhion thought. *What have you done all your life? Where did the left turn come from and why?*

"I don't understand. Why would you want to know the affairs of the Mothers?" Lena asked eventually. "Who in their right mind would want to meddle in such things? If you were caught..."

"Yes, well I clearly don't think things through as thoroughly as you. I was curious..."

"You did it because you were *curious*?"

"I've always wanted to know what lies around the corner, within the shadows, in unfathomable depths... I have only myself, Lena, and if I became afraid of the unknown then I'd make the most impossible company for myself. I see it most days- something that shouldn't be real, that shouldn't exist, and yet it does. I can't afford to be afraid of it."

Lena said nothing, but Rhion saw a faraway look in her eyes.

"Anyway, I allowed a small but potent miracle to be witnessed by enough people to cause a stir. I'd tried and failed on a few other occasions, but this time- helped by a longer and more chequered criminal record- I was taken to see the Voice. You probably won't know this, but one of the chief responsibilities of the Voice is to interrogate people like me, who may possess... *methods* that threaten the peace and the balance of the Citadel."

"But why would you do that?" Lena asked. "Why would you put yourself in that position?"

"I told you. I wanted to know the secrets of the Palace." Rhion shrugged. "You'll have to get used to my impulsive nature, Lena. I've always been drawn to that place, to the immense power hidden there- the Mothers and the secrets that I'm certain they keep. Secrets beyond anything you or I can understand."

"Then what good can they do you?" Lena reasoned.

Rhion ignored her. "None of the others interrogated by the Voice for similar actions had more than the slightest talent in anything... unusual, shall we say. He said so himself. I expect they had traces of the Great Power, enough to be caught, but no more than that. So, he expected nothing more from me, and I played my part until the time was right."

"What did you do to him?"

"I put him under a spell, made him fall into a trance. So, for a short while he was mine. I planted something of myself within him. But unfortunately, it worked both ways. He was able to find me only a few days later. I did fear that he might. After all, nobody can hide forever inside the Citadel if the eyes of the Mothers- or their first servant- are searching for them. I began to imagine what they would do if they were able to look inside my mind, and what they might find there."

"You make yourself sound like a monster."

"I am, in some ways. But I've always felt different. Even when I was too little to know what *different* really meant. You don't even remember the Great Power, do you?"

"I'd never heard of it until you mentioned it earlier."

"You must have felt it when you were little. Even if he never explained it to you."

Rhion saw a strange look in her sister's eyes- a recollection of something, perhaps, a dawning realisation.

"Let me describe to you one of my first memories, Lena. When I was four, Mother and I went into the garden area at the back of our house, one spring morning. Most of this garden is a grass lawn- it was then, anyway- it's overgrown with weeds and creepers now. But in the centre of that lawn stands a cherry tree. Blossom is falling gently in the breeze. I'm standing near the back door. I watch the blossom fall, I listen to the sound made by the tree as it yields to the forces

183

surrounding it in some areas and resists them in others. Even at that tender age, I know the science of the situation intimately, and yet I still marvel at the beauty of what the eye sees, despite what the mind knows. I know the speed of each piece of blossom as it falls slowly to the ground. I know the exact direction from which the wind is blowing. I sense the movement of tiny creatures that make their home in and on the tree. I know its height and its greatest circumference. I sense the movement of water and nutrients through its depths, and the rate at which they move. I even map the shape and direction of its roots through the rich darkness of the soil. All these things and much more I sense, in the two or three minutes I stand there by the open door."

Lena said nothing, her eyes wide.

"She told me things as the blossom fell," Rhion continued quietly. "About myself. About why we, and those that came before us- are different to other people. That, I think, was the first time she explained the Great Power to me properly.

"I remember other moments like this that happened over the next few years. Mother told me that the world is more than the sum of its parts. She said that it's a living entity. It is the Great Power, and the Great Power is it. But she didn't call the world *It.* She called it *She.* And although I could always sense it, this touch of elemental force was like a switch inside me, one that I struggled to use at first. The more desperate I became for that higher state of being that it unlocked, the more it would recede. I learned more as I grew older, and luckily for me I learned how to control it, up to a point. But of course, I told no one about this. It would have sounded insane, and besides, Mother forbade me to speak of it. Do I sound mad, Lena?"

"No. It sounds like something from a dream I might have had. A truth that was always just out of reach. Maybe a truth I'd forgotten, as you said."

"Mother allowed me freedom in some ways. Perhaps she gave me too much freedom. But she made sure I knew the things I needed to know. Meanwhile, you had a father, and a life that grew ordered and ordinary. Perhaps he wanted to forget about the Great Power altogether- I don't know. I don't know how anyone *could*."

"What did she tell you about him?"

"Not much. When I was little, she said that he died when I was still a baby. I didn't ask about him very often after that. I didn't think to, and she didn't want to talk about him."

"I wish I was like you," Lena said suddenly.

"Do you?"

"Able to sense and see the things that you can."

"I think that will happen soon. We're part of the same river and we hear a language that others can't. True nature surfaces sooner later." As Rhion paused, faint calls of wild dogs and cats came from out of somewhere distant.

"I believe that the Mothers fear something about us, or about the Great Power. They control everything within the Citadel to an obsessive degree through their hierarchy of servants and sycophants. They can't allow anything to jeopardise that. Of course, we both know that if I said such things within earshot of their spies or the Citadel Police, I'd be arrested..."

"I thought you hoped to be arrested."

"Not for that. They wouldn't have wasted questions on me. I would have been summarily executed. I would never glimpse the true faces of the Mothers, which few people alive have ever seen." She sighed, almost regretfully.

"Would you *want* to?"

"Why not? Do you think their gaze turns people to stone?"

"I wouldn't know, Rhion. Maybe it does."

"Anyway, I digress. I wanted to unravel the labyrinth, and finally the Voice provided me with a way to do that. Of course, matters didn't turn out as I hoped."

"They never do," Lena remarked.

"And what about *you*? I want to know about your life."

Lena looked nonplussed, and Rhion wondered if she had no idea what to say.

Lena began to speak at last, but the words that tumbled from her mouth were not the ones Rhion expected. "Maybe I *was* like you, when I was little. I imagined, I asked questions. I suppose I even touched the Great Power at times, but I had no idea what I was doing. Even then I saw things that other people didn't, but I barely remember those times now. You would have liked our house, Rhion. It felt full of mystery- and it *was,* but more than I could have ever imagined. When I was a little girl I would think beyond boundaries and... and the house was the centre of that, somehow. But as I grew older, I felt the Citadel press against the edges, telling me to abandon childish things. And Father didn't show me what your... what *our* mother showed you. He didn't discourage me from walking the other way and shutting my eyes to that side of my life."

"Maybe he'd become frightened of it," Rhion suggested.

"And maybe he thought it was for the best that I become a quietly dependable citizen, a helpful fixer of practical problems. So, I settled for the routine and the

186

practical. I trained as an engineer at one of the power plants. I suppose I had a talent for the work, because I was promoted four times."

"So you helped keep the Citadel warm and well-lit for those who can afford it."

"I regret the path I took. I regret a lot of things. If my childhood had been like yours, perhaps I would have become like you."

"How terrible."

"No, Rhion. Not terrible at all."

Rhion laughed. Lena's strangely phrased compliment made her feel uneasy, embarrassed. "You hardly know me, Lena. Reserve your judgement until you do."

Lena began to pace agitatedly again. "How did our parents decide which of us would go with who, or did they simply choose at random?"

"We'll never know, will we?"

"Do we have any other family? Any uncles and aunts, or cousins anywhere? Or are we all that remains of our lineage?"

"I don't know. I asked, more than once. I don't think there's anyone else. Tell me more about your home. You said it was full of mystery."

With a visible effort, Lena stood still. "When I was fourteen, Father showed me a flight of steps in the cellar. He asked me what I saw, other than the darkness. He wanted to tell me that this was a secret, an opening to somewhere. I think now that he was trying in his own way- at last- to bring me closer to this Great Power. But I wanted nothing to do with it. I knew how sad Father was when I made that clear. He felt that he'd failed. But maybe he was too frightened to do anything."

"As we grew older, they both grew more frightened," Rhion noted.

"I wanted to comfort him- and a small part of me even wanted us to leap into the unknown there and then- but I couldn't think of anything to say or do. I've always been awkward and useless with words, with emotions. And then, that last thread that linked me to some magical place... snapped. It happened that same morning. I went for a walk and I made a decision."

A prickle of unease washed over Rhion. "What was the weather like? Do you remember?"

Lena looked taken aback. "I don't know why, but I *do*. It was a bright morning. Cool but not frosty. It was the start of spring, I think. And there were lots of little clouds in the sky. More than I'd ever seen before."

"Yes." Rhion felt a lump rise in her throat and looked away. "Yes. I remember that day."

"After that, I went out of my way to avoid such things. He probably hoped to speak to me about it all at some later point. But later points don't always happen. We spoke of other things, of course- philosophy, history, even the Mothers sometimes. But never again the stairs and what lay beyond them."

"How did he die?"

"Slowly, over months. In bed. What do you want me to say? I watched him fade a little more each day. He had a disease of the brain- he was barely himself at all in the final weeks. It was like seeing something else inhabiting his body. Except for a few fleeting moments. Moments that I *wasted*." Anger flared in Lena's voice. "I should have said more. I should have... I don't know. Done something."

And then the defences you'd built up against yourself came crashing down, Rhion thought. She tried to imagine what their father had looked like and sounded like but was unable to conjure anything. It would be false anyway. She had never known him and never would. He was Lena's private memory.

"I got my apprenticeship at the power plant and became an engineer, then supervisor," her sister continued. "That's what I've done for the last six years."

"Bathed in the Citadel's effluent," Rhion said. "What about this door in the cellar?"

"It *did* go to another place. Somewhere horrific, wonderful, magical. I went through the door... I don't know exactly how many days ago⁻ and that's when I began to lose myself. I don't even know how I got back! I've lost track of time too, Rhion. Lost everything. Even that other place."

"I don't think so. I don't think it's *possible* to lose it." *I should have known,* Rhion thought. *Maybe I did know, deep within myself. She experienced something like what happened to me.*

"I even lost the house, because I burned it down."

"You burned your *house* down?"

Lena wiped tears from her cheeks. "This will make me sound like a madwoman. I had to burn it down because I needed to destroy the evidence that I'd killed one of the Ministry of Power's counsellors."

"I've met killers, Lena. You're not like any of them."

Her twin stared knowingly back at her. "I can believe that *you* would kill and have done. This was my first time. *Only* time. It wasn't easy or difficult. It wasn't even frightening. It just *happened.* A rage came over me..."

"Things like that don't just *happen,* Lena. What did he do?"

"He attacked me. He would have raped me. Something just... snapped inside me. Something else, or

189

some other part of me came to the surface and took control."

"How did it feel?" Rhion remembered very clearly how it had felt for *her*, more than once.

"I don't know. I can't properly remember, and even if I could I don't think I could describe it. But afterwards... when everything cleared- I no longer felt afraid. Even after I'd cut his body to pieces, I sat and calmly considered the best course of action."

"So you burned the house down..."

"And ran away. I wandered the streets and eventually I ended up at that guest house."

"No one should have to live there."

"It was cheap, Rhion. I didn't have many choices."

Neither of them said anything for a while. "Well, I went to another place too," Rhion said at last.

Lena stared at her.

"I don't know if it's the same as yours. Maybe it is and it just looked different when I went there. But I only found my way there because I was escaping from the Voice, he'd found me... and I jumped into the river, but then I was pulled down by a whirlpool that formed in the water."

"No one could have survived that."

"But if someone goes through and then falls into another world entirely... of course, I didn't make it all the way down to the bottom the river. I passed through some blank space, I guess- I don't remember any of it- and ended up in an empty version of the Citadel."

"That's where I ended up too."

"I had no way of measuring how long I spent there. It *felt* as if I was there for two or three days, but that couldn't have been possible. I didn't feel hungry or thirsty. Maybe I only imagined the time. It didn't get dark, and the light didn't change. The heavens were static, there was no sun- as if the sky was nothing more than a painting above the world. So maybe time stopped, and yet I didn't."

Rhion looked down at herself. "We winked out of existence and were remade somewhere else. Then we returned from wherever we'd been. That's the true miracle."

"I remember once I told Father I didn't believe in miracles."

"A miracle is just something we haven't understood properly yet." Rhion then told Lena about other conversations she had had with their mother- the rambling discussions, the existential questions and theories, and the secrets concerning the Mothers and their origins- handed down over generations.

"We're here together now because she intended for us to be. Our mother must have believed our eventually meeting again was important." Rhion shook her head, frustrated. "How can that be, though? We undermine the order of things, the two of us."

"Maybe that's as it should be. Maybe all of this is *wrong* somehow and needs to be remade."

"I like that idea, Lena."

"And maybe *you* caused the whirlpool in the river."

Rhion felt troubled. "The Great Power intervened to save me. That's *never* happened before. Not in such a huge way, at least."

"So, what now?" Lena shivered. "What next?"

"Mother told me some other important things that I've only just remembered in the last few days. I have to tell *you* those things now."

191

"She told me that the Mothers were once the chosen ones, the saviours of the old world. They defended her against a force- a *technology*, she said- that threatened the whole universe. It had already destroyed countless other worlds. In return, the Mothers were granted immortality, presumably so that they could preside over a golden age of civilisation. But the gift turned them. They have burned with evil for so many centuries that all their humanity has withered away."

"No one should live forever," Lena said.

"Quite. This knowledge- of a time before the Citadel- was handed down through our family and a few others. But for almost everyone else in the Citadel, that history was eventually erased. It was not taught to children. Books that related to it were destroyed. Over time, everything that had been, became forgotten. The Mothers made sure of that. Even their names passed out of history. The story of how the Citadel came to be was forgotten."

"And yet *our* family remembered and passed this on."

"Not only ours, Lena. As I said, there are others. Mother once said that we *never* seek out others like us, that it would be too dangerous. Our enemies would learn of it. Still, here we are- after I found you."

"What happens now?" Lena asked finally.

"I don't know. We try to survive." Rhion headed towards the door.

"I've only now realised," Lena remarked as she followed her sister. "I don't know her name."

"Elia," Rhion said quietly. "Her name was Elia."

The afternoon had grown darker and by the time Rhion and Lena left the wasteland of cracked concrete and rusted machinery, only a little daylight remained.

The moons were both full and especially bright tonight, Lena observed as they headed along a narrow lane bordered by scrub and the ruins of old huts and storage sheds. The derelict landscape appeared in almost daylit detail, alive with the continuous silvery glow. The moons appeared brighter or nearer than they ought. *Is that possible?* she wondered. *No, it can't be. How far away are they? Will we one day measure the distance to them as we measure the roads and tunnels of the Citadel? Perhaps the Mothers already have and keep that knowledge to themselves.*

"They had names once," Rhion commented.

"The Mothers?"

"The moons. I don't know what they were, only that they existed. Don't you think it odd that the people of the Citadel never knew them, or even gave them other names?"

Lena frowned. "No. But as I got older, I only noticed whatever was directly in front of me. They've always been the white moon and the red moon. That's just the way it is. Names are only given to useful things."

"Yes, nowadays."

"How do you even know that they had names?"

Rhion smiled faintly. "Mother told me. But she wouldn't tell me what they were. *Try to find their names,* she told me, perhaps to prove that they could no longer be found, that they'd been erased from the Mothers' revised history."

"One day, will you tell me everything about yourself? All your secrets?" Lena asked a little later.

They had left the open wasteland and hurried along a street of closed shops and storehouses whose buildings leered across at one another across the narrow gap, the older ones so bent that they almost touched. The area felt oddly familiar, although she was also certain that she hadn't been here before.

"No." Rhion sounded regretful. "No, I don't think that would be a good idea."

As Rhion and Lena navigated the quiet streets of the Citadel, clouds gathered, and a while later rain began to fall. Lena grew tired and Rhion suggested they rest on a bench in one of the trading squares. The rain came down harder than ever, and the cobbles glistened with moisture. Lamps hissed and spat as they struggled to remain alight, and somewhere in the distance a train screeched along, harsh and grating on the rusted rails of the Bay Line. *That will be headed towards South Hill,* Lena thought, and took out her pocket watch. Droplets pattered against the curved surface to stretch and skew the numbers out of proportion. *Last train of the night,* Lena mentally added. *It will stop at each halt and then stay at the terminus on South Hill until dawn. The sound of the rain at the terminus will be immense. The roofs of all those buildings are made of corrugated iron.*

Rhion was not thinking about train lines. "Something's happening, Lena. Look at the fountain and the statue."

Her sister put her watch away and looked towards the middle of the market square where the great stone statue and fountain that surrounded it rose fifty feet high. She couldn't make out the spray of water from the fountain, such was the deluge. "What am I looking for?" she asked eventually.

"Wait," came the terse reply. "You can't see it yet. Neither can I. But I *know* something's about to happen."

Lena wiped away wet hair that had fallen in front of her eyes. Moments passed. Then she caught sight of a slow movement in the darkness ahead, as if something unseen rotated or twisted the statue. No, the statue was *moving* of its own accord. "I see it," she whispered. "No, I can't just see it. I can *feel* it. How is that possible?"

"It's changing shape," Rhion said. "The force within the deeper world- the Halflight- has touched it. The stone has become fluid, for a time."

"It isn't possible." Lena rubbed at her eyes, but when she looked again, she saw the same slow, peculiar movements. One of the statue's arms reached slowly upwards to the low, dark rain clouds as if it made an unintelligible bequest to the heavens. "Why? What purpose can it have?"

"Do you still believe all things must exist for a reason after everything you've seen?" Rhion sounded amused. "It has no purpose that I know of. It simply *is*."

The arm became a thin needle of stone that reached ever higher until its apex became lost in the murk. "Do you know who that statue is a likeness of?" Rhion asked.

"Nobody, now." The head distorted like a slowly melting candle into a grotesquery without recognisable form. The gargoyle continued to shift, its evolving shape driven by whatever force compelled it and somehow moulded its stone nature. Lena felt her fear grow. If stone could be rendered malleable, even liquid, if holes could open and devour the greatest structures, if doorways could open that led into fathomless other worlds, then nothing was safe. This inexplicable change, this creeping chaos, might spread throughout the

Citadel. It could eat the Citadel, perhaps everything that existed in the outer world.

Where did it come from?

What did it want?

Lena tried to imagine a world that could willingly eat itself.

"A man from the old times." Rhion tilted her face upwards, closed her eyes and allowed the downpour to wash over her. "I don't know his name or his importance. Only the Mothers know the names from that age. They made this thing, sometime near the beginning of their reign- perhaps it was made in remembrance of a fallen comrade, who knows. I'm surprised it survived for as long as it has. But now the world is remaking it. Some of the Mothers' footprints are being erased."

"Why?"

Rhion shrugged. "Because of what they've done? Because they presume to maintain absolute dominion over us all and think themselves answerable to no greater force? I don't know. Perhaps they truly believe that they've mastered the secrets of the world. But those secrets cannot be mastered- not by ants such as us, scurrying blindly from mewling birth to shuddering death. And what are the Mothers except human ants that don't age?"

"You shouldn't give voice to such thoughts," Lena warned. "Those who do, disappear."

Rhion gave her a scornful look. "I've given voice to my thoughts all my life. I haven't disappeared." She laughed. "At least, not in the way you mean."

Lena recalled a time during her childhood- which until now she had forgotten- when every morning an odd fear would grip her for a short while, nameless and without identifiable cause. She would believe that the world outside had changed in some terrible and permanent way. She would even fear the simple act of opening her curtains.

In childhood, her waking moments had been filled with tiny miracles or nameless terrors. Together they had made life larger, punctuated it with bright shards of inexplicable beauty and great slashes of darkness. They had made her feel special, as if she possessed unique insight into the world's machinery.

The rain soon eased off and they walked over higher ground, where the elevation allowed them a panoramic view of the Citadel's Northern Quarter, although under the cover of night there was little to see except the lights scattered throughout the area.

"Some of the lights are moving," Rhion noted. "Do you see?"

"Lampmen or guides," Lena suggested.

"No. They're too bright. And see how quickly some of them move."

Lena looked again and saw that some of the lights were indeed moving swiftly and in odd directions. "Who is doing that?"

"Those are not the Citadel lights that other people see. They're different. I don't know what they are. I see them now and again. And now you see them too."

"When I was little, my father made up stories for me," Lena recalled. "I remember one about little creatures made of light. But he treated it seriously, and I could tell he wanted *me* to as well."

"Did you?"

"For a while. Then I grew up, and it faded."

They continued to watch the lights for a while longer, until they winked out of sight. "I want to show you the house," Rhion told her.

"The house?"

"Where I grew up. Do you want to see it?"

Lena nodded uncertainly. "If you want to show me."

They walked on for a while. As often happened in the winter months a grim smog began to develop, and the light of the street lanterns soon became an opaque, blurred haze. Rhion appeared to know her way even in these conditions and strode confidently ahead. Lena hurried along at her side, determined not to fall behind and become lost. She almost reached for her sister's hand at one point but stopped herself, embarrassed.

They came at last to a dilapidated house at the end of a quiet, narrow street. "After all this time, I still have the key," Rhion remarked, "and no one ever changed the lock."

"Doesn't someone live here?" Lena asked, although it certainly didn't look inhabited.

"No one has lived here in all the years since I left." Rhion turned the key and with some effort pushed open the door. "I would come back every few weeks just to see. I wanted to know if someone else had made it their home. But no one ever did. It stayed empty."

They walked down a hallway and through to a living room with large, wide windows. The air smelled stale and dust lay thick on the surfaces. Rhion went to stand by one of the windows and stared outside into the garden, part of which Lena could see even in the faint light. Maybe the garden had once been pretty but now it was almost entirely overgrown. The cherry tree still stood, skeletally bare.

Lena looked around and saw an armchair as her eyes adjusted to the gloom. It looked just like the one that had been her father's favourite, but of course his had burned to ash along with the rest of her past. Maybe their parents had bought two of the same chairs together and kept one each when they went their separate ways.

Lost for a moment in a sudden, unutterable sadness, Lena reached out and touched the chair. Then she jumped as Rhion abruptly spoke.

"Well, this is it, Lena. My childhood home. I grew up here. It wasn't always so sorry for itself. But then, neither was I."

Lena's gaze took in the scene of dusty abandonment. In many places, chairs and tables and bookcases were festooned with thick cobwebs.

"She died here," Rhion continued quietly. "Not in this room, but upstairs in bed. I wasn't here when she passed. Maybe I could have saved her or found a physician in time. Maybe not. I don't think she had long left anyway. Perhaps she knew that she was about to… expire. Some people…" Rhion's voice trembled. "Some people know when their time is up."

"That was the same day that she told me about you." Rhion turned to look at Lena, a silhouette against the faint outer light. "I think she made me forget. That was one of the many ways in which she could use the Great Power, a talent I inherited. I only remembered a few days ago. And as soon as I did, I began to look for you. All I needed was for the veil to be lifted. Then I felt my way along the web. Are you glad I found you?"

"Yes. Of course I am."

"You're supposed to say *why wouldn't I be,*" Rhion retorted bitterly, "and then I could tell you why."

Lena had no idea what to say to that. She got up and wandered around the room, then opened the door that led out into a conservatory area. She looked briefly around the array of old pots and planting trays, withered stick-like remains of plants and soil covered in dust or mould.

199

Rhion appeared to be lost in thought, slowly tracing lines in the windowsill dust when she came back into the living room. "Do you visit her grave, sometimes?" Lena asked tentatively. "Perhaps we could go there together..."

"No, Lena. I don't, and we can't. They took her body away, and I assume they must have buried her some days later, but by then I'd already left. They never found me, although I'm not sure they spent very long looking. One less problem for them to sort out. So I didn't attend the burial and I have no idea where she's buried."

"That's awful."

"Have *you* gone to our father's grave at any time after he was buried?" Rhion spat back.

"No. I haven't," Lena admitted.

"She died sometime in the afternoon," Rhion continued bluntly. "Perhaps at around the same time as I was fighting someone off in a low tavern somewhere. I'd been drinking too much as usual- but it's odd how a serious altercation can make you sober up just enough to get away from it. And when I arrived back here, she'd already passed."

"Are you *still* happy to have found me, Lena?"

VI

Exhaustion caught up with the twins. They slept in the living room- Rhion didn't want to go upstairs, nor did she want Lena to. Lena could tell that her sister was feeling brittle and resentful, and she had no idea what to say or if she ought to say anything at all. Likely she would worsen Rhion's mood further if she did.

"I wish I could make you feel better," she said nonetheless- but Rhion appeared not to hear.

She wondered why Rhion had wanted to show her this dismal place. No doubt it had once been filled with happy times, but there was nothing to show of them now, and she had never been a part of that life.

Lena fell asleep almost immediately. She barely noticed as Rhion placed a sheet of material over her to provide some warmth.

She woke sometime later. Rhion slept next to her, curled up with her arms folded. *I'll bet you wouldn't let yourself fall asleep in anyone else's company,* Lena thought. *And yet we've only just found each other. Will I ever know you properly? How similar are we, inside?*

Rhion woke suddenly and sat up, shivering.

"Bad dream?"

"Maybe worse than that. It felt... as if something was warning me about something, but it might already be too late." Rhion smirked. "Some warning *that* was."

"I dreamed of a place with thousands upon thousands of trees. It wasn't the first time."

"I've dreamed about them too. There are many such areas, far beyond the Citadel walls. They're called forests."

"How do you know all these things, Rhion? Words that I never knew existed?"

"Sometimes the words for things just come to me. Other times I simply *know* the words, and I can't say why. It's as if I've *always* known them."

"There was a house somewhere in the middle of this... forest," Lena said quietly.

"And?"

"And it's important, somehow. I don't know why, but I've had this dream before. I think it's something connected with our past."

"It may well be. There are many secrets yet to be unveiled. I doubt we'll ever know a hundredth of all the things that can be known, but even that hundredth will be a wonder far greater than we can imagine." Rhion pointed to the window. "Here's another for you. Imagine that we had a clear night. There are far more stars in the sky than any of us can ever see. Many millions, spread across a vast distance."

"Did that come to you in a dream?"

"No. Our mother told me about it. Maybe it came to *her* in a dream, I don't know. More likely it was passed down along with everything else."

"What about other worlds?"

"There were many, once. But no longer."

"Why? What happened?" Lena frowned. "Are you making up all of this?"

"No. Why would I? You're the last person I'd lie to. Perhaps the only one I *wouldn't* lie to. I simply know these things to be true, Lena." She glanced across at her sister. "You mentioned a forest with a house in the middle. Do you remember anything particular about it?"

"Yes. No one could get to the house. They'd spent years, maybe centuries, trying, but no one could ever find it even though they knew it existed. Paths through the forest invited them, but none led where they ought. People would walk into the forest, but the path took them in a circle until they ended up back at the edge of it..." Lena stopped, suddenly aware of Rhion's intense stare. "What's the matter?"

"I think your dream *is* important. Were you able to get to this house?"

"Yes. But I didn't use *any* of the paths. I stepped into some other place, took a diversion, a short cut· and ended up there. It's a frightening place, Rhion. I feel that it holds a key to... *everything*, maybe. It could bring light or darkness· it could make all good things prosper and bloom or it could collapse everything into the earth to be

202

crushed to nothing." Lena shivered and dug her hands deep into the pockets of her coat. "Maybe it depends who finds it."

"Do you believe it exists?"

"I'm certain of it." Lena yawned. "I'm thirsty. And hungry. I can't remember when I last had something to eat. Are you?"

Rhion pointed to the growing light in the east. "It's breakfast time. There's a bakery just off the market that sells the best meat pies I've ever eaten. It's always open early. Wait here- there are eyes and spies aplenty in that area, and I doubt they see twins that often. I won't be long."

Lena waited pensively as Rhion walked down the hallway and left the house. She had wanted to go with her and had almost demanded to, for fear of never seeing her sister again.

As soon as Rhion had gone, Lena felt strangely empty- and yet at the same time she could sense where Rhion was. *I'm waking up,* she thought, sensing their invisible connection, intangible and yet immense.

Maybe now they were together, she had started to become whoever she was supposed to be. She sensed the Great Power again.

What would happen next? They were both in danger, hunted by Citadel authorities. How would they evade them? Where could they live?

The guest house wasn't an option. Perhaps the owner had already submitted a report about her. Lena considered her belongings for a moment, but then remembered that she'd taken nothing more than some clothes, money and a few books from her house, as well as a little food. She still had most of the money in her pocket and had all but memorised the books- dry

203

engineering texts that she no longer wanted to look at anyway.

Lena smiled to herself. She could never go back to her work- why had she taken textbooks?

She sensed Rhion coming after a while and looked up just before the door opened. Her stomach growled as Rhion walked into the room, took a meat pie from the paper bag in her hand and gave it to her. "Don't eat too quickly, if it's been a while," she warned as Lena sank her teeth into the offering with a sigh.

"What do we do now?" Lena asked when they had both finished and drank some of the purewater that Rhion had also bought.

"I think one of the Guild libraries would be a good first step."

"What are we looking for?"

"Maps. My knowledge of the Citadel's layout is excellent, but a map will help us work out where to go and what to do. We need to think things through and work out how to stay ahead of our enemies. Together we'll find a way. We need to work quickly though. People always remember when they've seen twins."

They left the house. Rhion turned the key to lock the front door and stood, observing the threshold for a moment. "It looked different when I was little," she said finally. "I don't mean the state of the house. I mean its shape. Its dimensions."

Lena felt a cold shudder go through her.

The sisters headed away from the house and skirted around the Wood Lane area, where shops and small market areas were setting up for business. Morning sun began to burn through the dense fog, and more distant parts of the Citadel could be seen when they looked down the hill towards rows of densely-packed little houses, factory buildings and chimneys that belched thick smoke or wisps of steam into the icy sky.

They had walked down two more streets when Lena stumbled and had to lean against the wall of the nearest building. She gasped for air and closed her eyes for a moment, trying to swallow down the intense, nameless fear that had gripped her.

"It feels like my blood is boiling," Lena whispered faintly. "What's happening to me?!"

Rhion held her up with surprising strength. "The Voice. He's near."

"What? You feel it too?"

Rhion didn't reply, but she looked dazed and frightened. She looked around and gestured with her other arm to the open doorway of a tall residential block nearby. "This way. We must get out of sight. Higher up. More material between us. Then, maybe he won't find us."

They struggled through the doorway, up the first flight of stairs and halfway up the second. Lena gripped the cold iron banister of the staircase and tried to gather her breath. Rhion seized her arm. "He'll kill us both if he knows we're here," she hissed. "We have to keep going."

Explosions of colour bloomed and faded along the edges of Lena's vision. "I've had enough," she whispered. "Maybe I just want to die."

Rhion's grip tightened so powerfully that her sister cried out in pain. "Never, *ever* say that," she snarled.

They climbed the next ten flights of stairs. Even Rhion slowed down after a while, her energy sapped by the ascent. Their laboured breaths echoed harshly through the stairwell, a desperate hiss. Lena looked down at one point, and although she couldn't see their enemy through the gloom below, she felt his hatred, a potent concentration of rage directed at them both. Her legs almost gave way as that virulent force reached up towards them. A savage, sharp pain tightened around her heart.

Finally, the stairs ended at a rusty double door from which grey paint had mostly peeled and flaked away. Rhion pulled at the lever and then pushed against the door which opened to reveal a flat stone rooftop. As they stepped out of the stairwell into the open air, Lena saw that the weather had abruptly changed. Dark, angry clouds chased one another from out of the east, but the air felt warm, dead and still, accompanied by a bitter, acrid odour not unlike the aftermath of an electrical fire. The sky held a gloomy, dark yellow hue.

Rhion took Lena's hand and walked with her towards the edge of the rooftop. "What's happening?" Lena demanded. "What are you doing?"

"Are you ready?" Rhion's urgent voice cut through her fog of panic.

Lena tried to swallow as she realised with horror what her sister proposed to do. Her mouth was as dry as dust. She shook her head numbly. "No! I've only just found you!"

Rhion's hands touched her face and she looked her in the eyes. "The Great Power will protect us. We're *needed,* Lena. In return, we must have faith."

"Faith?" Lena laughed weakly. "You're mad, Rhion. We'll fall and we'll die."

"No. We won't. And even if we did, that would be a far better fate than one at the hands of the Voice and the Mothers."

The presence of the Voice loomed larger than ever, a malevolence that crept through the concrete. He could have been quicker, Lena reckoned, but he was being cautious, intent on making as certain of their destruction as possible. He had failed before. He could not allow himself to fail again.

More than four hundred hands below, people and vehicles passed heedlessly by. A cold, crawling sensation rose through Lena' legs and she trembled violently. "I can't. I can't do it!"

"Trust me," Rhion whispered.

"I *don't* trust you," Lena managed to stammer. "I don't trust anyone."

And yet, they stepped together from the rooftop.

That moment should have been their last in this world. It slammed by in a rush of air. Images of the sky and ground tumbled around the two women as they fell. Lena screamed out her terror. Rhion fell silently.

The impact never came, and darkness suffused with bursts of colour and impossible shapes bloomed around the sisters, carrying them to another place.

VI – The Finder

I

Teryn Hale silently observed the Assistant Minister for Power who sat across from him. The Finder reckoned that the Assistant Minister was about his own age, with a body that had started to protest and gripe. But while Teryn didn't have an ounce of undue fat on him, the Assistant Minister looked like someone who took great comfort from his food. Teryn felt a momentary pang of jealousy. He had often wondered what it might feel like to have that capacity- to thoroughly enjoy tedious, banal things and not spend his life in restless flux.

Had the official guessed something in the look? Appearing flustered for a moment, he cleared his throat and looked down at the papers on his desk. "Thank you for meeting with me so promptly. I hope you can help us. It seems that the Citadel Police worked on the matter for days but made no progress."

Teryn smiled. "That's usually how I hear about these things."

"It concerns one of our engineers. Her name is Lena Stone, as I believe you already know. Middle-ranking within the Ministry- well, *senior* for someone of her age. Twenty years old. Slim, average height, brown hair, blue eyes. No particularly notable physical traits. She's missing, and it's imperative that this woman is found."

"And why is she missing?"

"The circumstances leading up to her disappearance are strange. Five days ago, her house burned down."

"*Five* days? I'm surprised that my department weren't contacted sooner. What have the police been doing?"

The Assistant Minister pointedly ignored him. "I say *her* house- until recently it belonged to her father, who passed away recently."

"And you think she didn't burn with it."

"I sincerely hope not. Lena was... *is* one of our most talented assets. Human remains have been found at the house. But we don't think they're hers."

"Why not?"

"Based on the large pieces of bone that we found, we strongly suspect that they belong to a man. And this is where matters become... disturbing. Another of our employees is missing."

"Oh? You didn't tell me about that. Am I to investigate both?"

"Perhaps." The Assistant Minister did not appear to be sure. He shuffled some of his papers pointlessly, which only made him appear more uncertain. "His name is Faral Whitewood. He's one of our counsellors."

Teryn leaned back in his chair and sighed. "You sound as if you want me to find evidence to link the two events."

"I fear that they may indeed be linked. Our official position is that it's likely. But that must, of course, be proved."

The Finder pondered the matter. "Do you believe that the counsellor was at Lena's house?"

"It... remains a possibility."

"Were they friends?"

"I very much doubt it. Lena had no friends that we're aware of. Certainly none at her place of work."

"So it wouldn't be entirely normal for him to pay her a visit at home."

The Assistant Minister looked uncomfortable. "I wouldn't say it was entirely normal. But I feel you're perhaps missing the point I'm trying to make. Our fear is that Faral Whitewood met an unfortunate end."

"That's what I call a *convenient conclusion,* Assistant Minister. It's likely that a hundred or more people have gone missing throughout the Citadel in the last several days alone. The remains in Lena's house *could* belong to someone else. Man or woman, bone size notwithstanding. Did you measure the bones?"

The Assistant Minister frowned and placed his hands together almost apologetically. "Of course. I have a little more to tell you. A ring was found on a finger bone. This ring had a tiny crest and inscription embedded into it. We managed to clean this item, and it was identified by Counsellor Whitewood's family as his. Like many families they have a set of rings and other jewellery engraved with their unique crest."

"So, you think they're his bones."

The Assistant Minister flashed an oily smile. "As far as we know, no one else from their family has been reported missing."

Teryn thought for a while. "Did you know her well?" he asked eventually.

"Lena? I didn't know her at all. I only know her *value.*"

"I see. And you don't feel her *value* is diminished at all if it turns out that she murdered a colleague?"

"I..." The Assistant Minister floundered. "Obviously... if Lena was deemed to be a danger to the people of the Citadel, she would need to be incarcerated, or at least placed under medical supervision. *That*, I ought to point out, is not something that falls under my jurisdiction."

"I'm aware of that."

"But if the situation arose, we might still make use of her considerable talents. She could still conceivably work for the Ministry."

The Finder nodded. "An ingenious plan. A woman of possibly unsound mind working- probably with some reluctance- as a senior engineer from the bed of a secure hospital. How do the lights stay on? How are we not already plunged into darkness every evening of our lives?"

The Assistant Minister was not one of the brighter cogs in the Citadel's governmental wheel- Teryn knew that the man had obtained his position through family contacts and payments made by his father to the right people many years ago. But he clearly could tell when he was being mocked, and his lips tightened in disapproval. "I understand you've already been given clearance to search the remains of the house. We need Lena found within five days."

"What happens after five days?" the Finder wanted to know.

But the Assistant Minister would not tell him.

Teryn knew that he shouldn't have angered or belittled the self-righteous little rat. But, as usual, he hadn't been able to help himself. "Trouble happens regardless," he reminded himself, knowing that wasn't any sort of excuse, as he walked to the power station where Lena had worked.

At the dirty, sprawling administration area, he spoke with some of her colleagues. One of the men appeared keen to share his theory as to why Lena had disappeared. "She looked down on everyone," he claimed. "Didn't like any of us."

"No one at all?" *I don't like anyone much either,* Teryn almost said.

"Did her job, never said more than she had to, didn't want anything to do with anyone," the man‑ a thick‑set individual with angry eyes‑ summarised. "Thought she was better than us."

Maybe she was *better than you,* Teryn almost said. "Do you think she'd had enough and wanted to disappear?" he asked.

"Think *we'd* had enough of *her,*" the engineer retorted. He sat back, arms crossed, and laughed at his own summary.

A middle‑aged woman who the Finder interviewed next had a different perspective. "Lena was sad. When she came into a room it felt as if a cloud came with her."

Teryn recalled some of the information from the sketchy notes he had made. "She'd lost her father recently, hadn't she?"

"Yes, but Lena had *always* been sad. I remember the day she started working here. She was just fourteen. I remember thinking to myself‑ *There's a girl that doesn't belong here*‑ but the more I think about that now, the more I almost believe that..."

The woman paused, considering. "That she didn't really belong *anywhere.*"

Teryn walked to Lena's house later, following the route he reckoned she might have taken home from work. He made the journey slowly and took time to absorb the sights and sounds of the area, although he doubted that she would have done the same. Lena would have hurried home‑ under a cloud, as her colleague might have said‑ to hide away from the world, or at least slam her door on it.

This was a tired, down‑at‑heel neighbourhood, with its rows of small, cramped houses of red and grey

212

brick, its patched and potholed roads, most of which were unsuitable for steam-carriages or even horses. But it wasn't one of the Citadel's most run-down areas. *Dull,* Teryn mentally described the district as he looked to where the rooftops met the sky. *Insignificant.*

"Lena," he said as he paused at the corner where Downspiral Street met Lanterns Passage, whose length had been choked with refuse that leaked from torn sacks. A coalman pushing an empty barrow looked at him as he passed by, eyes bright and suspicious in his grimy countenance. "Lena," Teryn repeated as they both resumed their journeys in opposite directions. He hadn't heard the name until a day ago, and yet it sounded too plain to be rare. "Lena Stone. A woman without a heart? Cold and hard?"

No. Simply an unassuming name for an unassuming woman who lived in a little-regarded part of the Citadel. Lena had lived unnoticed, like a shadow.

But had she killed her counsellor? If so, then why? The Assistant Minister had shown no interest in her motivation. He had appeared more interested in her ongoing value to the Ministry of Power if she was found and apprehended. Teryn knew from experience that they would be disappointed in that regard. Firstly, the Ministry would find themselves in conflict with the Citadel Police, and Teryn already knew who would win *that* argument. Secondly, what motivation would Lena have to help her employer, which had arranged her incarceration?

Teryn arrived at the scene of the fire. Despite the extensive destruction, he could see from its remaining structure that Lena's house had been larger than the others nearby and set some distance away from the terraces. Its shape had also been different, irregular in comparison to its neighbours.

Teryn exhaled slowly as he drew nearer and surveyed the ashen, crumbled remains. His breath drifted visibly into the icy late morning air, which still held the tang of ash and char. Despite the damage done, some of the brickwork remained standing, although much of the remaining structure would clearly be deemed too perilous to stay in place, and the Council of Buildings would order for it to be knocked down.

Meanwhile, anything wooden had been reduced to fine ash, a shade of grey or deep black, except for a few larger beams which had somehow escaped partly intact.

The Finder picked his way through the rubble and breathed in the acrid stench of destruction. He stopped at the centre of what would have been the largest room in the house- a ground-level living room, he guessed.

He had seen many burned-out buildings before, and he felt certain that *this* inferno had roared with a particularly savage intensity. He noticed some remains of iron objects, melted into new, random shapes that made it impossible to guess their function. So, the fire had been hot enough to melt iron. A ring would almost certainly have been gold or silver. Why wouldn't an object with a lower melting point have also melted, given that the fire spread throughout the building?

He wondered what Lena might have used to start and accelerate the fire, if she had deliberately caused it.

Then, as he stood with his hands thrust into the pockets of his dirty greatcoat, Teryn wondered again why the Assistant Minister had chosen to reveal so little about the woman who had lived here. The Finder had, of course, already discovered as much as he could about Lena before his meeting- all the better to compare his own discoveries with whatever information the Ministry chose to feed him. Lena Stone had no record of criminality. She had lived in this house with her father for her entire life, until his recent death. She had been a quiet loner and a dutiful worker and described as such by her colleagues- albeit in differing ways. Lena appeared to have been the sort of woman who went out of her way to ensure her life remained as quiet and humdrum as possible. She would not have deliberately sought attention.

Instead, she appeared to have deliberately avoided it, living as a sad and timid shadow.

But there remained the matter of the counsellor. The Minister had failed to reveal that Faral Whitewood appeared to have met an unfortunate end *before* the fire started. Someone- perhaps Lena, perhaps not- had bashed his head in (judging by the skull fragments found by the investigators sifting through the ash in the main room), and then cut and chopped him to pieces.

"Lena, Lena," he murmured. "It doesn't sound like something you would do, does it?"

Then again, people were full of dark surprises.

Teryn walked on through the remains, as far as the pit that had opened where the cellar had stood. Wooden beams and parts of the roof and walls had collapsed into this area. He squatted down and observed the destruction and the silence for a long time. He breathed in the bitterness. The remains of this house deeply troubled him, and the fact that his unease came from something intangible, not the events that might or might not have played out before the fire, worried him further.

This was by no means the first time he had felt this way, but he had never become used to the sensation of being so disconcerted, so aware of possibilities that were beyond his control and understanding.

215

The more he experienced, the less those experiences made sense.

Teryn walked back to the street and looked back. He picked his way around the remains of the house, stopping occasionally to view it from a new angle. By the time he had made one circuit of the ruin he felt restless, eager to be somewhere else, which wasn't like him at all. He would normally sift for clues long after they were likely to turn up.

Troubled, he looked up and imagined what the house might have looked like. Almost immediately an image came to him of the intact building. Striking in its clarity, the vision took his breath away. He had experienced such vivid pictures before, but this was by far the strongest, the most detailed he could remember.

Lena's house had been built in a conventional way but then augmented idiosyncratically, fitted with odd new sections. *It was amended playfully,* Teryn thought. He touched a section of wall that still stood, and now he imagined the interior- the quirkily-shaped rooms, the passages that took frequent right-angles for no reason other than that they *could* (given the space and framework of their environment), the steps up that led to steps down before they eventually reached a higher floor- or occasionally a lower one.

Then, in his mind's eye he saw a door that led down a flight of steps into darkness. No, something greater and deeper than darkness.

Teryn recoiled and snatched his hand away from the brickwork. For a moment he felt certain that it was bleeding, that part of his skin had come away. But his palm and fingers remained unmarked. He wiped away the smudge of char from his hand and stared at the fragment of wall.

He had glimpsed something unknown in the gloom of his vision. An entrance to some other place? A hole that went deeper than could be possible? Teryn's mind whirled with increasingly unlikely possibilities.

He needed to think. He hurried away without looking back.

II

Teryn had worked as a Finder for thirty of his fifty-two years. His acute, often inexplicable perception - flashes of insight that he liked to call *leaps of instinct* - had served him well in his calling, but despite that (or perhaps because of it) he had spent his formative years within the profession as an unpopular outcast, and his seniority as a willing loner.

His superiors tolerated him because he was uniquely gifted in his occupation, and he was shunned by his colleagues for much the same reason. Teryn had long since ceased to care. There were far worse things than isolation and the long nights of silence. He'd seen more than enough human remains and heard more than enough unbearable stories of prolonged torture to know that. Beneath his unsmiling exterior he counted himself lucky, a man apart from humanity's seething morass of evil.

He had known since his childhood that the Citadel was a monster of many layers. No doubt he wasn't the only one to suspect this, but no one who valued their freedom ever spoke of such things. If they did then those who protected such knowledge would mysteriously hear about that transgression, and the guilty would be whisked away for questioning, incarceration and perhaps even rendering. After all, they would argue, once the information had been extracted, what was left but meat?

Of course, to prove any of the extraordinary things he sensed was impossible, because he had no understanding of that which, on some base animal level, he knew with absolute certainty. His insight could not be explained. It defied all logical scrutiny.

So, he had always put aside those little coincidences that never quite seemed to add up, the flickers of ephemeral darkness that sometimes gathered in the corners of his vision, the clear words spoken in an unknown language that he occasionally heard in the dead of night as he lay down and waited for sleep.

Teryn had no doubt that some of these phenomena were a consequence of slow but sure mental disintegration- after all, he was an old man who'd seen too much- but he remained equally sure that others were external manifestations.

Not that he could distinguish between the two.

Teryn's acceptance into the Finders' Academy without formal qualifications, almost unheard of thirty years ago, remained rare even now. The masters had decided that his raw and unusual talents and instinctive approach more than made up for his disappointingly average marks in tests, much as the idea of allowing such a maverick to enter their profession unnerved them. The authorities had been deeply suspicious of him, and Teryn quickly lost count of the number of interviews to which they subjected him. Nonetheless he concentrated through every one of them, remaining lucid, calm, reasonable. He had clearly shown that he was an asset rather than a threat.

But for years Teryn had shown only frustrating glimpses of his skills. He spent the gains of his vocation on drink and books. Some of his colleagues suggested that he considered himself a performance artist rather than a Finder, someone more interested in methodology and entertaining himself than resolving crimes and bringing perpetrators to justice.

"You take delight in the puzzle and gain little satisfaction from the result. The means to the end is nothing to you," a senior Finder accused him, many years ago.

"Without mystery there is nothing," Teryn had claimed.

"Mysteries exist only to be solved."

"I'm not sure that's right," Teryn had mildly argued. "Some mysteries just *are*."

Much of his enthusiasm for the lures of youth had worn away over the years. Plain in looks and not blessed with much verbal eloquence (except in his dreams, where he continually enchanted strangers with vivid descriptions of the Citadel's inner, secret life) Teryn spent great tracts of his life alone and in silence. He usually worked without the help of others (people tended to get in the way, and the talented sort got in the way more). He found that his more inspired moments came from those extended periods when he could concentrate on seemingly unfathomable tasks that everyone else had long since given up on. His perpetual despondency- *not* depression, he reminded himself, for he seldom despaired of himself, only of humanity- was something he wore almost like a second greatcoat, a shroud that could not be shrugged off even had he wanted to.

As a rule, and as he had almost admitted to Lena's colleague, Teryn didn't like people.

He had investigated (and, in most cases, solved) hundreds of murders and other felonies. He had seen at close hand humankind's incredible and boundless capacity for cruelty and depravity. Most people disgusted him, and those that didn't often bored him because they lacked imagination and were, in his eyes, about half the man or woman that they *could* be. It did not escape Teryn that the only way many people showed genuine imagination was through the ways they found to inflict pain and terror on others. Sometimes, usually after he had solved an especially vile crime and arranged the perpetrator's arrest, Teryn would picture their methodology as they committed the deed. He would imagine the fervour in their eyes and the ideas that raced through and lit up their fevered brains.

He concluded that at least some of them were genuinely happy and content doing what they did.

He slept poorly for days after he tasted success, oddly fearful that if he dwelt too much and too *vividly* on the internal abyss these people had opened, he might invite some faint part of it into himself.

Despite the unending solitude and near-silence of his life, Teryn still entertained random, pointless notions- daydreams rather than hopes. As he went about his grim work, he sometimes wondered what the chances were of accidentally encountering someone with whom he might share his ideas and beliefs, his wishes and desires (even though he would scornfully tell himself that this was nothing more than his restless ego trying to fight its way out).

He had no image in mind of such a person, physically- this mythical individual might be eighteen or eighty, female or male or somewhere between the two (Teryn thought of gender as a sliding scale, although this was not a popular opinion amongst his colleagues). Nevertheless, over the years he had sketched out a psychological profile in his head. Even this mental image had changed significantly over time, perhaps corresponding with his own, internal changes.

He had no idea *why* he allowed himself these idle thoughts but suspected that he was simply playing a cruel game with himself.

Yet Teryn spent so much time with the deceased and damaged, those who had brought death and ruin, or the loved ones of their victims (which was worse), that for long periods of time he thought very little about the *ideal*. His task was to sink his arms into human corruption and evil, so deeply that he could taste it, could understand the mindset and motivation of those he sought. That, much as he loathed the perpetrators of such malevolence, had become a curious addiction.

"When you've seen true darkness," a master of the Academy had told him long ago, "you carry a part of it with you, always. Those of us who cope with that stain have learned to set it aside and care a little less."

His investigations had never become routine- the peculiarity and uniqueness of the perpetrators and sometimes the victims saw to that- but Teryn nevertheless felt less human each time, as if evil deeds cast a shadow that ate a little piece of him.

On one level his increasing detachment made him uneasy, for he had no idea what its natural endpoint might be. But he also felt a growing sense of liberation. He didn't especially want to be human.

What happens if I become more shadow than reason? he had thought several times. *Can I still call myself an agent of law when I fully detach from the society I supposedly protect?*

But he had always- as far as he could recall- carried an inner shadow that sought to gain custody over him. Perhaps it had been there since his childhood. Certainly it had already been a part of him when he became a Finder. It manifested in odd ways. He felt deeply uncomfortable around children and especially around babies, although he had no idea why. He didn't like holes- this wasn't the aversion to clusters of holes that almost everybody shared, but simple, singular holes, particularly those beyond which nothing or little could be seen.

These were just a few of the blank patches in Teryn's life. He couldn't recall much from his youth, nor his childhood. He remembered his final day of schooling, the funerals of both his parents- he still remembered to visit the crematorium and stand by their memorials most months- and his first day of work as a Finder.

But he had drifted through those years.

And when I became a Finder I became too caught up in other people's vileness to notice myself, he would often think. *My work- or the things to which my work exposed me- became addictive. Now I'm just an old man, filled with aches and regrets.*

Most of his colleagues, with whom he shared such little information and time, counted down the days to their retirement. Teryn had no desire to do anything other than what he already did. He even wondered what he could do to *avoid* retirement, when the time came. He would work for less pay if he had to. Perhaps, if he had saved enough money, he could work voluntarily.

As he walked along Side Market Street towards his small, regularly shaped house, rain began to fall. Teryn listened to the hiss and rhythm on the gleaming cobbles, and wondered, as he reached his dark and silent home, how Lena's house had existed, unconventional and askew, in an area where almost all the other dwellings stood in neat rows and conformed with one another. Perhaps it pre-dated them, but even so...

222

It's as if the house was as unusual as Lena was unremarkable, Teryn thought as he turned his key in the lock.

Then he wondered, just for a moment, if Lena and her house were also like a key and lock.

III

When Teryn arrived at the wreckage of Lena's house again the following morning, barriers had been put in place to prevent access from the street. As he stepped around puddles and piles of rubble to get a better look at the ruin, an officious little man in a Council of Buildings uniform saw him and approached. "You won't be able to access the site today," he informed Teryn brusquely.

"Why not?" The Finder peered beyond the half-walls and towards the middle of the building. More parts of the remaining structure had collapsed. "Is it to be knocked down?"

"There... seems to be a sinkhole under the rubble. Under the cellar to be precise."

Teryn felt the hairs on his arms and neck prickle. "A sinkhole?"

The uniformed man shrugged and adjusted his cap to prevent the early morning sun shining into his eyes. The amount of surface moisture and bright, low sunlight made the day especially bright.

"How deep is it?"

"We don't know yet. At least six hundred hands, we believe. But we've had difficulties with the measurements. Technical issues. It may be that the soil and underlying rock is different here. Something is affecting our ability to be precise."

Teryn looked past him again, drawn to the area where rubble and ash had begun to fall into the

223

collapsed cellar. *It's moving,* he thought. *I can feel it moving, as if something wants to pull the remains of the house down.*

That made no sense, so he said nothing. The official walked away, having decided that the Finder's lack of response meant their conversation was done.

Teryn waited patiently until no Council employees were anywhere nearby. When he saw that they'd all retreated to an area behind the house to look through some paperwork and argue about how the area should be properly secured, he ducked under the flimsy barrier and quietly made his way over the rain-soaked ash and char, towards the cavernous hole that now occupied perhaps twice the original breadth of the cellar. He stopped when he had drawn near enough to peer over the edge, but he saw only darkness. A portion of a roof beam that had probably crashed to the ground during the fire slid ever nearer to oblivion. Teryn judged that it might make considerable noise when it fell, so he retreated to the street before the noise could attract the workers' attention.

He turned and looked in time to see the beam slide into the abyss. It made no sound as it fell, and although Teryn listened intently for the noise of it hitting the bottom of the hole, he heard nothing.

The Finder scratched at his close-cropped grey hair, puzzled. An estimated depth of six hundred hands couldn't be right. That was much deeper than any other sinkhole he had heard of, even those that appeared in the southern quarter after the spring floods.

He put the matter of the unmeasurable chasm to one side and decided to talk to some of Lena's neighbours.

An old woman answered the third door he knocked at, across the street and a few houses down.

Teryn presented his Finder's mark- a metal disc inscribed with the insignia of his Department- and allowed himself a resigned sigh when she gaped uncomprehendingly at it. "Did you know Lena Stone?" he asked. "The woman who lived at the house over there that burned down," he added when she paused.

"Yes. I knew her a little. Is she in trouble?"

"That remains to be seen. I need to find her." Teryn shivered suddenly and dug his hands further into the generous pockets of his greatcoat. Had the temperature dropped further? He thought it had. The weather had been more changeable recently.

She looked past him at the blackly skeletal remains of the house. The early sun had disappeared now, and low cloud had started to produce cold drizzle. Teryn wondered when it would turn to sleet or even snow. "I don't think Lena wants to be found," the old woman told him.

"Why would you say that?"

The woman folded her arms and glared at him. "Someone who burns down their house and runs away clearly doesn't want to be found."

Distance, Teryn thought as the hole loomed in his mind again. Was it still expanding or becoming deeper, eating up the sorry remains of Lena's life?

"I didn't say that she burned it," he pointed out mildly.

"I saw her run," countered Lena's neighbour.

Teryn chose not to point out the *leap of circumstance* as he called such assumptions, nor the fact that almost everyone would try to escape an uncontrollable fire if they could. "Did she look back at the house at all? Did she pause?"

The old woman looked confused. "I don't remember. I think she... stepped through the front door, closed it, and looked back for a moment. Then she ran."

"Which way?"

The old woman pointed in the direction of Wood Warrens and the main thoroughfare.

"Did she have anything with her? Any belongings?"

"A bag. A large one." She shrugged. "It was dark, even with the fire."

"Did she take anything else?"

"I don't think so. Like I said, it was dark." The old woman fixed him with a frosty glare as if to make clear that he'd stolen enough of her time. Then, just as Teryn thought she might be about to mumble an excuse and retreat inside, she added quietly, "The flames didn't *look* right."

Teryn studied her watery grey eyes for a moment. "How so?" he asked. "What do you think was wrong with them?"

The old woman took a nervous step back. One gnarled hand gripped the half-open door as if she might suddenly slam it in his face. "I watched from my front room. I opened the curtains just enough and peered through. I kept watching after Lena ran. But I wish I hadn't. The flames were all over the house by then. The windows were full of fire. The flames reached so high..."

Teryn turned his mark over and over in his hand and waited as she abruptly stopped talking.

"I saw colours that shouldn't have been there, and faces," she whispered finally.

"Faces?"

Her grip on the door tightened. Her hand shook. "Not men or women, or anything that I've seen before. They were... demons. Ghosts."

226

The Finder looked back at the shell of Lena's house, keeping his expression carefully neutral. "Are they still there now? Can you see them?"

She shook her head. "They disappeared with the flames."

"You mentioned colours that shouldn't have been there. Flames can be many different colours, depending on what happens to be burning. Which ones do you remember seeing?"

"The fire let me see through the veil. I saw colours I hadn't even imagined before." She smiled wistfully, until something pulled her back into the present and her expression tightened again.

Teryn decided not to try to make sense of that. "How well did you know Lena?"

"A little. Like I told you."

"Were you living here when they moved to this area?"

"Oh yes. It was just the two of them. Lena was only a baby. Her father told me once that Lena's mother had died during childbirth. I asked about her, you see. It's not often a baby has just her father and no mother."

"Did you speak with her often?"

"Often enough, at first. She would sometimes go for long walks around the area with her father. The last time was during the summer just gone. She didn't say much. But when she little... well, I'd never forget a conversation with that girl."

"Why?"

"Lena was a gifted child, full of enthusiasm for learning, and she loved to talk about the things that she'd learned, so much that her father would sometimes have to stop her talking. He was quieter than her, back then."

"Something changed," Teryn mused.

227

"Back then, Lena built worlds in her head and made rules for them. She challenged ideas that other children accepted. She had a *wildness* to her."

Teryn found that interesting. Lena's official profile and the accounts of her colleagues gave the impression of someone who would readily follow rules to avoid attention, rather than create their own set of rules. Still, people often changed dramatically as they drifted into adulthood. Hadn't he done the same? His recollection was vague, but his childhood had been very different to the years that followed. He hadn't been *wild* exactly, but certainly wilful.

"Sometimes," the woman told him, "you only need to see *properly* into someone's eyes, and there's the truth laid out for you. There's a look that can tell you more than a hundred or even a thousand words could."

The Finder silently agreed. He had met such people occasionally. Their inner truth shone from them-sometimes without their knowledge, and often to their detriment. "Lena saw the world differently," he said. "Is that how you remember her?"

"That's how I'd like to remember her. I wish *I* could see things as she once did. But Lena became sad. Long before her father passed. I saw that in her eyes, in recent years. She had a good job, didn't she? Lena was intelligent and she made use of it. You could say she was a good citizen. *Productive.* But she had that sadness inside her. She felt trapped, I think."

"Sadness is universal," Teryn heard himself say. "It often has little to do with one's station in life. Being trapped and discontented is also part of us. Why else do we yearn for things we don't understand?"

"The Citadel ate into her as it eats into us all." Lena's neighbour dropped her voice to little more than a whisper. "You look up at the stars and see an incredible distance, when the cloak hasn't yet fully settled over you. Then, reality and age pull you down into the dirt, and the stars... might as well be painted on a backcloth. We're part of the mud, you and I and millions of others. What purpose does that have? Do you know what I imagined, as I saw her running down the street? I pictured Lena growing wings as she fled- great, beautiful white wings- and flying high into the night, up and away from the Citadel forever. She would have been happy. She would have smiled into the dark."

Teryn was shocked to find tears prickling his eyes. For a moment he felt almost *less,* as if he might look down and find that he'd faded from the world a little. He looked down anyway but saw nothing except his own boots caked with ash, and the surface of the street gleaming wetly in the winter gloom.

"I shouldn't have said that," Lena's neighbour added worriedly. "I'm grateful for my life. We're all lucky to be here and not out *there* amidst the chaos. Don't say that you heard..."

"I didn't hear anything." Teryn wondered why his voice sounded different.

Abruptly he decided to curtail their conversation. He felt a nagging unease about where, if anywhere, it might lead- almost a fear that it might draw him nearer to some unwanted, dangerous revelation. And yet, why would he shy away from an opportunity to delve deeper? "Thank you for your time," he said abruptly, and walked on down the street.

Teryn didn't hear the door close. When he glanced back, the old woman still stood on the threshold, staring fixedly at the ashen remains of Lena's home as if the roaring flames still climbed into the sky, carrying the ghosts and demons of her imagination.

I can sometimes picture things as they once were, and as they might be in the future, the Finder thought later as he sat at his living room table, where papers relating to investigations mingled with unwashed crockery from his last several nights' dinners. *Is Lena similar in some way?*

Lena's isolation had made Teryn more aware of his own. He had been alone throughout his adult life. Not *lonely,* he reminded his colleagues on the rare occasions when such things were mentioned. *There's a big difference,* he had always told them, but almost nobody seemed able to understand that point. Most of them had wives or husbands, over half had at least one child, and almost all reacted with bafflement to his casual assertion that he not only survived but did very well by himself.

In truth he did well enough most of the time, and he rode out the dark passages of his life. He survived.

Now, as he sat at his table- where he read and reviewed his notes, ate and drank and occasionally slept, with his head slumped uncomfortably forward- the Finder looked up from his scribbles and diagrams and realised that he no longer felt alone- at least, not in the same sense as before this assignment. Something had changed, as if a mysterious energy linked him to Lena and had placed them both in the same vast web so that a movement or decision made by either of them might somehow be sensed by the other.

"No, that's not it," he said aloud, and took a sip of grain spirit from his chipped drinking glass. "If it were," he added, in the manner of someone talking to a companion across the table, "then she would remain several steps ahead of me at all times, and I can't allow that."

Teryn had already drank two large glasses of spirit that evening, and although this wasn't enough to radically change his mood- few things had the power to do that- the subtle chemical changes conspired to make him converse with himself, something that he never did when sober. His soliloquies would always end in bitterness, and frustration at being his own audience.

This connectedness to someone for whom he searched, albeit in a way he couldn't understand, was not entirely alien to the Finder. It was simply part of his nature. He didn't know its cause or origin. Other Finders shared it to a certain degree- in some cases it was the reason they chose to become Finders- but Teryn had always known that his had a strength and truth greater than theirs.

Might it be possible than Lena somehow *knew* about him? Perhaps not who he was or where, but an awareness of his existence on some deep level?

Other Finders, who relied on known facts and observations, would have laughed at the idea. Most were aware of his more esoteric methods, his hunches, even the bright and powerful visions he occasionally had. Not one of them believed such things to be credible, even when they helped solve a case. They would instinctively point to the more mundane tools in the armoury of every Finder including Teryn. *He likes to cloak himself in mystery,* they would say. *Perhaps he even makes up some of that nonsense for his own benefit. Old, lonely Teryn. He needs to tether himself more securely to society.*

His worries faded when he drank. But they also faded during those rare times when he abstained for days. Teryn concluded that the cycle of drinking just enough to feel better was also just enough to keep him sufficiently worried- tied down by routine and the fear of breaking protocol. The cycle ensured he acted as professionally as he needed to and with due diligence-maintaining his invisible status as an upstanding citizen with a roof over his head.

The Finder sat back and wearily told himself to stop overthinking. He stared at the patterns made by the grime and mould on the walls and ceiling- dirt that he had never bothered to clean properly, for he knew it would only return- and used them to imagine things into existence. Foreign lands on an old map, creatures, eyes in faces, weapons...

Teryn heard a faint sound like a hiss or a whisper come from the kitchen at the back of the house. After a moment he got up and made his way slowly through to the kitchen but saw nothing amiss. Everything remained as untidy- and unwashed- as ever.

He glanced at the window and walked a little nearer. He stared at his own vague reflection. Nothing could be seen nothing outside, and yet he felt oddly certain that had it been daytime he would have seen something unfamiliar- maybe a version of the path that ran past the back of his house, but changed and distorted somehow, so that it led somewhere different. Somewhere that had never been explored before.

Teryn looked at himself in the window once again. He imagined that his reflection appeared like a thin and grey husk, washed free of life and hue.

It's a reflection, idiot, he reprimanded himself.

But he looked too thin, his eyes too dark. *I ought to eat more,* he mused, but that sardonic observation failed to amuse him.

The Finder thought he saw something move behind his reflection, as if a formless shadow passed across the room. His skin prickled with fear.

Turn around. Turn around so you can see there's nothing there.

But he couldn't, ridiculously afraid that if he did turn, he would see something even worse- or nothing but a void, empty space.

Teryn continued to berate himself. Would this be how he spent his old age? Letting fear leak into him? Jumping at every little artefact his eyes tricked him with? Every false message generated by his tired, misfiring brain?

But no matter how much he engaged in this tirade, Teryn would not, could not turn and consign his apparitions to oblivion. He stood and faced the window for a long while, and when he felt too tired to stand any longer, he sat, still facing the same direction until he eventually slept, head bowed as if in submission to the impossible.

IV

The following morning, Teryn left his house without breakfasting and decided to find out what he could about Lena at the Department of Registrations.

An austere and unimaginative set of concrete buildings, its endless corridors of book-lined shelves appeared more like aisles in a warehouse than a library of information. Traversing the archaic and complex conventions of this place required considerable reserves of patience.

Teryn followed in silence as the clerk located the volume of births, deaths and marriages which contained (amongst many others) the details pertaining to Lena's family. The records he found were far from complete, and some appeared to have been duplicated unnecessarily or have the wrong information. He could locate nothing about her maternal or paternal grandparents, or *their* parents. A few sketchy details of Lena's paternal great-great-grandparents had been put together, but they were as scant as they were irrelevant.

"It happens sometimes," the young clerk apologised. "People fall through the net. We have so much information to collect and keep..." He shrugged his slim shoulders in defeat.

Teryn sat down at a desk to review the incomplete documentation as the clerk returned to his desk.

The facts of Lena's birth were straightforward enough. She had been born twenty and a half years ago, give or take a few days. She had been kept in the hospital for some time although whatever illness delayed her discharge wasn't specified. Then she and her father moved to the same house that she had (possibly) burned down. As Lena's neighbour had said, her mother had died in childbirth, which was far from unusual. A copy of a Certificate of Death for her had been attached.

"Daiana Stone," he said aloud. Little more than her name had been detailed in the certificate. She had had brown hair, blue eyes. Her height and weight had been average. "Like mother, like daughter."

Teryn sat back and thought for a moment, then looked again at the documents. But his view of the lettering began to blur so much that he had to look away, suddenly nauseous. *That's never happened before,* he thought as he rested his head in his hands and closed his eyes until the whirling sickness finally abated.

He wondered if he ought to consult a physician. If there was something wrong with him, he should find out what.

But, against all logic, Teryn felt certain, when he raised his head and dared to glance at Lena's papers again, that his sudden nausea was not the result of a medical condition but something caused by the documents themselves, as if they didn't *want* to be read.

He tried to ignore the prickling sensation that suddenly washed over his body. It reminded him of last night's experience.

I saw nothing, the Finder told himself. *I have no evidence.*

But over the last few days, evidence had begun to mean less than it ought.

Teryn walked the short distance from the Department of Registrations along a wide, cobbled street to a building that served as a construction and architecture academy where some of the plans for houses, residential blocks and factories were kept. The collection was nowhere near complete, and as far as he knew many plans over the decades and even centuries had been mislaid or accidentally destroyed- particularly those for buildings that had collapsed or suffered other catastrophic faults. But he wanted to see if a plan and record existed for the house that had been Lena's home- and her father's- and to ascertain that the layout matched the sharp, vivid picture that had come to him in the ruins.

The day clerk for the records section, a prim and fussy woman in her middle years, scribbled down the address he gave her and then led him through the maze of aisles in the main records chamber. She found the bundle of papers for the property sooner than Teryn expected. "You're in luck- these are complete," she remarked. He thanked her and waited until she departed before pulling open the string that tied the papers together.

Teryn stared in confusion at the main floor plan of the house.

This can't be right, he thought, but the address on each of the plan diagrams was consistent and correct and the building had not been demolished or rebuilt since that date.

The plans showed a slightly smaller house, the shape of which differed to that which Teryn's vision had shown. It also appeared to be a little nearer to the other houses in the street than when he had visited the site.

How was this possible? Had changes been made to the infrastructure? No, none were indicated.

So, had his vision been wrong?

Teryn shook his head. It hadn't. He instinctively *knew.*

He studied the plans again. They showed shorter staircases, a less extended back kitchen, and a main sitting room which appeared to be square rather than the slightly rectangular shape he had imagined. There were also far fewer passageways and ways in and out of rooms.

The plans were wrong, the Finder decided.

Or, they had been correct at the time, but the house had changed.

Teryn arrived at the headquarters of the Finders' Department later that morning to find that much of the electrical power had failed, for at least the fifth time in the month. Some of the desk lamps worked off a separate generator and still worked, but the interconnected lanterns that had been set up throughout the maze of narrow corridors fifteen years ago stood dark and cold.

As he walked slowly through the gloom, Teryn passed by several colleagues who were carrying old gas lanterns. "Here's to progress," one of them muttered- he didn't know the man's name- as Teryn shuffled past.

He made his way up three creaking flights of warped wooden stairs and along narrow, low-ceilinged corridors. Occasionally he reached out his hand to the wall when the light became especially poor, not trusting his balance as much as he once had. At one point he touched the wall only to snatch his hand away from it immediately, certain that the surface dripped with rivulets of cold, foul moisture.

Teryn eventually reached the large open room where he and five other Finders sometimes worked. He spent as little time as he could in this soulless place and came here only to collect papers and information about cases.

No one else was in. Some papers waited on his desk. Teryn sat with a sigh and peered at them by the dim light. They were related to a separate assignment, to do with the production and sale of illicit substances- a constant of Citadel life for centuries and one which the authorities had failed to tackle or properly control, no matter the approach they took. Teryn had been tasked with locating and apprehending a figure of importance in the transit of such goods throughout the Citadel. He had been unable to summon any enthusiasm for the task, knowing that for every such man arrested and put away, another would almost immediately take his place.

He gave the papers a cursory glance, put them to one side and sat despondently in the silence. The light flickered on and off continuously, interrupting any thought process.

Go for a walk, he told himself finally. *Don't just sit here when you don't need to.*

Teryn got up and left.

That afternoon, the Finder found himself near Brickworks, a long, wide road that bisected a run-down industrial area, once the main hub for rail construction. The industry had moved elsewhere, and the place left to slowly sink into ruin, although Teryn often chose to walk around such areas. He often found them peaceful.

Low grey cloud hung over the dismal scene today. Many abandoned shells of warehouses and factories stood here, places that were often havens for the homeless- mainly because the authorities seldom visited them. "They come here to die slowly, and they at least stay out of our sight," he had heard one enforcement officer say a few years ago.

Today he could neither see nor hear anyone. He stopped briefly in a narrow, pot-hole infested side lane that led onto Brickworks, then stepped out onto the wider street. Here the road was bordered on both sides by towering red brick structures whose many windows had all been broken. An unpleasant sensation of being watched, or rather, *monitored,* stirred within him as he surveyed the monstrous buildings. Teryn knew this might be nothing more than a product of his surroundings, but the strength of this crawling sensation took him by surprise, as if a thousand all-seeing, all-knowing eyes were trained upon him alone. *What will the old man do next? No one knows,* he imagined their concealed owners whispering.

He looked left and right, up and down, at the dark and glassless apertures.

He heard nothing but the wind as it sighed through the holes in the infrastructure. But he saw that one window space appeared darker than the others.

That could not be possible, of course, but when his gaze shifted to the others and then back to that space, it still looked darker. *Much* darker.

Teryn decided that there was something wrong with his eyes, and possibly even his mind. Earlier, he hadn't even been able to read from some archives.

He stepped closer to the dark mirage to inspect it in greater detail, until he stood almost directly under that space, which he estimated to be roughly thirty hands above him.

An open door creaked in the breeze a few dozen paces away. Teryn made his way over. Stone steps led up from a small, dank hallway in the gloom beyond.

Don't go in there, an inner voice warned.

He walked up the stairs anyway.

He arrived at the room with the window space that had played tricks with his vision and peered cautiously through the open doorway. The room- perhaps used for storage in the past, judging by the broken boxes scattered in the corners- looked no darker than it ought.

But as the Finder stood in the doorway and breathed in the abandonment, he saw something so extraordinary that at first, he decided his eyes were playing tricks on him again.

The floor had caved in slightly but in a regular way, so that it made a concave shape in the middle of the room. Towards the centre of this cavity a mass of something Teryn could only describe as a pool of darkness had gathered.

He crept forward and stared mutely at the phenomenon. *It's water,* he tried to tell himself, but knew that it wasn't. For a moment it rippled faintly, not in response to any external interference that Teryn could detect. But the ripples were slower than he would have expected in a liquid.

As he observed, Teryn began to wonder if it was a liquid at all. He could see the room reflected in it, and the reflection, once the ripples had ceased, looked brighter than the actual room. How could he see the contents of the room reflected so well, when the light here was dim?

The silence was absolute. He could not even hear himself breathe.

Impossible, he thought. *Am I going mad?*

Was someone playing an elaborate trick on him? Why?

Teryn closed his eyes, frustrated and more than a little fearful. He had no idea what to do, other than to leave this place and try to forget everything that had happened.

When he opened his eyes again, he found himself in the pool of darkness.

The Finder shouted in terror and instinctively thrashed around. Dark shapes detached themselves from the greater mass and moved through the air before falling soundlessly. Some landed on him and slipped across his body. Their touch was so cold that Teryn cried out in agony. He struggled to the edge of the pool and hauled himself out of it, shuddering with fear.

He looked down at himself and realised numbly that he wasn't wet.

Already the dark pool lay completely still again.

The Finder looked towards the window space and saw that the sky had started to darken. He stood up shakily and left the building as quickly as he could. His legs shook so much that he almost fell down the stairs.

I should write a report, Teryn thought as he stumbled outside a short while later. He almost laughed at the idea.

As he hurried home, snow began to fall. By the time he reached his house it was an inch thick. Teryn took several minutes to pull his keys from his pocket and open his door. He closed it behind him and sank exhausted to the floor. *Slam the door and close away the world,* he thought. *Just like Lena.*

He held his head in his hands and wept quietly.

V

Later, Teryn dragged himself upstairs to his bedroom. He lay down and waited for sleep, his confused thoughts whirling. He could no longer remember the order in which the events of the last few days had happened, nor could he figure a way out of this madness. Something had ensnared him. Perhaps something to do with Lena.

He slept uneasily for a while, woke with a start, slumbered briefly and woke again sometime in the small hours. His heart thumped and he could smell his sweat and fear, along with a bitter, unidentifiable odour.

Teryn lit his bedside lamp, picked it up and made his way slowly down the stairs, gripping the bannister more tightly than he usually did. He winced at the pain in his knees as he reached the hallway, one hand still on the end of the bannister. He walked slowly through to his kitchen and wondered morosely if he should eat even less and reduce the weight on his joints.

But if he ate any less, he would barely eat at all.

"What did I do yesterday?" Teryn asked the odorous gloom.

Had he ran? That would explain the throbbing in his knees and the tightness of his leg muscles.

Then he recalled a vast, derelict building with hundreds of windows. But he couldn't remember its location. He had gone for a walk as he often did. Had he become lost? He laughed quietly at the thought of a Finder who couldn't find his way around the Citadel, but then shuddered at the sound he made.

Teryn sat wearily at the kitchen table. He rubbed at the three days' stubble on his face and wiped away sweat from under his eyes. After a moment he noticed that the door to the bathroom, at the end of the passageway to his left, moved slowly back and forth as if a draught disturbed it. The Finder sat and watched until the movement became sufficiently irritating for him to get up and walk down the passageway.

He pushed open the door a little further and peered into the bathroom. The electric light hadn't worked in many years, and Teryn had never got around to finding someone to fix it, so the room was always gloomy. The small square window high in the far wall let very little light through even on sunlit days in the height of summer. An oil lamp stood on a chair next to the bath for the purpose of providing more light as and when needed. Teryn lit it to push back the shadows a little, picked up the lamp and moved slowly in a half circle to view the room properly.

Something about the bathtub looked different. The Finder stepped a little nearer, observed the iron taps and the corrosion they had wept down the edge of the porcelain. *Too dark,* he thought, and held the lamp closer.

Then he saw something so strange that he stared transfixed for an untold length of time, trying to figure out *what* he observed, and *why.*

The bathtub appeared deeper than it ought- much deeper. "Ten hands- no, twelve," Teryn estimated aloud, barely aware of his own words. But in fact it was impossible to work out the depth, because every time he tried the inside of the bath deepened further, as if it was gradually falling away into an impossible hole.

Like Lena's house, he thought, and for one mad moment he imagined that his proximity to that ruin had caused him to catch an illness that made holes appear wherever he went.

Teryn wondered if the ashen remains of her home had now fallen entirely and been swallowed up by the earth.

This isn't a sinkhole, he reminded himself. *That would cause anything and everything nearby to fall into it.*

Instead, a single object was changing shape. Nothing else nearby had altered in any way that he could see.

"Impossible," the Finder quietly declared, and he backed away to the door, which now stood still. He wondered if it had moved back and forth simply to draw him to the bathroom and make him witness this phenomenon.

"No. It's not happening," he protested, but he dared not turn his back on the room, fearful that if he did a chasm would open up behind and beneath and send him spiralling down into a place from where he would never escape. Teryn closed the door and backed away further down the passageway- was it now slightly longer than it ought to be?- keeping his eyes fixed on the bathroom door the whole time.

He stumbled into the kitchen table and somehow managed to sit down in his chair. *Still dark outside,* he noted. *What time is it? How long has it been dark for?*

A sudden desperate desire to see the morning light took hold of him. Had he ever welcomed the morning before?

"If it *is* happening," he reasoned, "then it's been happening for a long time. I've sensed it before. But now it's stronger. More obvious. I can look it in the eye."

"It *wants* me to look it in the eye," he added, although the door to the phenomenon was closed and he had no desire to open it. For all he knew, the door would now open on a chasm.

The kitchen window appeared taller and narrower now, and the section of ceiling above it curved upwards into shadow, as if an unseen force had pulled at the upper corner of the room and stretched everything towards that apex.

"Artefacts from a dream," Teryn said at last, contradicting himself.

He touched many different areas of the furniture, testing their substance and familiarity as he walked back to the stairs and began to climb them. "It's all right," he said finally. "It's all right. It's a bad dream. You need to rest." He gave an involuntary sob, perplexed and humiliated that he found such intense relief in familiar, ordinary shapes. "Sleep. It'll be morning soon." Hadn't his mother said that sometimes when he was little? When nightmares leaked into reality?

When he reached the top of the stairs and began to walk across the landing, Teryn realised that at the far end of the landing *another* flight of stairs now led upwards, and the door to his bedroom had vanished.

"No," he said blankly. "No. I need to wake up."

You can't wake up. You must climb the stairs first.

Whose voice was that, whispering in his head? Teryn thought it sounded female.

He walked as far as the second flight of steps and peered up. The stairs gradually disappeared into the gloom. He'd forgotten to bring his bedside lamp back up with him, but a strange fear took hold when he considered going back for it.

Teryn stretched out his leg and applied a little weight to the first step. Then he began to ascend the staircase, gripping the bannister tightly with his left hand, although he supposed he had no reason to believe bannisters were any more secure, any more grounded in reality than other parts of his house.

After six or seven steps he looked back down. The landing appeared further away- further *down*- than it ought. The single wall lamp that lit the area appeared to float in a void, and the stairs on which he stood might as well have been part of an altogether different structure, separated from the rest of the house by an abyss. It occurred to him that the house was being stretched by some supernatural force- as exhibited by the expansion of the bath into a fathomless pit, and an upper section that had spawned new stairs. He imagined the roof building on itself to escape the Citadel and reach the stars. *Keep going and you may escape,* he thought, and again he imagined Lena as her neighbour had-winged and ascending through the night.

Am I like her?

Teryn's hand gripped the bannister harder than ever. With an effort he resumed his climb, counting the steps as he went. He tried to list all the possible reasons for what he was experiencing and considered that the most likely of these was a mental collapse. He had, after all, touched the edge of a roiling, shapeless inner being before. During or after his worst excesses of alcohol or other substances, he had seen dark and formless entities bloom like flowers in the ceiling of his bedroom. He had been woken up in the night by the absolute certainty that his insides were melting, that the entire house and its contents- including the meat and bone from which he himself was made- glowed with evil heat and yet somehow retained its shape. A stench of burning wires and synthetic materials would accompany that dread as he cried out, sat up and clenched his sweat-drenched sheets.

The specifics of the dream would fade but the fear they generated would often last through the following day and beyond.

The *memory* of the fear never faded.

It was therefore not impossible that he'd taken a step too far towards that perimeter, and the chaos that ruled beyond it had snatched him from the comforts of reality. It was now engaged in disintegrating his observable world.

Teryn could see several stairs in front of him every time he took another step, but he couldn't tell where the light that illuminated them came from. The way the light fell, it looked as if it came from *him*. The lamp on the landing, meanwhile, faded to a lonely yellow dot in the dark. It could have been the most distant light in the Citadel, or even a feature of the night sky.

Teryn counted forty-three stairs before he finally reached another landing. He gathered his breath and peered ahead. Either his eyes had adjusted well to the gloom or the area had become marginally lighter.

If I keep going, he thought, *then I might never find my way down.*

He walked slowly along the landing. The floor had softened beneath his feet, as if he no longer stepped on floorboards but over soil, or grass. His feet made no sound. The air became colder, harsher with each step.

An inner voice implored the Finder to turn and go back or be lost forever, stumbling around in the heights or depths of this place that was no longer his home. His teeth chattered and the tips of his fingers were already numb.

The landing now widened out into a room. He saw oddly shaped furniture- tables, chairs and ornaments of a curious style. Through the windows he saw both moons shine. The air had grown warmer again and his fingers began to prickle.

I know this place, Teryn realised, dumbfounded. *I've been here before.*

Memories bloomed in his head. He stood, utterly transfixed by his sudden recollection, swaying in the darkness.

VI

He saw the man and the woman only vaguely in the fading light that seeped in through the window. "Come closer, Teryn," the woman said.

"I'll stay where I am." Teryn reached into the inside pocket of his coat to make sure he still had his gun but was dismayed to find it wasn't there. Worse, only a moment later he found that he had shuffled nearer to the two of them without realising.

He noticed a large cot further back in the room, and it was to this that the woman beckoned him. She wasn't there a moment ago, he thought confusedly. How did she get over there so quickly? How did I move to where I am?

The man, meanwhile, hadn't moved from his chair, but Teryn sensed that he watched him intently.

"*Your letter requested that I visit alone and tell no one,*" *Teryn said.* "*I wouldn't normally do that, but...*"

"*Nonsense. You do it frequently,*" *she interrupted.* "*You judge according to your instinct. That's one of many things that make you different. Do you have the letter with you?*"

"*Yes.*" *But when he pushed his hand into the left outer pocket of his coat, the Finder discovered that the note had been reduced to particulate matter. He retrieved his hand along with some of the residue but couldn't make out its nature in the gloom.* "*No,*" *he corrected himself.*

"*Good,*" *the woman said.* "*And you told no one of your whereabouts. We would have known if you had. We don't have much time, Teryn. Come over here.*"

He went to stand next to her. The moonslight improved a little- he couldn't have said how, because no lamps were lit, and it hadn't got any lighter outside. Teryn saw that two babies, both no more than a few months old, slept in the cot. "*My name is Elia. The man over there is my partner, Marim. These two are our daughters.*"

"*In your letter, you gave your names as...*"

"*Never mind what the letter said, Teryn. It's gone, and you're here. That's what matters.*" *Elia studied him, her expression inscrutable. Her hair had a silvery sheen to it, although she didn't look more than thirty years old. The light made it difficult to know the colour of her eyes- he thought they might be grey, or blue, or green.* "*Your methods are unusual for a Finder. You're closer to the horizon.*"

"*I can't possibly comment... what do you mean?*"

"*Your perception, your intuition, works on a higher level than that of your colleagues,*" *she explained.*

"That's very flattering of you, but I'd like to know what you require of me." Teryn rubbed the fine ash from his pocket between his fingers. Was it ash, or dust? *"Did you cause the letter to burn or disintegrate?"*

"Don't be silly- that would be quite impossible," Elia chided him. A hint of a smile creased her lips for a moment. *"I'll come to the point. We need to go our separate ways, Marim and I. The girls must be kept apart for the foreseeable future, and the best way for this to happen- though it grieves us to admit it- will be for me to take one and for him to take the other."*

"Why would you need to keep them apart?"

"Elia looked to Marim and motioned to the door behind them. "Does it hold fast?" she asked him. *"Are we truly separated from all things outside?"*

"It holds," he said quietly. *"They can't hear us. But let's be done quickly."*

Elia turned to Teryn again. For the first time her voice sounded as if it might break. *"The girls... must be kept apart for their own safety. As they grow, their natures will become... how do I explain this? Larger. More agitated. They will exert a greater pull on the Citadel's web, and sooner or later those not-so-tiny tremors will become powerful enough to attract the attention of the Mothers themselves. We can't allow that- at least, not until the time is right. We have a chance to break the cycle, Teryn- because these two have more potential than any before them. There's a presence- it works as a dream, for want of a better word- passed down through our families. A memory of what once was and what may be again. They have the power to fulfil that hope."*

"I don't understand any of this," Teryn told her, although on a lower, primal level, he did. *"Whatever*

your reason for wanting your babies to be hidden or kept apart- I'm a Finder. I locate people- I don't hide them."

"You can't be an expert in one without knowing a great deal about the other," Elia pointed out, "and we can't do any of this without your help. You have a hold on some of the Citadel's systems. You're a bridge between worlds, Teryn. You can do things- in terms of documentation, property, information held in archives- that we can't. If we so much as tried, they would know. We can't allow that to happen. Everything depends on the girls remaining hidden from the Mothers until the time comes. We don't know when that will be."

"But it will happen," she added softly.

Teryn looked down into the cot and as he did, one of the baby girls opened her eyes and looked sleepily up in their direction. Her eyes met his for a moment and then she looked away, but in that instant Teryn felt something indescribable stir inside him- unease, curiously mixed with something near to euphoria. He could have wept, or laughed- but he stood still, transfixed, caught in a dream.

"So, we require your help. Specifically, we need to disappear. We need new names- new surnames at least- for us all. The girls' certificates of birth will need to be replaced. We need to be accommodated somewhere under our new names- any serviceable houses will do, we don't have need of many comforts. And then we will live simple, uncomplicated- and unconnected- lives, hopefully without attracting the attention of authorities."

"You have the means to do these things," she pointed out when Teryn gaped at her.

"I could be incarcerated for even contemplating them." He shook his head. "No, I won't do this. Unless authorised by the chief of my Department, I can't..."

"Give me your hand, Teryn," she interrupted. The words were calm yet commanding, uttered in the knowledge that he would do as he was told. *"I will not..."* he began, but then saw that he had stretched his right arm towards Elia.

"Don't be afraid," she murmured. *"There are so many other things to fear. But not this."* She placed one hand on top of his and the other below.

Teryn gasped in astonishment as he felt something stir and lurch into life inside him, almost as if his blood had begun to flow in the opposite direction.

"You're filled with music," Elia said softly. *"She sings through you too. We were right, Marim. He's the one. He's the only one. And to think he became a Finder!"*

Teryn felt the man's eyes upon him without needing to turn and look. *"She made it so,"* Marim murmured.

"Who are you... talking about?" The words struggled unwillingly from Teryn's mouth. He wanted to pull his hand free and yet he also wanted Elia to hold it forever.

"You'll help us. Within yourself, you know why." Elia gestured to the cot. *"Look at our daughters again."*

Numbly he gazed at the sleeping infants, and he almost cried out as he sensed a concentration of writhing, unearthly power- magic, he thought for a moment. Magic, but also a living entity. This unspeakable, unknowable force was shared between them, forming a net, or a cloak, or a web- he could not know its form, and certainly not its function. When he finally looked up, he saw that threads of the same force linked the girls to Elia and to Marim.

He heard Elia speak, but she now looked like a glowing silhouette of a woman, sketched out in impossibly thin lines of light and energy. *"Marim and I*

251

met by chance, but of course it wasn't chance at all. The Great Power brought us together. We are both descendants of the Old Ones, those who defended the world against destruction in a forgotten Age- those betrayed by the women who would later call themselves the Mothers. We knew what might happen if we had a child- we knew that the Great Power would burn so brightly in that infant. And as luck decreed, we had two. Nothing like this has happened in a thousand years. Generations have lived and died and passed on the memories- the truth- without ever knowing when or even if anything would change."

Teryn let out an uncontrolled sob, unable to bear the inexplicable things to which he bore witness. "*Now do you understand?*" whispered a voice in his ear. He couldn't be sure if Elia or Marim or some third entity had asked the question- or even one of the baby girls.

"*What are their names?*" he whispered. "*Have you named them?*"

"*Our daughters are Rhion and Lena. But you'll forget those names for now. Perhaps for a very long time. You'll forget that you came here. You'll remember enough to do everything you need to do. Your own powers have awakened. You'll use them to find new paths for us and hide our trail, our records, and those of our daughters. And then you'll sleep again.*"

"*Sleep?*"

"*Until the time comes for you to wake. And you* will *wake, Teryn. Into the wider world. The world as it should be. When the time comes, find Rhion and Lena again. You must. They are the path to hope, but you are the map.*"

He could only nod in mute response, as he still held desperately to Elia's hand. Was it still Elia's hand? Gloom had settled again, and he couldn't be certain.

Teryn stumbled back, consumed with the shock of the memory that flooded his mind. For a while he couldn't see anything at all, and he thrashed about wildly until he turned and saw a light somewhere ahead.

Where am I? he asked himself frantically. He realised that he was kneeling, and he leaned forward, then began to inch his way towards the illumination, fearful that a precipitous incline loomed to each side of him. The ground began to feel harder again, more like a floor.

Eventually he realised that he was crawling across his kitchen floor.

"I can't keep hold anymore. I'm falling," Teryn mumbled, and he curled up on the floor and wept.

When he woke, he stared at nothing, still swept up in the shock of his unearthed memory. *I returned from touching the heart of all things to this grey void of a life, seeking out the vermin of the Citadel,* he thought. *I was sent back to this hopeless, dreary prison.*

"Why now?" he asked himself eventually. "Because of Lena? Yes. It has to be."

Because they're together again, came an answer from nowhere, and Teryn nodded in agreement. That made sense. They had been kept apart because of what would happen otherwise. Could it be that Lena had not only fled her old life but had also encountered Rhion?

"Why did you make me forget?" he asked the absent Elia.

If she had indeed clouded his mind somehow, she must have had her reasons. Perhaps, no matter how much Elia and Marim had revealed to him that day, they didn't fully trust him‑ why would they? He barely trusted himself most of the time. What if the Citadel's most insidious powers had learned of that brief display

253

of terrifying, exhilarating truth? His freedom would have ended. Teryn wondered how he would have stood up to interrogation by the Mothers' prime servants- one of the Lawmasters, the Chief Balancer or even the Voice.

So, briefly empowered, he had set about creating new, separate lives for the four of them, hiding his trail of activity. His inability to inspect Lena's certificate of birth was an after-effect of the powers he had used to engineer the melting away of Elia, Marim and their daughters, into the depths of the Citadel's web.

So what now?

He had no idea.

The lost man sat in his cold, drab kitchen and waited for the morning light. This night already felt as if it had persisted for a week. As the minutes wore on into hours he became certain that a vast, hidden apparatus that governed the natural order of things had begun to move certain people- including Lena and her sister, and himself- into the positions for which they had been made.

Players all, and yet *they* were being played by a universal force, the Great Power.

For the first time in his life, Teryn began to understand his place in the machinery of luck and strange forces of which the Citadel was only a fragment. He understood how it had come to be that his life had been devoid of meaning despite the evidence of his strange abilities that neither he nor anyone else could adequately explain. He had glimpsed- no, *tasted-* something so far beyond his comprehension, beyond the boundaries that defined his life, that his return to normality was to live in purgatory. He could exist, but he could not be happy- not until he did the things that he was destined to do.

Everything has led up to this, he thought. *I've been waiting without even knowing I was waiting.*

Sometime around dawn he left his house, painfully hungry but too nauseous to eat. As he closed the door he looked up, half-expecting to see the building rise like a tower far into the murky sky.

He walked as far as the nearest trading area, the snow squeaking under his boots. No shops were open nearby, and the market squares would be empty. Perhaps one or two of the more eager traders would be setting up in the chilly half-light. But Teryn had decided that he needed to walk out in the open- importantly, to keep *moving* and process everything he'd rediscovered.

How do I find them? he wondered as he stepped across the diamond-shaped flagstones outside one of the Guild of Engineering buildings. Then he stopped and looked up at the vast structure, all harsh cuboid blocks arranged in a sensibly functional way that offended his idea of architectural beauty. He wondered if Lena had studied here at any point.

He closed his eyes, suddenly nauseous, and it was then that a complex, intricate map of threads opened in his mind.

The threads represented all manner of things-paths, directions, relationships between people, histories of movements that people had made. The more he tried to study it in his mind's eye, the more it blossomed and bloomed into something even more complex, revealing further interrelationships and coexistences, a web of energy and objects held together by millions of people. Most of them appeared faint and dim, but some glowed, and a few even blazed like fire in the void.

"What is it?" Teryn mumbled. His eyes flickered open into the chilly dawn.

He had no name for it, but he knew that it must have come from Elia, all those years ago. Perhaps from Marin too- and even the twins, for all he knew. That sensation of suddenly being brought into a deeper, wider world of endless possibility surged through him. Elia had planted the seed of that intense, incredible sight and had given him a glimpse of it just for a moment- so that he might believe, so that he would help them disappear and allow the girls to live apart but in unknowing safety. Or might he always have had this ability, and Elia had simply coaxed it into germination?

Either way, he'd forgotten, or been forced to forget.

But now the Great Power spread through him. It offered a view of the Citadel's people for which any Finder would have killed. It showed cause and effect, the relationships and interactions between millions of citizens. It was both immeasurable and intimate, immense and intense.

It was, Teryn numbly realised, the answer to almost every question.

He leaned against a nearby lamp post, stupefied in his revelation as the world spun around him. He barely noticed the curious looks of the few people passing by, and dared not let his eyes linger on them, fearful of what he might now see.

"I can find her," Teryn whispered. "I can see where Lena has been."

And yet he couldn't see where she was now.

VII

Three hours later, Teryn stood outside a dilapidated guesthouse, shivering in the wind.

He would have searched places like this as part of his routine, although thousands of them lay spread throughout the Citadel. It would have taken too long, and in any case, he might no longer need to visit any others.

He opened the outer front door and stepped inside. The walls looked sticky, and the worn, reddish-brown carpet *felt* sticky under his boots. He saw dust and dirt that had gathered in the crevices and corners, presumably over many years. The odorous air somehow felt heavier than it ought, dense and oppressive, unpleasant to breathe. A stench of rancid cooking fat hung in the hallway. *Breakfast time, or just after,* Teryn noted.

He walked down the dismal hallway to where a little office stood. Sitting amidst a chaos of papers, keys and broken pieces of furniture was an old woman. She busily stuffed a paper with smokeweed as Teryn stood and watched her, but her shaking hands dropped most of it on the floor. She scooped it up and tried to prepare her smoke again, only to suffer the same accident.

At last she saw Teryn, flinched in fear and then stared wide-eyed at him. One painfully thin arm rose slowly and her hand placed the half-rolled (and now half-empty) smoke into the dry crack between her lips. Her nails were packed with dirt or another dark substance, and her eyes looked dull. "You need a room?"

"No. I need your help." Teryn showed her his Finder's sigil. She peered at it for a moment and then her eyes widened. "*Oh.*"

"Are you the owner of this establishment?"

"Forty-seven years." She sounded faintly proud, and for a moment she straightened her back and lifted her chin.

"Is there somewhere..."

"I *knew* someone would come." She stood unsteadily.

"You did?" Teryn prompted the guest house owner as she gradually emerged from the office and closed the door behind her with visible effort. He caught the odour of sour wine as she coughed and then wiped her hand on her other arm.

"Yes. You *will* help, won't you? It's all because of *her*, isn't it?"

"I have some..."

"Questions, yes. Through here." She wandered down to the end of the hallway and pushed open a door that led into a large common room.

The old woman gestured to a soft chair next to a low tinted glass table. When Teryn sat down, she went to a side cabinet and poured a glass of dark-coloured wine from a dusty bottle. "Drink?" she asked.

"No. Thank you." Teryn watched as she slowly made her way back over and sat in a chair opposite his.

The glass and its contents shook violently as she helped herself to a gulp of wine and then another. Looking at her in the softer light of this room, Teryn wondered if she might be younger than she appeared. Maybe circumstances had unfairly aged her.

For a short while she stared at him as if she'd forgotten why he was here. "My name is Jerra," she said at last.

"Mine is Teryn."

She took a deep breath and exhaled slowly. "I'm glad you're here. You can sort this out and stop anything worse from happening. I won't have my guests frightened out of their wits. Fear is a dreadful thing."

"I'm looking for someone who has been staying here. A young woman. Brown hair, blue eyes..."

"Yes. I know who you're looking for." Jerra shuddered. "I know *exactly* who you're looking for. I need you to arrest her."

"Is she still staying here?" *Only I can't see where she is,* Teryn almost added.

"I don't know. She hasn't said that she wants to leave. But people come and go."

"Tell me what she did."

Jerra sat back in her chair and stared towards the window and into the murky grey daylight. The dark shape of a bird flashed by.

Allowing her some time to gather her thoughts- or perhaps become lost in them- Teryn let his gaze wander around the room. This was a place of quiet despair, a refuge for those who had no lives of consequence and yet somehow possessed enough money to hide themselves away and rot in their insignificance until their weary hearts stopped.

People who were alive, but not living.

He might have ended up in a place like this if he hadn't become a Finder. He had no qualifications in any other line of work. What would he have wanted to do? He'd never had a desire to do anything else. Either way, it was so easy to slip down the ladder into hell. He'd seen it many times. Maybe that was how he'd managed to stay on the surface of life.

Still kicking, not drowning.

A guest wandered into the day room. A stooped man who might have been ninety or even a hundred, he walked slowly and shakily, supported by a wooden frame. He paid no heed to either of them but stared fixedly ahead as he continued his laborious progress to the far end of the room and sat with a loud sigh at a table. Jerra did not seem to notice him pass by.

"I'm frightened," she said at last. "I've never been so frightened. I wanted to tell someone what happened, but I couldn't tell the police. They'd think I'd gone mad and they would put me away. But *you* came instead, so things will be different."

"Yes. I came instead. But I don't know how different things will be." Spots and threads of colour and activity appeared before Teryn's eyes for a moment, an artefact of his earlier revelation. *I see the web and all the things that touch it,* he thought again. For a moment, as he looked around the dismal common room, splashes of light and concentrations of darkness bloomed and spread, linked by tenuous threads. In one corner, near to a bookcase and chair, he saw an especially powerful concentration of energy.

Lena, he realised suddenly. *Lena was there, reading a book. I should have known. And someone was with her...*

A moment later Teryn felt certain that the shimmering threads in his mind's eye were not only a residue of Lena, but of Rhion as well.

What would he do if he found the elusive engineer and her sister?

Why, out of everyone in the Citadel, were these two women the only people he *couldn't* find?

"I don't remember going to the Finders' offices to ask for help," Jerra suddenly told him. "I don't remember that at all."

"You must have," Teryn pointed out mildly as he turned his attention back to the landlady. "How else could I be here?"

She simply accepted the idea. "Yes. I suppose so. You *will* take her away, won't you?"

"Has she caused any trouble? Has she been violent at all?"

"Violent?" She almost barked the word at him, and then wheezed, her eyes wide as if the idea simultaneously amused and terrified her. "Has she done bad things in other places?"

"Did she attack you? Threaten you?"

Jerra shook her head slowly. "Not exactly."

"When did she arrive?"

"Two days- no, three days..." Jerra's wrinkled face crumped further in confusion. "Three days ago, I think. I don't know. She's jumbled up the days."

"Tell me what happened when you first saw her. When she arrived."

"Nothing, at first. I let her stay, of course. I knew she was troubled, or *in* trouble, but it's not my job to ask questions. If I did that, most of them would find somewhere else or have nothing but the streets. Those who have the money can stay for as long as they can pay or want to pay." She took another sip of wine and added defensively, "I don't charge much. I might turn a blind eye to a few things, but I need to make a living."

"What was the first thing that she said to you?"

"I don't remember. I spoke to *her* first, you see. I said she wanted a room. She didn't disagree. She seemed... a little confused. Thing is, *I'm* confused now, because of her. But she was calm. She wasn't aggressive like some of them. I told her the rules- there aren't many- and then I gave her the key to her room and off she went. I thought there was something odd about her even then, but I put it to the back of my mind. After all there's a lot of them like that." Jerra tapped the side of her head to signify her view that Lena's mental faculties had been compromised.

"Which room did you give her?"

"Thirty-seven. I remember *that*. I'm good with numbers." She drained the glass and promptly refilled it from the bottle. "Won't you share a glass or two with me?"

"No, thank you." Teryn noted again the sheen of grease and dust on the stopper and neck of the bottle.

"Will you stay for luncheon? I should like a bit of company."

"I'm afraid I can't. Something happened later that frightened you," he prompted her.

"She came downstairs..." The landlady frowned. "This was a different day, but I don't remember *which* day. That's very unusual for me." She leaned forward and wiped a thin veneer of sweat from her brow. Teryn caught a faint waft of complex odours for a moment - old perfume, perhaps applied several days ago, combined with urine. She idly dug some of the dark substance from behind her nails and wiped it on her shapeless skirt.

"I've been forgetting things recently, but I think it's to do with *her*. Something about that woman has disrupted me. Not just me but this place. *Physically,* I mean. I've always made sure that everything here runs in an orderly fashion, but it's started to fall apart. Is *that* a crime?"

"No. Not unless the building or its furnishings become dangerous." Teryn was relieved when Jerra abandoned her nail-picking and sat back in her chair. "She came downstairs," he reminded her.

Jerra nodded. "Yes. I was at the front desk. When I looked up at her I saw... something else. A kind of darkness that followed her, like a shadow - but no one's shadow."

The landlady's eyes had widened now, and she looked in Teryn's direction but clearly saw nothing except the nightmare she had witnessed. The Finder listened with unease as she continued, "The lights were still on in the stairwell, but they had no effect. Have you ever seen that before? They looked as if they were floating in the dark."

"I have," Teryn admitted. The memory of last night slowly surfaced.

"It was like one of those nights when the fog and soot come together, and you can see almost nothing because there isn't a light in the Citadel that can push through that gloom. *That* followed her, at least I thought it did. Then I thought, no, this thing is *part* of her. I remember thinking that even though I was terrified."

Teryn thought in silence for a while. He wondered what the cause of the phenomenon might have been. Why would she have seen *darkness* following Lena? His muddied, indistinct memory of events in the abandoned storehouse came back to him. *I was surrounded by a liquid void, held up by nothing,* he thought. *For a moment, there was nothing below me. Nothing at all. And yet I didn't fall.*

The Great Power held me, Elia would have said.

The landlady finally managed to light her smokeweed and continue her relation of events. "I saw something else behind her. It looked like a hole, a rip- as if everything was a painting and this was a tear in the canvas. I became so scared that I backed away, all the way to the storeroom at the back of the office. I wanted to get away but without running. And yet I couldn't keep my eyes off her. She... *transformed*, somehow."

"She transformed into what?"

Jerra shrugged helplessly. "I don't know. I mean, it happened on the inside. I can't describe it."

"Did the... darkness come with her to the desk? Did you see it hanging over her?"

The landlady shook her head vehemently. "No, no! I don't know *where* it went. But *she* changed. Her eyes became darker..." The landlady grabbed at her glass and drank the rest of the wine in two gulps. "I haven't seen her since then. But I know that she's been here. In this room. I heard her talking. I think she was talking to herself."

Teryn nodded. "I see." He wondered if Lena had been talking to Rhion. Might Rhion have a similar voice to Lena? Would twins necessarily have very similar voices? Teryn didn't know.

"Now some of the shadows are different," Jerra continued suddenly. "I lit a lantern in my bedroom earlier today and the shadow it made *pointed the wrong way.* And she did something else when she was upstairs. The upper floors of the house have *changed.*"

"How do you mean?"

"Some of the corridors and the rooms are different now. It took me the whole afternoon to find my way back down here. My own house!" She began to sob pitifully.

Teryn always felt uncomfortable in the presence of the distressed, no matter how often he sat with them. He wanted to provide comfort but didn't quite know how. He also felt baffled and even a little repulsed by the outpouring of emotion.

"I've people to look after. I think some of the guests might be lost upstairs. But I'm not sure which ones. My record keeping isn't so good now. It's all become..." She raised her shaking hands in frustration. "Muddled."

Teryn stood up and looked across the room. "Wait here, please. I want to ask your guest a few questions."

264

He made his way to the other end of the sitting room and sat across from the old man. The guest raised his head slowly and fixed his sad, suspicious eyes upon the newcomer. "I'm a Finder," Teryn said, showing the guest his sigil.

"I used to *know* a Finder," the old man grunted. "Many years ago."

"How long have you lived here?"

"*Lived?*" The old man chuckled quietly at that, although his eyes still held a cold, dismissive look. "Maybe three years. Maybe four. I was somewhere else before that, but it got closed. These places are all the same. You forget about time. Days rush by."

"Have you noticed anything odd lately?"

"I don't know what you mean. Not much is odd to me."

"Corridors not leading where they ought. Darkness that moves. Lights going out unexpectedly, perhaps. Anything unusual."

The guest sat back and fixed him with an unexpectedly sharp look. "Darkness that moves? What are you talking about?"

"Have you seen anything out of the ordinary?" Teryn asked mildly. "That's all I need to know."

"No." The old man sounded regretful, as if to see something unusual, no matter how horrific, would be welcome. "Everything is always the same. Nothing is ever *odd* anymore."

"I'm going up there to have a look," Teryn told Jerra when he walked back to where she sat, staring listlessly at the wine.

She gave him a horrified look. "You won't find your way back down!"

"But you want me to find her?"

"Yes! Take her away so everything can go back to normal!"

"I'll see what I can do. Have you any chalk?"

"Chalk?" She gave him a blank look.

"For me to mark the walls and find my way back if I need to."

"Oh. Yes. In the office."

They went back to her office. Teryn waited patiently as she rummaged in some drawers and finally found a thick piece of white chalk. She then opened another drawer and handed him a dark iron key with a slip of thick paper attached to it. The number 37 had been written on the paper.

"This is the spare key for her room," the landlady explained. "If you find it."

Teryn took the key. It felt heavy and ice cold in his hand. "Do you think I won't?"

Jerra shrugged miserably. "I wish you wouldn't go up there."

Teryn paused at the foot of the stairs to listen to the silence and observe the dim lighting. Jerra was nowhere to be seen when he turned around, but he hadn't expected her to linger for long. Perhaps she'd opened another bottle of wine and returned to the common room.

Is Lena still here somewhere? he wondered as his hand touched the end of the bannister and he placed his foot on the first stair. *If she met Rhion, where would the two of them have gone? Where would twins kept apart for their entire lives go?*

Teryn realised that he'd already made a mark on the wall with the chalk, just above the base of the bannister. It looked like an X, only lopsided and shaky as if a very young child might have drawn it. It reminded him of a time he had written letters in wax crayon on the walls of a room in his childhood home. They might even have been the first letters he'd ever written. He hadn't been allowed in that room but had found his way in regardless· although he couldn't remember how or why. He remembered seeing the entrance to *another* forbidden room across from him as he scribbled nonsense on the walls, but he had never walked over to find out what lay beyond that door, for his mother had found him and hauled him away.

She hadn't been angry at his scribbling on the wall, he recalled. Her anger had been at his being in the room at all.

But he couldn't remember any of the words she'd said, apart from one curious sentence.

Stop making doors everywhere.

Teryn put the chalk in his pocket and made his way slowly up the stairs. The memory of his ascent through his own house last night continued to come sharply back into focus. His shoes made almost no sound on the thick, dirty carpet. The lights remained dim but unwavering except for one that flickered madly and made an odd buzzing sound. When he passed by, the noise ceased, and the light stopped flickering.

He reached the top of the stairs and chose the passageway that led left, after making another mark with the chalk.

He studied the numbers on the doors that he passed by and soon concluded that they would not lead him to number thirty-seven. They had started at fifty-six and counted upwards on both sides of the passageway. Teryn turned back and soon found himself back at the top of the stairs. He chose the corridor opposite and this time found that the room numbers started at fourteen and counted upwards.

A short while later he arrived at the door to room thirty-seven.

He reminded himself that Lena might still be in her room, and Rhion might be with her. He listened for a moment but heard nothing from inside. Then he knocked on the door and again listened. No response or any other sound came from within.

Teryn turned the door handle and pushed. To his surprise the door opened easily to reveal a tidy, if dusty bedroom. The bed had been made, the covers smoothed down, but the amount of dust on the bedside cabinets was many days thick.

"Were you really here?" he mused.

He wandered slowly to the window, which offered a particularly dismal view of a street junction with the hideous structure of an Earthline station building behind it. Teryn wondered suddenly if Lena might have chosen to hide somewhere in the grimy tunnels and dark spaces of the Earthline or one of the other rail networks. In his view it made more sense than hiding out in a guest house where sooner or later the authorities (in the form of a Finder, in this case) would come calling. Might that also have affected his ability to detect them?

Teryn traced a finger through the thick dust that had gathered on the windowsill. Why was it so dusty in here?

He felt certain that if he did find Lena- not to mention her sister- something dramatic would happen. Something fundamental would change. Already he had seen places, objects and events that didn't behave as they ought. Might finding Lena make things even worse?

What if their meeting destroyed reality itself? What if Elia and Marim had intended this all along- that their daughters, unwittingly aided by him, were to bring down the Citadel, perhaps everything?

Teryn's vision swayed and his legs buckled. He leaned against the windowsill and closed his eyes, and suddenly the brightness in his head became unbearable. Now, at last, he sensed both women, as if they had blinked into existence. They were walking together along a street. They stopped briefly, and then walked in a different direction. No, they were *running* now.

Lena's thread twisted and turned viciously, along with the other- Rhion's- with which it was entwined. Teryn could sense a sudden panic coming from them both.

He saw the Great Power, raging through them both. But he also sensed something else drawing near to the sisters. It looked unlike the threads of anyone else in the Citadel- a concentration of absolute blackness, a complex, writhing mass of hateful energy.

He watched helplessly from his mind's eye as this entity bore down upon the twins.

"No," he whispered.

But it didn't reach them.

Instead, to Teryn's astonishment, the cores of light that belonged to Lena and Rhion winked out of existence altogether.

VII - The War Internal

I

Seneth knew that no broken bodies would await him on the ground below. Rhion and her companion would never reach it. A force he couldn't detect had spirited them both away, denying him his quarry again.

Enraged but exhausted, he walked almost to the edge of the roof, nauseated by the strange currents in the air and the swirling fragments of indeterminate matter- deposits of chaos, he thought, left by the two of them. He knelt and crawled the last few paces- for some reason he no longer trusted his balance- to peer down at the street far below.

"Gone," he whispered. "Where?"

The image of the two women standing together on the edge of the roof, hand in hand, wouldn't leave him. They had been dressed differently, but they looked the same. He had seen enough of their faces to know that.

So, Rhion had a sister. A twin.

Seneth returned slowly to the doorway that led back down from the rooftop. Faint swirls of colour and ever-changing shapes danced in the air. The temperature varied wildly from one moment to the next. *Those two women were part of this,* he decided. *They're part of the unfolding chaos. That's why the Mothers insist on their destruction.*

And he asked himself again- why couldn't the Mothers hunt them down?

Slowly the Voice's head turned, drooped so that his gaze was filled by the sight of his shaking hands. Their veins bulged like the roots of trees and shone like silver threads through the fabric of his skin. The Mothers had given him everything he needed to apprehend and destroy Rhion, and yet she thwarted him at every turn.

The pain coursing through the channels of his body formed a curious symphony with the residues in the air. Seneth felt certain that he ought to understand something of this. How could it be that he comprehended nothing?

He sat, watched and listened as the natural order of things gradually returned. The sun set behind him and the air grew still and cold. "Sooner or later the Mothers will destroy me for my failures," he quietly forecast, and shivered.

Seneth hoped for sudden oblivion but feared that when his end came it would be drawn out and agonising. It might not even be a finite process. He wouldn't be surprised if, when the Mothers eventually chose to be rid of him, they placed him teetering on the brink of whatever cold darkness or bright light or raging fire waited, sent him hurtling into that place and then pulled him back, perhaps as far as the life he had known, only to repeat that terrifying process.

He thirsted for the deaths of Rhion and her sister more than ever as he stared into the gathering dusk, lost in the heat of his hatred. He desired the extinction of the impossible force that compelled them- so much that he could barely resist the urge to get to his feet and run headlong over the rooftop and into whatever netherworld had pulled the women away, to tear the life from them.

But of course, he would simply fall to the ground- and perhaps even survive in some diminished, unspeakable state.

At last he made his way back down the flights of stairs, in almost complete darkness. He tried to console himself. Surely he would be given another chance- he would know when they reappeared.

But for now, that did nothing to lighten his mood. Nothing could. Submitting to his bright and shrieking rage, Seneth punched the concrete wall of the stairwell over and again until a wet, silvery gleam of blood and whatever else polluted his veins burst forth and filled the pungent gloom.

II

Three sat in silence with head bowed. To assist her use of the Great Power and keep her standing as she expended vast effort, her hands pressed against the grand marble columns. Inexplicably, vines, creepers and other growth once unheard of within the palatial halls had sprouted and spread over the stony perfection.

Restless even now, the vegetation entwined itself around the architecture and explored new areas of the vast room. Already it had turned much of the austerely white and grey hall dark.

This was not the first area of the palace where such an intrusion had happened. Other places frequented only by the Mothers had been invaded by a profusion of nature, their shining tiles cracked and forced upwards, their blankly grand plaster walls cracked as roots and tendrils found a way in through the cavities in the cold stone.

These were examples of the Spider's touch, reaching into their domain to remind them of her omnipresence- to warn them, perhaps, of her displeasure at the things they'd done. *Good,* they had all agreed. *Soon she will be more displeased than ever.*

Three's companions waited until she finally stirred. When her eyes flickered open, they looked almost black, and a faint trickle of blood dripped from their corners. As they slowly returned to their natural pale blue, she looked to the others and said quietly, "It's become more difficult to control. Her anger makes it so."

"What did you discover?" One demanded impatiently. "Did he find them? Did they escape?"

"Yes. They jumped to the Halflight again. Our slowdown of his faculties worked. But the other woman, with Rhion..." Three frowned and shook her head. "We ought to have known about her. How did we not? Her name is Lena. She is Rhion's twin sister."

One cursed loudly and struck the nearest column. Across from them, a dark, branch-like object snaked slowly up the face of the wall, loosing pieces of plaster to reveal old stonework beneath.

"This is hardly a problem. They've stirred the Great Power again," Two pointed out. "The disturbance will make the Spider weave new anomalies, and if the two of them are together- surely they're both conduits of the Great Power- matters have become even less predictable."

"How did they meet in a city of many millions?" Three wondered. "What would the chances be?"

"Chances!" One scoffed. "The Spider has a plan. Somewhere amidst the growing chaos is the kernel of a scheme. We must know its nature. Rhion and Lena can only have been the product of union between *two* descendants- who else could step into the Halflight, in a heartbeat?"

"How did they escape our attention for so long?" Three fretted.

"It doesn't matter now." Two leaned against a pillar and folded her arms, a smile upon her face. "All these things point to an awakening. The Spider's vengeance cannot be avoided- in which case, what do we have to fear? Death?!"

III

Seneth was summoned to one of the Mothers that afternoon. He knelt on the black tile and, at her command, told her what had happened when he almost caught Rhion and her sister. Then he listened incredulously as she told him he'd done well so far. *You know otherwise,* he thought. *Why would you say this?*

"Is there anything you wish to say, Seneth?"

"I..." Words failed him. "Majesty, I..."

"Say anything you wish, without fear for your life," she added generously, although that could only be a lie.

"How have I done well, Majesty?" The words tumbled from his mouth. "I've failed you. I almost caught her- and the other woman. Rhion's twin, I believe. She looked very much like her."

"She *is* Rhion's sister. Her name is Lena." The Mother paused for a moment and then continued, "Continue your efforts to find them, Seneth. Their movements, the ripples they cause have a certain signature. In time you will become better able to sense and locate them."

"And when I find them, Majesty? Am I still to destroy Rhion? And her sister?"

She sounded amused. "Yes. If you apprehend them, you may kill them both. Do you have anything else to ask me? Ask anything you like."

That doesn't mean your question won't go unpunished, came a warning whisper in his head. Yet he asked, "How is it that you command me to apprehend these two, when surely with all your great power you could easily do so yourselves?"

A pain gripped him, so precise and terrible that he could do nothing but remain entirely still, speechless. An unseen hand had appeared within his body and caressed and lightly squeezed his heart. "Do you live to serve the Mothers, Seneth? Do you live to follow our commands, with neither hesitation nor doubt?"

The sensation around his heart vanished, allowing him to reply. "Always, Majesty. Always!"

"Then do as you've been told."

"Of course, Majesty. Only they *vanished* from the Citadel, as far as I could..."

"They were taken to another place, certainly. A place we call the Halflight. But that realm is temporary for them. They can't remain there forever any more than people can spend their lives underwater. They will return."

"What if they always elude me, somehow? I have a fear of failing you, Majesty."

"As well you ought. But you can only do your best, Seneth. That's all we've ever asked. You may go now."

He bowed clumsily in his confusion, and almost ran from the room.

Questions whirled in Seneth's mind. The Mother had appeared almost *understanding* of his failure. He had expected nothing less than torture. But she had simply pointed out that he could only *do his best.*

Such mercy, such *reason* was unthinkable.

And why had she said that they were *taken*? To Seneth that implied that some other force was at play, one he didn't yet know about. Certainly he dared not ask about such a thing, if it lay beyond the Mothers' control.

Something was deeply wrong. But he couldn't work out what it might be.

IV

The three women stood around the glass cell and observed their prisoner in silence. Finally, Two said, "He is whole. His remaking is complete."

"Physically, at least," Three concurred. "Something accelerated it, clearly. A reaction to our work- Seneth's remaking. The stirring up of anomalies. Rhion and Lena. Some combination of all those things. It doesn't matter. He sees us now, and he knows us. Oh! The *look* in those eyes!" She paced around the glass cage, agitated, but the prisoner did not follow her movement, neither with his body nor his eyes.

"With luck, he'll still remember how the Spider destroyed his kind," Two remarked.

"The interrogation must begin." One traced a finger along the glass. "We'll need to unmake this material, but he must remain unharmed and held in place." She stared directly at the man in the glass cage. "You wouldn't try to kill us, would you? Perhaps in the hope of your own quick death?" She smiled. "I think you might. But it wouldn't work. You have *no idea* how quickly we regenerate these days. Only the Spider can destroy us, I fear."

The prisoner offered no response, nor did the Mothers expect one.

"I wondered when this day would come," Two remarked. "I always knew it would present a challenge."

276

"Do you think he relishes this as much as we do?" One peered quizzically at their prisoner. "He looks so *calm.*"

"A challenge- I'm almost glad to be alive," Three said. "Do you think *he* is?"

They brought down the temperature of the glass surface so much that frost coated it. Then they delivered a massive, invisible hammer blow to one side to shatter it into thousands of pieces.

But the structure held. Not even the tiniest of cracks appeared anywhere on the barrier.

The Mothers looked incredulously to one another. "Heat, then," One said, and the three together made the surface of the prison cell so hot on one side that it glowed white.

But it wouldn't melt, nor would it yield.

"Impossible," Two fumed, in direct contradiction to their observations.

They tried brute force again, by various methods. They brought to bear a vast pressure over the prison. They attempted to destroy the foundations beneath it, so that the structure might collapse and break, or at least be forced to move, but even that failed, for the area they tried to destroy remained intact no matter their efforts. Many of the methods they tried, had they worked, would have destroyed the precious contents of the glass cell (temporarily, at least) but in their rising fury and panic they gave no thought to that.

Their prisoner, conversely, showed no emotion whatsoever. He made no movement other than the slow rise and fall of his chest and the blinking of his eyelids, nor did his expression change.

When the Mothers finally crept away, defeated but swearing to return with a different approach- "A temporary setback," Three declared without much conviction- they went in separate directions. They could bear one another's company no more than they could tolerate the bitter notion that their irresistible force had met an immovable object.

The Mothers each spent that pensive evening in separate, far-flung places.

One sat on her bed and, armed with a surgeon's scalpel, cut herself in every conceivable place, then watched with a detached stare as her flesh healed in moments and scars faded away. She wondered if their accelerated healing had anything to do with the quickening recovery of their prisoner.

"The webs you weave," she said hatefully to the invisible, omnipresent Spider as she lay over once-white sheets steeped in her blood.

Two stood on a balcony high up in the far north of the palace. Beyond the many thousands of lights that wavered in the near distance lay the endless darkness of places beyond- a swathe of land only she and her two companions knew anything of. As she stared into the far distance some of that detail returned to her.

She absent-mindedly began to recite the names of towns and cities from that long-forgotten realm, rivers and forests, mountain ranges and great lakes, low swamplands and vast, labyrinthine caverns. She wondered what races claimed these as their own now. What stories and superstitions did they have concerning the Citadel? Did they know that the Mothers still ruled here? Might they even harbour notions of conquering it, or had they made their settlements as far away as possible and left the glowing metropolis to an existence even more isolated than its citizens believed?

Three's thoughts were of Rhion and Lena, surely distant descendants of those who had once been comrades of the Mothers. The twins were waking the Spider, and the Spider would see the abominations being created by the Mothers. Soon, her dark rage would engulf everything.

But surely, that universal force would make an end of the three of them before anything else.

I must have faith, Three told herself over and again. *I must believe it will end soon.*

She recalled a dream from several nights ago. She remembered it because she very rarely dreamed now. Rhion had been in that dream with her. Three had never set eyes upon the woman herself- she knew only what Rhion's *presence* looked like- but she felt certain that it had been her, that they had, inexplicably, shared a dream without knowing at the time.

I was different, she remembered.

She had been a version of herself from a very long time ago, or perhaps even the distant future. Either or both could be true. Didn't everything turn again, eventually?

She listened to the crackling of coal on her fire, and wondered if, when at last she and her two companions were utterly consumed, she would see all the stars of the universe, like she had in her dream, or a tunnel of joyous, thunderous light- or the eternally patient abyss.

V

Wake, half-man.

Seneth's eyes flickered open. In his dream, someone had stood by his bedside and mocked him. They had opened him up and shown him his insides, which bore little resemblance to human innards - objects with which he had long been intimately familiar. Then they had put everything back together but incorrectly, causing a wave of complications which he'd somehow survived.

"Good. You heard me. But we don't have a lot of time."

He looked to his left and saw a man standing in the gloom, blond-haired and grey-eyed, neither young nor old. "I *know* you," he said, nevertheless filled with disbelief. The prisoner's face and skull were whole. His reconstruction appeared complete.

"Of course you do." The figure stepped a little nearer, as pale and naked as Seneth himself. "You've been asking me the same questions every morning for years. I don't know which of us found that task more tedious."

The Voice got out of bed and looked for his clothes, but he couldn't find them. "You're not where you believe you are," his companion explained. "And so, things aren't going to be where you expect them. You're dreaming. How could I have escaped?"

Seneth went to the window and looked out over the Citadel's scrambled, jagged skyline. "Something is wrong," he reported. "Some of the buildings look different. There are no lights. Only moonlight. No, it's something else..." He turned to his companion again. "Who are you? Do you have a name?"

"Daniel."

"And why did the Mothers imprison you, Daniel?"

"This isn't about me. It's all about you, Seneth. You do the work of the Mothers - doesn't everyone in this place? - and yet you're nothing but a plaything sent into the mire to stir up the darkness."

"And *you...* you're my version of you. This isn't the first time. You've appeared before."

"It may be better for you to think of it that way. As you've seen, the lights are out and the sky looks different. I'm here to open your eyes to the truth."

"Truth," Seneth said flatly. He had seen glimmers of ghostly light out in the Citadel's depths, but their colour and movement disturbed him, and he looked away.

"You're the beginning of the end, my Lord Voice. At least, they hope you're the beginning of *their* end. And yet, right now, you're dreaming of the place they call the Halflight. The Mothers don't even know it. If they knew that you even *could*, they'd have destroyed you long ago. Certainly they wouldn't have done to you the things they did..."

"Wait. What did the Mothers do to me?"

"They combined your organic structure with an ancient, highly advanced technology. The Mothers have hidden the truth of what happened when this technology was last unleashed. They have almost entirely suppressed the past."

Trickery, Seneth decided. How could this man know the Mothers' motivations, their actions over so many centuries?

And yet, if the prisoner had telepathic capabilities, might he also harbour other powers, including the ability to explore the entire Palace and even beyond, from the confines of his cell?

Enough, Seneth told himself. *I'm dreaming. In a dream, nothing matters. When I wake, the dream dies.*

He looked through the window again and saw cold light gleaming on the cobbles of distant streets as rain poured down. Every one of Seneth's senses became amplified as he observed elements of the Citadel, near and far. The downpour made blurred silvery patterns on the flagstones, each one different. Here and there, lights appeared and were then doused. He knew the precise distance to each one of them.

But he looked internally as well, and visualised miraculous changes at a cellular level, a world that he alone had the power to witness.

I see it all now, Seneth reminded himself. *Something even the Mothers cannot glimpse.*

"There are two women I need to kill," he said suddenly.

The intense look in Daniel's eyes told Seneth that he knew exactly who he meant.

"Rhion has evaded me twice now. There's something inside her- and perhaps her sister- I don't know what it is. I sensed it on the rooftop... you won't know what I mean, but..."

"Confusing, isn't it? But I'll help you remember."

That didn't sound right. "Why would you help me? I'm a servant of the Mothers, who've held you captive for... I don't know how long." Seneth laughed. "Why would you make sense, anyway? I'm dreaming of you. Your words are coming from my mind. One part of me is talking to another part."

"*Yes*, Seneth. That's a more succinct and accurate summary than you know. Think of it as me helping *you* to unlock a room inside your head, if you like."

"Why would you help me?" Seneth repeated. "No, I mean- why would I *dream* of you helping me?"

Daniel walked over to the window to stand next to him. "Listen- and listen well. You've seen enough impossible things to have no excuse not to open your mind.

"The Mothers have ruled the Citadel, the place they call the last bastion of civilisation, for over a thousand years. The Citadel is, apparently, a guard against the inexplicable dangers outside the perimeters of reason and sense and safety. A sanctuary. Those who live within its walls are the luckiest people alive. Probably the *only* people alive. You know the doctrine as well as anyone.

"This is what happened, Seneth. What the Mothers did, changed you. *Improved* you, they would say. But you're just the start. They may soon seek to repeat the experiment over and over, in the hope of achieving a better result each time."

"So they'll make others like me? There has only ever been one Voice of the Citadel. When have they ever needed more than one?"

"No, you're missing the point. They don't care about the position of Voice any more than they care about the continued working order of the Citadel. You're nothing more than the start of a new journey- one that they hope results in a vast and terrible reaction. But therein lies the greatest danger. They're attempting to control and shape technology that they will ultimately lose control of. In fact, they *want* to lose control of it. They want it to bring the world into untold chaos. Even their predecessors would never have wanted that. And that is why there *must* and *will* be a reaction."

"What technology? Where did it come from?"

"A world that was already long gone before the Mothers were even born. Worlds come and go but ideas and possibilities remain. It's always the same. An infection is carried with this technology, entwined with its nature. A darkness. It matches the void that people carry within them. It's greater in some than in others." He stared meaningfully at Seneth. "It matched *you.* It fitted."

"But there is something else about you. It lies dormant, but you're a descendent of those who once defended this world. Comrades of the Mothers themselves, people who the Mothers now call the Forgotten. Rhion and Lena are also like you in that regard. And yet you're also a fusion of flesh and machine. One of a kind. This was not meant to be- and it will be rectified."

Seneth recalled the voice from the void- mechanical, utterly cold, ageless, the sum of all things and the absence of everything. He imagined a whispered promise drifting through his head- *I'll wait forever for you.*

Perhaps Daniel knew what he thought, because his companion leaned forward, eyes intent. "I won't let it take you," he said quietly.

Seneth had no idea what to say to that. How could Daniel protect him against something as omnipotent, as all-pervading as the abyss?

"When this virulent technology is stirred into action," Daniel continued, "the world fights it. The river of the Great Power flows more quickly, to put it another way, and overflows into the waking world. The two are fundamentally opposed. And that brings me to the Mothers and their scheme to bring about this collision- for I've listened to their rage against eternity for centuries.

"You see, my Lord Voice, those immortal creatures you serve crave only their own downfall. They dream of the world stirring itself into a rage of chaos so complete that it destroys them."

"Why?"

"Because they believe it's the only way they can be sure of dying."

"Rhion and Lena seem to *create* chaos," Seneth said finally. "Whenever I've drawn close to Rhion, something unusual has happened‑ in the air, or the water... the Mothers would want this to continue, wouldn't they? And that being so, why would they then task me with finding and killing Rhion and her sister?"

"Because, my Lord Voice, when you're close to them the barriers between the inner and outer worlds become more porous than ever. The Mothers *don't* want you to kill the twins. They want you to continue attempting to kill them, but to fail each time."

"But how would they..."

"They make certain that you will never be *quite* able to reach those women. They're able to manipulate you in ways that you can't even begin to imagine. But regardless of that, I don't believe that you‑ arch‑murderer though you are‑ have the capacity to kill them. There's something about Rhion and Lena, isn't there? Something intensely familiar."

Seneth said nothing, but his thoughts were still full of Rhion and his vain struggle to reach her in the river.

"If the Mothers meet their end in the way they want, everyone and everything else will end. That's no good for either of us, you'll agree. If, however, we find a way to destroy those women without the world erupting into mayhem as the skin between realities melts away‑ well, disaster is averted, and the Citadel becomes yours."

"Mine?"

"You do the work of the Mothers, with whom no one else ever has direct audience. No Voice survives beyond the end of their tenure for that simple reason‑

the Mothers cannot have a living man or woman able to describe them, spill secrets, make them smaller than the myth. Anyway· the Mothers don't have to *exist* for you to take orders from them, if you see what I mean."

Seneth laughed. "This is insanity. We can't destroy them. They're immortal. Even if it were possible..." The Voice could scarcely believe he was uttering these words. "...how could *we* do it?"

"You do yourself a disservice." Daniel's eyes searched his. Seneth shuddered under that scrutiny. "What if I told you that you could do the things that Rhion and Lena can do? What if I told you that, no matter what you may think, you are like them? Why else did you feel that intense affinity when you were with or near Rhion?"

"I would have killed her if I could."

"Would you? I think not."

"Nonsense," Seneth said, sitting back. "This whole dream is nonsense," he added for good measure.

"Give me your hand."

When Seneth did not, Daniel simply smiled. "Humour me."

Cautiously the Voice extended his hand. When Daniel held it between both of his, a jolt like electricity went through him. He opened his mouth to demand an explanation, but Daniel spoke first. "The elementary force known by some as the Great Power· it was taken from you when you were twelve. You'd all but destroyed that memory, hadn't you? Or it was made to gradually fade from you. Only fragments remain."

Seneth felt as if all the blood had drained from him. He stared back at his companion, open-mouthed. "How... how could you... I'd forgotten..."

And he *had* forgotten· he'd forgotten all but a few faint images, but now his memory of the day when his *secret magic* as he called it had been crushed to oblivion, flooded swiftly back.

"Please," he said, horrified at the sound of his own voice, which had instantly become that of a young boy. "Please don't make me go back."

"But you must go back, Seneth. You can't take a meaningful step forward until you've been back." Daniel's grip on his hand intensified˗ and the world exploded into fragments of colour and darkness.

The Pig was the undisputed head of the family, a patriarch with absolute power. Seneth lived in absolute fear of him, as did the fourteen others in the group. Some of them were children of the Pig, and the four youngest ones were both siblings and nieces or nephews. The Pig spread his seed far and wide. One of the most vivid images that Seneth recalled was of the Pig's daughter Amara, giving birth at the age of twelve, screaming as she was held down on the mattress in the back room. That room was even called the birthing room, amongst other things. As soon as a female in the group was able to become pregnant, inevitably she would˗ usually within a month or two. The Pig's main purpose in life˗ aside from the family business of smuggling and racketeering˗ was procreation, although many of the sickly infants he helped produce died after a matter of days, either from complications arising from the incest that created them, or occasionally from the Pig's lust. He would force himself upon any of his children, no matter their age. The back garden had grown full and rich from the sustenance of a dozen or more small bodies.

Seneth lived in that house not because he was the Pig's son˗ he wasn't˗ but because he was the son of a woman who lived there.

Nayen had been a prostitute. Seduced by the promise of a better life than the streets and the likelihood of murder- after all, most whores eventually met a client who went too far- she had been brought into the household. She had a talent for card and dice games, which was a subtle use of the Great Power. "You can't tell anyone about it," she had told him many times. "If you do, I'll be arrested or taken somewhere else and you'll be on your own. Here. And if you reveal anything of your own... talent, well..."

That threat alone was more than enough to ensure that Seneth kept his mouth shut. His own secret magic was a quiet thing of subterfuge and trickery- much like his mother's- but it had grown more difficult to control over the years.

Nayen observed his continued and increasing struggle, and grew fretful, worried that the Pig would somehow correctly interpret Seneth's erratic behaviour, although he knew nothing of the Great Power's existence.

Almost all the money she made from games of chance in various places around the neighbourhood was handed over to the Pig in return for Nayen and Seneth having a roof over their heads and enough to eat. Over time the Pig demanded that she game more and more, no matter her timid attempts to warn him that she risked being found out.

One day, when Seneth was twelve, the Pig came to the squalid room that they shared. Seneth felt the man's stare on him and tried to look away from the oversized creature with the great flat forehead, the wide-set eyes, the upturned and broken nose. The whole house stank, of course- mildew and dampness penetrated every corner of the sorry structure- but the

Pig's stench was unbearable, and Seneth's sense of smell was exceptional.

"*Think it's time we looked at our arrangement,*" the Pig said. His voice always sounded muddy and dense, as if the words he spoke bubbled up through some dark, thick fluid.

"*I can do a little more work,*" Nayen told him, "*but I need to be careful...*"

"*Not talking about more work.*"

Seneth felt a prickling sensation wash over him. He didn't need to look to know that the Pig's stare was still fixed on him, not on his mother.

"*I don't understand. I already give you all the money I make.*"

"*Your boy. I don't want him sleeping with you anymore. He'll sleep with me.*"

Seneth's heart jumped and he stared open-mouthed at both in turn.

Nayen shook her head. "*He's not yours.*" She appeared calm, but her voice trembled.

"*Doesn't matter. My house, I say what's mine. You want to be difficult about this, I break all your fingers, so you never hold anything in your hands again...*"

"*You can take me,*" she said, and a low, deep laugh emanated from the Pig's fetid mouth. "*Wanted you, I would've taken you already. Don't touch whores.*"

"*Mother,*" Seneth whispered desperately. They could leave, couldn't they? They didn't have to stay here. Surely they could find somewhere else? They'd lived in other places from time to time- none of them pleasant, but anything would be better than this.

"*He's not yours,*" Nayen repeated.

The Pig's fist slammed into her jaw with such force that she was sent flying backwards into the side of the bed. Blood spattered the floor. Seneth looked in horror at the broken mess that her lower face had become as she struggled to sit up.

"*I'll do it again and again,*" rumbled the Pig. "*I'll smash your face to pieces. Won't look like a face when I'm done. Just meat.*"

Nayen uttered a faint, keening sound which could have meant anything.

The Pig motioned for Seneth to come with him. The boy took one last look at his mother. "*Don't be like her,*" the Pig warned. "*Do as you're told and you stay pretty.*"

For perhaps a month or more, Seneth endured the Pig's attentions, sometimes more than once a day. Each time he would return to the room he shared with his mother and she would put her arm around him. They would sit together for a long time, saying nothing.

Her jaw healed eventually- Nayen had a sturdy constitution that belied her slight frame- although she had lost several teeth. Even the enhanced healing ability gifted by the Great Power couldn't restore those.

But slowly the determined look that Seneth was used to seeing in her eyes was replaced by a dull, lifeless glaze.

Then one day Nayen said quietly to him, "*I'm going to set you free.*"

He looked questioningly at her.

"*Listen to me and say nothing. Only listen. He may already suspect that you have unusual powers...*"

"*I thought he didn't know about...*"

"*He doesn't know what it is, but he thinks there's something odd about us. If only we could use it to protect ourselves from men like that- but no, we can't. The Great Power is a curse, Seneth. It's brought the two of us nothing but ruin.*"

290

"*So, I'll set you free from it‐ I can do that‐ and then you must go your own way. When you're next sent out on an errand, don't come back. Do you hear me? Don't come back.*"

He shook his head, astonished. "*But you must come too. We both have to escape...*"

"*Seneth, if we both try to escape, he will come after us. He needs me. And if he finds us, our punishments...*" She wouldn't complete the sentence. "*You need to promise me, Seneth. At your next opportunity, you get as far from here as you possibly can. And you never, ever come back. Promise me.*"

He couldn't speak.

"*Promise me!*" Had he ever seen such desperation in her eyes? Suddenly, she looked alive again.

"*I promise.*" He could barely whisper the words.

"*And now I have to do something else for which you'll never forgive me,*" she said, grasping his wrist. "*I have to set you free, so that he can never use me to find you. We will no longer be linked, Seneth.*"

He had no time to ask what she meant before every part of his body began to crawl with a terrifying sensation. It felt as if his skin and even his flesh was being slowly lifted from him, one part separated from another. He was being ripped apart from himself.

He couldn't cry out. He couldn't even move.

When the ordeal was finally over, Nayen laid him down on the bed and stared sorrowfully at his exhausted, depleted form. "*Rest,*" was all she said.

Seneth slept for a few hours, and when he woke later, the lantern light had grown dim and his mother was nowhere to be seen. She had probably gone to one of the taverns or gaming halls to work the tables.

The Great Power was no longer inside him.

The sheer emptiness and despair he felt was overwhelming. The one thing that had made him feel alive, had made him almost believe that life was worth living, had been taken from him, either destroyed or taken to some other place. All that remained now was a gaping hole, as if his entire existence had been drained free of all colour, all hope.

His mother had told him to leave and never come back. Not only that, but she had ripped the Great Power from him. How had she managed to do that?

He wept. He screamed. Hours passed.

Nayen returned much later. She said nothing to him as she lay down, exhausted, and eventually drifted off to sleep. Seneth stared at her, still disbelieving.

After a while one of the Pig's children came with a message. Seneth was to go to an address in Whitetower Chimneys, an industrial area not far away, to pick up some packages. "You're to go now," she said, "and take them straight to my father."

Seneth walked outside minutes later and breathed in the cold night air.

Never return, he thought.

He made his way to the end of the road. From there he took the turning that led directly away from his destination. He continued, through the night and for many hours. At first light he was still walking, his feet raw. He hoped for nothing. But he kept moving.

One day, he swore to himself, he would no longer be powerless. He would rely on no one. He would have his revenge, whatever it took.

He would fill the void.

Seneth's eyes flickered open. Daniel sat across from him at the table. A force that he knew intimately coursed and surged through him. He could only sigh as that familiar energy filled him, unlocked from the tiny kernel that had stayed hidden, unseen and undetected for over thirty years.

"She couldn't destroy it," Daniel explained softly. "It *cannot* be destroyed. She simply reduced it in scale, so much so that even *you* believed it had disappeared. But it protected itself."

Seneth pulled his hand away. Daniel's eyes had changed colour, he thought, but he had no idea what colour they now were. They had become brighter. Something lurked behind them, a primal force that mirrored his own rediscovered power.

"You're not him. You're not Daniel," Seneth managed to say eventually. "What are you?"

It smiled. "Does it matter what I am? After all, you're dreaming."

VII

Seneth woke suddenly.

Nothing from his dream faded as he got up, dressed and looked outside over the Citadel. Instead the details grew sharper with each passing moment.

"It can't be," he murmured, as the revelations concerning the Mothers flooded through his mind.

"No," he added a moment later, as he felt the Great Power within him, a quiet potential, sleeping but ready to wake, potent and alive. How had that happened? How had it been restored as he slept? He stood still, open-mouthed in sheer astonishment at the sensation of the quiet river‐ the secret magic. He'd forgotten so much about how it felt, but as each moment passed, he remembered more.

Inevitably, Seneth's thoughts turned to fear of discovery by the Mothers. They would surely be able to detect the Great Power in him.

The rigid control that had always marked his adult life evaporated in an instant.

Seneth panicked and fled.

He ran to the north of the Palace, and down to the lowest levels. He rushed along abandoned corridors, through empty rooms where the dust lay thick and on, further and deeper, consumed by fear. He did not tire. The technology that had spread to every part of his body carried him quickly and almost effortlessly through the distant warrens of the Palace. At the same time the Great Power seethed and roiled through him, like a caged creature demanding to be set free- but he had no idea how to do that.

He'd forgotten how to use it.

Finally he reached a bricked-up wall at the end of a tunnel, and when he turned to head back to the last turning he'd taken, Seneth saw the Mothers appear at the mouth of the passageway.

Instinctively he collapsed to his knees and began to beg them for mercy, desperate for them to listen to his hurried explanation. He had to tell them that none of this was his fault. Somehow, he had unlocked his latent power through a dream, but he would not use it- no, he would never use it!

When it became obvious that no mercy would be granted, he tried instead to summon the Great Power. He had managed to many years ago, as a child. It had come easily to him, then- almost as simple as moving or speaking. Surely it would protect him. What use could it have if it didn't?

But nothing happened, and the Mothers reached him, impassive and wordless.

A searing pain crashed through his skull, and Seneth's world went black.

"How has this happened?" One demanded. "Seneth is more machine than man." In an act of sudden fury, she hurled her glass across the hall. It shattered on the tiled marble floor, the violence casting fragments far and wide. Sunlight poured through one of the windows for a moment and the shards glimmered in the sudden brilliance.

"Clearly he is a descendant. But his nature had been hidden‐ perhaps the Spider hid it, just as she must have restored or enhanced the same." Two began to pace around the hall. Her boots made harsh, almost whip‐like sounds against the tiles until they crunched on the broken glass. "What is her plan?!" she demanded, and stopped suddenly, trembling with cold rage.

"She reached into Seneth as he dreamed. Whatever power he had was too small even for us to detect‐ and yet from that atom she has made something much greater. Why?" One considered the matter at length. "But the fool has no idea how to use it. Did you see how he tried to, in his desperation, when he realised that we'd give him no mercy?"

"Why does he mean so much to her?" Three slumped forward in her chair, perhaps exhausted‐ but the others paid her no mind.

One pondered the matter. "We no longer need to pursue the twins. We have a more direct route. If our loyal servant is a descendant of the Forgotten, then with enough coercion, perhaps he can generate enough mayhem himself‐ with our... assistance."

Two smiled. "You mean torture him."

"What better way to stir her displeasure‐ if he's one of *hers*?" One argued. "Perhaps we should have done the same to the twins- if they hadn't been so difficult to find."

"Retribution will be swift," Three said with a shudder.

"Yes. She will tear us apart. Our annihilation will be total. And it will come far more quickly than it would were we to persist with hounding Rhion and her sister to stir the outer world into chaos. If the end can come sooner, then let it be sooner."

"We must do this as soon as possible," Two declared. "What if, in time, his dim power grows? What if he becomes able to reach the Halflight? Rhion and Lena seem to have discovered how to, after all."

"Precisely. We submit him to processing again- mix the hybrid further, or better yet, invoke the Great Power- then the fabric will burst, the wall will melt away. The Spider will come. We'll take him apart, slowly, in the most imaginative way possible- and wait for her wrath to crash over us."

The Mothers' eagerness for oblivion became a blind panic. They rushed to the prison room where they had placed Seneth, bound in unbreakable chains, and took him to one of the processing rooms. His fear mounted as they approached- he even had the temerity to beg not to be returned to that area. "The process disturbed him greatly," One observed as their highest servant was cast into the chamber and held in place. "He saw many things during his first transformation. Things that we've never seen, perhaps. What were they, Seneth? What revelations came to you?"

"Majesty, I beg you..."

Two shook her head in disgust. "Don't beg! We can't let you go. You should know that by now."

One stepped closer to the Voice, fascinated, eager to understand a glimmer of the things he must have seen. "What frightened you so, during that process?" she asked softly.

VIII

The abyss yawned before him in his mind's eye, unutterably vast. He could not frame the words to describe this immense, pitiless *absence* of hope and light.

"Well, it doesn't matter." The Mother's stony expression did not change. "Perhaps you'll experience it all over again."

Seneth stood strapped into the rusted apparatus, but the Mothers didn't energise the dreadful machinery that had inflicted such agony on him before. They regarded him in silence. "That it may come down to this moment," one of them remarked. "How will she react to the dismantling of a prize pawn?"

To his own surprise, the Voice found steel from some inner reserve. "I have always been your loyal servant. Why do this to me?"

"But Seneth, you don't *know* what we're doing," another replied. She smiled and then the expression grew instantly cold before it transformed once again into a grin of delight. *She is mad,* he thought distantly as cold ice curled up inside him. *They are all mad. But you always knew that, didn't you?*

"He deserves to know," another of the women said. Seneth had never seen the three of them as closely as this before. They had always appeared in the distance or in shadow, in the palatial halls. The one who had spoken looked younger than the other two, he thought- which didn't make sense as all three of them had an ageless look to them. But she didn't share the triumphant, almost gleeful look of the other two women. Why not?

"Please," he said, addressing her directly. "Please tell me what I've done to displease you."

"Nothing," she said, and looked away.

The third woman then addressed him, impatient and dismissive. Dark-skinned and orange-eyed, she had a look of almost desperate cruelty about her. "You're a means to an end. We don't have time to produce a hundred others like you and hope the ensuing chaos is enough. We no longer *need* to. We're taking a short cut, Seneth- and you're the path."

I don't understand, he almost said- but then he recalled words from his dream, spoken by whatever had taken the shape of the Mothers' prisoner. The Great Power seethed quietly inside him- placid, useless, just as it had been during his childhood. Why had it been restored at all?

"You want to die," he whispered. "You think that killing me will destroy *you.*"

"Killing? Perhaps. But it's a matter of process more than result. It seems that you were always special, Seneth- even before we changed you. The force that *made* you special had remained dormant for so long... but the Spider clearly wants you for something." She regarded him for a moment longer. "How was it subdued for so long? Ah." She looked more closely. "Family? A few did possess that rare power to diminish it in another of the same blood."

I will set you free, and then you must make your own way.

"It doesn't matter now," he whispered.

She smiled. "Now we'll see what value you have to the Spider. As for what *you* will see..."

They gave vent to the Great Power, their hands linked together. They loathed one another's touch, but the ecstasy and bitterness of the primal force they hadn't dared to use more than tiny droplets of for so long overcame that animosity.

The three forms around Seneth glowed with a light so fierce he feared it would peel his skin and melt his innards. Even amidst his fear he imagined what he might look like as the radiation revealed them.

Then the agony hit.

Every nerve, every blood vessel, every tiny thread of the alien technology that had become part of him turned and twisted in violent reaction to the Great Power. Sharp pins slowly forced their way outwards through his flesh. Liquid dripped down his body, along with something else- parts of his augmented interior that were being slowly expelled, bursting from him with agonising slowness. Seneth's ragged shrieks filled the room, but soon he no longer heard himself.

His sight deteriorated, shot through with flashes of intense colour and intricate patterns. Low, deep roars and rumbles echoed around him. Had he the strength and the freedom he would have reached out and seized his tormentors, ripped the meat from their bones.

Soon he stared through a red film, vaguely aware that he stood in a pool of his slowly coagulating blood. When his head dropped, he saw a silvery sheen on the floor. It moved like a live thing, and although it was no longer attached to his body, savage pain swirled inside him as it shifted through the gloom.

Still connected, he thought numbly, and then his vision faded to a curtain of deeper, darker red as the Mothers resumed their torture.

Over time he felt himself slowly fall, disconnected from his body. He looked up through darkness and saw his physical form turn and twist, racked with agony as the Mothers' merciless onslaught continued. But as he fell, Seneth's pain eased. He became an exhausted observer, as the scene played out above him like a grand canopy painted in a night sky. The room where the Mothers tortured him begin to change. Walls shifted, and holes opened in the floor and the ceiling. Items in the room developed the properties of viscous liquids. Those that were nearest to his body appeared most distended, as if the very fact of his torture pulled at their nature.

He heard faint shrieks of delight. The Mothers were, perhaps, within reach of their objective.

Then Seneth sensed an enormous, universal presence as he floated, bodiless in the dark. He recognised it. He knew it intimately.

It belonged inside him. It belonged everywhere.

COME TO ME, it whispered.

But then another entity responded. *He is mine.*

The vast, cold blackness of the void responded with implacable, icy rage. I AM UNIVERSAL. I AM THE END OF ALL THINGS. THIS CREATURE BELONGS TO ME.

This one is mine for all time, came the reply of the other. The words floated through him, calm but imbued with absolute authority. Seneth listened in astonishment as the void responded only with wordless fury. It writhed and shrieked its hatred but could do no more than that- as if the abyss had been presented with irrefutable logic than even *it* could not deny.

Seneth remained encompassed in gloom and absolute silence, held in a place that was nowhere. He imagined that his constituent parts had now spread over an impossible distance. Perhaps the Mothers and even the entire Citadel had been obliterated now, twisted beyond recognition.

Am I dying at last? he wondered. But no answer came.

One stared in bewilderment at the space which only a moment ago had been occupied by Seneth's tortured form. The straps and chains hung slackly from the wall and glistened with the leavings from his torture.

The anomalies that had appeared around the Mothers slowly faded. Reality had been twisted to almost unrecognisable extremes, but now normal shapes seeped back and familiar structures snapped into place once more.

The three women stood in mute disbelief as the tide of chaos receded. In a short while they occupied an entirely ordinary, dusty chamber in the palace catacombs. The world they yearned to leave forever hardened around them. Their hope had disappeared, winked out of existence.

"How?!" One screamed. She beat her fists against the wall until they were broken and bleeding. As they healed, she sagged to the floor and uttered a low sob.

Two looked across at her. "He couldn't have shifted on his own- not in such pain. Could he?"

"He was helped," Three said quietly.

"By *what*? By *her*?"

"What else?" Three turned furiously to the others. "Have you not even *considered* the idea that she might somehow *know*- on some base level- our desperate desire for oblivion? That she works actively against every step we take towards it? That's the grand *plan* that we've long suspected."

"Either we go after the twins ourselves, into the Halflight- or we prepare for eternity," she spat, and left them to their own despair.

IX

His baking hot body pressed against savagely cold stone.

Seneth couldn't tell if he lay on top of the surface or had become adhered to its underneath with a yawning chasm below him, or if he clung to the side of an icy cliff.

He remained still as his head spun and a residual force tugged him one way and then another. He drew breath after ragged breath. Finally, he summoned the strength to raise his head.

He lay in an ancient building of massive grey stones and ornate pillars, vast wooden beams and panes of intricate painted glass through which dim but persistent light poured. The air felt bitterly cold one moment and oppressively warm the next. To his left, the light was green hued, and to his right the illumination held a silvery tinge. Where the colours met, there was only shadow, and he looked out from that gloom.

The Voice sat up and looked down at himself as his body cooled. The physical signs of the torture that the Mothers had inflicted upon him had, if anything, worsened- and as the memory of that torture loomed large in his thoughts, Seneth heard a distant roar and felt the ghost of that agony stir.

This place bore no resemblance to any building that he knew of in the Citadel. The painted windows depicted people and events that meant nothing to him.

"What are you?" the Voice murmured. "What do you want with me?"

He stood, swaying. A large door stood on the side of the building to his left. He went over to it and pushed against the surface. After a moment it yielded and swung slowly open.

Before him and to his left and right an arid, rocky landscape stretched away. Above, so many stars filled the sky that their points of light almost drowned out the patches of darkness between them.

"Where am I?"

When Seneth closed his eyes the way before him glowed in his head with a pure white brilliance. He visualised a further sequence of paths beyond that snaked across the alien landscape, all of them lit up as if a fire glowed beneath the ground. A way to somewhere was being mapped out for him and the route burned into his mind.

He opened his eyes. He tried to tell himself that this- like so much else he'd encountered recently- was an elaborate trick, a lure.

And yet he couldn't imagine that it would be worse than what he'd already escaped.

"Can they reach me here?" he murmured at one point. He stood uneasily in the eternal dusk for a moment, to see if sudden, savage punishment came. But the earth didn't subside. No lightning bolt struck improbably from the clear sky to turn his insides black.

Seneth set off along the track. When he looked down at the ground it glowed faintly, as if with a residue from the bright glow he'd seen in his head.

The deep silence unnerved him. Here the only noises to be heard were those he made himself. Maybe this was the Halflight that the creature in his dream had spoken of.

The Voice set off across the dark desert. He had, after all, no other way to decide what direction to follow, in a world he knew nothing about. The path scythed through this darkness like a narrow strip of land with a chasm to either side.

Here and there the remains of lonely, petrified trees bent acutely towards some distant point at the end of the path as if they pointed the way. A light breeze had stirred, and it flowed past him down the narrow path. It pushed gently at his back as if gently cajoling him to make haste towards his unknown destination.

Faint cracking noises sounded from the surrounding gloom, as if parts of this world were being stretched to breaking point by the strange pull of whatever ushered him forward.

His body began to fight itself. The technology that the Mothers had weaved into him rippled and moved. It coiled and lashed out against the Great Power, and Seneth moved back and forth, up and down, a ragdoll over which two opposing powers fought with increasing fury. His sight melted away and was remade over and over. The wind howled, desperate to cast him into the unknown gloom beyond the path. But the technological infestation railed against it with increasing rage- which Seneth, even in his bewildered horror knew that should not be the case.

How could a work of miniscule engineering feel rage at all?

Even with his eyes tightly closed the Voice could see the world around him begin to change. He was being carried, taken deeper into the Halflight, a slave to antagonistic forces that threatened to tear him apart.

Dark, fleeting patches appeared on the earthen trail, as if those areas were under the cover of a deeper night. They moved, in the manner of shadows cast by objects somewhere above. But when Seneth looked up he saw only the half-lit sky.

The shadows rose into the air in front of him and danced like black flames. The Voice shrank back in fear but could not look away. Something invisible but possessed of terrible power held his head in place. He could not close his eyes.

Seneth involuntarily wept with fear, and when he wiped at the tears that streamed down his cheeks, he saw that something darker than water stained his hands. "I'm dying," he croaked. But then, wasn't he already in hell?

Seneth's environment melted. Everything became unbearably bright, as if an unseen sun bore down upon the world, but at the same time the shadows expanded to fill his view, so that he was surrounded by scorching brilliance and infinite darkness at the same time.

He toppled forwards. He imagined that the ground had softened so that his hands and knees sank gently into the cold, dark morass beneath. In his mind's eye he saw a writhing mass of strange horrors burrow through the earth towards his pale and helpless flesh. Some had complex forms he couldn't describe. Others existed in continuous flux, fluid in nature but united in their utter determination to feast upon him.

You mustn't fear the cycle, he thought a voice whispered, but terror had already consumed him.

Finally, as Seneth lay in subservience to his torment, he felt a faint but undeniable presence, like tiny concentrations of faint light, somewhere across the vastness of the unknown landscape.

He stared sideways as his face was pressed against the mud, although his sight had become bordered with a filmy redness. The bitterness of blood and earth filled his mouth.

The pain ebbed sufficiently for him to raise his head at last.

The Voice lay alone in a barren desert, still shuddering as forces fought for control inside him.

"Why?" he croaked at last.

But he knew no answer would be given.

VIII – Liquid Darkness

I

"Rhion? Where are you?"

Lena sat up. She could see nothing around her.

"Rhion?" Lena called out again. Fear rose swiftly as she heard the tremble in her voice. "Can you hear me? Are you there?" Tentatively she put her hands down at her sides and felt soft grass.

"Here," came a murmur from somewhere to her left. Lena reached out blindly and after a moment she felt the ground slope gradually away. She inched her way carefully down the incline.

"Down here." Rhion's voice sounded closer this time, but Lena still flinched and cried out when she reached out again and touched Rhion's arm. "Where are we?" she whispered as the shock subsided.

"Where do you think?" came her sister's reply, perhaps mocking her, although Lena heard a tremor in Rhion's voice not unlike her own.

"I can't see you. I can't see *anything*."

Rhion's hand found hers and held tight. "*Now* do you believe me?"

The memory of their fall from the rooftop came rushing back to Lena, so powerfully that for a moment she felt as if she was falling again. "You couldn't possibly have known..."

"I *did* know. I told you. I wouldn't have killed us both."

"This is all a mad dream," Lena whispered.

"Well, whatever it is- we're here."

The twins sat in silence. Over time, outlines and shapes emerged around them, and stars appeared in the sky. But as the light strengthened, a landscape appeared that Lena had never seen anything like before.

Then she realised she *had*, in dreams, most of them from her childhood. All those dreams, no matter how different, had occupied this common terrain and were related to one another by it. The silent, twilit world that came into view was simultaneously alien and familiar- a patchwork from her subconscious.

The grassy ground sloped away before them. It extended for many thousands of steps into the interminable distance, a gentle downward curve that revealed mysterious features wherever she looked.

She had run through some of the enclosed areas of grass- *fields,* Lena thought as the word came to her- in her sleep. She had sat by the silvery rivers that snaked through the vast wilderness. She had followed winding paths through distant woodlands. She had even seen other cities from a distance, their complex shapes and multitude of lights like beacons of hope and dread.

"The Halflight," she murmured.

"Look behind you," Rhion said. Lena turned, noting how clearly she could now see her sister. They sat with their backs to the edge of a woodland. Tall trees reached towards the sky, silhouettes against the bright heavens. Nearer the ground, the darkness was almost total. A path led from where Lena and Rhion sat, directly into the mass of trees.

"What do you suppose is in there?" Rhion asked. Something in her sister's voice made Lena think that Rhion already knew or thought she did. Lena opened her mouth to reply when a faint sound of material cracking- perhaps the wood of the trees being pulled or stretched- came from somewhere in the forest.

Paths being made and unmade, Lena thought, as she recalled her dream of the vast forest and the house in the middle. Here, everything was in flux. Liquid masqueraded as solid- and things that ought not move, could. New possibilities emerged.

"I think we should get away from here," she said.

"You're probably right," Rhion admitted. "But I think we *need* to do the opposite."

Somewhere in the thickness of the trees, Lena heard something that might have been a vast sigh, the sound of centuries of regret. A picture bloomed in her head, so clear that she saw every tiny detail. "The *house*," she said. "The house is in the middle."

"The house?"

"From the dream I told you about. A dream I've had several times."

Rhion gave her a thoughtful look. "What do you suppose happens if we find this house of yours?"

Lena blinked in sudden shock. *This house of yours.* The words circled in her head.

"That's it, Rhion. It *isn't* just mine. It belongs to us both." She paused, agitated. "Something happened to the version of it in the... the world we know. It belonged to our ancestors, many centuries ago. But... some force visited them. They had powerful enemies."

"The Mothers."

"Yes, although I think they were called something different then."

"They were. And this is all from your dream?"

Lena nodded. "Scenes from it are coming back to me. That shouldn't happen, should it? Dreams ought to fade quickly in the morning and are then barely remembered."

"Not where the Great Power is concerned, Lena."

"The Mothers saw our ancestors as a threat. They lived outside the Citadel for a long while- longer than most others. But then the Mothers came and destroyed their strongholds, including the house in that... what's the word? Forest. But some of them escaped. Obviously- we wouldn't exist otherwise."

"Where to? Oh! The Citadel. Where better to hide than in plain sight."

"And the stories have been passed down over the centuries, in secret where possible. Just like you said."

Rhion looked thoughtfully towards the wooded border again. "So, a version of their house is *here*?"

Lena considered. "Yes. I don't know why. But I'm sure of it."

"Time for *me* to believe *you,* then." Her sister got up and stretched and offered her hand. "Let's go."

As the sisters stepped into the dense woodland the path ahead glowed faintly. Wherever they looked, branches of trees, tendrils of bramble and thickets of vegetation moved restlessly back and forth. Occasionally the wall would thin sufficiently for the women to glimpse the forest beyond, a mass of tall trees, spiny bushes and moss-covered boulders.

"I think it's been waiting for us," Rhion whispered, transfixed by the ever-moving scenery.

"To do what?"

"I don't know, Lena. I was hoping *you* might."

"This isn't my dream, Rhion. This is only what my dream told me about. Everything that happens here matters, more than you or I could possibly imagine. We're being cradled in the hand of a vast creature."

Rhion shivered, and Lena gave her an appraising look. "You're as frightened as I am. That's probably a good thing."

"I'm *not* frightened. You've spent your whole life in fear," Rhion scoffed, but she wouldn't meet her sister's gaze.

The direction, height and width of the path changed continually. The nearby foliage shrank back at their approach, as if initially repelled, only to then creep towards them as they passed by. "Don't touch it," Lena warned when she saw Rhion stretch an exploratory arm towards the silently writhing mass.

The track took them in every direction. It sloped up, then down. It became perilously thin, only to widen so that a horse-coach or steam-carriage could have been driven along it. Three times it even bent around in a tight spiral that wound upwards or downwards, although Lena and Rhion never caught sight of the path they had trodden anywhere above or below. If they glanced back, the way behind appeared dim and forbidding after their recent steps, a road whose purpose had been fulfilled and which would never be used again.

At last, they turned a corner and a house stood before them, no more than fifty paces away in a clearing of long grass. The revealed sky had become fiercely bright with unfamiliar constellations, and the house gleamed faintly in their cold light.

A garden had once grown in front of the house, but like the building itself it had withered and decayed. The roof of the house had caved in, no window glass remained and where a door should have stood, now an opening gaped blackly, revealing nothing of the interior. Little remained of the threshold other than a few pieces of soft, rotten wood partly hidden by a tangle of ivy and bramble. Nature in her patience had gradually reclaimed this place.

Rhion and Lena walked to the doorway. The remains of the door lay rotting in the long grass. The air hung heavy and silent over the area. "Do you think it's the same in our world?" Rhion wondered aloud.

Lena didn't answer. She stepped into the hallway and Rhion followed.

Three doorways led from the area into desolate rooms. Great foundation cracks made ugly courses through the walls, and cold, faint light filtered in weak shards through the schisms. Vegetation had taken a firm foothold inside, and saplings grew through the floor. "This isn't sunlight," Rhion murmured as she stared at the plants. "Why would they grow towards starlight? There's no light and day here, is there?"

"There's something important here," Lena said as she looked slowly around. "We need to find it."

"How do you know? Did you dream of that too?"

Lena didn't hear the question. "Parts of this place are like the house where I grew up. The house I burned down." She wondered suddenly if every home of every one of their ancestors had taken on subtle features in common with this house as it had once been- as if a ghost of this building had echoed down the hundreds of years, affecting the places where the descendants of those people lived their lives.

It sounded too strange to be plausible, but Lena reminded herself that she'd seen much recently that she would never have believed before.

She stood still as her sister waited pensively. *Think,* she told herself. *Think back to the dream.*

Then she realised what it was they were looking for. A picture of it opened and bloomed in her head. "It's a *book.* There's a book somewhere here. It was sealed away and kept hidden. Even if someone found it, the book's nature would remain masked."

"How?"

"It would appear to be something else entirely. Something innocuous. The location was protected- *blurred* somehow. But the book had such power, it caused the house to change over time, making it larger in some areas and smaller in others. In the middle of the house, the walls bent inwards around a specific area. A cavity. The house was drawn slowly into this peculiar chasm. The book even pulled on reality. It changed things over time. The shapes and features of the places where we lived. Our thoughts, our actions. It's been doing this for hundreds of years, waiting for someone to find it."

"Why *houses*?"

"I don't know. Maybe because that's where we spent most time- at least, when we were young. Without us knowing, maybe the book pulled on *us*, influencing us through the Great Power- and in so doing affecting the places we called home. Maybe it even helped pull us through into this place- the Halflight. It's like the centre of the web, Rhion."

Rhion said nothing. She watched as Lena walked slowly around the remains of the room and continued, "I think a ghost of this place echoed down the centuries, through our family. The house where Father and I lived- that also changed slowly over time, although I didn't realise at first." She shook her head. "Or maybe I did, but I simply accepted it."

The upper rooms and staircase had long since fallen through, and the twins had to step over broken masonry, timber and other debris to search the house.

Finally, they reached the rear of the building where the walls had caved away and opened out into a large overgrown area, once a back garden, which merged with the surrounding clearing.

313

Faint, yellow light seeped from a corner of the room. When they went over to it, they saw that the illumination came from a book. "That was easy," Rhion murmured. "I thought you said the book would be hidden."

"Not from those who are meant to find it."

The cover bore no title or markings. The floor under the book had given way a little so that it lay in a dark, earthy basin, surrounded by debris.

Lena slowly stretched out her hand towards it, and Rhion quickly seized her wrist. "Wait. We should touch it together. At the same time. If something happens to you..." She looked flustered. "If something happens to you, I want it to happen to me too."

A sudden, powerful fear gripped Lena. "Maybe we shouldn't touch it at all. Maybe we should just leave."

But when Lena said that, it seemed to her that the shadows around them grew darker and a faint sound like a low, world-shuddering rumble reverberated through the air.

The twins looked to each other, wordless.

Had an observer stood in the ruins, they would have seen the women's subsequent movements mirrored perfectly in the other‑ as they reached out towards the book and its light covered them.

That observer would have then witnessed the twins as they sat still, bathed in the illumination, looking directly at each other‑ almost as if a mirror bisected the world.

But Lena no longer saw her sister, or the book, or anything of her surroundings.

Lena looked up. Lines of standing stones stretched away in every direction for as far as the eye could see. *Graves,* Lena thought as she stood and surveyed the grim scene.

The house, the woodland, and Rhion- all had disappeared. She had been taken somewhere else, pulled into a dream or a deeper reality by the book's immense power.

She willed herself not to succumb to panic, and walked slowly between the dark stones, pausing to read the carved epitaphs on each. She understood none of the inscriptions, and yet when she passed by each grave a seething force stirred- inside her, inside the stone and between them, potent threads of the Great Power that strove to bind with one another.

Lena stopped by one of the tombstones and this time, when she reached out, that same force pulled at her so powerfully that she fell forwards and the palm of her hand pressed against the stone.

Simultaneously icy cold and searing hot, the touch was agony. A soundless scream left her lips and a moment later Lena was thrown back onto the dark ground. Something shivered through her- a memory, a ghost. Lena cried out fearfully but again she could make no sound.

The invisible shadow of something that had once lived seeped into her mind, and Lena saw through its eyes a murder from the distant past.

He walked as he always did, to the very heart of the forest.

Down in this secluded place, all the light appeared green, filtered from far above and brought softly to earth. The depths of the woodland were always cool, but never chilly. Respite from baking summer heat and harsh winter frost could both be found here, no matter the season.

He made his way down a narrow path he had walked a thousand times before, to a lake whose waters, as he reached them and rested at the shore, lay calm and silvery in the late evening sunlight.

Death came swiftly.

He saw a shadow from the corner of his vision, swift with murderous intent. He had no time to defend himself.

He staggered and knelt at the water's edge, bemused. His hands reached to his throat where blood gushed and spattered on the shore. He stared at the swirls of crimson as they mingled with the water.

A familiar figure crouched at his side. She watched and savoured his final moments as he fell into the shallows, cast in soft evening light.

Lena shuddered and as the scene faded into the back of her mind, she picked herself up and walked on, compelled by the Great Power and now also by the spirit that lurked within her.

There are others, she thought it whispered.

And there were *many* others.

Lena knelt by stone after stone, and ghosts of the past leaked into her. The dreadful, violent ways in which the men and women they had once been met their end, were indelibly marked in her mind. Helpless, she became a conduit for them all· dozens who had once stood with the Mothers and were then murdered by them, perceived as threats.

These vengeful spirits stirred and whispered their hatred inside her, and as Lena reached the centre of the vast cemetery, the visions of a hundred or more atrocities became a single mass of rage, a desire for revenge that was stronger than either life or death.

They could not rest until the Mothers were pulled into their own black existence, torn apart and made to suffer eternally.

Lena's eyes flickered open, and Rhion shrank back, afraid of what she now saw.

"Lena?" she managed to say at last.

"I could have fallen into those memories," her sister murmured. "They're not properly dead, nor are they alive‑ and yet they *continue*, somehow. Their need for vengeance burns too brightly for them to rest. Their hatred is our hope."

"Who?" Rhion managed to ask, fearing the answer.

The smile on Lena's lips was barely her own. "All of them."

She fell forward and lay unmoving on the ground.

II

Why am I back here? Teryn wondered.

He sat in a stationery Earthline train carriage, sandwiched between his parents. He wore his best shoes, trousers and shirt, which meant they were on their way back from his school. The train had suffered a mechanical fault and the guard was making his way through the carriages to inform the irritated passengers they would need to be towed to the nearest station by a second locomotive unit.

"When?" someone demanded to know.

"Soon. As soon as possible. I can only offer my apologies." The guard mopped his brow and pressed on along the carriage, then through the door into the next one. Summer had reached its height and an uncomfortable, oppressive heat filled the train. Some of the small, oval windows were open, but the subterranean air was almost as hot outside as inside.

I'm dreaming, Teryn told himself. *This happened a long time ago. I was seven.*

He remained a passive observer inside the head of his much younger self, transfixed as he watched events unfold.

The minutes wore on, and seven-year old Teryn had observed and gathered numerous pieces of information about their environment. He had always possessed the curious ability of knowing intricate details of his surroundings that couldn't be easily observed or measured, and this was, he judged, the perfect time to exercise his unusual skills, given that their train was stuck in a deep tunnel and they could do nothing but wait to be rescued.

He heard another child in the adjoining carriage, clearly in a state of distress at the protracted stoppage. *Panic won't help you,* he wanted to call out. *Distraction might.*

He concentrated on everything else around him. Observations and facts, whatever they were and wherever they could be found.

"Three hundred and fifteen hands separate us from the surface," Teryn whispered to his mother. "The temperature there is twenty-four percent less than in this tunnel. Give or take half of one percent."

She glanced at him and smiled, perhaps a little nervously. Neither she nor his father knew quite what to do when Teryn behaved this way, although his mother had her own special abilities as well- ones that she kept to herself. His father, who didn't know of such things (and never would, as far as the adult Teryn could recall), simply thought that Teryn loved to make up his own facts and information. Sometimes he indulged his son- other times, he worried about him.

"The driver is forty-one years old and his name is Allin," Teryn continued, and his mother squeezed his hand a little too hard. *In your head,* he heard her say. *Keep your hidden facts to yourself.* Her lips didn't move. She had spoken to him in the way she wanted his trivial discoveries to be kept- in his head, out of earshot. No one else would have heard her.

Teryn glanced up and met his mother's eyes. The look she gave him confirmed that she wouldn't put up with any disobedience.

Further along the carriage, a middle-aged man with an angry face began to curse and mutter to himself about public transport services. His complaints grew more furious as he saw that none of his fellow passengers sympathised with his tirade. Teryn watched as they looked away, pretended he didn't exist and perhaps inwardly wished they'd picked another carriage when they boarded the train. They dabbed at their foreheads and under their eyes using handkerchiefs already grimy with coal dust.

As the man's outburst became more enraged, however, Teryn noticed that the other passengers' eyes grew more restless and their breaths came more swiftly. It was difficult for them to pretend that things were as they'd been a moment ago, when the level of danger had abruptly changed.

Look away, Teryn heard his mother remind him. He knew he ought to, but he couldn't help glance furtively at the enraged traveler when he felt that he might not be noticed.

319

Then the man pulled out a knife from the inside pocket of his coat.

Teryn was rooted to his seat now, staring helplessly at the awful, crazed face of the knifeman. He looked grotesque, as if something that was not human fought to burst out from beneath his skin. *He's different to the others,* Teryn thought, although he had no idea what that meant.

Their eyes met. He saw the man's eyes as clearly as if he stared into them from inches away. The man recoiled, his pupils suddenly enlarged. Teryn felt helpless, as if he was caught in front of an onrushing train, not stuck in a stationery one.

He knows what I am. He knows what I can do.

And then panic *did* help Teryn.

Something invisible but immensely powerful left his body and surrounded the knifeman. Was his mother helping him too? Teryn thought she must be. Her hand in his felt almost red-hot. Something writhed where their hands met, a shared invisible force.

Harm yourself, not others, Teryn silently begged the man, but the words sounded as if his mother uttered them at the exact same moment.

A brief, dreadful struggle followed, as if the knifeman had become a puppet quarreled over by two different masters.

Then his head jerked back to bare his neck. His shaking hand reached up, the knife glittering faintly in the gloomy light.

In one violent movement, he slit across his throat with the knife. Blood spouted over his shaking hands. The weapon clattered to the floor.

Screams of terror and disgust flooded the carriage. Teryn sat and stared, until his mother covered his eyes, and his parents ushered him through the door at the other end and into the next carriage.

"Rules of the house," someone muttered.

Had one of the other passengers said something? Why would she say that? Teryn peered down the carriage, but the lights had grown dim, and he could no longer make out people's faces. Shadows lengthened and spread across the dirty floor. The windows dripped with sweat or oil, or maybe something else- a destroying substance that leaked in from the tunnel to eat reality.

"Mother," he said worriedly, and turned to her- but she was no longer there, although he could still feel his hand being held. His father had also disappeared.

Everyone had gone, leaving him in the carriage as his surroundings melted.

The train began to disintegrate, a blacked-out shell that crumbled away, unable to maintain its shape. Whoever or whatever had held his hand slipped invisibly away into the surrounding space, leaving nothing but warmth that soon vanished. "I don't want you to go," Teryn whispered.

"Rules of the house," came the voice again.

Teryn's eyes flickered open.

He lay on the carpet in the common room of the guest house.

The Finder rolled over and eventually managed to sit up. How had he ended up here? The common room appeared different, as if the colour had leeched from it. *Something's wrong with my eyes,* he decided, but closing and rubbing them did nothing to change the dismal scene.

Jerra stood across the room, clad in a dirty dressing gown. Her face appeared slack but distraught, her expression one of restless, mindless confusion. Her fingers were dark, dirty and scratched, as if she'd pulled herself up out of a grave.

She stared in his general direction but hadn't seen him.

Teryn stood up, keeping his eyes on the landlady the whole time. "Jerra," he said quietly, and again a little more loudly when she failed to respond.

"Things turn up eventually," the landlady said finally. She turned and walked to the other end of the room and stood facing the wall. "They've gone into the cracks," he heard her mutter.

Teryn turned and left the room. The front door at the end of the hall was open and creaked quietly back and forth in the breeze.

Beckoning him, the Finder decided, towards a changed world.

III

Outside, the silence was far deeper, far more *complete* than it should have been.

Something fundamental had, as he suspected, changed.

Teryn walked out into the street. A damp mist hung over the area. Here and there figures appeared in the distance before melting away, never getting close enough for him to identify them as male or female, or even human. Shapes of vehicles loomed further down the road, but these too were gone the next moment. *Here but not here,* he thought. *I'm near a crossing-point, a bridge.*

He began to walk, not sure where he was walking to.

All around, the grey and half-shrouded landscape of streets and buildings looked much the same, drained

322

of colour and with shapes that leaked and dissolved into the monochromatic fog. Tall structures with open doorways and broken windows materialised and faded as he walked along. Lamp posts with their lamps missing stood forlornly at junctions whose roads went nowhere he recognised. The mist came and went, swirling soundlessly to reveal a cityscape in sketchy detail before hiding it from view.

Even his footfall sounded dull and lifeless.

"Lena," he muttered. "Lena. Rhion."

He had to find them. Why else, he reasoned, had he now remembered that fateful afternoon when their mother showed him a tantalising glimpse of the Great Power- and her daughters' astonishing potential? Why else had an ability to see the interconnectedness of everything bloomed inside him?

They are the path to hope, Elia had told him. *But you are the map.*

He wasn't simply caught in the web- he had started to weave and shape it.

I should stop, he worried suddenly. *I mustn't become lost.*

Immediately he recognised the stupidity of that idea. He had become lost the moment he woke up on the floor of the guest house. No, long before then. Perhaps his fate was sealed the moment he took on the mysterious case of Lena Stone.

Everything had changed, so it made no difference where he wandered.

Better, perhaps, that he simply walk. Anything but stand and do nothing.

"Until you reach somewhere," Teryn said, and shuddered at the odd tone of his voice. He was out in the open and yet his voice sounded as if he was locked in a small, enclosed space.

323

He peered down one alleyway from which breaking, crunching sounds came. The mist thinned enough to reveal robed figures that might or might not have been human, gathered around something unmoving and shapeless. Teryn saw bones being snapped and pulled and glimpsed the whitish length of a femur gleaming through the murk, held in a dark hand.

He hurried away.

The Finder tried to reach the intricate web that linked all the people of the Citadel, a lattice built for him by the Great Power. But it had become muffled, indistinct. He sensed some people but not others, and those who he could detect appeared far away and faint, as if he'd started to fade from their reality into another place.

"Elia," he muttered. "Did you do this as well?"

The buildings around him became more spaced apart as Teryn continued, until finally he no longer walked through a built-up area but over grassland with thick fog on all sides. Whatever mysterious currents had carried it previously were not active here. The air lay still and silent.

The Finder shivered, dug his hands into his pockets and walked on. No path lay before him or behind him. All directions were now equivalent, he decided.

The grass became wetter and muddier until eventually he struggled through thick mud. He almost slipped over three times. On the third occasion he saw that several paces ahead of him the ground abruptly ended.

Teryn went down on his hands and knees and inched his way along, then peered over the edge. As the mist cleared the sheer distance between himself and the land at the bottom of the cliff made his vision swirl.

Thousands of steps separated him from the land below. He glimpsed paths and roads, areas of open land and groups of trees together, rivers and lakes. *This is how flying birds view the land,* Teryn thought. But nausea cut through the sense of wonder, and he had to close his eyes for a moment.

The cliff was formed of hard, jagged black stone. A flight of steps cut from that rock zig-zagged their perilous way down the cliff. After a moment Teryn made his way over to where their route began and stared down at the stone stairs. They had no supporting rail or structure of any kind, and only the rock face to hold onto on the inward side. The mist rolled here and there, sometimes revealing a dozen steps, sometimes a hundred or more. Occasionally Teryn again glimpsed the ground far below, a grim reminder of how far he could fall. The descent was precipitous, and any mistake or slip could easily be his last. He'd be dead and broken long before he reached the base of the cliff.

Find another way, he urged himself, but he already knew that no other way existed. He had to reach Lena and Rhion as soon as possible, and something-perhaps a residue of the insight the Great Power had given him- told him they were somewhere beyond this chasm, and the only way to cross it was to descend these steps. An almost impossibly faint presence lurked somewhere in the distance far beyond the ravine, and no matter how weak that binary signal, he believed it belonged to them.

"No fool like a dead fool," the Finder muttered, as he began to make his slow, uncertain way down the stone steps.

The descent challenged his balance as much as his nerve. The steps were not uniformly wide and occasionally they became so narrow that Teryn had to press himself against the cliff wall and hope that he didn't lose his footing and tumble through the abyss. *No one will mourn you,* he chided himself as he almost stumbled and somehow managed to recover just in time.

He couldn't have said how long it took him to work his way down the cliff. His legs and knees ached and burned, and he frequently had to sit on one of the steps to recover and wait for the pain to subside before he continued. His heart hurt. A few times he wept with the sheer misery and fatigue. Maybe the land he'd seen below was a façade, a trick. *I'm in hell,* he thought. *I'll descend these steps for all time.*

But at last Teryn glimpsed dry and earthy flat ground below. He reached it a short while later and sank to his knees in exhausted relief. The mist had lifted, although he couldn't see the top of the vast cliff. The ground appeared parched, the earthy surface riddled with cracks. In places, great slabs of dark rock rose from the broken desert. A dried-out riverbed cut through the grim landscape- not a river of water after all. None of the rivers and lakes that he'd observed from the clifftop were anywhere to be seen.

A sky trapped in perpetual twilight overlooked this mournful, abandoned land, with no part lighter than any other, no moons visible, no stars anywhere to be seen.

Somewhere in the far distance, the ground rose again towards mountainous peaks. The thought of walking all the way across this vast valley almost made Teryn's legs buckle.

But he began to walk anyway.

A sly voice in his head whispered that the lights, the combined essence he thought he sensed, might be nothing more than the twins' remains, slowly fading as the essence of their lives leaked away. Maybe they *were* here, it theorised, but had perished.

Teryn didn't want to think about that.

The rocky growths became larger and more frequent, although the weak light remained. Eventually he walked between two vast cliffs of dark, smooth stone, both over a thousand hands high. It was in this dismal corridor that he found a man sitting in the earthy desert, slumped forward with head in hands, shuddering.

As Teryn approached he noticed that the man was not only wounded but *changed* somehow. Deep cuts and gashes marred his body and something both metallic and fluid mingled with the exposed flesh. Light, and a silvery mesh that pulsated and changed shape in subtle ways, leaked from these wounds and between the man's fingers.

Teryn felt certain that if this stranger looked up, his head would look like the sun.

But then he did look up, as if he'd sensed that someone else had joined him in this barren purgatory, and he turned slowly to face the Finder.

The man's hungry, desperate gaze remained fixed upon him, unwavering. The orange-brown eyes- like polluted mud and chemicals leaking from factory waste pipes, Teryn thought- did not blink. Veins pulsed and pressed against the stranger's mottled skin so tightly that the Finder wondered how they didn't rupture.

He barely looked human at all.

The stranger opened his mouth wider than should have been possible, and a cracking sound emerged, as if his jaw was resetting itself. His throat rippled and bulged. When that unsettling process was done, the man shuddered, then coughed and spat.

327

Whatever emerged from his mouth, it glistened darkly on the ground and moved independently for a moment.

A veil lifted from in front of Teryn's eyes. He knew who this man was- or who he had once been- no matter that the horror before him bore little resemblance to how he must have once looked.

"How can *you* be here?" the Finder heard himself ask.

The Voice continued to stare directly at him. A multitude of emotions flashed through his eyes. "How can you know who I am? Who are you?" The voice sounded ragged and hoarse.

They faced each other in silence. Wind, or something that uttered the same sound, sighed around the vast cliff walls, but down here the air remained still. Teryn wondered dismally why he should be condemned to the abyss with this monster. What had he done that so displeased or enraged the world? Was this the price to pay for his miraculous insight- for being able to see everyone as they truly were, emmeshed and linked in the Citadel's great web?

Why was this creature his reward?

Some incomprehensible science had changed the Mothers' highest servant, made him part man and part something else. But even now, that virulent technology fought against the Great Power. That war raged throughout his body and mind, and Teryn saw it painted in his pain-maddened eyes.

The Voice was- unbelievably- a man like him, a creature of the Great Power, whatever else he had become.

Teryn sat on a granite boulder nearby. "My name is Teryn," he said at last.

"Mine is Seneth- I am, or *was* Voice of the Citadel, but you already know that. Why are you here? No one is lost in the Halflight without a reason."

Don't tell him about the twins, a quiet voice whispered in Teryn's mind. "I don't know why I'm here," he replied with a shrug.

Teryn had no desire to see the lattice of events, deeds and circumstances that made up this man's inner light, yet he was drawn helplessly to that diseased and terrible thing, a bundle of ruin caught up in strands of something vile whose centre was nothing but a black, slowly expanding hole.

That chasm expanded with immeasurable slowness, eating the Voice from the inside out. It had all but consumed his life, and any goodness that might once have been a part of him.

Seneth's intent stare did not abate. "You can *see* me. Inside me- and others. That's your curse."

Teryn nodded reluctantly. Fragments of the Voice's life flashed past. On their own they meant little, but brought together, they made sense. Circumstances had conspired to make him who he was. But that was always the way.

Seneth had been special. Like Rhion and Lena. Like himself, perhaps. But someone- his own *mother,* Teryn discovered- had attempted to crush the Great Power from him. "To protect you," he said aloud.

"What?"

"Your mother did it to protect you."

One of Seneth's eyes darkened almost to black, as the other flared with a bright yellow hue. Shadows made by nothing that Teryn could see passed over the man's face seemingly at random to accentuate his lurid malevolence. "She tore out all the hope I had in the world," he said at last.

"But now, the Great Power has me," he added quietly. "It brought me here. One way or another, I'm a slave. You saw the void?"

"Yes. I saw it." Teryn again pictured the slowly growing abyss and fervently wished he could unsee it.

"It's ageless, a thing out of time. It belongs in us all, and it can't be destroyed. It will take me eventually, no matter what she said."

It's eating you, Teryn thought.

"It hides in the technology that the Mothers revived, and yet it's not *unique* to it." He smiled, but to Teryn it looked as if an unseen puppeteer pulled at the corners of his lips. "At first, I didn't notice. How *do* you see the absence of something?"

"But you can feel it."

"Always."

Teryn's thoughts were alive with questions. "Why did the Mothers do this to you?"

"To die- they hoped."

As Teryn struggled to understand, the Voice continued, "The Mothers tortured me. But the Great Power didn't kill them as they hoped. Instead it brought me here. It saved me, because of my heritage." He laughed hoarsely. "It cares only for that- and nothing for who I am or what I've done."

Perhaps that's just as well for you, Teryn almost said.

"The void wanted me..."

"Maybe *you* want the void."

Seneth's lip curled contemptuously. "I desire only one thing- to destroy the Mothers for what they did. But they *want* to die. How do I satisfy my needs *and* deny them theirs?" He grimaced as a surge of movement under the skin on one side of his body pained him.

330

Teryn had no answer. Why would the Mothers wish to end their own lives? How *could* deities die? Were they not all-powerful, in which case didn't they also have the power to destroy anything, including themselves?

These were not questions he had ever expected to ask or try to answer.

How many people had the Voice murdered? How many executions had he ordered? Teryn felt a sudden urge to put an end to this central cog in the Citadel's machinery.

Could he destroy him?

Teryn's eyes were drawn to several medium-sized stones nearby- small enough to throw a short distance, maybe large enough to kill with. He hadn't noticed them before. For a moment he wondered if they'd materialised to coincide with his dark thoughts and to tempt him.

What would happen if he smashed the man's skull? What might be released?

Then Seneth said something that gave him pause. "My blood is their blood. What's left of it. I've been chosen."

"Chosen." Teryn had lost count of the people he'd helped incarcerate, who believed a higher power had urged them to commit atrocities.

"The Great Power made me recall things I'd forgotten." Seneth fixed him with an intent, luminous stare. "Have *you* remembered things recently that you'd forgotten? *Yes*," he added before Teryn could reply. "I can see it. But you have no idea why you've been chosen either."

"No." Teryn looked away, along the chasm between the dark cliffs, fearful that the Voice might read something in his eyes. "I'm like you. Lost."

331

IV

Seneth stood slowly. He staggered for a moment and then righted himself. "The Mothers will come here soon. I'm certain of it. But I think they'll hunt the twins now. Killing *them* would be a sure path to their own annihilation."

Teryn felt his stomach leap and a cold knot of fear stir inside him. "*Oh,*" the Voice murmured, leering closer. "You know who I mean. You've had dealings with them."

Teryn said nothing. *What now?* he thought desperately.

"They're still here, aren't they?" Seneth looked thoughtfully at him. "And you're a Finder, aren't you? I've always been able to tell. How do you know those women?"

Teryn studied the Voice's expression, to work out what his motives might be regarding Rhion and Lena. But the light behind his eyes, the criss-crossed veins and nerves visible through his skin, the flickering shadows that might or might not be a part of him, all combined to make it impossible.

At the same time, the clarity of the sisters' distant lights grew stronger, their identity more certain. He became acutely aware of the lie of the land for many thousands of steps in each direction, as if he had mapped it out in his head without knowing.

Empty land, mostly, but within it the light of the twins writhed and pulsed. He knew where they were now.

Teryn's vision slowly cleared and he saw the Voice looking down at him, a murky shape set against the red-tinged gloom. He remained still for a long while, breath spiralling periodically into the cold air.

"I can't do this alone," Seneth told him. "I can't destroy the Mothers by myself. I need your help. I need *their* help."

When Teryn didn't reply, the Voice smiled knowingly at him- or *something* did.

The Finder wearily tried to stand and flinched as Seneth grabbed his wrist and hauled him upright. The touch of his hand was like fire. "No one can destroy them. They're..."

"Not deities. Things are only deities if you let them be."

They faced each other and the Voice said quietly, "I think you *already* know where to find the twins. You were going to them when you saw me. Did you think you could hide that from me?"

Teryn looked bleakly past him and into the distance.

"We can only survive by giving the Mothers the death they crave. The four of us, together. We both know it."

The Finder recalled the dizzying moment long ago when he had stood by the two infants in their cot, granted sight of their vast potential, the incredible force that flowed in their veins.

But what about the Voice? The Mothers had unwittingly forced him here- or forced the Great Power to pluck him from their grasp- but might there be another reason for his presence in the Halflight? Had he a role to play?

Teryn looked at the dim shapes of the stones again.

"I don't trust you," he said bluntly.

"I don't care if you trust me or not." Seneth gestured along the dark ravine. Were the cliffs higher now, and shaped a little differently? Teryn thought they might be. "You were headed this way," the Voice prompted.

Reluctantly he nodded. His nightmarish companion had already begun to walk away.

As he limped after him Teryn wondered if, given the choice, he would turn his back on this and return to his unknowing, docile existence that now felt like a past life.

But there was no normality to return to.

Just lonely madness.

They arrived, perhaps a day or more later, at the foothills of a vast mountainous area silhouetted against the dim sky.

Teryn sat wearily and grimaced as he pulled off his boots to inspect the blisters on his heels and feet. Acute exhaustion filled him. Every part of his body ached, and his feet felt as if they were on fire.

He looked up at the mountain range in their way, a black and jagged mass set against perpetual twilight. How high would they need to climb? Just as importantly, how deep and far did this barrier extend? Might the dim horizon be the first of many?

It could take days to traverse this miserable landscape- not that they had any way of properly measuring time. The sky didn't change. Neither of them had needed to sleep or developed a thirst or hunger in this static hell.

Teryn pulled up the grimy sleeve of his coat and peered at his wristwatch. It had either slowed down or speeded up, and the minute hand and hour hand were nowhere near their correct places relative to each other. Did it still work at all? Teryn held it to his ear and listened for the familiar ticking but heard nothing.

"Time is irrelevant," Seneth told him. "All that matters now is distance."

Teryn silently agreed. The things that ground them to the reality they'd known, that chained them to the familiar world, were absent.

"And the land changes." The Voice's sudden iron optimism surprised him, spoken through gritted teeth and with fists clenched so hard that Teryn thought his knuckles might burst through the ravaged skin. "Distance for us isn't necessarily what we think it is. Maybe the Great Power will help us."

Teryn considered the idea. Was their journey towards Rhion and Lena being helpfully shortened? Conversely, might the Mothers' determined march towards them‑ assuming they followed as Seneth seemed to think‑ be lengthened in some small way? Perhaps.

He looked again to the hard, glassy surface of the climb before them. *If I fall on that, my bones will shatter,* he thought morosely, *and I'll slide and tumble through the dark like a bag of beaten meat.*

Teryn felt the despair of defeat claw at him. He tried to steel himself against it and consider the possibility, however small it might be, that he was imagining all of this, that he'd become a prisoner in his own mind.

But the pain was too savage, the fear too real. How many times had he already implored himself to wake up, knowing that he couldn't because he wasn't asleep?

"Are you ready?" Seneth's impatience cut through his thoughts.

They began their ascent. No path to the distant summit existed nearby so they clambered and staggered over the jet landscape.

As they climbed, the Voice became visibly weaker, his rests more frequent. Why not attack him when he least expected, Teryn mused more than once, and leave him battered and incapable on this lifeless mountain for the Mothers to find and do with as they pleased? Perhaps then they might pause to torture and ruin their highest servant, giving Teryn time to reach the twins, warn them of the Mothers- assuming they didn't already know- and at least make a stand against their enemies.

He glanced at a piece of loose rock he stepped past, and almost picked it up.

But this once-man, crippled and in agony as he was, might still prove to be more than a match for him. Teryn could fight- even in his advancing years he remained more than useful- but he had no idea if he could defeat his condemned companion.

And truthfully, he was afraid he might lose that struggle, and die here. What then? Teryn had never subscribed to any theory of what (if anything) happened after the corporeal form expired, but here the natural laws of existence had been subverted. Everything he thought he knew was either wrong or simply the starting point of an altogether wider, more astonishing truth. Through Elia, through his pursuit of Lena, through the blossoming of his insight, the Great Power clearly had a plan for him- and for all he knew, a plan for Seneth too. What would happen if he deliberately thwarted it?

Occasionally, Seneth's internal chaos would manifest itself in one way or another when they rested. He would sit still, unblinking, perhaps even unaware of anything nearby. It was then that thoughts of murder loomed persuasively in Teryn's mind.

Or he would shake uncontrollably and scream so loudly that the Finder wondered if the twins or even the Mothers could hear his agony. Perhaps the Mothers sensed the light of people's lives in much the same way as he did and felt their way along the web that bound people to one another and to the world. Such insight would make controlling an entire population easier.

Or Seneth would engage Teryn in conversation, only for it to quickly become apparent that his words made no sense. Sometimes they didn't sound like any language Teryn could understand- and the Finder knew all the dialects of the Citadel.

He is dying, Teryn decided. *So how can there be a plan for him?*

When lucid, the Voice spoke sparingly, and only of his hatred for the Mothers. Teryn was darkly amused that a man whose callous disregard for human life and eagerness to torture and murder must have made him an ideal candidate for Voice, raged coldly against his employers, who had treated him as he treated the rest of humanity.

Nonetheless he listened, fascinated in an awful way by the utter absence of compassion and remorse. He had heard monologues like this before, powered by ego and indignation- confessions used as opportunities.

"What turned you? Losing the Great Power?" he asked at one point.

Seneth gave him a contemptuous look. "It cares nothing for the way we live our insignificant lives, only that we do what we need to when the time comes."

"We are what we are," Seneth added later as they rested about half-way up the black slope.

Teryn had been staring up at the sky as he regained his breath. He wondered how it was that faint stars had now emerged, as if his and Seneth's grim ascent had brought them nearer to the heavens. He glanced across at his companion and wondered if some revelation would be forthcoming.

But all the Voice said was, "I don't care for the way you observe me, like a specimen. The Mothers did that. Some people are made for saving lives, others are made for ending them. What have *you* done with your sorry life?"

"Nothing," Teryn admitted.

"Nothing," Seneth flatly repeated, and looked away.

They reached the summit of the mountain at last. The ground sloped gently away on the other side, into a vast, shallow valley where numerous tall stony structures protruded like huge, shapeless statues. Beyond these, a dark curtain rose from the ground. Teryn eventually realised that this was made from trees- hundreds, perhaps thousands of them.

And the twins were somewhere within that mass of trees. When he closed his eyes, he saw their light- separate and combined at the same time.

I don't know what I'm doing, he thought helplessly. *I don't know what will happen when we reach them.*

"Are we near?"

Teryn felt uneasy at the eagerness in his companion's voice. He looked across the Voice. Had he healed a little? It was difficult to say in this light.

He set off down the slope, and Seneth followed.

V

Rhion sat by Lena's still form, tears of misery and frustration rolling down her cheeks.

Her sister had collapsed to the ground without uttering a single word. Her eyes were closed now, the beat of her heart fearfully slow, her skin cold- as if she straddled an invisible bridge between life and death.

Rhion reached out and stroked her cheek. She could do nothing but wait and hope beyond hope that Lena stirred.

The book had done something to her- infected her with something. Rhion was certain of it. She glanced pensively at the volume, which had now mostly disintegrated into dust. As she looked, another fragment crumbled away, seemingly of its own accord.

Rhion felt a shudder go through her, a familiar warning. "No," she whispered. "That's impossible."

How could the Voice have followed her *here*?

She took one last look at her sister and stood up, then faced the direction from which he would come. She couldn't leave Lena. Even if she could, where would she go in this empty world?

"I'd rather die," Rhion said, knowing that likely she would.

She didn't have long to wait until the Voice appeared. Another, slightly older man walked with him. They appeared on the other side of the clearing, beyond the grounds of the house.

Rhion stared apprehensively at them and took shallow, deliberate breaths as adrenaline coursed through her. But the Great Power lay quiet. Why wouldn't it come to her defence?

Seneth looked barely recognisable. Something had twisted him inside and out.

The Voice and the stranger walked slowly across the grass towards her. Rhion tried to swallow down her growing panic as they approached. *Calm,* she told herself.

"You must be Rhion," the older man said. "My name is Teryn." He looked unremarkable at first, until Rhion's eyes met his and her heart lurched. A world of knowledge lay in that steady gaze. "Do I know you?" she asked.

"We've met before, a long time ago."

"I don't remember." Rhion turned cautiously to Seneth. "What happened to *you*?"

All sorts of different emotions danced in his eyes. He didn't answer her question, but eventually he said quietly, "I didn't expect us to meet again, Rhion. Not until I met *him,* anyway."

"Neither did I."

"The Great Power brought me here. It turns out that I'm not unlike yourself and Lena. Hard to believe, isn't it?"

"Very." Rhion's steady gaze did not waver.

"The Mothers intend to bring about their own end by destroying *you*- and invoking the fury of the world. They will also find a way here, and- assuming the ground doesn't disappear from under their feet or they're not redirected to the bottom of the ocean- they will sense where you are."

Rhion turned to Teryn. "Is that true?"

"It's very likely."

"And what about you? When did we meet? I don't remember you."

Teryn said nothing for a long while. He appeared to be recalling something. "I'm like you," he said simply.

"When I was a child, I used the Great Power, without really knowing what I was doing- my mother could use it too- but then it left me, or *I* left *it*... until I remembered a meeting with your mother and father, twenty years ago."

Rhion listened in astonishment as Teryn told her about an afternoon when he had gone to Elia and Marim, and things had been revealed to him that he wouldn't remember until many years later. His struggle to describe the things he had seen was evident.

"I helped them- and the two of you- to spend the last twenty years hidden from the Mothers," he said at last. "They knew that they had to live apart, and that you and Lena would need to be separated. The forces within you- within all four of you- would have been too great to remain undetected. But I think they also knew that one day you'd be reunited. When the time was right, your mother told me."

Rhion couldn't think of anything to say.

"They chose me for a reason. Your mother said that the two of you were the path, and I was the map."

Rhion smiled faintly.

"I think she meant my ability to see the threads of the Great Power that bind everyone together without their knowing- the collections of energy that make up each man, woman and child."

"You can see *that?*"

"In the Citadel, I could see everyone. *Here,* I can see everyone."

"Do the Mothers know about you?" Rhion wondered.

"I don't know. I hadn't thought about that."

Rhion heard a faint sound behind her. When she looked around, Lena was struggling to sit up, weak and exhausted.

341

"Lena!" Rhion knelt and carefully helped her up.

"The Mothers have one weakness," her twin told them, "and it lies in the past."

VI

Even as Lena spoke, the Great Power surged and coursed through Rhion's veins. She could even sense it in her companions. A jolt like electricity went through her, an amplification of the Great Force that roiled agitatedly.

Three figures materialised on the other side of the open ground, where the long grass met the trees. Rhion's stomach felt as if it had turned upside down. Her legs trembled and almost gave way.

Close your eyes, something whispered to her, maybe from out of the ruined house or even the ground.

When she did, the Mothers appeared as silhouettes cast in absolute darkness, as if their shapes had been cut out of the gloomy terrain. At their combined core something cold and empty writhed, a shape that that was all absence and no substance.

Abruptly something invisible slammed into her and threw her backwards. Instinctively she curled up on the ground. The Great Power leapt to her defence, but the sheer terrifying rage of the Mothers would not be denied. When she looked up, nothing but absolute gloom filled her vision. The stars had disappeared, as if an abyss had opened in the sky. Rhion imagined that this was their void, released from the Mothers into the Halflight and cast like a blanket over them all.

She had never known fear like this. Their enemies' baleful darkness threatened to drown her. She was less than nothing, not even a droplet of water in that expanse.

Misery and defeat clawed at Rhion, pulled her down, dissolved away her defences. She sobbed and hugged herself even more tightly, lost in despair.

She would die unremembered.

She was worthless.

She had let her own mother die alone and in pain.

Rhion knew that this desolate emptiness was simply using her against herself. But she could find no escape. It played on self-loathing and lonely bitterness, and it burrowed insistently into her.

Then Lena's presence flared and bloomed like a flower, a beacon of searing light in her head. Rhion reacted instinctively. She desperately reached out to her sister across the howling chaos that now swirled around them all, but then she stopped- for she saw terrible, unliving things writhe within Lena, baleful remnants that sought only vengeance on the Mothers.

What has happened to her?!

She screamed her twin's name, but the sound was like a whisper in a hurricane, so faint it could have come from the other side of the world.

Someone else's voice swam through the seeping void. *Rhion.*

"I can't see you!" she screamed as absolute terror clawed at her. "I don't know where you are!" Who was she talking to? It no longer mattered.

She shrieked even more loudly when a hand grabbed her arm, then recoiled as she realised who that hand belonged to, simply by the familiar force that rippled through it. *Seneth!*

Rhion almost pulled away as she felt the Great Power flow between them, a surge of immense force that rolled like a wave, far stronger than the two of them by themselves. Then she stopped. Unbelievably, he wasn't

343

trying to harm her. He was trying to *link* with her so that the two of them combined could fight the Mothers.

"I can't *see* anything!"

"Stand up," he told her. "Keep your eyes closed."

Now the abyss retreated, and outlines emerged from the dark. As Rhion staggered to her feet she saw the Mothers clearly. They remained by the treeline. Malevolence poured like a poison from them, a corrupted strand of the Great Power that reached out towards her and the others.

Rhion shuddered and almost collapsed as immense force raged and tore at her and left her body and Seneth's at the same moment. Her vision leaped forward with it and surrounded Lena.

Savage light now made a barrier between her sister and their enemies, and for the first time she heard the Mothers' own frustration and rage.

Whatever happens, protect Lena.

That was Teryn's voice, faint and distant. It could have come from deep under the earth or across the vastness of space. Rhion now saw the Mothers as complex structures of light and force, changing all the time. *This is how the Finder sees them,* she thought. *He's shared it with us somehow.*

That bewildering insight allowed her to know exactly where and when each of the Mothers was about to strike at the same moment as the Mothers themselves.

The fury of their enemies struck at them, and Rhion screamed in agony. She felt Seneth's pain almost as intensely as her own. Together they fought desperately, yet they grew weaker, and the force applied by their enemies more insistent.

But within moments the Mothers' rage became tinged with horror and disbelief.

344

Dozens of ethereal, constantly shifting entities swirled around them, a swathe of light and colour. Transient faces loomed briefly, twisted with hate. Ghosts that had somehow been written into the book over time and then caught inside Lena, released at last. Her sister stood swaying, head drawn back, the light inside her now growing dim.

As the Mothers desperately turned to these new enemies, a terrible cacophony stirred. Trees cracked and burst apart as if under great pressure. The ground shuddered and vast cracks and trenches appeared, leading down into a deeper, perhaps infinite darkness.

The ghostly forms released by Lena had stirred the world into chaos.

Wasn't that what the Mothers wanted, though?

The world utters a great sigh and holds her arms aloft, Rhion imagined Elia saying. Their mother wouldn't have been afraid. She had never feared the outer world, nor even the insidious powers of the Citadel, for almost all her years. She had only ever feared her own demise.

How I wish you were here with us now, Rhion thought as all the strength left her and she collapsed to the ground.

No matter the destruction we've unleashed.

Teryn witnessed the same unfolding struggle between the Mothers and the vengeful, silent spirits, but he saw that they had begun to *steal* parts of the Mothers' consciousness and rip away fragments of it that were invisible to his companions.

These ghosts tore ravenously at the threads and pulses of energy, casting them into the darkest corners of the Halflight.

It's what they want, Teryn thought as he stared in wonder.

But then he saw that rather than being destroyed, the three women were being assimilated into the fabric of the world by these impossible, terrible spirits. Piece by hateful piece, the Mothers disappeared like soil or dust whipped by the wind. If these were truly ghosts of the wronged from the distant past, now was the moment of their vengeance.

The Mothers are not dying, Teryn observed in astonishment. *They're dissolving into the world, trapped and rendered helpless, bodiless- yet their consciousness remains, to be scattered throughout the Halflight.*

They're becoming ghosts too- but powerless and condemned to a place of eternal unrest.

Seneth stood and watched the Mothers' demise. He neither knew nor cared what the creatures were. He possessed nothing of Teryn's deep insight. But as the unfathomable process continued, the parasitic technology within him finally withered to nothing. The Great Power had asserted control over his mind and body and linking with Rhion to defend himself better against the Mothers had only accelerated that change.

His healing was almost done. Even the accompanying pain- excruciating at times during his journey here- now ebbed away. Instead of dying, he was being remade.

A smile of grim satisfaction creased his lips as the Mothers' slow but sure destruction continued. When at last their physical forms and their *emptiness* were no more, and even their destroyers had faded away to some other place, he became fully aware of the chaos around them.

Tracts of ground swelled and rose in the clearing, through the remains of the house and further away in the woodland. The unstable walls and rotten timbers of the building groaned and fell. The ground rumbled and roared as if to celebrate the Mothers' disintegration.

A path through the dark woods lay before him, newly opened, inviting. Seneth stepped towards it, then looked back. Lena lay unmoving on the ground. Rhion crawled slowly and painfully towards her sister. Teryn stared at the space the Mothers had occupied only moments before.

Seneth walked on towards the path a little way, and only turned again when he sensed Teryn's gaze upon him. "She told me something, in a dream," he shouted to the Finder above the noise of rupture. "She said the Citadel will be mine."

Teryn didn't respond. The Voice could read nothing in his expression, but the look in the Finder's eyes nonetheless disturbed him.

"Stay away. Return and you die," he continued, desperate to set foot upon the track through the woods. It appeared wider now, but the ground hadn't been riven with schisms along its length. Without doubt, this was his safe path back to normality.

To eternity.

"As you say," he thought the Finder said, but the continuing destruction drowned out the words.

Teryn went over to Rhion, stepping over cracks in the ground.

Seneth watched them for a moment, then turned and walked away.

VII

When the Voice emerged from the forest and the path led him into open land, he looked back and saw that the entire landscape had changed. Maybe Rhion and Lena and Teryn had been buried under it. For a moment, the memory of linking with Rhion rushed back to him, a euphoria that he couldn't describe. With an effort he crushed it.

Seneth turned and made his way up the head of the wide, grassy valley, heading towards a patch of lighter sky. Strength soared through him as he strode along. The Great Power hummed calmly in his veins. He felt almost entirely at peace.

The world didn't care which of its servants survived, he noted later as he rested and observed a distance riven with precipitous dark slopes, sharp mountain peaks and abyssal rifts that snaked through the alien landscape like black rivers. It cared only for the destruction of the Mothers. Now it would sleep once again. Already the land around him lay quiet and still.

Meanwhile, *he* had been awakened. Not only had the Great Power been restored to him, but the taint inflicted by the Mothers had withered away to nothing.

"Thank you," he said softly. "Should I worship you?" He laughed and touched his face. The deformities caused by the battle between those forces had already disappeared. He felt as good as new. No, better.

Seneth walked for a long time. He tired, but only a little. Sooner or later, if he kept going the same way, he would step back into the world he knew, through a place where the barrier was weak and the Halflight embraced the world of the sun and the seasons.

What will I call myself, he wondered, *when I take my place as master of the Citadel?*

Father?

Seneth's return to the palace felt detached, automatic. It held a dreamlike quality. He couldn't tell, at times, if he still walked in the Halflight or the world he'd known his entire life, or somewhere in between.

For a while he went amongst people, with the sun on his back, and heard everyday sounds of conversation and commerce as he walked across flagstones and steam-carriages hissed past. But the people appeared grey and formless, as if they were painted onto a canvas he happened to be crossing. Their faces looked much the same and were instantly forgotten. None of these faded citizens appeared to notice him.

At other times he walked in shadow, under a night sky, and the firmament above was unfamiliar-stars of numerous colours and unknown configurations glittered down on streets that bent and twisted in strange directions, while great castles and fortresses that dwarfed the Mothers' domain loomed over the cold and silent city. *One day I'll build higher and wider and greater than this,* he vowed.

Like a mist that burned away in the morning, the otherness of his surroundings dissipated over time and Seneth was drawn fully into the hard reality of the world he knew.

He arrived at the Palace gates and smiled at the sight of the familiar, obsequious guardsmen who hurried to allow him swift passage through the barriers and into the grounds. Numerous murmurs of "My lord Voice" filled the air as his lackeys bowed and averted their eyes. Seneth caught sight of his reflection in a polished shield. He looked, as he felt, better than ever.

The Voice soon discovered that parts of the Palace's internal structure had changed radically.

Passageways sometimes went in different directions and joined to one another in new ways. The dimensions and shapes of some rooms had changed. The walls and ceiling of one hall were half as high as he remembered them being before, and in another the upper ramparts couldn't be seen at all, for the walls appeared to converge on some distant, impossibly high point. In another chamber, a bitter chill filled the air on one side and caused frost to form on the walls. A humid, overpowering warmth lingered on the other side, and foul moisture dripped.

All residues, he decided, of the chaos stirred by the Mothers, and the Halflight almost reaching into the outer world.

He encountered servants and administrators, many of them babbling with terror- for they had also seen some of the inexplicable changes around the Palace. "What is the matter with you people?" he demanded, inwardly enjoying their distress.

"Please, my lord Voice, all these impossible things...." one of them had the temerity to say.

"There's bad magic let loose," another, a woman who worked in the kitchens, added. Then her face drained of blood as Seneth fixed her with an incredulous stare. "Fool. There is no such thing as magic."

I am your God now, he wanted to tell his cretinous subjects- but even in this, the moment of his triumph, Seneth knew that he had to ensure everyone assumed the Mothers still existed, that their collective all-seeing eye roamed continually around every dusty nook and abandoned corner of the Citadel. For now, he would need to rule in secret.

But he could live with that inconvenience.

Seneth left his underlings to their frightened babbling. If they fled, as some apparently had, so be it.

Soon the chaos would come to an end, now that the Mothers were no more. The fear would ebb away. He would find enough servants for his needs from amongst the teeming masses in the Citadel.

He savoured the beauty of each moment as he strolled the length and breadth of this, his domain. He observed and enjoyed the distress and confusion he saw everywhere.

But he reserved the good sense to wash, shave and dress in new clothes before summoning the Chief Balancer. Nonetheless, he noted with amusement that Moran still gaped at him like an imbecile.

"Have I grown some deformity?" Seneth asked mildly. "Perhaps a second, smaller head?"

"I..." The Chief Balancer appeared lost for words - or perhaps simply *lost,* much as Seneth had been when he bowed like a frightened child before the Mothers. "My Lord Voice, you... you seem different."

"Better, or worse?"

"Better! Most assuredly so."

"Why, thank you. But I'm quite the same as I've always been. Are you ill, Moran?" He leaned forward and adopted a solicitous tone. "If you're not well enough to conduct your duties, perhaps you deserve a few days' rest. Time away from the cut and thrust of your demanding work. I could have a word with the Mothers and see if they might permit it."

"I'm..." The Chief Balancer shook his head in the manner of someone trying desperately to clear a fog of confusion. "I'm not ill, my Lord Voice."

"I'm most glad to hear it." Seneth sat back and observed the man for a while. *I can do anything I want with him now,* he thought idly.

"There's a certain amount of unrest in the Citadel," Moran said abruptly. "I wanted to deliver a full report before now, but no one in the Palace was able to find you."

"The Mothers have claimed all my attention recently, Moran. You know how it is. What manner of unrest?"

"It's... difficult to describe."

"Try."

"I can only give you examples. Parts of the infrastructure have become unstable. Sinkholes. Puddles and pools of water which are far deeper than they ought to be. Fissures have opened in buildings, which appear to go to... deep places where the geology is different. Some structures have moved suddenly with people inside them or nearby, and those people have become... *amalgamated.* Part of the reformed structure. Loud noises that can't be attributed to anything..."

Seneth's expression remained implacable. "I assume you have witnesses. This does sound quite difficult to believe."

"Many hundreds, my Lord Voice. And on a related note, over ten thousand deaths have been reported." Moran's eyes strayed to the corners of the meeting hall. "Even *this* room looks different. Other parts of the Palace appear to have changed as well."

"Have they? I've been busy, Chief Balancer. I haven't noticed."

"You haven't *noticed?*"

"I'll ensure that the Mothers hear about this. I'm sure a plan to reassure the people and restore order will be forthcoming. And I'm equally certain that everything will soon become calm and return to normal."

"Have faith," Seneth said with a smile when the Chief Balancer stared at him.

"The guards. There are no guards," Moran noted. "Where are they?"

"I honestly do not know. Perhaps they became as frightened as *you* appear to be and decided to leave their stations. I will, of course, ensure that every man is skinned alive in front of his family if they're found to have abandoned their duties."

"We're done. You may go," Seneth added when Moran simply blinked in confusion.

The Voice realised, as he glanced at the large clock in a corner of the meeting room after Moran's departure, that it was around the time of morning when he would have gone to the prisoner in the cell.

"One last time, to say farewell," he said aloud, "and then I'll have the entire area bricked up. I don't need to see your face again."

He went to the prisoner's chamber and stood at the entrance for far longer than he had anticipated.

Both the glass cell and its contents had vanished.

VIII

It shouldn't surprise me, Seneth mused as he finally turned away and headed back along the dimly lit passageway. *Other parts of the Palace changed or even disappeared because of the chaos stirred up by the Mothers. He'll be somewhere.*

Or will he?

Seneth laughed for a moment, wondering if the prisoner and his cell had fallen into the Halflight.

The Palace seemed quiet this morning, almost entirely abandoned. Once everything had stabilised here and out in the city, he would recruit for every department. A new Chief Balancer would be the first appointee.

Seneth went to the hall where in the past he would grovel before the Mothers. He walked to the single black tile and spat upon it. He walked the length and breadth of the room and observed the ceiling far above, then walked to the chairs that the Mothers had used. He smiled. Everything looked so *ordinary* now. He had to remind himself that his tormentors were gone, dissolved into the earth for all he knew.

Then the light began to fade.

The lanterns sputtered and their glows shrank.

Shadows formed and leapt from the distant regions of the hall.

Seneth's vision quickly adjusted to the miniscule level of lighting. He turned to face the entrance and saw Daniel standing there. "You," Seneth said.

As Seneth stared at him he took a tentative step nearer. "I had thought I might even forget how to move," he murmured, "but it seems I haven't. Did *you* destroy the Mothers? They don't seem to be here anymore."

Seneth struggled to overcome his shock and sense of immediate, virulent danger. "No," he heard himself say at last. "No, but something else did."

"They won't be coming back then. That *is* a shame."

Seneth had no idea what to respond to that. For a moment, a look in Daniel's eyes distracted him. Somehow it reminded him of the Finder he had travelled with in the Halflight.

"I suppose you're wondering how I escaped," Daniel remarked.

"Am I?"

"My prison simply disappeared *or* moved to some other place." Daniel smiled. "Perhaps it was inevitable- the forces that imprisoned me were made by the Mothers- and the Mothers are no more."

"The Great Power appeared as you, in my dreams," Seneth remarked. "I still have no idea why it chose *you*." He thought for a moment. "How is it that I can understand you, a man from a thousand years ago? A feature of the Great Power, perhaps."

Daniel only smiled.

This was simply one more enemy to be destroyed, Seneth reminded himself. After he killed him, he would be lord of everything at last, as he had promised himself so many years ago.

"Can we coexist, do you think?" Daniel wondered aloud.

Seneth had nothing to say to that.

The two men faced each other, waiting, watching for a moment of weakness.

Then, at the same time, they rushed at each other.

A struggle followed that would have astonished and reviled anyone unfortunate enough to bear witness to it.

Animalistic roars of fury were given voice at last as the two men fought. Daniel seized and crushed Seneth's fingers until the bones broke in a dozen places. In the heat of his rage Seneth barely felt the pain, although he sensed the digits of his fingers fuse and repair swiftly only moments later.

Seneth gouged at Daniel's left eye, plunging two of his fingers deep into the warm, wet socket.

Daniel screamed and grabbed at Seneth's throat, digging into his skin and then the flesh of his windpipe with an iron grip.

The grotesque battle continued for hours. Blood and gore decorated the floor and walls. The combatants slipped and staggered amidst the leavings of their struggle. Their appearance took on a ghastly reddish hue as their healing processes struggled to keep up with the grievous wounds they sustained.

But then, as they fell against each other and continued to bite, gouge and rip at each other's flesh, howling with rage, something happened that neither had expected. In the haze of their fury they failed to notice until it became too late.

Their bodies began to fuse together.

As their combined flesh melded the process intensified until even their bones began to merge. The combatants screamed their horror at the sudden and near-total amalgamation of their limbs, torsos and eventually, their heads.

The single, writhing mass stumbled, fell, and tried again and again to rise, struggling against itself. A mouth formed in its oversized, patchwork head, and from that gaping maw issued a low bellow of terrified misery. The amalgam tore at itself as the remnants of both combatants fought to extricate themselves from the nightmare. It threw itself against the walls, ripped at its flesh, mutilated its body only to roar in agony as skin, meat and bone swiftly healed.

They were trapped. The restorative process of each had grown too powerful. The combination of Daniel and Seneth could not kill itself.

It lay quietly, at last, shuddering in the low light. The oversized, misshapen body would heal again, whenever this hybrid abomination tried to harm or even kill itself.

It could not speak, nor would it ever be able to. The creature would have no way to express the sheer horror and misery of its existence. Immortal yet powerless, it would never command authority.

In time, the Palace- haunted and full of terrors according to the stories of men and women who lived through the time of the Mothers and just after- would lie entirely abandoned by people, and nature's sinuous fingers would prise open the cracks of the infrastructure. The story of its lone inhabitant, the unnamed monster, would grow ever more fanciful with the passing of years. The beast was the true form of the Mothers- a creature that could occasionally split into three and roam around the Citadel, but which had none of their powers. Or it had once been their prisoner, and it wandered the catacombs beneath the vast building, searching for its absent tormentors. Or it had come from another world entirely.

The monster knew nothing of these tales. It crept through the distant depths, in shadow and silence. In the sunlit world, generations came and went, the cycle turned and eventually even the myths that came from ancient history were put aside. In the vastness of time, even the monster would be forgotten.

And still, somewhere under stone and earth, it lived.

IX · Threads

I

The earth grew quiet under the stars and a deep silence suffused the Halflight.

"I won't leave you," Rhion whispered, over and again. She cradled Lena's head in her arms. Her sister's breaths came slowly, and she looked as grey as stone in the cold gloom. *She'll wake,* Rhion stubbornly asserted. *She did before.*

But that had been for a purpose.

After some time, she became aware of Teryn nearby. "Are they really gone?" she asked.

"Dissolved into the world," he said quietly. "They're with those they murdered now, spread across the Halflight. Perhaps condemned to remember their grim misdeeds for all eternity."

"They can't harm us?"

"No, Rhion. They can't harm us."

She gave him a long, considering look. "Where's Seneth?"

"Gone. A path opened for him. By now, he may well be in the Citadel. He seemed to think he'd been promised it."

"We need to find somewhere else to go then."

A smile flickered briefly on his lips. "Yes, although perhaps not for the reason you think."

Lena stirred suddenly and her eyes flickered open. "Rhion?"

"I'm here," Rhion murmured, exhaling in relief. "Are you in pain?"

Lena stared up at her as if she hadn't understood the question at first. "No. I don't think so."

A strange panic gripped Rhion, stirred by the fear that the ghosts they'd released were not done with her sister yet. But she could no longer sense them. Their threads, their collective essence had gone. Sank back into the fabric of the world, and with them the hateful fragments of the Mothers.

"You're all I have," she told her, more forcefully than she intended.

Lena smiled weakly.

Rhion helped her up, and the twins walked with Teryn through the broken woodland to the point at which the ground fell away to the vast open plain below. In the extreme distance, another, larger forest could be seen, stretching to either side of the observable horizon. Between that barrier and the companions, hills rose, and rivers cut through the silent landscape.

Rhion remembered that Teryn had not entirely satisfied her questions about the Voice. "Will Seneth rule the Citadel now?"

"You seem to think I have all the answers, Rhion. I think there's a plan for all of us, the Voice included. But I don't believe *that* will be his destiny." The Finder's eyes held a faraway look.

They stood together in silence for a while. "Where do we go now?" Lena asked finally. "What will have happened by the time we return?"

Rhion gave her an amused look. "Did you have a life worth returning to, Lena? You didn't tell me about that."

"But we can't stay *here*. We don't belong here."

"No. Not truly." Rhion turned to Teryn. "What about you, Finder? Anything to return to? Any*one*?"

Teryn didn't answer the question. He pointed into the distance, where the open land met the great forest. "That's where we need to go."

The companions walked down the slope and through silvery twilight across the undulating plain below. They walked near to a wide river and found that the water didn't move at all- as if it formed a lake in the shape of a river. The still water gleamed faintly and offered an eerily perfect reflection.

"Where are we going?" Lena asked Teryn as they headed along a path that partly followed the river, towards the distant dark wave that marked the forest.

"Back," was all he said.

"But not to the Citadel?"

"No. Not to the Citadel."

Before them, hours or perhaps even days later, stood the vast woodland.

To their left and right the trees appeared to extend forever, a wall of close-packed trees and tangled vegetation, a seemingly impenetrable barrier with neither weakness nor limit. And no creatures, Rhion noted. That was another reason why the three of them didn't belong here and never could. They were living beings, and this was the realm of ghosts.

Exhausted, the companions rested at the forest's edge. They fell asleep, and when they dreamed, their dreams were shared.

They soared, borne by currents that swirled and took them upward, away from their sleeping forms and over the dense carpet of the forest. Somewhere far above black clouds lingered. Below, in the thickness of the trees, there were movements of dark, oddly shaped entities and baleful eyes cast stares towards the airborne companions. These were not living things, but the remnants of creatures that had once lived- spirits that lingered on in limbo.

Further ahead, in the distance, light split the sky, a continually glowing presence that shone through a tear in the fabric of the world.

The three companions flew amidst a juxtaposition of stormy gloom and alien light. Over time the woods below them grew sparse and eventually gave way entirely to the ever more extreme slopes of savage mountains, where snowy peaks and black ravines formed the backdrop to their flight. When they finally passed the great peaks and lower grasslands stretched away below them, the companions flew higher still, and into the greater darkness of space.

The universe opened before them to reveal a million truths and a million more secrets.

Great towers of colour and cloud appeared, columns that stretched an immeasurable distance, inside which tiny points of light gleamed like mica in dark rock. Some carried worlds around them.

Through the immeasurable distance of space they drifted, and formations of millions of stars appeared around them, some in whirlpool or spiral shapes, others stretched thin or elliptical.

Worlds in abundance wheeled past in the blackness of the void · dead now, but some had once flourished with life. The companions witnessed the greatest epochs of these forgotten places, then their dramatic decline, and the long eons of arid stillness that followed.

Unchanging deserts, or rocky landscapes burned to char.

Poisoned and suffocated hells, or dark and icy wilderness across which deathly winds had stripped all sustenance.

And *their* world lived on, alone.

II

Lena woke first.

The first light of dawn cut across the landscape. The air had a slight chill to it and a faint breeze blew from the east.

We're no longer in the Halflight, she realised.

They were still at the edge of the forest, but now when she listened, she heard wildlife and the sound of the river, its waters now moving. She watched, unaware that she was smiling, as a flock of large birds flew overhead in a formation, calling to one another.

Lena wondered why they had experienced that powerful dream. Was it something to do with their passing together through the interface between the Halflight and this world? She sat and meditated on the miraculous things she had seen.

Teryn stirred across from her. He looked different now, Lena thought- younger, somehow.

She felt thirsty. "Do you think the river water is safe to drink?" she asked.

"It's passed through no cities," Teryn remarked, stretching with a grimace. "It comes from a lake high in the mountains to the north. It'll be safer than any tap water in the Citadel."

Lena went to kneel by the river's edge and drew water from it in her hands. The sensation when she swallowed it was so icy that she gasped with the shock. After a while she glanced across to see that Teryn had joined her. He drank and then stared into the river. Lena followed his gaze and saw the silvery flash of many small fish darting around.

They sat by the river for a while longer as the morning light strengthened. "Do you remember anything about what happened? How the Mothers were destroyed?" he ventured at last. "The ghosts?"

Lena thought. "No. Not really. It feels like a dream, but one that's already faded."

"I suppose I'll be your last ever case," she remarked after a while.

Teryn smiled at that. "I would think so, Lena. One I'll leave unsolved."

"Are we really never going back?"

"*I am the map and you are the path,*" Teryn murmured. He smiled when Lena looked blankly at him. "There's a different road for the three of us, Lena. I don't know what's on that road. I only know it exists and it's up to us to find it."

"Will you miss the Citadel at all?"

"No. I have no one there. I don't expect you will either."

Lena shook her head. "No. I don't know what will happen to us now. But I feel intensely happy and frightened at the same time. Does that make sense?"

"It shouldn't. But it does."

"As if I might grow wings and fly," she said.

Later that morning they walked along a track bordered by fields of grass in which flowers bloomed· more kinds than Lena had ever imagined, even in her dreams of places beyond the Citadel. The companions drank more water from the streams and small rivers they passed, and Lena wondered if any of these rivulets ended up in the vast river that cut through the Citadel's brick and concrete landscape. A haze of small, buzzing insects hovered over the bubbling water in places. In the distance, the faint blue-grey contours of great mountains rose to meet the azure sky.

Over the next few days, they travelled through a mountainous, wooded area. Lena drank in the sights, sounds and smells of the rich landscape. Whenever she saw something for the first time, its name came to her, along with information that unlocked itself in her mind- much like the swiftly blooming flowers that carpeted the grass. The tall trees were pines, or sometimes larches. The furtive, four-footed creatures that peered nervously from the cover of trees and bushes were deer. She inspected leaves, herbs and grasses and their names and properties came to her instantly- information that her ancestors would surely have known, in the time before the Citadel. Within two days she knew everything that could be eaten or made use of and everything poisonous or to be avoided.

The Great Power continued to change her. With almost every passing moment, she learned something new about the wider world.

"How big is it?" Lena wondered aloud as they now followed a broad river that headed east through a winding valley, picking their way carefully along a boulder-strewn path by the water's edge. Snow-capped peaks rose into a sky dotted with white clouds, and the lower slopes of the mountains were thick with conifers. The sharp, cool air warmed as the sun appeared above the mountain tops and its light painted the valley.

The wooded ravine opened out gradually into lowlands, and the following morning they drew within sight of a vast settlement in the distance, a walled city not entirely unlike the Citadel, except that a road led to vast entrance gates which lay open.

The companions walked slowly closer, along a hedge-bordered track on either side of which fields of crops stretched away. "No closer," Rhion said pensively, as they finally drew close enough to see tiny figures and vehicles passing in and out of the city's perimeter.

"Are you going through those gates?" Rhion asked Teryn.

The Finder shook his head. "I've lived behind walls for long enough already. I don't wish to die behind them, no matter what that city is like. And to know *that* is too complex a question for me- even now."

Lena stared at the distant metropolis for a long while. "A normal life ending in a normal death," she heard herself say. "We should accept it. Shouldn't we?"

Rhion fixed her sister with an intense stare. "Such a life is yours, if you want it- not that you can know what that city and its people are like. As for me- I don't even want to know who holds power there... how can I live by their rules, now that we've glimpsed the secrets of the world? I can't turn my back on the things I'm now aware of. She has a plan for us, Lena. Everything that's happened to us is only the beginning."

Her twin said nothing.

"Could you oil the wheels of industry again, and forget? Could you become a tiny insignificant cog in a machine that cares nothing for you? The cycle may change but it never truly ends. What do you think might lurk *here*, a thousand years from now? Do you want to have been a part of it?"

Lena shook her head numbly.

"And do you remember all those stories told in the Citadel of monsters and demons with evil powers, lurking out in the wilderness?"

"I remember," Lena said.

"*We* are those monsters now."

Yet even after her sister and Teryn had turned and walked the other way, Lena remained for a short while, her eyes fixed on the walls of the alien city. She imagined finding joy in small things again. The comfort of routine. The familiarity of neighbourhoods. The pointless talk of people whose lives were lived to a set of unchallenged rules. The sheer bliss of never over-thinking, of being the mud and never the sky.

Copulation. Rearing children to be just like oneself, watching the light of imagination slowly die in their eyes. Conformity. Regulation. Capitulation.

Lena's smile faded. The cold breeze chased itself across the meadow and sighed through the trees. The sun darted in and out of view.

"What do you see, other than the darkness?" Lena asked herself as she hurried after her companions.

"Now, I see everything."

Author's Note

Thank you for reading this book. If you enjoyed it, please do take the time to review on Amazon, even if it's just a few lines. Every author appreciates a review of their work and I'm no exception.

You can also browse other works of mine here:

https://www.amazon.co.uk/Simon-Williams/e/B00P0ZZYS8

Thanks for your support!

Simon Williams

9 781787 234570